P9-DEM-638

Richard Laymon was born in Chicago in 1947. He grew up in California and has a BA in English Literature from Willamette University, Oregon, and an MA from Loyola University, Los Angeles. He has worked as a school-teacher, a librarian and as a report writer for a law firm. He now works full-time as a writer. Apart from his novels, he has published more than sixty short stories in magazines such as *Ellery Queen*, *Alfred Hitchcock* and *Cavalier* and in anthologies, including *Modern Masters of Horror*, *The Second Black Lizard Anthology of Crime* and *Night Visions 7*. His novel *Flesh* was named Best Horror Novel of 1988 by *Science Fiction Chronicle* and also shortlisted for the prestigious Bram Stoker Award, as was *Funland*. Richard Laymon is the author of more than twenty acclaimed novels, including *The Cellar*, *The Stake*, *One Rainy Night*, *Darkness Tell Us*, *Blood Games*, *Savage*, *Alarums* and *Endless Night*. He lives in California with his wife and daughter.

Also by Richard Laymon

The Cellar
The Woods Are Dark
Night Show
Beware!
Allhallow's Eve
The Beast House
Flesh
Resurrection Dreams
Funland
The Stake
One Rainy Night
Darkness, Tell Us
Blood Games
Dark Mountain*
Midnight's Lair*
Savage
Out Are The Lights
Alarums
Endless Night

*previously published under the pseudonym of Richard Kelly
Dark Mountain was first published as Tread Softly

In the Dark

Richard Laymon

Copyright © 1994 Richard Laymon

The right of Richard Laymon to be identified as the Author of
the Work has been asserted by him in accordance with the
Copyright, Designs and Patents Act 1988.

First published in 1994
by HEADLINE BOOK PUBLISHING

First published in paperback in 1994
by HEADLINE BOOK PUBLISHING

A HEADLINE FEATURE paperback

10 9 8 7 6 5 4 3 2

All rights reserved. No part of this publication may be
reproduced, stored in a retrieval system, or transmitted,
in any form or by any means without the prior written
permission of the publisher, nor be otherwise circulated
in any form of binding or cover other than that in which
it is published and without a similar condition being
imposed on the subsequent purchaser.

All characters in this publication are fictitious
and any resemblance to real persons, living or dead,
is purely coincidental.

ISBN 0 7472 4509 6

Typeset by CBS, Felixstowe, Suffolk

Printed and bound in Great Britain by
Cox & Wyman Ltd, Reading, Berks

HEADLINE BOOK PUBLISHING
A division of Hodder Headline PLC
338 Euston Road
London NW1 3BH

THIS BOOK IS DEDICATED TO

BRIDGET ANN

THE KANGAROO ISLAND GIRL

Thanks for the letter and photo.
My regards to Roy and Long John Silver.

Your address went missing.
Please write again.

Chapter One

Jane Kerry noticed the envelope when she stepped behind the circulation desk. Her first thought was that it didn't belong on the seat of her chair. She hadn't put it there. Had it fallen from the top of the desk? She wondered if someone might've lost it, and whether it contained anything of importance.

She ignored the envelope as she checked out half a dozen mysteries to old Agnes Dixon. Agnes was one of her regulars, a retired school teacher, and the first person to make Jane feel really welcome in her new job as head of the Donnerville Public Library.

While they chatted in quiet voices, a few more people drifted over to the circulation desk. Others wandered out the door. As usual, the library was beginning to empty with the approach of its nine o'clock closing time.

The envelope.

Jane slipped a dated card into the pocket of Agnes's last book – a Dick Francis – flipped the cover shut, and set it atop the woman's stack. Even as she said, 'That's one of his best,' she took a small step backward. Feeling the push of the seat's edge against her right buttock, she reached down without looking. She fingered the envelope and picked it up.

'Hi,' said a teenaged boy who looked vaguely familiar. 'I'd like to get this, please.'

'Sure thing.'

He pushed a book toward Jane, cover open, and held out his library card for her. She took it with her left hand.

She brought her right hand up and glanced at the envelope.

Handwritten in the center, in black ink, was one word:

JANE

What?
Me?

She felt mildly surprised and perplexed, and a little bit anxious.

What could it be?

At least the envelope apparently hadn't been lost by anyone, so she wouldn't need to worry about trying to catch its owner.

She tossed it back onto the seat, and returned to business. She tried to focus entirely on the patrons, getting to know them better, hoping to show them that she was friendly and always ready to help in any way possible.

The mysterious envelope didn't preoccupy her thoughts.

Instead, it lingered just off to the side where her mind seemed to glance at it from time to time, and wonder.

An invitation? A greeting card of some kind? A love letter or poem from a secret admirer?

A complaint?

Maybe a bit of hate mail from someone I shushed.

Could be anything, she told herself. Don't worry about it. You'll find out as soon as everybody's cleared out.

'If you like that one,' she told a pony-tailed girl, 'we've got a lot more by the same author.'

As the girl thanked her and headed for the door, Jane swept her eyes over the remaining people. Quite a bunch. Maybe six still lined up, a few on their way out, a dozen others scattered about the main reading room. No telling how many might be upstairs in the stacks. Nobody in sight seemed to be paying any special attention to her.

Whoever left it will probably stay behind to see if I open it.

Hope he's cute.

Don't hope for cute, she told herself. Just hope he's not a weirdo.

By the time Jane was done checking out books, only a handful of people still lingered in the reading room. She recognized most of them as regulars. They all seemed busy with their own projects. Don, her assistant, was making his way among the tables, gathering up books and periodicals that needed to be put away.

She checked her wristwatch.

Ten till nine.

She picked up the envelope again. Holding it at waist level so that the desk would hide it from the view of anyone who might be watching, she flipped it over.

As she'd thought, nothing on either side except the handwritten JANE.

The envelope looked clean and unrumpled.

Its flap was sealed.

From the envelope's thinness, she supposed that it contained nothing more than a sheet or two of folded paper.

She picked at a corner of the flap, tore it upward, thrust her forefinger into the small hole, and worked her finger along the seam, ripping upward.

As she tore at the flap, she lifted her gaze. Nobody appeared to be watching.

Looking down, she removed a folded sheet of paper from the envelope. Lined, three-hole paper of the sort that students use for filling their looseleaf binders. It was folded into thirds. She could see the raised, dark scribbles of the handwriting on the other side. And a darkness within. A darkness caused by an extra layer of paper. Paper the size of a bank check or a dollar bill.

Somebody sent me money?

Suddenly, she felt like an idiot.

This was not a message from a secret admirer. Nor was it a threat. This was nothing more than payment for a lost book or an overdue fine.

Jane felt silly. A little relieved. And a little disappointed.

She unfolded the paper.

Inside was not a bank check, but a stiff, unwrinkled fifty-dollar bill.

Must've been a mighty *expensive* book, Jane thought.

She moved the bill aside and read the handwritten note:

Dear Jane
   Come and play with me. For further instructions, look homeward, angel. You'll be glad you did.
Warmest Regards,
MOG
(Master of Games)

Jane read it again. And again. Then she looked around. The few people who remained in the reading room were paying no attention to her.

'We'll be closing in about five minutes,' she announced.

She refolded the note around the fifty-dollar bill and tucked it back inside the envelope.

'Don, would you come here for a minute?'

The lanky graduate student hurried toward her. He looked worried. Or guilty? 'Is there a problem, Miss Kerry?'

Jane shook her head. 'I don't think so.' She raised the envelope. 'Did you happen to see anyone put this on my chair?'

He rolled his eyes upward as if an answer might be written on the ceiling. Then he shook his head. 'No. I don't believe so.'

'Anyone hanging around the circulation desk when I was away from it?'

Again, he shook his head. 'Not that I noticed.'

She shook the envelope. 'This isn't from *you*, is it?'

'Me? No. What is it?'

Jane hesitated. How much should she tell him? She'd known Don for a couple of months, and she didn't *really* know much about him. Only that he'd been a part-time helper at the library for a year before her own arrival, he was going for a PhD in English literature at the university across town, that he was single and lived in an apartment a few blocks from the library. She also knew that he was agonizingly shy and apparently had no social life.

Maybe he's trying to start one up with me, she thought, by way of a mysterious message and a chunk of money.

'It's an anonymous letter,' she said, and decided not to mention the fifty dollars.

His eyes widened. 'From a secret admirer?'

'Not exactly.'

His jaw dropped. 'Not a threat, I hope!'

'No. Just a . . . strange sort of message. But you haven't seen anyone wandering around with an envelope

5

like this, or acting in any way furtive near the circulation desk?'

'I certainly haven't.' He eyed the envelope. 'May I?'

'Thanks, but . . . I don't think so.' Seeing the dejected look on his face, she added, 'It's rather personal.'

'Personal?' He suddenly blushed. 'Oh. Well. Never mind. If I'd known it was personal . . .' He grimaced and shook his head. 'I'm sorry.'

'Don't worry about it, Don. Really.'

'I . . . may I have your permission to leave? I haven't quite finished picking up, yet, but . . . I'm not feeling especially well. My stomach.' He pressed a hand against it.

'Sure. Go on ahead.'

'Oh, thank you.' He scurried around the end of the circulation desk, entered the office, reappeared moments later with his briefcase, gave Jane a cramped smile and a wave, and hurried for the library doors.

'Hope you feel better,' she said.

Then he was gone.

Jane wondered if she'd had a hand in causing his sudden illness.

Not unlikely. After all, she was his boss *and* a woman, on top of which she had almost (but not quite) accused him of perpetrating the anonymous letter. Plenty to give a person of Don's temperament a nasty case of upset nerves.

Describing the letter as 'personal' had apparently been the final straw.

Shouldn't have told him that, she decided. The thing isn't what you'd normally call personal. Didn't ask my income, didn't get sexy.

It's not personal, it's just plain screwy.

She glanced at her watch. Five after nine. 'We're

6

closing up, now,' she announced. 'Time to hit the streets, folks.'

When the last was gone, she locked the front doors and returned to the circulation desk. She knew that she ought to go upstairs, make sure nobody was lingering in the stacks, and turn off the lights. She wasn't eager to do it, though. Neither she nor Don enjoyed that particular task. Just too creepy up there when you went alone.

Too quiet. Too many shadows. Too many hiding places. Just plain spooky.

But made a great deal worse because you knew about old Miss Favor, the librarian, Jane's predecessor. She'd died up there. Dropped dead from a bad heart. Dropped dead while she was alone, closing for the night. And there she'd remained until morning when a part-timer had opened the library and discovered her body. According to Don, a rat or two had 'been at her.' He knew the unlucky worker who'd stumbled onto Miss Favor. 'Oh, she was totally freaked out. Totally. She hasn't set foot in this library ever since.'

The upstairs stacks weren't so bad in the daytime. They weren't so bad at night, either, as long as a few people were up there searching the shelves or working at the study carrels. But they were usually deserted when you went up at closing time.

Through some sort of unspoken acknowledgement of their mutual fears, Jane and Don had fallen into the habit of accompanying each other on that special job. It helped. A lot.

But tonight, Jane would need to do it alone.

Thanks a heap, Don.

Well, there was no hurry.

Back behind the circulation desk, she picked up the

envelope. She removed the note and the fifty-dollar bill, and studied them both.

She had rarely seen any denominations higher than twenty dollars. The fifty seemed a bit alien. On one side was a portrait of President Grant, on the other a rendition of the U.S. Capitol. She supposed it was real.

She also supposed that she was meant to keep it. After all, the thing had come in an envelope with her name on it.

Why would anyone want to give me fifty bucks?

Was it supposed to be a gift? she wondered. Or maybe payment for some real or imagined services?

Payment in advance?

Cute, she thought. Maybe now he expects something from me. Figures I've taken the money, so I owe him.

That's what he thinks.

She read the note again:

Dear Jane,

    Come and play with me. For further instructions, look homeward, angel. You'll be glad you did.

                    Warmest Regards,
                    MOG
                 (Master of Games)

The 'come and play with me' sounded sort of like the eager request a child might make. *Will you come out and play?*

Of course, 'come' was also a rather vulgar euphemism for an orgasm. 'Play with me' also carried some strong sexual implications. Maybe this was an invitation – payment enclosed – to mess around with its sender.

He wants to fuck me.

The idea blasted away Jane's composure. Anger,

8

humiliation, fear, revulsion, and an unexpected surge of desire seemed to hit her all at once, stealing her breath, making her heart race, surging heat through her body.

'The bastard,' she muttered. Here's fifty bucks, now come and play with me.

Maybe that isn't what he means, she thought.

And maybe it is.

She suddenly looked up. She turned her head, scanning the entire room.

She saw nobody. What she saw were countless hiding places: in among the rows of bookshelves, down low behind the tables and chairs, behind any of the several shoulder-high card catalogs, behind the photocopy machine.

In front of my desk.

She pushed her feet against the rung of her chair and raised herself off the cushion. Hands pressed against the desk top, she leaned forward and gazed past the edge.

Nobody there.

She settled down onto her seat again.

I oughta get out of here, she thought.

Then she thought, How dangerous can a guy be if he's giving me fifty bucks?

Also, he must be familiar with literature. The 'look homeward, angel' business was definitely an allusion to the Thomas Wolfe novel – one of Jane's favorites.

She read that part of the note again. 'For further instructions, look homeward, angel.'

Further? He sees this note as the initial instruction. He has more for me. Maybe the *further* instructions will be given face to face.

Maybe not.

Maybe I'm supposed to go home and look in my mailbox for the further instructions. Look homeward.

Maybe I'll find an envelope with another note inside – and another fifty dollars.

Maybe I'll find it in the book.

Tucked inside a copy of Look Homeward, Angel.

The library's copy, if not checked out or misplaced, should be on a shelf in the fiction section.

In the upstairs stacks.

I need to go up there anyway, she reminded herself. I'll just take a quick look at the book.

What if he's waiting for me there?

Chapter Two

Jane folded the note around the fifty dollars and tucked it back inside the envelope. Her hands were trembling. She felt a little crawly in her stomach. As she walked into her office, she wondered if she *really* planned to go upstairs all by herself when there was a real possibility that the author of the note might be lurking there.

What am I *supposed* to do, leave?

Leave without shutting off the upstairs lights, without making sure everyone has cleared out? No way.

She crouched beside her office desk and slipped the envelope into her purse. Then she stood up. From the top drawer of the desk, she took her switchblade knife.

She'd found the knife a day before her seventeenth birthday, while hiking in the woods near Mount Tamalpias. The point of its slim, three-inch blade had been buried in a redwood trunk. She'd worked it loose and kept the knife.

It made quite a nice letter opener.

She released the lever at the base of the blade, then folded the blade into the handle, where it clicked into place.

If I need to take something like this with me, she thought, I shouldn't be going at all.

She looked at the office phone.

Call the police? That'd be very cute. Explain that

11

somebody gave me fifty bucks, so now I'm afraid to go upstairs and turn off the lights.

They'll think I'm a weenie.

Bringing in the cops over a matter like this would be foolish. But she tried to think of a friend she might ask to come over.

Hello? I'm a little bit spooked about going upstairs here at the library, and I was wondering if you'd maybe like to come over and keep me company? Shouldn't take more than five minutes.

She did have a few friends who would be quick to respond if she called – but none who lived in Donnerville. Most of them lived at least an hour away. She certainly couldn't ask any of them to drive out here on such a lame pretext.

And it really *is* lame, she told herself. For one thing, this Master of Games character might be long gone. For another, he's probably harmless.

Maybe nothing but a twerpy kid. MOG, Master of Games. Sounds like the brainchild of a nerd who's spent too much time playing Dungeons and Dragons, or something.

Well, she thought, we'll soon find out.

For better or worse.

Just in case of worse, I've got my trusty knife.

On her way out of the office, Jane rubbed the switchblade against her right thigh, trying to slip it into her pocket. Having no success, she looked down. She was wearing her denim skirt, not her culottes. The culottes had pockets, but the skirt didn't.

Her only pockets were on the front of her blouse. The white blouse, big enough to be comfortably loose, had a large pocket on each side of the chest. As she headed for the staircase, she unbuttoned the flap over the pocket on the right, lifted it, and dropped in the knife.

The plastic handle bumped against her breast. It turned sideways as it slid downward. From the tip of her breast, it fell to the bottom of the pocket. It hung there as if caught in a hammock, swaying back and forth as she walked.

Terrific, Jane thought. She'd forgotten how *enormous* these pockets were.

The damn knife won't do me a lot of good if I have to spend five minutes fishing it out.

She was already at the fire door, so she went ahead and pushed it open. The lights in the stairwell were still on. The bulbs gave off enough light to illuminate the stair treads. Just fine for safety. But they were dim and yellowish.

Not exactly cheerful.

I really should get them changed, she told herself. Just buy some new ones myself. Might help the dismal atmosphere in here.

While I'm at it, have the stairs de-squeaked.

Every one of the old wooden stairs groaned or creaked or squawked as she climbed.

This is a regular spookhouse. Why did I ever take this job in the first place?

Cut it out, she told herself. The job's just fine.

Right. It's the building *that sucks.*

As Jane arrived at the landing, halfway up, the swinging bottom of her pocket reminded her that she wanted to retrieve the knife.

Get it now, while the getting's good. If you wait till you need it . . .

I won't need it, she told herself.

Lord, I hope not.

Continuing to climb, she shoved her fingers down into

the pocket. Her thumb didn't go in with them, but she didn't think she would need its help.

She worked her fingertips between the knife handle and the bottom of her pocket (felt like some sand down there – where'd that come from?) and began to raise the knife. Having no grip on it, she could only bring it up by sliding it against the underside of her breast.

As she set her foot on the top stair, the door burst open and a man charged at her.

She yelped, flinched, reached for the banister.

The man gasped, 'Whoa!'

As Jane grabbed the banister with her left hand, her right squeezed the knife in her pocket.

She felt the hard nub of its button sink down.

Uh-oh!

She dropped the knife as the blade sprang from its handle. It whipped up against her nipple while she stumbled backward and the man skidded to a halt and clamped a hand on her shoulder.

The hand stopped her, held her steady.

'I'm sorry,' the stranger blurted. 'Are you okay?'

Jane nodded. She tried to catch her breath. Her heart was thudding quick and hard. Her nipple tingled and burned. She looked down, half expecting to find the pocket of her blouse soaked with blood.

No blood.

But half an inch of shiny steel point jutted out from the side of her pocket.

The stranger looked at it, too. Then he met her eyes and said, 'Are you sure you aren't hurt?'

'I'm all right.'

'You didn't cut yourself, did you?'

He's talking about my boob! Man!

'It sort of felt like it, but I don't see any blood.'

14

He still held Jane's shoulder.

She wanted to get away from him, wanted to hold her hurt, wanted to check the damage. 'Were you on your way down?' she asked.

He nodded, but didn't take the hint. 'I shouldn't have been in such a hurry. Afraid I didn't realize it'd gotten so late. You're the librarian, aren't you?'

'That's right.'

'Coming up to shoo me out?'

'I didn't know anyone was up here.'

'I'm really sorry.' He released her shoulder, turned around and opened the door for her.

'Thanks,' she said.

She expected him to head on down, but he followed her out of the stairwell. She looked back at him.

He gave her a smile that looked friendly and a little sheepish. 'Do you mind? Maybe I could help you pick up, or something. I hate to leave you alone up here. Especially right after I've arranged to scare the daylights out of you.'

Jane knew she shouldn't trust him. What was he doing up here after closing time? He might even be the man who called himself MOG. But nothing about him seemed threatening. He looked very normal: his hair slightly unkempt; his clean-shaven face attractive but not handsome in any striking way; his shirt and jeans casual but neat and clean.

For the first time, Jane noticed that he was carrying a book. It must've been in his left hand all along.

A very thick book.

The nape of her neck began to crawl.

Look Homeward, Angel. Has to be. Can't possibly be anything else.

'What's that?' she asked.

The stranger raised the book. '*Youngblood Hawke*. Wouk? I've been meaning to read it for . . . too late to check it out tonight?'

'No. No, that's fine.' She released a shaky breath. 'You can either stick around, or wait downstairs. This'll only take a couple of minutes.'

'I'll walk along with you, if that's all right.'

'Fine.'

From the stairwell door, an aisle stretched the length of the room. To the aisle's right, study carrels lined the wall. To the left stood row after row of bookshelves that reached to the ceiling. The stranger stayed at Jane's side, but half a pace behind, allowing her to lead the way.

Except for their footsteps and the creaking floorboards, there was silence.

'Was anybody else up here?' Jane asked.

'Just now? I don't think so, but I was reading. I tend to block everything out when I'm in a good book. Want me to grab these?' he asked, gesturing toward several books that had been left at one of the carrels.

'They can wait till morning. Thanks, though.'

'Welcome. My name's Brace, by the way.'

Jane looked over at him. 'It's what?'

'Brace. Brace Paxton.'

Deciding not to question him about his unusual name, she went ahead and introduced herself. 'I'm Jane Kerry.'

'I thought it might be James Bowie.'

'Are you a wise guy, Brace Paxton?'

'Sorry. But maybe you oughta take that knife out of your pocket. I'd hate to see you trip and fall with it open like that.'

'Me, too, actually.' Halting, she turned toward the gap between two rows of shelves. Her back to Brace, she

16

delved into the pocket of her blouse. 'It's a switchblade,' she explained. 'That's how it opened. Its safety thing doesn't work.'

Carefully, she fingered her nipple through the fabric. It felt a little tender, but the pain had faded away. The blade must've given her no more than a harsh, stinging flick. 'I was trying to take it out when you rammed through the door, and I pushed the button by accident.'

'Hope it didn't do any damage.'

A blush spread sudden heat through Jane. She quit fingering her breast and reached deeper into the pocket. 'I guess I'm fine.' She curled her fingertips underneath the knife handle.

'Be careful taking it out.'

'I'm trying to be.'

This is a lousy idea, she thought. He can't see my hand, but he sure knows where it is. Next thing you know, he'll be offering to help.

'If I'd been keeping better track of the time,' he said, 'none of this would've happened.'

'No harm done.'

'I'm glad we met, though.'

Wish I could say the same, she thought. Then she said, 'Well, thanks.'

She tightened her precarious grip on the knife. Then she pushed her knuckles against the pocket, bulging the blouse away from her body to put her breast out of harm's way, and drew the knife upward, sliding its blade free of the slit. 'There. Got it.' She turned around and showed him the weapon.

'You're sure you aren't hurt?'

'I'm fine.' She folded the blade shut.

'Where'll you put it, now?'

'Guess I'll just carry it.'

They continued on their way down the aisle, Jane checking between the rows of shelves, Brace walking slowly beside her.

As they made their way toward the end of the room, Jane realized she was growing more and more tense. At first, she wasn't sure why. Then she knew.

Because they were almost to the Ws.

Should she check for *Look Homeward, Angel*?

Why not?

She'd spent enough time reshelving books up here to know the exact location of the Thomas Wolfe novels. She would be walking right past them.

What about Brace? she asked herself.

If you don't want to do it in front of him, you'll have to go all the way downstairs with him, usher him out, then come back up here by yourself.

Or wait till tomorrow.

She couldn't wait, just couldn't.

'Maybe I'll pick up something for myself,' she muttered, then sidestepped out of the aisle. She found herself facing shelf after shelf loaded with hardbound novels. She crouched down. Wolfe was lower still – level with her knees.

'Are you going for Wouk?' Brace asked.

'Wolfe.'

'*Bonfire* boy, or . . .?'

'Thomas.'

She spotted two copies of *Look Homeward, Angel*, followed by an empty space, after which was a single copy of *The Web and the Rock*, another open space, then two copies or *You Can't Go Home Again*.

Jane pulled out a copy of *Look Homeward, Angel*. Elbows on knees, she opened the book and flipped through it.

'That's just about my favorite book of all time,' Brace said.

'It is?' She looked up at him.

Her heart thudded hard.

What the hell.

'Did you leave a note on my chair tonight?'

'Huh?'

'Master of Games?'

Frowning, he shook his head. The confused way he looked, Jane might've been speaking jibberish.

'The what?' he asked.

'Are you the one who left the note?'

'What note?'

'I mean, it's all right. I'm just curious, okay? It's not very often I get mysterious notes with money in them.'

'I don't know anything about any note.'

'You don't, huh?'

'What sort of note?'

'"Come and play with me? For further instructions, look homeward, angel?" *That* sort of note. With a fifty-dollar bill in it?'

He looked mystified. 'It wasn't from me. If I *had* a fifty-dollar bill, I wouldn't be giving it away.' A smile suddenly lit his face. 'Well, maybe to *you*. If you needed it very badly. Maybe.'

If this is Mog, Jane thought, he's got an odd way of lying.

'Okay,' she said. 'Maybe it wasn't you.'

'Anything in the book there?' he asked.

She returned her attention to the novel, riffled through its pages, and made sure that nothing was hidden in the dust jacket. As she slid it back into its place on the shelf, Brace said, 'I think that's another copy . . .'

'I know.' She dragged the second copy forward. Even

before lifting it from the shelf, she spotted a strip of white paper protruding from its top like a bookmark.

'There y'go,' Brace said, sounding pleased.

Jane opened the book. Tucked into its gutter was an envelope.

The envelope looked identical to the one she'd found downstairs on her chair. Even her handwritten name looked the same.

She plucked it out and shut the book.

'Woops,' Brace said.

'What?'

'Maybe it was there to mark a passage.'

'You *sure* you don't have anything to do with this?'

'Honest. Just trying to help.'

'Did you notice the page number?'

'No. Sorry.'

'Neither did I. Well, maybe it won't matter.' She returned the book to its shelf and stood up.

The envelope was sealed.

'Want me to leave?' Brace asked.

'No, that's all right, I already told you everything about the other one.' She looked at him. 'You're *sure* you don't have anything to do with this?'

'Pretty sure.'

'Only pretty sure?'

'Almost a hundred per cent sure.'

'You mean, like you don't want to rule out that it might've been done behind your back by one of your alternate personalities?'

'That's about right.'

'Okay. Well, here goes.' She thumbed the button of her switchblade. The knife jumped slightly as the blade sprang out and locked. She slipped its tip under the envelope's flap and slashed the top seam.

To free her hand, she reached forward and set the knife on the edge of a bookshelf. Then she spread open the envelope. Inside was a folded sheet of lined paper. She removed it, unfolded it, and pursed her lips.

'Whoa,' Brace said. 'Looks like you've earned a raise.'

Jane slipped the hundred-dollar bill aside and read the handwritten message aloud.

'"My dear Jane, Congratulations! You've taken your first, minor step on the road to fun and riches. More is waiting. Do you have the will to proceed? I hope so. At midnight, horse around. You'll be glad you did. Yours, MOG."'

Chapter Three

When Jane finished reading the note, Brace said, 'Looks like the game's still on.'

She nodded. She felt *awfully* strange.

'You don't have any idea who's doing this?' Brace asked.

'No idea at all.'

'He's generous.'

'Let's get out of here,' Jane muttered. She tucked the message and money back into the envelope, then picked up her knife. 'Keep your eyes open, okay? He might be up here.'

'Hope so. Maybe he'll give *me* a hundred bucks.'

'As long as that's *all* he does . . .'

Brace stayed at her side as she walked the remaining length of the aisle, turned around and headed back. He said nothing. He seemed watchful and tense.

He's worried, Jane realized. That was good. It confirmed her own take on the situation: anyone who would write such notes and give away that much money to a stranger was certainly abnormal – possibly dangerous.

You'd think he might want to see my reactions.

Is he watching us? Hiding up here?

If he was lurking in the stacks, however, he succeeded in staying out of sight. And he made no sounds. Jane only heard herself and Brace as they walked the old, noisy floorboards.

Maybe he's waiting in the stairwell.

She grew more tense as they approached the stairwell door. Moving ahead of her, Brace opened it. Nobody leaped out. While he waited, Jane stepped over to the panel of light switches. She flicked one after another, dropping sections of the room into darkness until no light was left except for the glow from the stairwell.

Jane hurried over to Brace. It was good to have him holding the door open for her.

Instead of starting down the stairs, she waited for him to shut the door.

'Do you want me to go first?' he asked.

'If you go first, I'll have to take up the rear.'

'Ah.' Smiling slightly, he shifted *Youngblood Hawke* into his right hand, took Jane gently by the forearm with his left, and turned her around.

'I hate this sort of thing,' she said as they started down the stairs.

'What sort of thing?'

'Feeling spooked. Being afraid somebody might jump out at me. I'm not usually such a chicken.'

'You have every right to feel nervous. I'd be pretty shaken up, too, if somebody was sending me anonymous notes. Money or no money, it's weird.'

At the bottom of the stairs, Brace let go of Jane's arm and swung open the door.

She hurried into the bright lights and kept moving, wanting to put distance between her back and the stairway to the stacks. When she heard the door bump shut, she whirled around and smiled at Brace. 'Thanks for the moral support,' she said.

'My pleasure.' He raised the novel. 'Will you let me

check out the book? I know we're past closing time, but . . .'

'Happy to.'

She took up her position behind the circulation desk. Brace stepped to the other side.

'I really am grateful,' she said as he slid the book toward her.

He handed over his library card, 'What are you going to do about midnight?' he asked.

The question made Jane's stomach go cold. She shook her head. 'I don't know. I'm not even sure what I'm *supposed* to do.'

'Horse around.'

'Whatever that means.' She slid the book back to him, his library card on top.

Brace tucked the card into his wallet, then glanced at his wristwatch. 'Not quite nine-thirty yet. You've got a while to figure things out.' He met her eyes. 'I'd be glad to help. Do you need to be anywhere right now, or . . .?'

'What do you have in mind?'

'Maybe we could go to a restaurant, or something?'

She stared at him.

She liked his looks. Especially his eyes. They seemed warm and friendly, intelligent – and they looked like the eyes of someone who had known many troubles but had never forgotten how to laugh.

He had the looks of a good and decent man.

But she hardly knew him at all. She wasn't sure she *wanted* to know him. He seemed all right, but he might be the man behind the peculiar notes. For that matter, he might be a rapist or a killer. You just never knew. Even if he was harmless, he could turn out to be jealous and possessive enough to make her life miserable, or a womanizer who would get what he could and dump her.

He might be none of the above, but already married.

All sorts of ways for Jane to get hurt – or worse – by this guy.

Then again, she thought, he might be just what he seems.

Figure it one chance in a thousand.

'A wedge of pie,' he said. 'A cup of joe, and thou.'

Her small cough of laughter took her completely by surprise.

'What do you say?' Brace asked.

'Sure, why not?'

At Ezra's, a block from the library, they sat at a corner booth and Brace plucked two menus out from behind the napkin holder. He handed one to Jane. 'Hope you don't mind if I order a full meal. Do the same, if you'd like. It's on me.'

'What happened to the wedge of pie and cup of joe?'

He grinned. 'I only said that for effect. Thing is, I skipped my supper tonight.'

'On purpose?'

'Forgot about it.'

'You forgot to *eat*?'

A waitress came to the table. Jane ordered a Pepsi and chili-cheese fries. Brace ordered a bacon cheeseburger, seasoned curly fries, and a root beer.

When the waitress was gone, he said, 'I suddenly got this bug to read *Youngblood Hawke*. Does that ever happen to you? There's some book or author you've always wanted to try, and all of a sudden you *have* to?'

'Oh, yes. Sometimes, I need an 87th Precinct fix. Or I get a sudden a craving for a Travis McGee. And there are times I feel like I can't get through the night without reading a Hemingway story.'

'Really? Unusual tastes for a woman. But I did have you pegged for a book nut.'

'Must've been quite a leap, considering I'm a librarian.'

Brace laughed. 'Takes one to know one. I teach lit. over at D.U. Anyway, I got the urge to read *Youngblood Hawke*, so I went over to the university library. Their only copy was checked out, so then I tried the B. Dalton – no luck – the Waldenbooks – no luck. Finally, I gave your library a try. Success! I grabbed the book and hurried over to the nearest carrel to start reading. Thus did I miss my supper.'

'And thus did you miss closing time.'

'My powers of concentration are awesome. And often a pain in the rear. Give you an example. I picked up an F. Paul Wilson novel at an airport gift shop last Christmas. I was supposed to fly home to spend the holidays with my family. While I was waiting for the jet to start boarding, I began to read the book there in the waiting area by the gate. A very *crowded* waiting area. When I came out of the book, the crowd was gone. So was my flight.'

She saw the glint in his eye. 'You're kidding.'

'It's the truth. Stuff like that happens to me all the time.'

'But that's awful!' she gasped, trying not to laugh.

'Oh, everything balances out. Tonight, for instance, my little problem introduced me to you.'

'Lucky you.'

'You're quite an improvement over your predecessor.'

'You knew her?'

'Oh, yes. Old Phyllis Favor. An awful thing.'

'Her death?'

'Her life.'

Jane laughed. 'That's *terrible*.'

'You never met her, did you?'

'No, but . . .'

'I know people who stayed away from that library because of her. Real book-lovers, too. Including myself, when I finally couldn't stomach any more of that woman. I've seen her make people burst into tears by the way she *looked* at them. Not a nice person, may she rest in peace.'

'I've heard she was . . . unpleasant.'

'The earth is a far a better place, now that she's beneath it.'

Jane tried not to laugh, but couldn't stop herself. 'And you seemed like such a *nice* man.'

'People are often mistaken that way.'

The waitress arrived with their food and drinks. When she was gone, Brace lifted his glass of root beer toward Jane. 'Here's lookin' atcha, Madame Librarian.'

She raised her Pepsi and winked at him.

And wondered if she had ever before in her life winked at anyone.

For the next few minutes, she sipped her drink and forked chili-cheese fries into her mouth and watched Brace devour his burger and fries. He didn't say anything, just ate and looked at her and sometimes smiled. From the expressions on his face and his occasional moans, he seemed to be relishing every moment.

Done, he wiped his mouth with a napkin. He sighed. 'Good eatin'.'

'Would you like to polish off my fries?' She had plenty left. She pushed the container toward him, but he shook his head.

'Gotta watch my figure,' he said.

Jane blushed. She couldn't help it. Brace was slim and trim and looked as if he didn't need to lose an ounce. Jane was the one who should be watching her figure, who'd been neglecting it for way too long. She hadn't allowed herself to grow *fat*, but the extra weight and lack of exercise had thickened her, softened her.

Enough so that Brace's mention of 'figures' had triggered the rush of heat. With her fair complexion, a blush never failed to turn her face bright red. Brace couldn't help but notice it.

'So,' he said, 'what do you want to do about your mysterious friend?'

'I'm not sure,' she said, surprised that he'd made no comment on the blush. You *are* a good guy, she thought. 'I guess I'm pretty curious. Who is he? Why is he doing it?'

'He or she,' Brace said.

'It *might* be a woman.'

'Of course, he doesn't call himself "*Mistress* of Games."'

Jane nodded. 'So it probably *is* a man.'

'A man with money to spare.'

'Yeah. Jeez. Fifty bucks. I mean, I'm not exactly rich. To me, that's a lot of money. It's a pair of decent shoes, or a week's worth of groceries. It'd pay my telephone bill for a couple of months.'

'He gave you a *hundred* and fifty.'

'I *know*. Fifty in the first envelope, a hundred in the second. Which means he *doubled* the amount the second time around. What if I find the third envelope, and he's doubled things again? There might be *two* hundred in it. Or even three, if he doubles the whole amount instead of just the previous installment.'

'Or there might be nothing,' Brace said.

'What do you mean?'

'Maybe there isn't a third envelope. Maybe you'll figure out where it's supposed to be, go there looking for it, and he's waiting for you.'

'Yeah.' Though she was aware of that possibility, she didn't like hearing it spoken. The words, especially coming from Brace, seemed to give the idea more weight. 'If he wanted to jump me,' she said, 'he could've done it in the library.'

'I was there. And you left with me.'

Jane suddenly smiled. 'Ah! But at the time he left the message telling me to "horse around" at midnight, he couldn't have known I'd be leaving with you. Which means he never intended to attack me in the library.'

Brace nodded.

The waitress came to their table. 'Will there be anything else, folks?'

'I'd like a cup of coffee,' Brace told her. 'How about you, Jane?'

'Sure.'

As the waitress walked away, Jane shivered slightly though the restaurant was warm. She was nervous, but excited. She had goosebumps. She pressed her thighs together. She wanted to rub her arms, but that might draw Brace's attention.

The waitress returned quickly with two mugs of coffee, and set them down in front of Jane and Brace.

Brace raised his mug. He blew a soft breath at its top. 'So you're fairly sure you want to go ahead with this?' he asked.

Jane shrugged. Her shoulders trembled slightly. Her shivers didn't seem ready to go away. *Just don't get any worse, or Brace'll notice.*

'Is that a maybe?'

'More of an "I think so."' She gritted her teeth to stop her jaw from shaking. She hadn't attempted to drink her coffee yet. She didn't dare lift the mug. Not while she felt like this.

29

Brace took a few sips from his. He watched her closely, concern in his eyes. 'Are you okay?'

'Just a little nervous. *Very* nervous, as a matter of fact.'

'I know a great way to get over it.'

'How's that?'

'Choose not to play the game. Keep the money you've gotten so far, and forget about going after any more.'

You're probably half-right. There'd still be the problem of you.

I could follow the same advice with Brace, she told herself. Choose not to play. This thing with him doesn't have to go anywhere. It can end right here.

A corner of Jane's mouth twitched. 'Quitters never prosper,' she said.

'You want to go ahead with it?'

'I have to, don't I?'

'You do *not* have to,' Brace said. 'All it would take is a decision against acting on the second note.'

'But then I'll never know what might've happened.'

'Do you think it's worth the risk?'

She grimaced and rubbed her chin. Her fingers felt like ice. 'I guess so. Up to a point. You know what they say: nothing ventured, nothing gained. I wouldn't want to get hurt, though. You know? I don't want to get myself . . . attacked by some lunatic. It wouldn't be worth it, not for a couple of hundred bucks. But maybe this guy *isn't* a lunatic.'

She picked up her mug. It shuddered, coffee sloshing up its sides but not quite spilling over the brim. With the help of her other hand, she managed to bring the mug under control. As she took a drink of the coffee, she met Brace's eyes.

'You won't have to go alone,' he told her. 'Okay? If you

want to follow through, I'll go with you. I'll do whatever I can to protect you.'

She set down her mug, but didn't let go of it. 'That'd help,' she said.

Brace reached forward. He lowered his hand down onto Jane's left wrist, wrapped his fingers around it, and gently squeezed. His hand felt warm. It didn't tremble at all.

'That'd help a lot,' she added. She could feel her tremors and chills subsiding.

Because he's touching me? she wondered. Or because he's coming with me?

'I wouldn't be able to *guarantee* your safety,' he said.

'So when do we ever get guarantees?'

'When we buy a wristwatch.'

She smiled. 'When we buy *anything* from L.L. Bean.'

Brace laughed softly. He squeezed her wrist again. 'Feeling better?'

'A little bit.'

'Anyway,' he said, 'we have no reason at all to believe that your mysterious Master of Games has any intention of harming you.'

'I know, I know. But if it's not something like that, why *is* he doing it?'

'Could I have a look at the notes?' He let go of her wrist. It was warm where he'd been holding it, and now it felt bare and cool.

Jane turned aside. Her purse stood upright on the seat cushion, close to her hip. She reached into it and pulled out both the envelopes. She passed them to Brace. He studied the outsides of the envelopes. Then he plucked out the folded sheets of paper. He removed the fifty-dollar bill and the hundred-dollar bill, and handed them to Jane. 'Why don't you go ahead and put these in your wallet?'

'Should I?'

'They're yours.'

'Guess so.'

While she searched her purse, found her wallet and slipped the money into its bill compartment, Brace unfolded the two notes and held them side by side.

Jane dropped the wallet back into her purse. 'So, what do you think?'

'Same paper, same handwriting, same *mind* behind the notes. On the surface, it all seems fairly straightforward. He calls himself Master of Games, and these notes are basically instructions to the player.'

'Me.'

'You. In the first note, he invites you to play the game with him. The fifty dollars is the hook, of course. With money like that coming to you out of the blue, you can't help but be intrigued. He's hoping it'll be enough to tempt you into giving his game a try. Your instruction is to "look homeward, angel." The clue is fairly ambiguous, but not at all difficult. He wanted to make things easy for you, I think. He wasn't trying to confuse you, just get you to play along.'

Jane nodded. She liked Brace's interpretation of the note. It agreed with her own view of it.

'To encourage your participation, he writes "You'll be glad you did." That's a hint that there's more money waiting for you up ahead. The guy keeps his promises, doesn't he?'

'He came through with the money. I'm not sure how glad I am about it, though.'

'Glad enough to continue playing.'

'I guess so.'

'Okay, the second note congratulates you. "You've taken your first, minor step on the road to fun and riches. More is waiting."'

'So there's a lot more money ahead.'

'But to get it, you may need to take some *major* steps.'

'I can quit any time I want to, right?'

'That's sure how it looks.'

She laughed softly, and without any humor. 'It's crazy. Why's he doing it? And why me?'

'He doesn't say.'

This time, she had humor in her laugh. 'I know *that*, dingus.'

'Why do *you* think he's doing it?'

'Who knows?' she said. 'He's probably just a harmless twit with nothing better to do.'

'Might be.'

'I guess just about anything is possible. But I'll never find out what's going on if I quit now. And I'll miss out on all those riches. You, too.'

'The riches are for you,' Brace said.

'I'll share.' She smiled and shrugged. 'I'd probably quit right now if I had to go it alone. How about this: whatever we find tonight at midnight, we'll split fifty-fifty?'

'The money doesn't matter to me.'

'Really? What are you, already rich?'

'Oh, not hardly. It doesn't concern me, though.'

'What does concern you?'

'You.'

That one knocked most of Jane's breath out. Her face felt crimson. 'What do you mean?' she asked. Her voice sounded strange to her, muted and husky.

A corner of Brace's mouth tilted upward. 'I'd rather be your friend than your business associate.'

'You won't take *anything*?'

The other side of his mouth tilted up. 'Your undying gratitude will be sufficient recompense, my dear.'

She broke into laughter.

Brace grinned and drank his coffee.

After Jane had settled down, he said, 'The thing now is to decipher the clue. "At midnight, horse around."'

'I don't suppose he means the obvious.'

'The obvious?' Brace asked.

'You know, horse around. Like monkey around, goof around, mess around, *screw* around.'

'We might try it and see if an envelope turns up.'

Jane knew she was blushing. She tried to laugh. 'Hey, come on.'

'I'm sorry. Forget I said that, okay? Anyway, I think you're right. The sort of horsing around that you're referring to is an activity, and he's probably trying to give you a location.'

'Someplace where there's a horse,' Jane said.

'I don't imagine he's trying to send you into the countryside to hunt out stables or a farm. This horse is probably here in town someplace.'

'And not necessarily a *real* horse,' Jane added. 'Maybe just a place with "horse" in its name, like the White Horse Inn, or . . . we could check the telephone directory and see what we can find.'

'I don't think we'll have to hit the reference sources just yet. I think I might know where he wants you to go.'

Chapter Four

After leaving Ezra's, they walked back to the library parking lot. 'Why don't we take my car?' Brace said. 'No point in both of us driving.'

'Fine,' Jane said, and followed him toward an old Ford near the end of the lot.

She felt jittery. Climbing into a car with Brace might be a big mistake. She'd decided to risk it, however, even before he had made the suggestion.

Because she agreed with his theory that the campus statue was probably where they would find the envelope. The campus was two miles from Ezra's, a fairly long walk but a quick drive, and she could think of no good reason to insist that they go in separate cars.

Only one reason existed: climbing into Brace's car would amount to surrendering control to him. If he turned out *not* to be the good guy he seemed, Jane could be letting herself in for a world of pain.

She *wanted* to trust him, though. She liked him, and hated the idea that he might be a threat.

Also, she figured there was at least one logical reason to trust him: if he had evil intentions, he could've nailed her earlier, when they were upstairs together in the library's stacks. A perfect place for an assault, but he'd behaved just fine.

There's no reason not to trust him, she reminded

herself as she waited for Brace to unlock the passenger door.

Except for the fact that he's a guy.

He opened the door, then ducked in and began to clear the seat of books, magazines, file folders, and loose papers. 'We could take my car,' Jane suggested.

'No, that's all right. This'll just take a minute.'

'You aren't used to passengers, huh?'

'Sort of a loner.'

Oh, that's a wonderful sign.

She surprised herself by saying, 'Oh, great. I'm about to get in the car with a loner.'

'Don't be afraid, my pretty.'

'Very funny.'

'Sorry.' He stepped backward with the materials clutched to his chest. 'Could you open that?' he asked, nodding at the rear door.

She opened it. Brace leaned in and dumped his collection onto the back seat. 'All set,' he said. He gestured for her to sit in the passenger seat.

Jane climbed in, and he shut the door for her. While he walked around the front, she leaned over and unlocked the driver's door. He pulled it open and climbed in.

'Excited?' he asked.

'A little, maybe. Mostly just nervous.'

He started the car, put on the headlights, and began backing out of the parking space. Jane pulled the safety harness down across her chest and lap. She latched its buckle into place by her hip, then wondered if she might be safer without it. If she needed to make a quick getaway . . .

Hey, cut it out. I'm trusting him, remember?

'I hope it's where it's supposed to be,' Brace said.

'What do you mean?'

'The statue. I haven't actually *seen* it since the thing was banished from the quad. I know where they originally *put* it, but who knows?' The headlights swept across the rear of Jane's parked car, then left it in darkness. She turned her head. Her little Dodge Dart looked dreary sitting all by itself in the lot.

'How long ago did they get rid of it?' she asked.

'Ah . . . three years ago? Right, three. I was one year away from tenure, so the administration threatened to give me the bounce if I didn't shut up about it.' He checked the street, then pulled out, turning right. 'I didn't shut up about it. They kept me, anyway. They kept the statue, too, but safely tucked out of sight so it wouldn't offend anyone.'

'If they found it so offensive, why didn't they melt it down, or something?'

'They almost did. There were suggestions that it should be destroyed and recast into a giant peace symbol, for one thing. Fortunately, the sculptor was an alumnus. Also, there were a few of us who argued that history might be unkind to those who went around destroying works of art because a ludicrous political trend happened to make the subject matter unpopular. They finally compromised and hid it. Just hope it's still there. It's possible that the statue was moved or destroyed or something after the controversy finally died down.'

'If that's the case,' Jane said, 'it obviously isn't the horse we're looking for.'

'It's the most obvious one, though.'

'Not if it's gone.'

Brace looked at her and nodded. 'It'd *better* be the Crazy Horse statue. The only other horse I know about is in front of the Safeway market and goes up and down when a kid drops a quarter in its slot.'

'We might have to give that one a try.'

'Let's hope we get lucky with the statue,' he said.

Brace parked on the street in front of Jefferson Hall, the humanities building. 'This is about as close as we can get in the car,' he explained.

They climbed out.

'Where is it?' Jane asked.

'The other side of campus,' Brace said as they started walking. 'Just this side of Mill Creek. There's a fenced-in area where the maintenance crews keep equipment and things. That's where it's *supposed* to be. More than likely, it hasn't gone anyplace. The thing's a monster – took a construction crew with a giant crane to move it there in the first place.'

On their way through the campus, they encountered several students. Some were alone, while others walked with friends. All of them recognized Brace and spoke to him. Some even stopped and chatted.

'You're pretty popular around here,' Jane said as they reached the far side of the quad.

'It's you they're curious about.'

'So I noticed.'

'Hope you'll forgive the fellows who drooled.'

She laughed. 'Nobody drooled. A couple of those *gals* looked ready to kill me, though.'

'You'll be okay. Just don't turn your back on them.'

She looked behind her. The students who'd stopped and talked were no longer in sight. Nobody seemed to be nearby, or approaching, or watching from a distance. 'I wonder where *he* is,' she said.

Brace turned around. His eyes narrowed as he scanned the walkways and trees and shadows.

'He must be watching,' Jane said. 'He must be. Otherwise, what's the point?'

'I don't know.'

'He *must* be watching.'

'He wasn't in the stacks,' Brace reminded her.

'He might've been. You know? Just because we didn't find him doesn't necessarily mean he wasn't there. Maybe he had a good hiding place.'

'It's possible, I guess.'

'You're *not* him, right?'

Smiling, Brace raised his right hand. 'Honest Injun.'

'Oooo. I heard that.'

'Sorry. I'm evil – the demon who thought it wasn't a sin to call our team the Warchiefs.'

'I don't think *that's* so bad. Warchiefs. It's not like calling them the Redskins, you know? But I'm not so sure about Crazy Horse as a mascot.'

'He was great. You should've seen him, galloping down the sidelines at the football games. And the statue . . . it's magnificent. You'll see.'

'Hope so.'

'We're almost there,' Brace said. He left the walkway and walked on the grass, leading Jane toward the side of a low building.

Though Jane had been on campus a few times, she had never done much serious exploring of the university grounds. She was aware of the wooded area behind the buildings on the western side of the quad, but she'd never ventured into it.

You're about to do it now, she told herself.

She didn't much care for the idea.

Mill Creek was back there someplace.

She had probably noticed a few things from the park on the other side of the creek. Storage sheds? A greenhouse? She couldn't really be sure what she'd seen. Mostly, she remembered seeing thickets and trees. She clearly remembered that the area had seemed desolate and gloomy.

'This is where the statue is?' she whispered, nodding toward the darkness ahead.

'Back behind the science building. Can't see it from here.'

'Terrific.'

'Don't worry.'

'You know what?' she whispered. 'I'm not so sure we oughta keep going. I mean, it's pretty stupid. We don't know what this guy wants.'

Brace halted and turned to face her. She wished she could *see* his face. In the darkness, it looked like a gray smudge. He took hold of both her hands. 'You don't really want to quit, do you?'

'No, but . . . it's getting scary again. We really *should* quit. It's stupid not to.'

'I tell you what. Suppose I go on ahead and check out the statue?'

'What am *I* supposed to do?'

'Go back to where the lights are and wait for me. You should be safe there.'

'And let you do the dirty work?'

'My pleasure, ma'am.'

'No way. What if it's some sort of a trap?'

'All the more reason . . .'

'Oh, sure. I can't let you get hurt, or something, on account of me.'

'Should we give it all up?'

'No, but . . .'

Brace squeezed her hands. 'Let's go ahead, then. Money or not, it'd be a shame to come all the way out here and not get to see Crazy Horse. Especially since I risked my job to save him from oblivion.'

'Okay.'

He let go of one hand, but held on to the other as he turned around and led Jane deeper into the trees behind the building. Her heart was pounding very hard.

Nothing's going to happen, she told herself. We'll find the envelope or we won't, and that'll be it. Nobody's going to ambush us.

In a loud voice that trembled only slightly, Jane announced, 'If any shit *does* go down, the game is over. I'll quit. End of his fun with me. So he'd better think twice before he pulls anything cute.'

'That's telling him,' Brace said.

'I meant every word of it.'

'Do you think he's near enough to hear what you said?'

She felt a tremor slide up her spine. 'Jeez, I sure hope not.'

Brace laughed softly.

'I'm glad you find me amusing. Maybe I should hire out for parties.'

'If you want to know the truth,' he said, 'I think this whole business is great. It's like you and I have teamed up for a treasure-hunting adventure. There's mystery, suspense, excitement, untold riches in the offing, the possibility of danger and romance . . . It's wonderful, in a way.'

Possibility of romance?

With me?

Who do you think *he means?*

Jane blushed. She was glad that Brace couldn't see it in the darkness.

'If he murders us under the statue of Crazy Horse

tonight,' she said, 'we can die happy in the knowledge that he gave us a few such precious moments.'

She heard Brace laugh again.

Then he halted. Jane stepped closer to his side. She felt his arm brush against her. 'The light's off,' he whispered.

'What?'

'There's supposed to be a spotlight on the gate. For security.'

'Where?'

He pointed straight ahead. Squinting through the darkness, Jane found a vague shape that she supposed might be a high, chainlink fence beyond the trunks of several trees. She couldn't see through the fence. Nor could she see a gate.

'That's where the statue is?' she asked. 'In there?'

'That's where they put it.'

'Are you sure there's supposed to be a light?'

'It's always on at night. I mean, I don't keep track of it, but I've seen it often enough when I've been around campus after dark. You can see it from the quad when you walk past the science building.'

'And tonight it's out.'

'I don't see a light, do you?'

'No.'

'I'd say our friend has been here,' Brace said.

'Yeah,' Jane muttered. 'And added a little darkness to the game.'

Chapter Five

'How are we going to get in?' Jane asked as they approached the fence.

It reminded her of fences she had sometimes seen around tennis courts: as high as a one-story building and draped on the inside with tarps.

'I can't climb over that,' she said.

'Sure you can.'

'Well, I'm not *going* to.'

He laughed. 'Me neither. But there might be another way to get in.'

They passed a corner of the enclosure, and walked along the front. Here, moonlight found its way through breaks in the trees. It showed broad, double gates at the center of the fence, and a lane of asphalt that led away toward the quad. Fixed high on the fence was the spotlight Brace had mentioned. It was apparently aimed down at the asphalt directly in front of the gates. A curve of its fixture glowed with moonlight, but its bulb was dark.

'Might've just burnt out,' Brace said as they walked closer to the gates.

'I bet he climbed up there and unscrewed it a little.'

'Whatever, it's just as well. I wouldn't want to be fooling around back here with that light shining on us.'

Jane had hoped the gates would give her a view inside the fenced area, but now she saw that they, too, were hung with tarps. 'Somebody sure doesn't want people looking in,' she muttered.

'It's probably to avoid tempting the students.' Brace stepped toward the padlocked chain that was wrapped around the center posts of the gates, binding them together. He crouched slightly and lifted the padlock. Then he began studying the chain. 'The last thing the college needs is for some guys to break in and boost a tractor mower or some Porta-potties, or . . . all *right*!' He moved his hands together, and the chain parted.

'How . . .?'

'Someone clipped one of the links.'

'I wonder who.'

Unwinding the chain, Brace said, 'Maybe he figured you'd give up if you had to climb over the fence.'

'He was right.'

Brace let the chain and padlock fall to the ground. He pulled at the gate on the right, and it swung toward him. 'Just slip in,' he whispered.

Jane hesitated. 'Could we go to jail for this?'

'Only if we're caught.'

'I mean it.'

'We'll be all right. For one thing, we aren't the ones who cut the chain. For another, I'm on the faculty. I'd have some explaining to do, that's all. Probably.'

'I wouldn't want to get you fired.'

'You won't. In, in.'

Jane sidestepped through the narrow gap. Brace followed, then quickly pulled the gate shut.

The surrounding fences and the high limbs of trees just outside the enclosure blocked out much of the moonlight. Jane could only see dim shapes – some black, others in grays of varying darkness. The shape directly in front of her was apparently the tractor mower Brace

44

had mentioned. Off to the right was something that looked like a golf cart. And a bird bath. And half a dozen Porta-potties standing all in a row near the fence.

Her heart gave a lurch when she spotted the man.

He stood absolutely motionless just in front of the nearest toilet. Though his figure was vague in the darkness, he seemed to be naked.

'Brace!' She pointed.

Brace looked at the man. 'Don't worry,' he whispered. 'I know him.'

'You *know* him?'

'It's Dave.'

'Who's Dave? What's he doing here? Why's he *naked*?'

'Dave the statue. Michelangelo's David. A miniature reproduction. They stuck him away last year after a co-ed brought a sexual harassment lawsuit. She alleged that walking by him on her way to class was offensive and stressful.'

'Oh. Okay. I was afraid it was . . . him.'

'I don't think he's in here. He couldn't have done that with the lock and chains from the inside. So unless he climbed over the top afterwards . . .'

'Wouldn't rule it out.'

'We'll keep our eyes peeled, just in case.'

Jane scanned the area. 'What is all this stuff, anyway?'

'A little bit of everything. Sort of like the university's version of a junk drawer.'

'I don't see Crazy Horse.'

'Over there,' Brace said, pointing toward the far left corner. 'Behind all that stuff. I hope.'

He led the way.

The statue *could* be back there, Jane realized. A Bradley tank could be tucked out of sight in that corner behind the accumulation of clutter.

So could Mog, Master of Games. Or he might be hiding anywhere along the way.

Most of the dark shapes over there were too indistinct to identify. But Jane thought she could make out a collection of park benches standing on end; at least a dozen cages of various sizes, all stacked up like castoffs from a traveling zoo; plywood trees that she imagined had served as props for a stage production (*A Midsummer Night's Dream* came to mind); and a small forest of standing Doric columns, twice Jane's height, that looked dirty gray in the darkness.

She turned sideways to follow Brace through the columns. She brushed against some, rubbed against others as she squeezed between them. They felt cool and rough like concrete.

She almost asked Brace if he knew what they were for.

But she didn't want to know. Not that badly.

Not badly enough to speak and invade the silence with her voice.

He might be anywhere.

Near enough to hear Jane whisper, close enough to touch her. She reached out for Brace's arm, but he kept moving, unaware, and her hand found only air.

Don't leave me behind!

She hurried after him. Her footfalls were nearly silent in the soft, dewy grass. Good. You want to be silent, she told herself. But her breathing sounded awfully loud. And her denim skirt rasped as her buttocks rubbed against the rough grain of a column. Another column thrust against her left breast as she squeezed by. It didn't hurt her and it made no more than a whisper against the fabric of her blouse, but gave a tug that popped her top button out of its hole. As she reached up and fumbled to refasten the button, the maze of columns ended.

She halted. She lowered her arms. She glanced at Brace. His head turned toward her and his hand reached out. She took hold of it, squeezed it.

In front of them stood the statue of Crazy Horse.

It loomed high over them, nearly double the size of a real horse and rider, black in a bright glow of moonlight.

Black and magnificent.

The black stallion at full gallop was stretched out long and sleek, mane afly, tail aloft, only a single hoof at the left rear grounded to the pedestal, the other three airborne as it raced through frozen time.

And on the stallion's bare back rode Crazy Horse, war chief of the Sioux. Naked except for a loincloth, lean and muscular, hunched over, hugging the mount with his knees, one hand raised in a fist, the other bearing a lance. His mouth was wide in a warcry, his long hair and the rear flap of his loincloth high up behind him, lifted by the same ceaseless wind as the stallion's mane and tail.

'What do you think?' Brace asked.

'My God.'

'Yeah.'

They moved closer together, and Jane leaned against him. He slipped an arm across her shoulders.

'Who was the alumnus, Frederic Remington?'

'A guy named Pat Clancy, class of thirty-nine. This was the only major piece he finished before the war. His plane went down somewhere over the Himalayas in forty-three. He's up there now, near Mount Everest somewhere, always will be.'

For a while, Jane didn't trust herself to speak. She knew her voice would falter. After wiping her eyes, she took a deep breath and said, 'It shouldn't be hidden away

47

back here. It should be where everybody can see it.'

'Yeah. Well, maybe someday.'

'I didn't even know it existed. If you hadn't brought me here . . .'

'I helped a bit,' he admitted. 'But it was your friend Mog who *really* brought you here.'

Jane gazed up at the statue of Crazy Horse. 'You're right,' she whispered. 'How weird. I've been afraid of him, and what has he done? He's given me money . . . he's led me to a copy of a great novel like *Look Homeward, Angel* . . . and he's brought me over here to see this fabulous statue. What's to be scared of?'

'Maybe nothing,' Brace said.

'Maybe plenty, huh?' Jane said. 'He might be trying to lull me into trusting him. Then *wham!*'

'It's possible.'

Jane nodded. 'Anything's possible, isn't it?'

'Pretty much so.'

'But, you know? Even if he turns out to be some vicious, bad-to-the-bone creep, I might never have seen this Crazy Horse statue if he hadn't sent me here. Might've missed getting to know you, too.'

'I know *I'm* grateful to him,' Brace said.

They faced each other.

Jane knew that he was about to pull her into his arms. Knew. Felt it. Any second, now. He wouldn't stop with embracing her, with kissing her, wouldn't stop at all.

Oh, my God. I'm not ready for this. No! It's too soon, way too soon.

We can't!

'So,' Brace said, 'where do you think he left the envelope?'

'Huh? Oh. I don't know.'

'Somewhere around the horse, more than likely. "At midnight, horse around."'

'It isn't midnight yet, is it?' Jane asked.

'Are you okay?'

'Yeah. Fine. Just a little nervous. What time is it?'

Brace checked his wristwatch. 'Only eleven-thirty. It shouldn't matter, though. If this is the right place and he did that to the chain, he's already come and gone.'

'Maybe.'

'You don't want to leave and come back at midnight, do you?'

'No. I guess we should go ahead and look for it.'

'It's probably up on the statue somewhere,' Brace said, 'but let's check the easy places first.' He started to make his way around the pedestal, Jane following. He walked slowly, crouched over, head turned toward the statue.

His trousers were gray and slightly baggy. He had a bulge in the rear left pocket. Jane supposed it was his billfold.

'This used to be on top of a huge concrete base in the middle of the quad,' he explained as he moved along, inspecting the pedestal, the horse's legs and underside. 'They kept the base where it was, at least for a while. Figured they might put a new statue on top of it to replace Crazy Horse. Problem was, they couldn't come up with any ideas that didn't have a potential for negative political ramifications. I mean, there are campus and community activists who will find something wrong with *anything*. So when somebody figured out that they could remove the concrete block and put up a tree instead of a statue, that was it. Now we've got a Sequoia growing in the middle of the quad where Crazy Horse used to be.'

49

'What did they decide to call the football team after all the problems they had?'

'The Chargers.'

'Oh, that's it. Couldn't think . . . And their mascot is a credit card?'

He laughed. 'No, but maybe it should be. They don't have a mascot. And we don't seem to have an envelope down here.' He stood up straight and tipped back his head. 'I'd bet anything it's up there someplace. Maybe smack on top of the chief's head.'

'Wouldn't surprise me,' Jane said.

'Okay, well, make yourself comfortable and I'll . . .'

'Oh, no you won't. If somebody has to climb the statue, it'll be me. This is *my* gig, remember?'

'Well, sure, but . . .'

'You may come up, too, if you like. But I want to go first.'

'Fine.'

Jane suddenly felt annoyed with herself, certain that she'd been too abrupt with him. 'I mean, I just don't want you doing the hard part for me. It wouldn't be right.'

'That's fine. I didn't want to climb up there. High places make me queasy.' He reached out and gave her shoulder a gentle squeeze. 'Be careful, okay?'

'Don't worry, I won't fall.'

'Glad you've got so much confidence.'

'Hey, why do you think they call me Jane?'

'Why?'

'Tarzan, Jane, Edgar Rice Burroughs?'

'You were named after *that* Jane?'

'You bet.'

Brace laughed. 'If you say so.'

'I've been a climbing fool all my life. And I swing from vines.'

'Okay. If you say so.'

'You believe me, don't you?'

'Sure.'

'You do?'

'Sure.'

'Whoo. You're sort of gullible.'

'Maybe I'd better do the climbing.'

'No. I was serious about that. I'll go up and find the envelope. Or try, anyhow. You just stand by and catch me if I fall.'

'Jane would never fall, would she?'

'This Jane might.'

She made her way to the rear of the statue, stepped onto its pedestal, and reached for the horse's tail. Stretching, standing on her tiptoes, she could just touch her fingertips to the tail's cool bronze. So she jumped. She caught hold and struggled to pull herself up.

'Give you a boost,' Brace said. Not waiting for a response, he moved in from behind, hugged her around the thighs and hoisted her.

Instead of keeping her grip on the tail, she twisted and pressed herself against the horse's hindquarters. She reached her right arm across the rear flap of the chief's bronze loincloth. Grabbing it, she gasped, 'Okay.'

Brace released her legs.

She kicked up her left leg.

Giving him a great shot up my skirt.

It's too dark, she told herself. He can't see anything.

Can't see much, anyhow.

Gasping, thinking how silly it was of her to blush at a time like this, Jane squirmed and pulled at the shelf of loincloth until she straddled the horse's back.

'How is it up there?' Brace whispered.

51

Like doing the splits, she thought. But she said, 'Okay, I guess.'

For a while, she remained sprawled there, trying to catch her breath. Her face trickled with sweat. The statue felt cool underneath her, but the back of her blouse and the seat of her panties, soaked, were glued to her skin.

After a couple of minutes, she brought her legs closer together and lifted herself. On her knees, she crawled forward until the flap of the loincloth went in between her thighs and underneath her skirt. She sat on it. It felt as wide as a teeter board, but wavery. The bronze was chilly against her overheated skin, and she could feel it through her panties. It felt good.

She leaned forward against the chief's cool back, and wrapped her arms around his waist. From there, she looked down at Brace.

So far down!

'Oh, jeez,' she muttered.

Pressing her forehead against the chief's back, she thought, I'm doing this for two hundred dollars? I must be nuts.

There might not even *be* two hundred dollars!

This isn't for the two hundred, she reminded herself. It's for that, but it's also for the clue to the next step. The next step . . . if there is one . . . if the game goes on . . . might lead to four hundred dollars.

And the one after that to eight hundred.

Then sixteen hundred.

I could get rich.

If the game goes on long enough – if the Master keeps doubling the ante and if I don't quit.

Anyway, I'm already up here.

So where's the envelope?

Easing herself backward slightly, she checked to the right and left. The chief's back appeared to be nearly four feet across. From her seat on the loincloth in the middle, she might be able to take a look past one side or the other if she leaned over far enough. It would mean a major shifting of balance, though. If she should loose her grip . . .

No, I don't think so.

She leaned forward again. With much of her weight against his broad, solid back, she relaxed the grip of her thighs against his sides. She shoved her feet down against the horse and straightened her legs, raising herself off the loincloth. Her leg muscles trembled. She blinked sweat out of her eyes.

Then she was standing on the horse, clinging to the bronze sloping back of the hunched warrior chief. She rested her face against him and shut her eyes and gasped for air.

You still down there, Brace? she wondered. Sure wish you'd say something.

Maybe he decided it was time to go home.

Maybe Mog crept up on him and slit his throat.

'Take it easy,' she whispered to herself. 'Everything's cool.'

Get this over with!

She stepped up onto the loincloth with one foot. Pushing against it, she slid herself up the chief's back, stretched, and clutched the curved ridges of the trapezius muscles on each side of his neck.

Hanging on to them, she squirmed higher and higher.

And bashed her head. The pain slammed down through her body. Her vision flashed. For an instant, she imagined a vicious dwarf perched atop Crazy's Horse head, armed with a tomahawk – guarding the chief, gleefully whacking the heads of trespassers.

Through the pain, she felt herself slip downward a bit. *NO!*

She flinched rigid, locking her arms, freezing her fingers in their grip on the bronze shoulder muscles.

'My God,' Brace blurted in a harsh whisper. 'Hang on!'

'I am,' she murmured. In a louder voice, she said, 'I'm okay.'

Sure, she thought. Just great.

What she really wanted to do was let go and rub the top of her head. The urge was almost great enough to make her try, but she told herself that a little bump on the head would be nothing next to the pain of falling from this height.

Tipping back her head, she looked up.

Just above her, a sheaf of blackness jutted out from the rear of Crazy Horse's head.

His hair, flowing out behind him.

His bronze hair.

'Do you want me to come up?' Brace asked.

'No! Please don't. I'm okay.'

By this time, the pain from the blow had faded, leaving behind a hot place on her scalp and a dull ache inside her skull.

Jane pulled herself higher, squirming over to the right and tilting her head sideways to avoid the outcropping of hair. Soon, she was able to hook her right arm over the top of the chief's shoulder.

When she looked around, her stomach seemed to fall. *Oh, man, this is too high!*

She was way up in the moonlight, slightly higher than the chainlink fence, higher than many branches of the nearby trees. Through the treetops, she could glimpse bits and pieces of some university buildings. Mostly, however, the limbs blocked her views of the regions beyond the fence.

She had an aerial view of the odd clutter within the enclosure. She spotted the statue of David. Nothing else resembled a human.

Mog has to be down there, doesn't he? Why does he put me through this if he can't watch?

She sure couldn't see him, though.

Of course, she couldn't see Brace, either. She supposed Brace was somewhere behind her.

Maybe Mog, too.

She didn't dare change her position to look for either of them.

While looking about, she'd been vaguely aware that no envelope was attached to the statue below her. But she hadn't actually focused her attention on the search.

She did that now.

The way Crazy Horse was hunched over, she couldn't see much of the stallion; its head, most of its mane. To see more, she would need to climb higher and hang down over the chief's shoulder. That should give her a top view of the stallion's withers, the chief's chest and belly, the front flap of his loincloth and the tops of his legs clamping the stallion's sides. And maybe the missing envelope.

She wasn't ready to do that, though.

The less I have to crawl around on this guy . . .

She checked his right arm and the lance he carried. No envelope there.

Most of his left arm, fist high, was out of sight on the other side of his head.

Let's just check on top of his head.

Clamping herself more tightly against the chief, she twisted and reached up with her left hand.

55

She patted the top of his head.

Nothing.

The envelope had damn well better be somewhere up here after all this!

Halfway down the furrowed slope of Crazy Horse's hair, Jane's hand touched a papery packet. She explored it with her fingertips. It felt like an envelope folded in half, every edge taped down against the bronze.

She ripped it free.

Though her body trembled with the strain of keeping herself clamped to the statue's shoulder, she took a few moments to inspect her find.

The square was a folded envelope, all right. It looked grimy gray in the moonlight, and the cellophane tape along its edges gleamed silver. It had a comforting thickness.

In the middle of the square was one word: JANE.

'Got it,' she called down in a loud whisper.

'Yes!'

'I'm tossing it down. Ready?'

'Be careful.'

She reached across herself and dropped the envelope into the night beyond her right shoulder.

Chapter Six

Jane was drenched with sweat and every muscle in her body seemed to be twitching by the time she made her way down to the horse's tail. As she struggled to lower herself from it, Brace caught her dangling legs.

He eased her toward the ground, letting her slip gradually through his arms.

Jane felt her skirt being rucked up, felt his hands on her bare legs.

She accepted it. Brace was helping her down, and this sort of thing was probably unavoidable. Or maybe he meant to have his hands under there, the better to cop a feel. Either way, Jane didn't much care. She was out of breath, sopping wet, aching and shuddering from the exertions of the climb, still scared. She'd been so high up. She'd come so close to falling. But now she was almost to the ground. It didn't matter where Brace's hands were.

They were high on her thighs, pressing her against him, when they lost their grip. Jane gasped and dropped abruptly a few inches. She felt a soft tug between her legs. Then Brace clutched her hips and pulled her sharply, forcing her rump tight against his chest and bringing her to a halt.

He bent his knees. The moment Jane's feet touched the ground, he released her. As his right hand went away, she felt a gentle snap of elastic and realized his fingers had been inside her panties. Under the front panel. They must've gone in from the side when Brace lost his hold and had to make the quick grab.

It probably wasn't on purpose, she told herself.

Maybe he didn't even notice.

He noticed, all right. Are you kidding?

'Sorry about that,' he whispered.

Just pretend it's nothing. No big deal.

Jane turned around. She rested her hands on Brace's hips and bowed her forehead against his chest. She was too winded to talk. Good. It gave her an excuse for ignoring where his hand had been.

As she gasped for air, she realized that she could pretend *she* hadn't noticed.

'How's the head?' Brace asked.

'Sore.'

'Do you feel dizzy or anything?'

'No. It wasn't . . . that bad. Just that it . . . almost made me fall.'

'Thank God you held on.'

'Yeah.'

She felt both his hands gently caressing her back. She couldn't imagine why he would want to do that, considering the sodden condition of her blouse. The touch of his hands felt good, though. Soothing, comforting.

'About ready to get out of here?' he asked after a while.

She nodded. 'You've . . . got the envelope?'

'Sure do.' Taking her hand, he led her on a meandering route to the gates of the fenced enclosure. There, he eased one of the gates open slightly and stuck his head out. 'Coast is clear,' he told her, then opened it wide.

While Jane waited behind him, he wrapped the chain around the gate posts and hooked it together. 'I'd like to really secure the thing,' he whispered. 'Can't do it without a key for the padlock, though.'

'They'll probably fix it tomorrow,' Jane said.

'Yeah. Let's get out of here.'

They made their way through the darkness. Soon, they rounded the corner of the science building and walked toward the lights of the quad. Brace dug the folded envelope out of his pants pocket. 'We can stop under the lights and . . .' When he looked at her, his words died. 'Uh-oh.'

Jane lowered her head.

She had known that she must look a mess, but this was worse than she'd expected. Her blouse was not only filthy with a mixture of grime and bird droppings from her climb on the statue, but it was completely untucked and mostly unbuttoned. Plastered to her skin with sweat, it was twisted askew so that the wide gap in front showed the side of her right breast.

Turning away from Brace, she pulled her blouse shut and fumbled with the buttons.

'This is really the pits,' she muttered.

'Hey, you got the envelope.'

'What if somebody sees us?'

'Would you rather take the long way around? We can stay behind the buildings and avoid most of the lights.'

'Yeah. I don't want to be seen like this.'

'Might make people suspicious,' Brace said. 'Especially if we run into campus security.' Taking her arm, he led her toward the dark area at the rear of the building. 'Not that we did anything wrong.'

'They'll probably think we did. I'd hate it if you got into any sort of trouble over this.'

'It would've been worth it,' he said.

'Think so?'

'Definitely.'

She was surprised to feel a smile spread across her face. 'It has been quite a night.'

They moved through shadows and encountered no one. When they reached Park Lane, Brace hurried off to fetch the car. Jane waited near the bridge, staying out of sight in a stand of trees.

As she waited, she shivered.

The night was very warm, but her sweaty clothes felt chilly. She pressed her legs together and crossed her arms and gritted her teeth.

It isn't so much the cold, she thought. It's everything else.

Nerves and excitement.

Soon, Brace's car came along. It passed on the other side of the street, slowed down on the bridge, then made a U-turn and came back. It swung to the curb in front of Jane's hiding place. It stopped and the passenger door opened.

Jane walked quickly over to it, climbed in and pulled the door shut. 'That was pretty quick,' she said.

'I hurried along. Where to now, the library?'

'Let's see what's in the envelope.'

'Here?'

'Sure. You never know, he might send us back to the statue, or something.'

Brace dug it out of his pocket and handed it to Jane. She tore off the strips of tape and unfolded the envelope. As she ripped open its flap, Brace reached to the dashboard and the car's courtesy light came on.

'Thanks,' she said, removing the note.

The lined sheet of paper was folded into thirds, just like the others. Inside, she found a fresh pair of hundred-dollar bills. She showed them to Brace.

'Very good,' he said. 'The guy came through.'

'I'd be a mighty unhappy camper if he hadn't.'

'Well, I'd say you earned it.'

'*Worked* for it, that's for sure.'

'And he doubled it, so he's sticking to the pattern.'

'Right,' Jane said. 'The next should be four hundred bucks.'

'Maybe two's the max.'

'Oh, I sure hope not.' She set the money down on her lap and raised the handwritten note. '"My dearest Jane,"' she read aloud, '"The game goes on. Troll for your next treasure tomorrow, midnight, under Park. You'll be glad you did. Yours, MOG, Master of Games."'

'Tomorrow night,' Brace said.

'That's a relief. I've about had it for tonight.'

'Shall we be off?'

'Guess so.'

He started driving. Jane folded the note and tucked it back inside the envelope. She picked up the money. 'How about taking one of these?'

'Nope.'

'Are you sure? I never would've gone into a place like that alone. Hey, I wouldn't have even *known* enough to go there.'

'Glad I could help. But it's your money. I don't want any, really.'

'Okay.' She slipped the bills into the envelope. Bending over, she reached down between her knees and lifted her purse off the floor. 'If you change your mind, let me know.' She dropped the envelope into her purse.

'Are you planning to go on with all this?' Brace asked.

'I guess so. I don't see why not. Will you come with me tomorrow night?'

'You bet. Want me to meet you at the library?'

She considered it for a moment, then shook her head. 'I think I'll go home first and change clothes.'

'Good idea. You messed up your blouse pretty good tonight.'

'Yeah.' She blushed at his mention of the blouse. Even though she was fairly certain that her nipple had stayed out of sight, Brace had definitely seen a lot of her breast – and he was well aware that she wore nothing at all underneath the blouse. 'I'll get into some grubbies for tomorrow night,' she said.

Soon, Brace slowed his car and swung into the library's parking lot. Ignoring the lines on the asphalt, he steered directly toward Jane's car.

'Maybe I should follow you home right now,' he suggested. 'It's pretty late. Make sure you get there safely, and it'll save me from having to hunt for your house tomorrow night.' He stopped beside her car.

He wants to go home with me. Then what?

He's okay, she told herself. He's fine. Hell, he's terrific.

Yeah, right, this terrific guy just so happened accidentally to slip his hand in my panties.

It was an accident. I was all sweaty and he lost his hold, that's all.

Yeah, right.

It wasn't on purpose, I know it.

'Sounds good,' she said.

'Fine. I'll be right behind you.'

That seemed very much like her cue to leave – but not at all like a farewell. As Jane lifted her purse and opened the passenger door, she realized that Brace intended to do more than follow her home and drive off.

He'll want to come in.

'See you later,' she said, then shut the door and went to her own car.

Brace stayed a safe distance behind her as she drove from the library to her rented house on the outskirts of town. She pulled into the driveway, and he stopped at the curb.

It came as no surprise when his headlights went dark. But it made Jane's heart pound harder, made her stomach go squirmy.

Brace strode up the driveway while she climbed out of her car. She slung the purse onto her shoulder, shut and locked her door. Then she turned to face him.

'Thought I'd better find out what time you want me here tomorrow night.'

'I'm not sure. I don't know exactly where we're supposed to go.'

'Maybe we should take a closer look at the note, see what we can figure out.'

Jane reached into her purse. She pulled out an envelope, saw that it didn't have a crease in the middle, put it away and came up with the envelope from the statue. She handed it to Brace.

He removed the note, leaving the money untouched. 'We'll need some light on the subject,' he said, and led the way toward Jane's porch.

Standing under the porch light, he unfolded the note and read it. 'That's what I thought.'

'What?'

He grinned. 'I'm here to lend help, not to do all the thinking for you.' He handed the note back to Jane. 'Take a look and tell me what *you* think.'

She gave the note a glance, then met Brace's eyes. He's a good guy, she told herself. He won't try anything.

Right. Sure.

I want to trust him, she thought. So here goes.

'Would you like to come inside?' she asked.

'Oh, I suppose so. Can't stay long, though. I'm already way past my bedtime.'

'Well, we'll have to make it quick, then.' She unlocked the door, and Brace followed her into the living room. She turned on a lamp, then tossed her purse onto an easy chair. In the bright light from the lamp, she saw that more than her blouse was filthy: her hands, her blue denim skirt, her bare legs, even her white socks and gray Reebok shoes were smudged and streaked with grime.

She suddenly wanted very badly to get out of her clothes and under a hot shower.

Not while he's here.

She dropped the note onto the coffee table in front of the sofa. 'Would you like something to drink?' she asked.

'Thanks. Whatever you're having.'

'Beer okay?'

'Beer's great.'

He followed her into the kitchen. There, she washed her hands with soap and hot water, dried them on a paper towel, then removed two cans of Budweiser from the refrigerator. She carried them to the counter, set them down and popped their tabs.

'Maybe we'd better take a look around the house,' Brace said. 'Just to be on the safe side.'

'Oh, great,' she muttered.

'You never know.'

'You think Mog might've used this little game of his to keep me away from the house – so he could be sure I wouldn't show up and surprise him?'

'Anything's possible,' Brace said.

'Yeah. When nothing makes sense, anything *is* possible.'

'Why don't you give me a tour?'

They took their beers with them and started to walk through the house. Right away, Jane found herself less worried about running into an intruder than encountering castoff undergarments or other such surprises. But the house seemed reasonably clean and tidy. The clutter wasn't half as bad as it might've been. And she hadn't left any dirty clothes scattered around.

Still, she felt a little embarrassed that Brace was getting this opportunity to see so much – the mementos on top of her dresser, the pictures on her walls, the bed where she slept, her toilet, her bath tub.

My God, she thought, this guy has already seen and touched more of me – my body *and* where I live – than the last five guys I went out with.

Finished with the search, they returned to the living room. 'It was sort of a longshot,' Brace said. 'Glad he *wasn't* here, though.'

'Me, too.' Jane sat down on the sofa. Brace sat down beside her – nearly a foot away.

Close, but not too close.

Maybe *he's* the timid one, she thought. But probably not.

Leaning forward, he reached to the coffee table and picked up the note. 'So, what's your take on this?' he asked, passing it to Jane.

She read the note to herself. 'Okay,' she said when she was done. 'At midnight tomorrow . . . or tonight, actually, since this is *already* tomorrow . . . I'm supposed to "troll" for my next treasure. Troll under Park. And Park is capitalized. So it's a proper noun, possibly the name of the street we were on tonight. Park Lane?'

'Sounds about right to me.'

'So this could mean I'm supposed to troll under Park Lane. By "troll," I don't think he means I'm supposed to go fishing or sing a song. He probably wants me to *make like a troll*. Traditionally, they dwell under bridges, right?'

In a deep, menacing voice, Brace said, 'Who's that walking across my bridge?'

'It's own-wee me,' Jane baby-talked. 'Wooddow teeny-weeny Baby Behwwy Goat Gwuff.'

Laughing, Brace rocked sideways toward Jane and gently bumped against her upper arm before swaying away. 'You oughta be in pictures.'

'That was actually my Chicken Little impression.' She took a deep breath. 'Anyway. I think what I'm suppose to do is go where the trolls are – underneath a bridge. Probably the Mill Creek Bridge on Park Lane.'

'Strange,' Brace muttered.

'I know. We were just there. Jeez, we should've gone down and checked around.'

'Want to go now?'

'Are you kidding? All I want to do is get out of these disgusting clothes and take a shower.'

Terrific. Talk to him about getting naked.

She turned away from Brace and took a drink of beer.

'If we went now,' he said, 'it'd probably be a waste of time. I don't think Mog would risk leaving his envelope down there a day ahead of time. The wrong person might find it.'

'Yeah. Good. Because I've got no intention of looking for it now. Midnight'll be plenty soon enough.'

'And you want me to pick you up here?'

'That'd be nice.'

'What time?'

She thought about it. She usually arrived home from the library by nine-thirty. If Brace came over then, they'd have at least two hours before it was time to leave for the bridge.

Two hours in the house with each other . . .

No way.

'Maybe if you come by at around eleven,' she said. 'How would that be? We could have a beer or something before we hit the road.'

'Sounds good.' He tipped his head way back and drained his can of Budweiser. Then he leaned forward and set the can on the table. Rising, he said, 'I'd better be off.'

Jane stood. She walked with him to the front door.

As he opened it, he turned and faced her. 'I'll bring a flashlight. We could've used one tonight, huh?'

'Yeah. This time, we'll have to be better prepared.'

He gave her a parting smile and nod. 'Take care of yourself,' he said, and started to leave.

Jane caught hold of his arm. 'Hey,' she said. He turned toward her. 'Thanks. I don't know what I would've done.'

'My pleasure.'

Keeping her grip on his arm, she curved her left hand behind his neck and drew his head down. She gazed into his eyes as she brought his face closer. They looked different. Gone was the sharp intelligence, the alertness, the spark of mischief that she'd grown used to seeing there. They suddenly seemed dark with longing and maybe sadness.

Then they were so close that Jane lost focus on them. She shut her eyes and kissed him.

His lips were open and warm and moist.

They didn't move. Brace seemed motionless except for his breathing.

Then he moaned into her mouth.

Then he wrapped his arms around her and hugged her hard, squeezing and kissing her until she squirmed against him, out of breath.

Can't let this happen, she thought. No. Can't let it.

As if Brace could read her mind, he eased his lips away from her mouth and relaxed his embrace. A corner of his mouth tilted up. His eyes looked normal again. 'Well,' he said.

'Well?'

'Whew.'

She glanced down at his chest. 'Now you've gotten your shirt all dirty.'

'Oh, that's okay.'

'I could wash it for you.'

'What, now?'

'Sure.'

'Thanks. I've really got to be going, though. And you need to take that shower.' He gave her a quick peck on the forehead. 'Goodnight, now.'

Jane stood in the doorway. She watched him walk out to the street, enter his car and drive slowly away.

Chapter Seven

Jane shut and locked the front door. Then she stood motionless. The house seemed very silent, now that Brace was gone. Silent and empty.

Though she was accustomed to being alone, though she *needed* to be alone now so she could shower and go to bed, she suddenly felt more lonely and vulnerable than usual. The house didn't seem as safe as usual.

Don't get spooked, she told herself. There's no reason to feel spooked.

She took the two beer cans to the kitchen, drinking from hers along the way. It was empty by the time she reached the sink. She rinsed out both cans, then tossed them into the recycling bin beside her oven.

Before leaving the kitchen, she double-checked the back door. It was almost never unlocked, and she was fairly certain that neither she nor Brace had touched it tonight, but she wanted to make absolutely sure it was secure.

The lock button in the knob was turned horizontal.

She tried the knob, anyway. It rattled slightly, but refused to turn. She pushed at it. The door didn't budge.

As she left the kitchen, she flicked off its lights. She entered the living room, prepared to turn off the lamps. But she changed her mind about that.

Not tonight.

Tonight, she didn't want the living room dark while she showered.

Silly, she thought. But so what if it's silly? I don't want it dark in here, so I'll keep the lamps on. It's what I want to do, and nobody's exactly keeping score.

With her back to the lights, she walked up the hallway and past the bathroom. She stopped at her bedroom, reached around the door frame and found the light switch.

We already searched the whole house, she told herself. There's no reason to be so nervous.

She couldn't talk herself out of it, though.

After the lamps came on, she stepped into her bedroom and looked around. She checked inside the closet. On her knees, she checked under the bed. Then she shut the window curtains.

'Nobody here but us chickens,' she muttered. *'Brawwwk brawwwk brawwwk!'*

She took off her blouse and held it up by the shoulders.

It didn't appear to be torn or snagged. But the stains! *Soak it in Clorox?*

The hell with it, she thought. If it doesn't come clean in the wash, I'll just buy a new one and keep this for yard work, or something.

She tossed the blouse into her hamper, then added her socks, skirt and panties. She set her Reeboks on top of the hamper, figuring she would wipe them with a wet rag in the morning.

Her bathrobe hung from a hook on the back of her closet door. She took it down, but didn't put it on. The robe was for after her shower, when she would be clean.

Leaving her bedroom lighted, she walked down the hall to the bathroom. She reached in, clicked the rheostat and turned its knob until the lights were as bright as they could be. Then she entered, shut the door, and hung her robe on its hook.

As she turned around, she saw herself in the mirror. She looked away quickly, but not fast enough to avoid glimpsing the stringy mess of her hair, her dirty face, or the thickness of her waistline.

God, what a wreck!

At least Brace saw me before calamity struck.

She knew that she normally looked pretty good. Clean, well-groomed, and the extra weight was hardly noticeable when she wore the proper clothes.

Just gotta always keep my clothes on.

I shouldn't have let myself go, she thought as she crouched and turned on the water.

Hey, the hell with that. If Brace doesn't like my looks, tough tacos. Who am I trying to impress? No one, that's who.

Anyway, I'm not all that fat. Pleasingly plump.

He can like it or lump it.

Jane smiled. Pretty obviously, Brace *did* like it. Or at least he didn't seem to be put off by anything about her.

Her smile died. *Don't get all hot and bothered. He's a guy. When it comes right down to basics, he's probably a creep like the others.*

She touched the water gushing from the bathtub spout, adjusted the flow of cold to ease the burning heat, then twisted the shower handle and stepped into the tub. Quickly, she rolled the glass door shut.

She turned to the hot spray. Eyes shut, she took it full in the face. It seemed to engulf her. It tapped her eyelids, filled her mouth, spilled down her chin. It soothed her, made her feel drowsy.

After a while, she bowed her head. The spray soaked and matted her hair, heated her scalp, but also drummed her sore bump where she'd thudded her head on the underside of the chief's bronze hair.

Enough of that.

She turned around. Now, the water hit the back of her head and neck. It splashed her shoulders, flowed heavily down her back while numerous trickles meandered down her front. It felt very good, now that it was no longer striking the bump on her head.

She stood motionless for a while, savoring the feel of the water. Then she began to soap herself.

She wondered if Brace would someday be standing here with her.

Taking a shower with a man had always been one of her favorite fantasies.

She'd never done it.

Not that she hadn't been asked.

But you don't jump into a shower with just anyone. Especially when you're a little too plump. You don't want just anyone to see your fat unhidden.

Sliding the soap over her skin, she wondered if she would allow Brace in.

Say he shows up right now, she thought. He comes into the bathroom starkers, with a boner that doesn't quit. What do I do? Squeal and try to cover up? Or slide open the shower door and say, *Come on in, honey, the water's fine?*

Forget it, she told herself. Won't happen.

But what if it *did* happen? Make it easy on yourself — say you've lost fifteen pounds, or even just ten. And you're in here all lonely and hot and bothered, and you look through the shower door and there he is, coming at you, naked as the day he was born, all huge and stiff.

Jane turned toward the glass of the shower door. It was steamed up, white except in a few places where drops of water made clear streaks.

Though she couldn't see much through the fogged glass, she could easily see that nobody was approaching her from the other side.

But maybe Brace is in the hallway now, undressing, about to come in.

With both hands, Jane gripped the aluminum runner above the door. She leaned forward until her breasts touched the glass. It felt slick, and surprisingly cold. She rubbed herself lightly against it, and watched the tips of her nipples mark clear strips across the fog.

How would this look from the other side? she wondered. What would Brace think if he saw this? Better yet, what would he *do*? What would he do if he showed up right now and saw me like this?

Come over, maybe, and lick the glass.

Then slide the door out of the way, and I would hold on up above while he does it, feeling the glass slide against me, and then feeling his mouth.

Jane let out a small moan.

Hey, let's not get carried away. He isn't here, he isn't likely to be here in the near future, if ever. And if he did walk through the door buck naked right now, you'd probably give him hell and maybe throw the bar of soap at him.

'More than likely,' she muttered.

She leaned her head against the glass, pressing it with her brow and the tip of her nose.

So much for fantasies, she thought.

She rolled her head slowly from side to side, liking the rub of the cold glass.

Of course, she thought, I could make it come true if I wanted to. Just one telephone call.

Why not?

Who knows?

Because it would spoil things, she supposed. One way or another, things were sure to be ruined by a move like that.

It's too soon, anyway. Way too soon. By the time I know him well enough, maybe I'll hate him.

She realized she had slumped against the glass door, was holding herself in position by her grip on the aluminum runner at the top. So she straightened up.

And her eyes came level with an oval of glass that had been wiped clear of fog by her forehead.

The door to the hallway stood open.

Okay.

Jane was certain she had shut it, had heard the clack of its latch.

Okay.

So a gust of wind hadn't shoved it open. Nor had a settling of the house. Nothing short of a major earthquake could've opened that door.

Nothing except a hand.

Someone's in the house.

Okay.

Just dandy.

Forcing herself to look away from the door, she raced her gaze across the bathroom.

Nobody. Not yet.

She again fixed her eyes on the door.

Someone's probably just on the other side.

She tried to tell herself that it might be Brace. Might be. Just like in her fantasy. She couldn't believe it, though. Brace wouldn't sneak back and break into the house in hopes of delighting her with a surprise appearance. She was sure of it.

So sure that she felt no eagerness.

She felt only fear. She was gasping for breath as her heart galloped. Her insides seemed to be shriveling and twisting. Her skin crawled.

It's not Brace.

Maybe Mog, hotshot Master of Games, showing up to do whatever it is that he does.

Or someone else.

A burglar, a peeping Tom who got carried away with his hobby, or better yet, a rapist or serial killer.

Maybe none of the above, she told herself. Maybe it's something . . . perfectly innocent. Something I'll laugh about tomorrow.

And maybe tomorrow I won't be alive to laugh about anything.

'Not if I can help it,' she muttered.

Slowly, she rolled the shower door aside. Though it made a soft rumble, she doubted that the sound could be heard by the intruder lurking in the hallway. Not over the rushy noise of the shower.

Steadying herself with one hand on the wall, Jane stepped over the edge of the tub. She stood on the bathmat, panting for breath, trembling and dripping. Her purple robe still hung from the hook on the door.

The door stood half-open, showing a small section of the hallway beyond it.

She saw nobody out there.

What's he doing?

Maybe he's gone.

Sure, fat chance.

In two seconds, he'll probably come charging in to nail me.

Her mind raced. Should she charge the door, herself, smash it with her shoulder and make a dash for safety? Or jerk the door shut, lock it, and try to escape through the bathroom window? Or wait? Or what?

Try to run, she thought, and he might get me from behind.

She could almost feel a knife blade slicing down her spine.

And then she pictured herself making a brilliant escape, dashing outside in the buff, only to discover after some major embarrassment that nobody had been inside her house, at all.

Even as she thought about her options, Jane began to sidestep toward the sink. Two steps, and the bathmat was no longer under her feet. The tiles of the floor felt cool and slick. Water dribbled down her body. She blinked to keep her eyes clear, and never looked away from the door.

After a while, her rump met the edge of the counter. She moved sideways a little more, and stopped. Reaching back with a hand, she found the front of the sink.

She spun around.

Glimpsed a wild, wet Jane in the medicine cabinet mirror. Her foggy portrait darted sideways and vanished as the mirror's hinges squawked.

Most of what she saw on the narrow shelves would be of no use at all. Too many tubes, cardboard packages, bottles and jars made of lightweight plastic.

But the bottle of cough syrup was made of glass.

She grabbed it.

Then she snatched down an aerosol canister of OFF! insect repellent and struck its top against the edge of the sink. The big, plastic cap fell off. She took a moment to figure out which way the spray hole was pointing, then turned it away from her body and positioned her fingertip on the button.

Armed, she rushed the door. Though her wet feet

skidded and slipped, she stayed up. She hunched low and rammed the door with her shoulder.

It flew wide. It pounded the wall behind it.

She lurched into the hallway, skidded on the carpet and whirled herself around, ready to hurl the bottle at her assailant, ready to spray his face with bug repellent.

But no one was there.

She stood motionless. She held her breath and listened. She heard only the thumping of her heart and the hiss of the shower.

Maybe the door *had* opened by itself, she thought. If it hadn't really latched . . . I suppose I could've been wrong about hearing that.

Or maybe he's in another part of the house.

She resumed breathing.

She considered what to do next. Get out of the house? Go looking for the intruder? Call the police? Call Brace and ask him to come over?

There might not be anyone here.

'Screw it,' she muttered.

She stepped back into the bathroom. Her robe had fallen to the floor, so she crouched, set down her two makeshift weapons, and picked it up. She hung it on the hook again, then shut and locked the door.

If somebody *is* out there, she thought, maybe he'll be gone by the time I come out.

She half expected to find the bathroom flooded. In spite of the open glass door, however, most of the shower's spray had stayed inside the tub. She climbed back in and began to shampoo her hair.

It was probably just a false alarm, she told herself. I bet nobody's in the house but me. The door opened on its own. They do that sort of thing all the time when the latch doesn't quite catch.

Regardless, she knew she would be compelled to search the house carefully as soon as she finished her shower.

Make your first stop at the kitchen, she told herself. Grab a good, big knife.

She certainly didn't relish the idea of searching the house all by herself. It seemed better than the alternatives, though.

After rinsing, she shut off the water, rolled the door open and climbed out of the tub. She spent a long time drying herself.

No big hurry.

She hung up her towel. She used the bathmat to mop spilled water off the tile floor, then draped the mat over the side of the tub. She used the toilet. She brushed her teeth.

When she could think of no other delaying tactics, she went to the bathroom door. She unhooked her robe, swept it around her back and slipped her arms into its sleeves. Then she closed it around her. Holding it shut with her left hand, she reached with her right for the cloth belt dangling from its loop by her hip.

She wasn't watching her right hand.

But she looked at it fast when one of her fingertips brushed against a small corner that felt like paper.

A white envelope stood on end, a fraction of an inch protruding out of the pocket of her robe.

Chapter Eight

Brace arrived a few minutes early. Through her living room window, Jane watched him stop at the curb, climb from his car and stride toward her house. He wore dark clothes. He carried a flashlight. He walked with a light step, almost a bounce, as if he had to restrain himself from prancing like an eager kid.

She opened the front door as he bounded up the porch stairs. He stopped abruptly and smiled. 'All set for another big adventure?' he asked.

Nodding, Jane stepped backward. Brace followed her into the foyer and shut the door.

'Actually,' she said, 'more like yes and no.'

'Having second thoughts?'

'Hundred-and-second.'

'But I see you dressed for it.'

'Yep.' To blend in with the night, she wore black jeans and a navy blue chamois shirt. The shirt was too heavy and hot for a night like this. But she needed the dark color and the long sleeves, and this was the best she could do.

'You're going to be mighty warm in a shirt like that,' Brace said.

'Already am.' She led him into the living room. 'Would you like something to drink?'

'Thanks, but I'll pass. You go ahead, though.'

'Nah.' She sat on the sofa and patted the cushion at her side.

Brace took the offer. But then he scooted farther away, turned sideways until one of his knees almost touched her leg, and rested his elbow on the back of the sofa. He looked into her eyes. 'What is it?' he asked. 'Something isn't . . .?'

'We've got a little problem,' she said.

'A problem?' His eyebrows lifted slightly. 'What sort of problem?'

She leaned toward the coffee table and picked up an envelope. She showed it to Brace. 'This came "special delivery" last night. Apparently hand-delivered to the pocket of my bathrobe.'

Suddenly, Brace looked concerned. 'Your robe? Where was it?'

'On the bathroom door.' She was blushing, but she continued. 'I hung it there when I took my shower last night. Just after you left? He must've opened the door and slipped the envelope into my pocket while I was in the shower.'

'Oh, man,' Brace muttered.

'It shook me up pretty good.'

'He was *in the house*?'

'He had to be. But the doors and all the windows were locked. After I found the note, I looked everywhere. I couldn't find him. I couldn't even figure out how he got in. Everything was still shut and locked up tight.'

'You must've been scared half to death.'

She gave a little shrug with one shoulder and tried to smile. 'It wasn't so bad. I was scared, but . . . he'd passed up a great chance to attack me. I mean, nobody else was in the house, and he'd already opened the bathroom door. He could've nailed me right there in the shower, if

80

he'd wanted to. That's why I wasn't as frightened as I might've been. I think he was just here to deliver the envelope.'

'I *really* don't like it that he was in the house.'

'I'm not thrilled about it myself.'

'No idea how he could've gotten in?'

She shook her head. 'All I can think of is that he either picked a lock or had a door key. I mean, how else *can* you get into a house without breaking something?'

'I don't know. The police might've been able to figure out how he did it.' Brace laughed softly. 'You didn't call them, though, did you?'

'Almost. The thing is, he *didn't* attack me. And I don't think he stole anything. Except for how the bathroom door opened and I ended up with the envelope in my pocket, there's no sign that anyone was even here. I couldn't call the cops about something like that. And I'd have to show them the envelope he left, and they'd end up reading the note and finding out about the Game.'

Brace slid his arm off the back of the sofa, reached out and gently squeezed Jane's shoulder. 'So you just . . . searched the house all by yourself?'

'Me and my knife.'

He made a face. 'That little switchblade?'

'It isn't so little. But anyway, that isn't the knife I used. I grabbed me a big old butcher knife from the kitchen.'

Rubbing her shoulder, Brace shook his head and looked a bit like an exasperated but rather proud parent about to say, *You monkey, what're we gonna do with you?*

But he didn't tell her that. Instead, he said, 'I would've come over, you know. All you had to do was call. I could've been here in ten minutes.'

'Maybe if you'd given me your phone number . . .'

His hand went rigid on her shoulder. He groaned.

'You're unlisted,' Jane said.

'So you *did* try to call?'

'Well, I got as far as a talk with an operator.'

'Damn it,' he muttered. 'I'm sorry. I had my number taken out of circulation so long ago, I hardly ever think about it anymore. If only I'd . . .'

'It's all right. I could've used some moral support, but everything turned out okay. I mean, Mog was nowhere to be seen. I'm perfectly fine. No harm done.'

Brace released her shoulder. He pulled an old, battered black wallet out of his rear pocket, opened it and found one of his business cards. 'Here, keep this. It has my office number *and* my home number.'

Jane took the offered card. It looked as if it might've been dropped onto a floor and stepped on. 'Is it an antique?' she asked.

'Pretty near. I had them printed up in a burst of naive enthusiasm when I first got hired. *Before* I started getting calls from students at all hours of the night.' He reached up and tapped the back of the card. '*Nobody* gets these anymore.'

'I'm honored.'

'I just wish I'd given it to you last night.'

'So do I.' She slipped it into a pocket of her shirt, and found a grin spreading across her face. 'I guess we'll never know what might've happened.' When the words came out, she blushed.

'We'll never know,' Brace echoed. 'And I'm beginning to wonder if *I'll* ever know what's in the envelope. Did he bring you more money?'

'Afraid not.'

'What? Or is it supposed to be a secret?'

'You aren't going to like this. I know *I* don't.' She sighed, then picked up the envelope. She opened it and removed the note. '"Jane,"' she read aloud. '"Ours is a game built for two. Three's a crowd. If you have any desire to continue with me, lose Brace. I must insist. Mog."'

She handed the note to Brace. His eyes seemed to darken as he read it. 'The plot thickens,' he muttered.

'What do you think?'

'Obviously, he wants me to butt out.'

'It also means he watched us last night,' Jane said.

'At least part of the time,' Brace agreed. 'And he knows my name. How could he know my name? Maybe he's a student. Or someone on the faculty. That'd make sense. Look where he's sending you: to the Crazy Horse statue, to Mill Creek Bridge – places on or near the campus. And there's the literary angle.'

'He could've picked up your name by listening to us last night.'

'Eavesdropping?' He frowned. 'Most of the time, nobody was close enough for that.'

'Nobody we *saw*, anyway. But someone might've been . . . when we were inside the fence, there was so much junk around.' The skin on the nape of her neck suddenly prickled with goosebumps. 'I *felt* like we weren't alone in that place. I'll bet he was there.'

'It's possible,' Brace admitted.

'And he wanted me there by myself.'

'I don't like this one bit.'

'Neither do I,' Jane said. She realized that the goose-bumps weren't just on the nape of her neck. Her forehead and arms and nipples and thighs felt crawly, too.

'I can only think of one good reason,' Brace said, 'for wanting me out of the way.'

83

'Yeah.' Jane slid her hands slowly up and down her thighs, rubbing them through the legs of her jeans. 'But that doesn't make sense, either. If he wanted to attack me, he could've done it last night when I was in the shower. Would've been easy.'

'Then why *does* he want me out of the way?' Brace asked.

'Who knows? Why does he do *any* of this?'

Brace shook his head, his cheeks and lips puffing out as he expelled a deep breath.

'Maybe,' Jane said, 'we need to take the whole thing at face value. Maybe it really *is* a game, and he thinks of himself as the big boss, or something, and he doesn't want anybody playing it except me.'

'Sounds like a good time to quit.'

'I know. It does. But on the other hand . . .' Grimacing, she slid her shoulders up and down. 'I sort of want to keep going with it.'

'He broke into your *house*.'

'I guess so.'

'There's no telling *what* he might do.'

'Well, you know . . . If his past actions are any indication, he'll probably give me more and more money.'

'But *why*?'

'To keep me playing his game.'

'He's up to something,' Brace said. 'He's gotta be. Up to something no good.'

'We don't know that. Maybe he's some sort of mysterious benefactor. Like that creepy guy in *Great Expectations*? The fellow who popped up in the graveyard and scared the hell out of poor little Pip?'

'Magwich.'

'Right, Magwich. Maybe it's something like that.'

'You're not going to be talked out of this, are you?'

'Nope.'

'Well, it's your call.'

'I want to go ahead with it.'

'Alone?'

She nodded.

'Well, at least I can drive you over there. Why don't I do that? If you're still absolutely sure you want to play by his rules, I'll park and wait on the bridge while you go down after the money. That way, at least I'll be close by. If something goes wrong, you can yell.'

'That'd be nice,' Jane said. 'But I don't think so.' She shrugged again. 'I've thought a lot about all this. He wants you out of it, Brace. If I let you chauffeur me over there and hang around, he might just drop me. No more envelopes, no more clues, no more money. I don't want that to happen. I want to play this out – as far as I can, anyway.'

'Why should he care if I drive you over . . . ?'

'The thing is, he might.'

Wincing as if in pain, Brace shook his head.

Jane clasped his knee. 'It'll be all right.'

'I'm sorry,' he said. 'This is . . . it's none of my business. I mean, whatever you want to do. It's just that I don't want you to get . . . in trouble or hurt. I feel like I need to take care of you, but . . . crazy, huh?'

'Yeah, crazy.'

'We hardly even know each other.'

'Hardly even.'

'And you're pretty good at taking care of yourself.'

'Pretty good,' she whispered, and by now she was twisted around on the sofa, facing him, her hands on his sides. She brushed her lips against his, then murmured, 'You stay here. Okay? I'll go to the bridge, and you stay here, and you'll be here when I get back. Okay?'

'If that's what you want.'

'It might be a while. He might give me something else to do. You know? There might be more than one thing.'

'Might be.'

'But you'll stay?'

'Sure.'

Smiling slightly, Jane straddled his legs, sat on them. 'Have yourself a little party while you wait,' she whispered.

'Oh, that'll be fun.'

'Eat, drink, watch TV, read something.'

'I've got my book in the car.'

'The Wouk?'

'The Wouk.'

'If you get tired of reading, take a little nap.' She leaned into him and wrapped her arms around him. 'Only one rule.'

'Uh-huh?'

'Stay away from the bridge.'

He stiffened slightly in her arms.

'Promise. You've got to promise.'

He hesitated. 'All right.'

'That means no following me, no surveillance in any way, shape, or form. You stay completely out of this business tonight.'

He didn't say anything. Jane felt his chest rising and falling against her chest as he breathed.

'Promise.'

Brace sighed. 'But what if he tries something?'

'He won't.'

'Then why do you have your knife?'

It came as no surprise that he knew about the switchblade. Jane could feel it herself, down at the bottom of her shirt pocket, sideways just under her breast, the handle pressed tight against Brace's ribcage.

'It's just in case,' she said. 'I wouldn't go if I thought . . . you know, that I'd be in real danger.'

'The thing isn't gonna open by accident, is it?'

'Not this time. I put a good, strong rubber band around it.'

'Will you be able to get it open if you need it?'

'Sure. But I won't need it. And you changed the subject on me. I'm still waiting for your promise.'

'I promise,' he said.

'You promise what?'

'To stay out of it tonight. I won't leave your house. How does that sound?'

'Sounds perfect.'

Jane kissed him long and hard on the mouth, then eased herself away. With the back of her hand, she wiped the moisture off her lips. Then she checked her wristwatch. 'I'd better get going.'

Brace looked at his own watch. 'If you leave now, you'll get there fifteen minutes early.'

'The sooner I get there, the sooner I'll be back.'

'You don't want to break the rules, do you? He said midnight.'

'We were early last night and he didn't complain about that. It probably doesn't matter to him, a few minutes one way or the other.'

'Maybe not.'

She climbed off Brace's legs, then pulled him off the sofa. 'Come on, you can walk me out to my car.'

Chapter Nine

On the way from her home to Mill Creek Bridge, Jane saw only one car in her rearview mirror. She wondered if Brace had broken his promise, after all. But the car turned off, and the road behind her remained empty.

She parked under a streetlight near the bridge – exactly the same place, she realized, where Brace had pulled over last night to pick her up.

She removed Brace's flashlight from her purse, then set her purse on the floor where passersby wouldn't be likely to see it. Keys in hand, she climbed out. She locked the door and shut it. As she walked toward the bridge, she dropped the key case into a front pocket of her jeans.

They were good, loose jeans.

She gave the other front pocket a try, and found that it was large enough to hold the flashlight. The flashlight was a big ribbed metal job, probably a foot long, with a heft like a club. She was surprised that it fit.

It softly bumped her right leg as she walked.

And it tugged her jeans lower. She stopped walking, reached under the hanging front of her shirt, pulled up her jeans and tightened her belt.

Now, the jeans felt nice and snug around her waist.

She walked on to the middle of the bridge. Stopping there, she leaned against the concrete parapet. In the light from the nearby lamps, she could just barely make out the creek straight down below her, the rocks and bushes along its shores, and the wooded slope beyond the far side of the bridge. The footpath down the slope wasn't visible, but she knew it was there. She'd followed it once, on her first free day after moving to town for the new job.

She'd spent all that day exploring, but the path had been one of her first discoveries. She'd spotted it from about here while crossing the bridge early that morning. And it had beckoned her.

Nothing beckons like an unexplored path, she thought.

She'd followed it down to where the creek went under the bridge. On the way to the bridge, the creek was shiny with sunlight and slipped around trapped dead branches and gray rocks. Under the bridge, the shadows turned it dark and cool.

You could walk alongside the creek and go under the bridge, and come out in the sunlight on the other side.

Jane had taken only a few steps into the gloom – and was thinking how fresh and cool the air felt – when she realized that a dark shape at the foot of one of the concrete pillars wasn't a bush after all.

It was a man. He wore filthy rags. He sat with his back to the pillar, his knees up against his chest, his arms around his knees, his head pillowed on one knee but turned in Jane's direction. His head was a tangle of filthy brown hair and beard – he seemed to have no face at all.

Shocked, Jane had gaped at him for a few seconds. Then she whirled around and scampered back up the path.

She'd returned many times to Mill Creek Park and had spent hours by the shore of the creek. A few times, she had even taken a look underneath the bridge. Except for that first morning, she'd never seen anyone lurking there. But she'd stayed out from under it, anyway.

Jane pushed herself away from the parapet and continued across the bridge.

I'm really going under there by myself? At midnight, no less?

The notion made her feel shriveled and tingly somewhere low inside.

It's for four hundred bucks, she told herself. Four hundred, if Mog sticks to his routine. As much as I make in a whole week at the library.

Just hope the creepy guy isn't down there.

My own private troll.

'It's own-wee me,' Jane whispered. 'Wooddow teeny-weenie Baby Behwwy Goat Gwuff.'

She grinned and shook her head.

Cute, she thought. Real cute. Can't believe I did that in front of Brace. Lucky thing he didn't throw up.

She pictured him lounging on the sofa in her living room, *Youngblood Hawke* propped up on his lap.

Wish I was there, she thought.

I just hope *he's* there, she told herself. If he broke his promise about coming . . .

She looked up and down the street. A car was approaching from behind, but it wouldn't be here for a while. She doubted that it was Brace's car. She wanted to trust him.

Other vehicles were parked along both sides of the street. A few scattered cars, a van or two, a pickup truck. Jane was pretty sure that they'd arrived before her.

She supposed that Mog might be in one of them.

Watching her right now.

'Naw,' she muttered.

If he's anywhere, he's down below. Waiting for me under the bridge.

She ducked into the trees beyond the end of the bridge. Crouching behind a trunk, she waited for the car. Her heart gave a nasty lurch when it came into sight.

A police car.

But it didn't slow down or stop.

She watched it for a while. When it was far away, she turned her back to the street. She pulled the big flashlight out of her pocket, switched it on, and used its beam to locate the top of the path. Then she shut it off.

Without the flashlight on, she couldn't see much of the path. But she kept it off. Better to have trouble finding her way down the slope than to make herself conspicuous.

Somebody might very well be down there. Her own personal troll. Or Mog. Or God-knows-who.

She carried the flashlight dark. Ready to flick on if she had to. Ready to swing if someone should leap at her.

She moved slowly, watching the steep ground just in front of her feet, trying to stay on the vague blur of the path. She supposed that the path must have fairly regular foot traffic. Its foliage – grass, weeds, whatever – was skimpy from being trampled down.

It was probably used now and then by students from the college.

Adventurous couples seeking someplace dark and private.

She wondered how many of them fell on their asses.

Jack fell down and broke his crown . . .

The last thing I need is a good fall, Jane thought.

All day, she'd been suffering with sore muscles. Climbing on Crazy Horse had done it. Left her with an aching stiffness in her neck and shoulders and arms and back and sides and belly and butt and legs. Even in her toes.

All I did was climb on the thing. Didn't fall off it.

Did almost break my crown, though, she reminded herself.

And gasped as she planted the heel of her left shoe on the slope, started to shift her weight forward, and felt the slick ground jerk her foot out from under her.

Her rump hit the earth. It sent a jolt up her back and into her head.

She felt a quick stab *underneath* the lump on her head. With that and the sting to her rear end, she felt her throat go tight. Her eyes began to burn and spill tears.

'Wonderful,' she muttered.

She shut her eyes. She took a deep, trembling breath. With the back of her empty hand, she wiped tears from her cheeks.

No pain, no gain, she thought, and sniffed.

Small price to pay for four hundred bucks.

Then she felt cool moisture seeping through her pants.

She struggled to her feet. Standing precariously on the dewy slope, she plucked the seat of her jeans away from her buttocks. Then plucked again to nip her panties through the denim and unstick them.

Not that it helped.

They resumed clinging the moment she took her next step down the embankment.

Could be worse, she told herself. I could've sat down on a sharp rock. Or a broken bottle. Or a board with a nail sticking up.

Quit it.

She moved more slowly, more carefully. Before she

reached the bottom of the slope, several muscles in her rump and legs began to shimmy. But she didn't fall again.

At last, she found her way to level ground. She leaned back against a tree near the shore of the creek and huffed for air.

Gotta get in better shape.

Do enough of this stuff, she thought, and I'll either shape up or ship out.

As her breath returned, she realized that her mouth was parched. She licked her dry lips. She looked at the creek. It was a broad, black strip, sprinkled here and there with silver bits of moonlight.

She wondered if its water was clean enough to drink.

It sure *sounded* wonderful. It blurbled and hissed and sounded icy cold.

Take a sip, and I'll probably drop right where . . .

'Jane!' A man's scratchy voice.

It knocked her breath out. Rigid, she pressed her back hard against the tree.

What'll I do? He's seen me!

Run?

'Huh?'

'That's what she says here. Jane. J-A-N-E.'

He's spelling, she thought. He's reading. *He's reading off the envelope!*

There're two of them and they have my envelope.

But at least they don't know I'm here, she told herself. I don't think so. The guy wasn't calling my name, just reading it.

'Jane,' he said again. 'See that? Plain as the nose on yer face.'

'Nothin' wrong with *my* nose,' said a second male voice. 'Open 'er up.'

93

'Don' know if I oughta. Thing's meant for ol' Jane. I ain't Jane. *You* shore ain't Jane.'

'Fuck Jane. Open 'er up.'

'Likely just a birthday card, some such shit.'

Jane bent her shaky legs. The bark was rough through the back of her shirt as she lowered herself to a squat. Getting down on all fours, she turned herself around and peered past the side of the tree.

At first, she couldn't see the men at all.

Then she found two figures under the bridge, black against the lesser darkness beyond them. They seemed to be standing. One of the men looked tall and skinny and seemed to have a horribly huge, misshaped head. The shorter man looked broad and bulky. His head looked odd, too, but Jane figured its unusual shape was due to a hat.

They were farther away than she'd expected.

That's how come they didn't see or hear me, she thought.

She wasn't sure why she'd been able to hear *them* so well. Loud talkers, she guessed. Or maybe being underneath the bridge amplified their voices.

'Shore ain't no birthday card. Strike up a match there.'

A moment later, light flared.

Jane flinched.

No!

It can't be him, she told herself. But of course it is him – almost had to be, huh? When it comes right down to it? Wouldn't you just *know*?

The ruddy flutter of the matchlight showed that the awful size and shape of the tall man's head wasn't caused by bulging deformities of bone and flesh. It was hair. Thick, filthy tangles that massed around his head and mingled with his eyebrows, moustache and beard so that he seemed to have no face at all.

My own personal troll.

Why him, of all people?

He stood with his side toward Jane, and the other man stood in the way, blocking much of her view. They both wore long, heavy coats.

Must be sweltering in those things, Jane thought.

Good. I hope they drop dead of the heat.

Though she couldn't see much, she was fairly sure that her own personal troll was the one opening her envelope while his short friend held the match.

'Shit,' said the short one. 'Them things real?'

'Shore look real.'

'*Four* of 'em?'

'One, two, t'ree, four. That's right, Swimp.'

'Fuck me twice. What's that letter . . . Ow!' Swimp jerked his arm and killed the light. A couple of seconds later, another match flared. 'Read me what she says, Rale.'

'Read 'er yourself,' said the tall, faceless one.

'Haw haw.'

'Awright. Here she goes. "Dear Jane, you sweet thing. This here's them C-notes you asked us for. We all chipped in."'

What? Jane thought. That can't be right. He's making this up.

Rale continued, '"Now you gotta come across with yer crack t'morra night."'

'She spose t'fuck 'em?' Swimp asked.

'Naw. They're buying *crack* off her.'

'Ain't that what I just said?'

'Ya moron.'

'Ain't no moron.' Swimp swept off his headgear – a

95

straw cowboy hat with most of the brim missing off one side – and swatted Rale on the shoulder with it. As he did that, his second match went out. In the darkness, he said, 'This here Jane, she shore don't come cheap. Course, what you said about 'em *all* chippin' in, guess there might be a whole slew of fellows. Maybe she's fixin' to fuck the baseball team. Whatta they call 'emselves? Use t' be the Warchiefs, but . . .'

'The Chargers,' Rale explained.

'Yeah.' Swimp lit another match. 'Well,' he said, 'bad luck for them, good luck for you 'n' me.' The hat was back on his head. He nudged Rale with his elbow. 'Bad luck for ol' Jane, too.'

That's for sure, Jane thought. The idiot didn't know what he was talking about, but he was right, anyway.

Bad luck for ol' Jane.

And then some. Losing the four hundred dollars was bad enough, but losing the note could put a stop to the whole game.

If that damn Rale had just read what was there instead of making the whole thing up . . .

Maybe Rale can't read. Maybe he's as illiterate as his buddy, Swimp.

Wait, she thought. No. He read my name. If he knows Jane when he sees it . . .

'How we gonna split her up?' Swimp asked.

'You mean ol' Jane? Reckon I'll have me the front 'n' you take the back.'

Swimp snorted and gave Rale another shot with his elbow. 'Go awn. The *bread*, the *moola*. We gonna split her even-Steven, right?'

'Well, now . . .'

What if I just step out and show myself? Jane wondered. Tell them they're welcome to the money, but could I please have the note?

Brilliant idea.

'Reckon that'd be a fair split,' Rale said.

He wants my front and Swimp gets my back. Real nice.

But maybe it's just talk, she thought. Just a couple of horny, drunk bums talking big.

The match died.

I've gotta get the note!

No, I don't. I can just forget about it. Forget about the whole thing. Go home and see what Brace is up to. Consider myself lucky to be out of it three-hundred-and-fifty bucks to the good, relatively unscathed, and with a fine new friend who might be just the sort of man . . .

Swimp lit another match.

During the short period of darkness, the two had changed positions. Now, they stood facing each other, their profiles to Jane. Swimp was holding both hands toward Rale. He kept the match in his right. Jane could feel no breeze at all, but the match flame shivered and wobbled, casting a crimson glow that made the two men look ghoulish.

They aren't ghouls, Jane told herself. Just a couple of dim-witted bums. *And they're screwing up everything!*

Swimp's left hand was open, palm up.

Rale dealt him two bills.

Two hundreds.

Mine!

'All fair 'n' square?' he asked.

'Fair 'n' square,' Swimp said, his head bobbing up and down.

Rale tucked the other two bills back into the envelope, folded the envelope and shoved it into the side pocket of his long, bulky coat. Then he said, 'Let's scat.'

Swimp shook out his match. 'Spose Jane's gonna show up?'

'Shore.'

They began to walk alongside the creek. At first, Jane thought they were walking *away* from her.

Chapter Ten

'Wanta hide 'n' see her?' Swimp asked.

'Wanta get us shot dead? She ain't no whore, y'lamebrain. The gal's a *drug* pusher, and folks like that . . .'

They're coming!

Not walking away, but heading straight toward Jane. She was on all fours, the tree trunk between her and the two men.

It won't be between us for long!

Run!

But which way? she wondered. Up the slope? It's so steep and slippery! I'll fall flat on my face and they'll grab me by the ankles . . . Run up the shore? I'm probably faster than them. But what if I'm not? I'll be running deeper and deeper into the park . . .

If I try running anywhere, they'll see me and chase me and . . .

Here they come!

She eased herself down flat against the ground at the foot of the tree, and lay motionless.

They won't see me, she told herself. I'm dressed in black (well, not *really* black but close enough), and if I lie absolutely still they'll walk right on by without even knowing I'm here.

Maybe.

Please!

Their voices came closer and closer. Jane couldn't follow what they were saying; she could only think about the distance. Ten or twelve feet away. Now maybe six. Now probably just on the other side of the tree. Now coming alongside the tree.

They can see me now. If they look, they'll see me. Don't look!

Just keep walking and don't look down over here!

'Jumpin' shit!' Swimp blurted.

The footsteps stopped.

'She dead?' Swimp asked, his voice hushed.

Don't panic!

Though her face was turned away from the two, she shut her eyes. She strained to control her breathing, to take small breaths so her movement might go undetected in the darkness.

'She don't appear real frisky,' Rale said.

Someone stepped on her. A shoe pressed against the seat of her jeans, pushed down on her buttocks and began to jerk back and forth quick and hard. She stayed limp, letting her whole body wobble with the rhythm of the shaking foot.

'Spose it's Jane?' Swimp asked.

'Might be,' Rale said. The foot lifted off her rump. 'Let's see what she's got.' He groaned and a couple of his joints crackled as he squatted beside Jane.

She felt a hand push down into the left rear pocket of her jeans. She knew it would find nothing there. But it rubbed and squeezed her before coming out and entering the other pocket. The hand stayed longer in that empty pocket, kneading her buttock.

Done, Rale said, 'Let's turn her over.'

Hands clutched Jane's left shoulder and arm and hip

100

and leg. They pulled and lifted, rolling her onto her right side (where the pocketed flashlight shoved painfully against her wrist), then onto her back. She kept herself limp – let her head wobble, her legs flop lifelessly.

'Hey,' Swimp said, 'wanna see her?'

'Shore.'

She heard the snick of a match. A shimmery, pinkish glow soaked through her eyelids.

'Wah!' Swimp blurted. 'She's a hon. Ain't she a hon?'

'A beaut. Ain't no more dead 'n you 'r me, but she's shore a beaut.'

'Ain't dead?'

'At's okay,' Rale said. 'Reckon she's passed out, 'r somethin'.'

She felt a tug at her waist. Her belt went loose.

'Whatcha doin'?' Swimp asked.

'Jackin' her belt.'

'No, you ain't.'

Rale laughed. Then he unbuttoned the waist of Jane's jeans and she snatched the flashlight out of her pocket and both men made surprised noises and flinched. Swimp, crouched by her arm, dropped the match. Rale, by her hip, had both hands on her zipper. Just as he let go, the flashlight crashed against his temple. The blow knocked his head sideways, spit flying. The falling match died. Swimp yelled in the sudden darkness. The hot matchhead found Jane's skin just down from her throat and she gasped, 'Ah!' Rale tumbled backward, arms flung high. Swimp, still yelling, scurried backward on his knees. Jane rammed the flashlight at his belly, but missed, so then rolled toward him, rising onto her left elbow as Rale splashed into the creek, flinging herself over and stretching as she jabbed. But Swimp was out of range. Jane sprawled facedown. She drove both hands against the ground and pushed herself up fast. Her jeans fell down around her ankles. Swimp didn't notice. Or didn't care. Whimpering, he stumbled to his feet and started to run away.

As he fled, Jane clamped the flashlight under her arm and pulled her jeans up. She fastened the waist button. She buckled her belt. Then she turned her attention to the creek and looked for Rale. Unable to spot him, she grabbed her flashlight and thumbed its switch.

Nothing.

Must've busted it when I whacked him.

Keeping the flashlight in her hand, she stepped to the edge of the creek. The water looked black except for bits of silver from the moon.

Still no sign of Rale.

I hit him awfully hard. What if I knocked him out, and he drowned?

What if he's just fine, thanks, and already out of the water? Hiding somewhere?

That can't be, she told herself. He hasn't had time to get out. And I've been right here. I would've seen him.

He hasn't had time to drown yet, either.

Jane suddenly waded into the creek. The chilly water filled her shoes, wrapped her ankles, climbed past her knees and up her thighs. Though the current was slow, she could feel its gentle push. She turned her back to it and trudged a few steps closer to the bridge.

Too slow.

She shoved the flashlight into her jeans pocket, took one big step and lunged, leaving her feet, plunging forward, diving down below the surface. Her shoes and heavy clothes dragged at her. Instead of gliding, she was almost stopped. She kicked to the surface and swam hard.

But only for a few strokes.

Then her right hand swept down and slapped a sodden tangle.

Got him!

Him or maybe a beaver.

As her blow submerged whatever it was that she had struck, her left hand collided with a sunken object that might've been Rale's chest.

With both hands, she grabbed.

By his coat lapel and beard, she raised Rale to the surface of the creek. He was limp.

Playing possum?

Jane doubted it.

She waded backward, towing him, then dragged him onto the dirt and rocks of the shore. When only his feet remained in the creek, she let go. She was huffing for air. She dropped to her knees beside him and pushed the wet hair away from her eyes.

Though Rale didn't seem to be moving, she pulled the flashlight out of her pocket. Holding it in her right hand, ready to strike him, she reached into his coat pocket with her left hand and pulled out the soaked envelope that he'd put there.

He still lay motionless.

What if I killed him?

He can't be dead. Can't be.

She needed both hands to open the envelope, so she clamped the flashlight between her thighs. She picked at the torn, wet opening at the top of the envelope, spread the edges, and fingered what was inside.

Two dark bills.

And a folded sheet of paper.

Mog's note.

Got it!

She knew that the bills would be okay, so she tucked them into a pocket of her shirt. Then she carefully unfolded the note. She thought she might have to peel the paper away from itself, but it opened easily. It seemed damp, but certainly not sodden. For the brief amount of time that it had been submerged, the envelope must've kept most of the water out. She doubted very much that the handwritten message had been ruined.

This was no time to read it, though.

She shook a few drops off the paper. Putting it anywhere on her body would be risking further water damage, so she placed it on a nearby slab of rock. She pinned it down with a smaller rock.

Taking the flashlight from between her legs, she leaned over Rale's sprawled body. With her left hand, she shook him by the shoulder.

Oh, my God, if he's dead . . .

'Rale! Hey! Wake up!'

She shook him harder.

Nothing.

Hunkering down, she put her ear close to his mouth. She heard no breathing, felt no air against her ear.

With her left hand, she fingered his thick growth of facial hair until she found his lips. They were slightly parted. She forced his mouth open wider and reached in deep with two fingers. They rubbed against the edges of his teeth, slid over the slimy flesh of his tongue.

If he's faking it and bites . . .

Nothing seemed to be blocking his airway.

She pulled her fingers out, wiped them on the shoulder of his coat, and again slipped the flashlight between her legs. With her right hand, she delved through his beard and reached his neck. She found his carotid artery, felt its beating pulse.

At least I didn't kill him, she thought.

But he isn't breathing.

She tilted his head back, pinched his nostrils shut, and held his jaw open.

What am I, nuts? He was all set to rape me. Maybe he would've killed me. And I'm gonna do this?

Apparently yes, she thought.

And took a deep breath and covered his mouth with her lips and blew her air into him. When she lifted her mouth away, the air rushed out of him, flapping his lips.

She blew into him again.

Again.

Again.

Come on, she thought. If you die on me . . .

Where the hell is your good buddy Swimp? Ran off and left you. Some friend. One of us could've gone for help.

She again blew her breath into Rale.

He puked. It happened fast. Jane had no time to get her mouth away. There was a sound like the muffled bark of a dog, and up came a belch loaded with vomit.

It filled her mouth.

She lurched back, head down, his sour fluids spilling out of her. She spit and spit. She gagged. With Rale coughing behind her, she scurried into the creek, waded out until it was knee-deep, bent down and cupped water into her mouth. She didn't swallow any, but spit it out and rinsed her mouth again and again.

Turning around, she found Rale on his hands and knees, head hanging as he coughed and gasped.

Jane rushed for the shore, kicking at the water, splashing it high.

Rale twisted his head around and looked over his shoulder.

'Don't move!' Jane snapped. 'Stay right there! Stay right there!'

He stayed on his hands and knees, still coughing but not so much as before, and watched Jane as she splashed ashore and crouched to grab her flashlight. With the flashlight in her hand, she didn't feel so vulnerable. She shook it at Rale. 'Stay right there,' she warned.

She bent down and plucked Mog's note out from between the rocks.

Anything else? she wondered. Have I got everything?

Everything but the two hundred bucks Swimp ran off with.

At least I got half the money, she told herself. And the note. The note was the important thing.

Is it? she wondered. Maybe the important thing is that I didn't kill anybody. And nobody killed me.

'Stay right there,' she told Rale again. Keeping her eyes on him, she stepped backward toward the slope. The ground began to rise behind her. She turned to the slope and started climbing. After a few strides, she looked down over her shoulder. 'Stay right . . .'

He was gone.

The shock almost knocked her breathless.

Flashlight in one hand, note from Mog in the other, she bounded up the steep, slippery hillside. Halfway to the top, she fell. She started to slide downward on her elbows and knees. Letting out a whimper of fright, she scurried and found footing and made it to the top.

She ran all the way to her car.

Chapter Eleven

Jane stopped on the front porch. Keeping the note from Mog in one hand, she used her other hand to pull off her muddy shoes. As she crouched to set them beside the welcome mat, Brace opened the door.

She smiled up at him.

Her smile seemed to require a ton of energy.

'What happened?' Brace asked.

She felt too weary to answer. So she shrugged and shook her head as she straightened up.

Brace looked ready to reach for her. She shook her head again. 'You don't wanta touch me,' she said. 'Take this.' She thrust Mog's note at him.

'So you got it,' he said, taking it from her hand. 'Are you all right?'

'Not sure.' She waved him aside. He moved out of her way and she entered the house.

'Are you hurt?'

'No. Just . . . yucky. And I don't feel too hot.' She turned toward the hallway, but looked over her shoulder at him. 'Can you stick around? I've gotta shower and change. Okay?'

'Sure.'

'Thanks. I'll tell you all about . . .' She stopped. She turned around. 'Gotta have a drink.'

'I'll get it for you. What do you want?'

107

'Jim Beam. It's in the cupboard by the fridge. And a glass. Want a glass. One for you, too. If you want.'

'Ice?'

Jane shut her eyes and shook her head.

'I'll be right back,' Brace said.

'I'll be in the john,' Jane muttered.

As Brace hurried toward the kitchen, Jane staggered down the hallway and entered the bathroom. She left the door open. Standing by the counter, she removed the flashlight and key case from the wet pockets of her jeans. She set them on the counter, then dug into her shirt pockets. She fished out the soggy pair of hundred dollar bills, the switchblade knife, and a flimsy, damp card.

Confused, she stared at the card.

Brace Paxton, PhD, Instructor of English, Donnerville University . . .

'Ah!'

His business card.

Jane added it to her collection on the counter, then shambled over to the toilet, lowered its lid, and sat down. Groaning, she bent low and peeled off her wet socks. Her feet looked pink, and a few bits of grass were pressed into her skin. How did *they* get there? she wondered. How'd they get in my *socks*?

'Just one a those things,' she murmured.

Then raised her head as Brace came in with the bottle and two glasses.

'Ah,' Jane said.

'A wee bit o' cure for what ails ya,' he said.

'I'm gonna want more than a wee bit.'

He set the glasses on the counter near the collection from Jane's pockets. As he started to pour, Jane said,'I broke your flashlight for you.'

'No problem.'

'I'll fix it. Or buy you a new one.'

'Looks like you only got two hundred this time.'

'Somebody else got a share.'

He handed one of the glasses to Jane.

'Thanks. Anyway . . . a long story. Tell you later.' She filled her mouth with bourbon. She sloshed it around and held it, feeling its heat soak into her tongue and gums and cheeks. After a while, the inside of her mouth started to tingle and burn. Her eyes watered. She swallowed, and sighed.

Brace watched her. He looked concerned.

Jane filled her mouth again.

'Are you sure you're all right?' Brace asked.

She nodded. 'Just worn out. Drained.'

'You aren't going to fall down in the bathtub, are you?'

Jane fell down and broke her crown . . . and a troll threw up down her throat.

I didn't swallow any, she told herself.

Hope not, anyway.

She shook her head and took a small swallow of the bourbon stored in her mouth. It scorched her throat and slipped downward to join the heat in her belly.

'Want a refill before I go?'

She nodded and held out her glass. Brace added enough for another mouthful.

'All set?' he asked.

She nodded again.

'See you when you're out,' he said, and stepped into the hallway and shut the bathroom door.

Jane thought about locking it. She decided not to bother. Brace wouldn't try anything funny.

Might be nice if he would, she thought.

No.

Don't want any messing around. Don't even want to

think about it. Too tired. Too sore. Too fat . . .

She swallowed the last of the bourbon in her mouth, then took her glass to the counter and set it down. Keeping her eyes away from the mirror, she took off her wet clothes. Then she stepped over to the tub, spread the bathmat, squatted down and started the water running.

She felt so terribly tired.

Tired all over, sore in every muscle, filthy, half numb inside her head.

When the water was ready, she climbed into the tub and shut the glass door. The strong, hot spray felt good, but it sapped away even more of her energy. Though little effort was needed to soap herself, her arms ached and grew heavy as she washed her hair. Finally, she sank down and sat on the bottom of the tub. Hot water splashing down on her, she folded her arms around her knees and hung her head.

The water felt wonderful.

So wonderful.

She could almost sleep . . .

She woke up shivering, gasped out 'Yah!' as she found herself being drenched by ice cold water, lurched forward and twisted the faucets until the shower shut off. Teeth chattering, she hurried out of the tub. Her dripping skin felt tight and hard. It was spickled with goosebumps. Shuddering, she snatched her towel off the bar. She started with her hair, and worked her way downward.

By the time she was done drying herself, the tremors had subsided. She draped the towel over her shoulders, stepped to the counter, and took a couple of swallows of bourbon.

Oddly, the mirror wasn't fogged up. The cold shower

must've cleared away the steam.

Jane's reflection was sharp and clear.

She started to turn away, then hesitated, surprised.

I don't look all that bad, she thought. Not really.

Of course, the thick towel hanging from her shoulders to her waist hid plenty.

Watching herself in the mirror, she brushed the tangles out of her hair. When her short, damp hair was smooth against her head, she set aside the brush and pulled the towel away.

It's really true, she thought. I'm changing. I've already changed.

No doubt about it, the mirror showed that she looked less soft and pudgy than usual. She doubted that she'd lost much weight, but the physical exertions that had caused her to be sore and weary had apparently also tightened her muscles.

You've still got a long way to go, she told herself.

But this is pretty good for just two nights of chasing after Mog's envelopes. Pretty amazing, in fact.

Keep it up, and before long I'll look as good as I ever did.

Yeah, great. Just what I need. I was *so* happy then. Everything was *just so wonderful*.

Screw it. I oughta stay fat.

She took another drink. She turned around, gazing at her reflection.

No matter what, it felt *good* to look better. It would be great to look the way she used to – like throwing aside an old disguise that had outlived its usefulness.

Who says I don't need it any more? she wondered.

And who says it's even a disguise?

Don't think about it, she told herself. Why bother? I'm looking better, and I wasn't even trying. It's just the way

111

things have happened. So I'll just let things happen as they happen.

Maybe Mog wants to make me slim.

She smirked at herself in the mirror.

Sure, that's it. You've been looking for his Big Plan. Well, maybe that's it. The whole point of the Game is to wear the pounds off Jane, shape her up.

Ship her out.

Play hard, die young, have a good-looking corpse.

The corner of her mouth curved higher.

Sure, she thought. That's got to be it.

She laughed softly, then frowned.

A silly idea, she thought. Interesting, though. Sort of like Hansel and Gretel in reverse. In the fairy tale, the old witch fattened up Hansel so there'd be more of him to eat. Maybe the point of the Game *is* to whip me into shape . . . make me slender and firm and more good-looking.

But why?

Some sort of Pygmalion thing? Wants to shape me into his idea of perfection?

She sighed and shook her head.

I'd better finish up and get out of here.

She swung the mirror open on its hinges. From the medicine cabinet behind it, she took her toothbrush and tube of paste. She swung the mirror shut.

She started to brush her teeth.

And suddenly remembered the feel and taste of Rale's vomit. She gagged and her eyes watered.

Stop it! Don't think about it!

Think about something nice.

Brace waiting for me in the living room. Probably wondering what's taking me so long.

Done with her teeth, she put away the brush and

paste. She drank some cold water, dried her mouth and hands with the towel, then turned toward the bathroom door.

Where her robe didn't hang.

You never got it, you idiot. Came right in here, did not pass Go, did not go to your bedroom and grab your robe. Where was your mind?

Probably back by Mill Creek Bridge.

No big deal, she told herself.

She shook open her bath towel, wrapped it around her body, and tucked a corner in between her breasts to hold it up. The towel was wide enough to hang past her groin and rump. But just barely.

A terrific night, she thought. A really wonderful night. What'll be next to go wrong?

She inched open the bathroom door. The hallway looked clear. Brace was probably in the living room, sipping his drink and reading while he awaited her arrival.

The house sounded awfully quiet, though.

How much noise would he make, sipping and reading? None, that's how much.

Jane stepped out into the hallway. It was dark in the direction of her bedroom. At the other end was light from the living room. She stood motionless and stared into the light. She could see the carpeted foyer and the front door, but nothing else. She listened very hard.

Why doesn't he cough, or something?

Because he's gone, that's why.

He got tired of waiting and he went home.

She began to walk slowly toward the light.

He wouldn't just leave like that, she told herself. Something's wrong.

What if Mog got him? Mog was here last night. Maybe

113

he came tonight, too. Maybe he snuck up on Brace . . .

Where the wall ended, Jane halted. She pressed a hand against her chest to make sure the towel didn't slip loose, and felt the quick hard pounding of her heart.

This is dumb, she thought. Brace is fine. I'm making a big deal out of nothing.

Leaning forward, she peered around the corner.

The lamp on the end table partially blocked her view down the length of the sofa. She could see enough, though. Brace wasn't there. He wasn't across from the sofa on the reclining chair, either.

Maybe he'd gone into the kitchen, or . . .

Jane saw fingertips on the floor beyond the coffee table. She shuffled toward them, sliding her feet over the carpet, trying to make no noise. The rest of the hand came into sight. And then the rest of Brace.

He lay on his back, sprawled alongside the coffee table, legs spread slightly apart, left hand curled by his side, right arm away from his body and bent at the elbow as if he'd extended it past the table to help Jane find him. His shirt was untucked. Open at the bottom, it showed a triangle of bare skin just above the belt of his dark gray trousers.

His face was covered by one of the big, blue pillows from the sofa.

Jane's mind screamed, *NO!* as she rushed toward him.

Dropping to her knees, she grabbed the pillow and hurled it away.

Brace's eyes leaped open and he gasped.

Jane's mouth dropped. So did her towel. She caught the towel and lifted it and clutched it to her breasts. 'You . . .!' she gasped. She scurried backward. 'You were

114

sleeping!' she blurted, and scrambled to her feet and ran for her bedroom.

She felt like a fool as she ran.

Now I've done it!

In her bedroom, she slammed the door. Then she fingered the wall until she found the light switch. She leaned back against the door and gasped for air.

I've really done it. God! What was I thinking?

'Jane?'

She flinched. She hadn't heard him approaching. She pressed her back harder against the door, and clutched the towel more tightly to her chest.

'Jane?' he asked again. 'Are you okay?'

'I thought you were dead!'

Silence for a few moments. Then his quiet voice said, 'Why?'

'You were on the floor! You had . . .'

'I was just taking a nap.'

'On the *floor*? That's what the sofa is for!'

'It feels better for my back. I like to lie on floors sometimes.'

'With a pillow over your face?'

'Sometimes.'

'I thought you'd been *suffocated*!'

'Oh.'

'Murdered!'

'I'm really sorry, Jane. I just stretched out on the floor to rest for a couple of minutes. I put the pillow on my face to block out the lights, you know? I had no idea you might come along and think . . . anything was wrong.'

'Well, I did! I thought you were dead! I thought Mog had gotten in and killed you!'

'I'm really sorry. I am.'

'And my towel fell down,' she blurted. 'I bet you're all sorry about that, too.'

'Yeah, I am.'

'I'll just bet you are.'

'I'm sorry if you're embarrassed about it, that's all.'

'I thought you'd been killed.'

'I know.' After a few moments, he said, 'Would you like me to leave?'

'Yes! Please.'

'Okay. Well . . . I guess . . . so long, then.'

'I didn't mean *leave*! Brace? You still there?'

'Yeah.'

'I only meant you should go back to the living room. Will you? I'll be out in a few minutes.'

'Sure. Whenever you're ready.'

Chapter Twelve

When Jane entered the living room, Brace stood up in front of the sofa and smiled. 'Hey, you look great.'

'Thanks.' She knew that she didn't look great; not with her hair still plastered down flat from the shower and her eyes red from crying. But she did feel nicely dressed in her fresh white shorts, white blouse and moccasins.

She and Brace sat down beside each other on the sofa.

'I got a little crazy,' she said. 'Everything's been so weird, you know? None of this was your fault, that's what I'm getting at. I mean, you can stretch out on my floor any time you want. I promise I won't go nuts next time.'

'See that you don't,' he said.

She saw the look in his eyes, and laughed. 'Creep,' she muttered.

Turning toward her, Brace brought his knee up onto the cushion, leaned sideways and rested his arm across the back of the sofa. 'What *I* want to know,' he said, 'is what happened at the bridge. You must've had quite an adventure.'

'Maybe I could use another drink.'

'Your glass still in the bathroom?' He started to rise.

'Don't bother. We can share, can't we?' She leaned

forward, lifted the bottle of bourbon off the coffee table, and started to refill Brace's glass.

'Fine with me,' he said. 'You aren't wearing lipstick, are you? I hate the taste of lipstick in my bourbon.'

She put down the bottle. 'See for yourself,' she whispered, leaning toward him.

He laughed softly, pulled her up against him and kissed her on the mouth. He kissed her for a long time. Then he eased her away and said, 'Guess you don't have any lipstick on.'

'That was quite a test,' she murmured, and rested her forehead against his shoulder.

He moved his hands softly up and down her back.

'It's okay,' he said, 'if you don't want to tell me about tonight. If you're too tired, or you'd rather just not talk about it.'

'No, it's not that. I want to tell you. But maybe first you'd better test me once more for lipstick.'

Brace laughed. Laughing, the movements of his chest and belly jiggled her. She raised her face and met his lips again.

When it was done, she whispered, 'That's a lot better. Thanks.' She took a very deep breath. 'What a night.' Turning away from Brace, she leaned forward and picked up the glass. She took a drink, and passed the glass to him.

'So anyway,' she started, 'I parked on Park Lane right at the same place where you picked me up last night.' She leaned back, sinking into the soft cushion of the sofa, and propped her feet up on the coffee table. 'I left my purse in the car, but I took your flashlight with me. Good thing I did, too.'

And she went on, telling Brace every detail she could remember about her quest for the envelope, describing

118

Rale and Swimp, mimicking their speech, leaving out nothing.

Almost nothing.

She made no mention of Swimp's confusion over the sale of 'Jane's crack.' It was irrelevant, crude, and way too personal.

She also said nothing about Rale vomiting into her mouth.

She was afraid she might gag if she had to tell him about that. And she was afraid he might not want to kiss her again for a very long time.

Brace listened to it all, sometimes taking a sip of bourbon and passing the glass to Jane, sometimes looking very worried, but never interrupting her story.

After she finished, he remained silent. He looked very serious.

'So, what do you think?' she asked.

He scowled. 'I should've gone with you.'

'Wrong.'

'My God, Jane.'

'It worked out okay.'

'Oh, it worked out just great. You nearly got yourself raped. And they probably would've beaten you up, at the very least. They might've *killed* you. And you damn near did kill that Rale bastard.'

Jane made a weary smirk. 'Don't forget Swimp got away with half my money.'

'That's the least of it.'

'Well, at least they didn't get all the money – or the note. It was the note that really had me worried. If they'd ended up with that . . .'

'It might've been a lucky thing if they *had* gone off with it. Maybe that would've put an end to all this.'

'I don't think so. What I think is, I would've gone after

119

them and stayed with them and gotten it back one way or another.'

Brace blew softly through his pursed lips. 'You are *really* hooked on this thing.'

'I want to get as much out of it as I can. And find out what's going on.'

'But look at what happened tonight.'

'I know. Are you kidding, I was *there*. I was scared out of my wits. But it was just one of those things. An accident, you know? Those two bums just happened to be at the wrong place at the wrong time. It was a fluke. I could go chasing down Mog's envelopes from now till doomsday and never have anything like that happen again. You know?'

'No,' Brace said. 'First, he's sending you to lonely places in the middle of the night. You're bound to run into more trouble if you keep at it. Second, you can't be sure it was a fluke.'

'Well . . . I can't be *sure* of anything, but . . .'

'Maybe Rale and Swimp were sent by Mog. For all you really know, one or the other of them might've *been* Mog.'

She let out an uneasy laugh. 'It's possible, but I sure doubt it. I mean, I think those things are both *very* unlikely. These guys just happened to be there.'

'Maybe, maybe not. The thing is, it got bad tonight. It could've gotten a lot worse. You were lucky. One of these times, you might run into more trouble than you can handle.'

'Trying to cheer me up?'

'Trying to make you quit.'

'I'm not going to quit.'

'At least let me go with you next time. I can stay out of sight . . .'

'No.'

'Rale saw the note,' Brace reminded her.

'Yeah, but it was pretty dark. He might not've been able to make out everything it said. The stuff he pretended to read for Swimp didn't have anything to do with what was really written. And even if he *did* manage to read it all, that doesn't mean he could necessarily figure it out and remember it well enough to go there.'

Leaning forward, Brace lifted the note off the coffee table and unfolded it.

Jane sat up and looked at it with him.

The paper was dry, slightly rumpled from all the handling, a little warped and bulgy here and there where the creek had gotten to it through the envelope. A few of the ruled, blue lines had small smears – almost as if someone had wept over the note. Three or four drops of moisture had also struck the handwritten words, making the ink of certain letters dark and fuzzy.

It had still been wet when she'd read it the first time.

After racing to her car, she'd tossed the paper onto the passenger seat, keyed the ignition and sped away – eyes on the rearview mirror, watching for Rale and Swimp. Only after driving halfway across town had she pulled to a curb and stopped. There, she'd turned on the courtesy light and read the note.

She'd read it four or five times.

She read it now as Brace held it open over his lap.

Dear Jane,

Glad this wasn't a bridge too far. How far *will* you go? To the moon? To the stars? To the pits of hell? Or all the way to Paradise?

121

Tomorrow, when churchyards yawn, see the Babe.

Love and kisses,
The Master

'I don't think we need to worry much about *Rale* showing up,' Jane said.

'Showing up where?' Brace asked.

'Yeah. That's what I mean. He might've read this thing once – in the moonlight. He'll never figure it out. Just hope *we* can. What do you make of it?'

'I know when churchyards yawn.'

Jane grinned. 'When's that?'

'At "the very witching time of night,"' Brace said.

'Like about the time of night "when churchyards yawn and hell itself breathes out contagion to this world"?'

'That's it! Most excellent, Jane! You do know your *Hamlet*.'

'Obviously, so does Mog. But tell me this, professor – what exactly *is* the witching hour? Midnight?'

'Yep.'

'Midnight again. Okay. At midnight, I'm supposed to see the Babe. Babe Ruth?'

'Paul Bunyan's blue ox?'

'Any statues I need to know about?'

Brace shook his head. 'Not anywhere around here. I think we're getting ahead of ourselves, though. Why don't we start at the beginning and work through from there?'

'Okay. The beginning. "Dear Jane."' She shrugged.

'*A Bridge Too Far*,' Brace said, 'might be an allusion to the Cornelius Ryan book . . .'

'We have it in the library.'

'Maybe the envelope's in the book.'

'Check the index for a Babe?' Jane suggested.

'Doubt if that's even close.'

'Same here. I think he's just being cute about the bridge too far.'

Brace shook his head.

'What?' Jane asked.

'You don't suppose he knew you'd have a battle at the bridge? That's what the book is about, you know – a disastrous World War Two attack on . . .'

'Saw the movie. I still think it's Mog being cute.'

'Let's go on. "How far *will* you go?"'

'The jerk.'

'What?'

'Him and his innuendos.'

'Oh. Okay, how about "To the moon?"'

'Maybe the guy's a Jackie Gleason fan.'

Brace grinned. 'Think so?'

She waved her fist in front of his nose. Trying to sound like Ralph Cramden, she said, 'One a dese days, Alice! To da moon! To da moon!'

Seeing the look on Brace's face, she laughed.

'You *are* a little nuts, aren't you?' he asked.

'Maybe a smidgen.'

He bumped her softly with his shoulder. 'It's all right,' he said. 'I sort of like little nuts.'

'Ho!'

'What?'

'Never mind. "To the moon? To the stars? To the pits of hell?" Very nice. The pits of hell. I'll pass on that, thank you.'

'You draw the line at the pits of hell?' Brace asked.

'I do believe so. We should be up to eight hundred bucks for this one, right? Well, that ain't enough for a visit to the pits of hell.'

'Glad to hear it.'

'Wouldn't want to try for Paradise, either. The place has stiff entry requirements.'

Brace nodded. 'Like being virtuous and sinless?'

'Like being dead.'

They both laughed for a while. Wiping her eyes, Jane sighed. 'It's getting late. *I'm* getting giddy.'

'We'd better wrap this up.'

'I'd say the envelope will be waiting for me in Paradise. In a Paradise I can visit alive. Maybe there's a Babe at the place, and he, she or it will have the next envelope.'

'It's probably something like that,' Brace agreed.

Chapter Thirteen

At two minutes before midnight, Jane swung open the door of the Paradise Lounge and stepped inside.

It was dimly lit and smoky. The air smelled bad. Off to one side, pool balls clacked. The juke box played Mary Chapin Carpenter.

Could be worse, she thought.

She'd expected it to be pretty bad, the address being on Division Street. In an area of town known for its high crime rate, thrift shops, pawn shops, porno shops, hookers, winos and druggies, the Paradise Lounge was certain to be a dive.

'I bet it's that lounge on Division,' she'd told Brace last night after looking up Paradise in the white pages of the Donnerville telephone directory. There were only four listings: the Paradise Drive-in, an outdoor movie theater north of town; Paradise Gardens Memorial Park, a cemetery; Paradise Lanes, a bowling alley; and the Paradise Lounge, certain to be a dive.

'What makes you think it's that place?' Brace had asked.

'Tomorrow'll be Thursday. The drive-in is only open on Friday, Saturday and Sunday nights. I doubt if the bowling alley is open at midnight on a Thursday, but I'll give it a call tomorrow just to make sure.'

'What about Paradise Gardens?' Brace had asked.

'It's a bone orchard.'

'I know. Seems like just the sort of place I'd expect Mog to send you.'

'I don't want to go to a place like that.'

'Nobody does.'

'Very funny. Damn. It probably *is* the cemetery. All this stuff about hell and paradise and yawning churchyards.'

'Churchyards *are* graveyards.'

'I know, I know.'

'This one's probably got plenty of babes in it.'

'Jeez.'

'Babe is probably someone's name, though. You'll have to read the tombstones.'

'Just what I want to do.'

'Nobody's forcing you.'

'What I think I'll do is try the other places first. If I don't have any luck, I'll go to the boneyard.'

'Such is life.'

'Oh, you're awfully fine and jolly.'

'That's because I'll be back in my apartment, getting a good night's sleep for a change, while you're out in the night hunting through sleazy bars or whatever. Unless you'll let me come with you.'

'I wish you *could* come along.' After saying that, she'd kissed him and snuggled with him there on the sofa. But it hadn't lasted long.

Out on the porch, he'd said, 'Call me when you get done tomorrow night, okay? Let me know how it went.'

'You don't want me to wake you up, do you?'

'You won't wake me up. You don't really think I'll be able to fall asleep, do you?'

'You said you would.'

'I lied.'

Walking into the Paradise Lounge, Jane wondered if Brace had also lied about his intention of spending the night at his apartment.

She almost hoped so.

She would be furious with him, but she knew for certain that the cold hard knot in her belly would loosen and go away if she found Brace here at the Paradise Lounge.

She scanned the place, looking for him. She didn't see him. He wasn't sitting at one of the tables, or standing by the pool table, or perched on any of the bar stools.

Neither was Rale, the bum she had nearly killed last night.

She spotted three women. One of those was the barmaid.

Two female customers, she thought. I make three. Terrific.

Maybe one of them is Babe.

Babe could easily be a man's name, though.

She didn't bother counting the men, but guessed there were at least fifteen of them.

More than a few were watching her.

Studying her.

She started for a corner table, where she could sit in the shadows and wait. Maybe Babe would come to her table and hand the envelope to her.

But what if the wrong person came over, someone who wanted to bother her? Over there at the table, a lot of things could happen without anyone even noticing.

She decided she would be safer at the bar.

She walked toward it.

She was very glad that she had decided to wear a bra. She disliked the things, and avoided them when she could. But making a midnight trip to a bar in a sleazy section of town required one. So did her tight shirt, which would've shown every jiggle.

The bra didn't stop the men from staring at her, though.

Partly, she guessed, they were staring because she was a lone woman coming into the bar at midnight.

More than that, it was probably because she looked so very out of place. There was just no way for her *not* to look out of place. Even though she wore an old shirt and faded blue jeans, she was too well-dressed.

Too well-dressed, too clean-cut, too well educated, too well employed, too young, too innocent, too pretty, too almost *everything* for a joint like this. And all of it showed, she was sure of that.

I don't belong here. They all know it, too.

Would've been better off going to the graveyard.

I'll probably end up there, yet, she thought, and imagined how Brace might laugh if she told him that.

She found three empty barstools in a row, went to the one in the middle, and climbed onto it. Leaving the strap on her shoulder, she rested her denim purse on her lap.

The bartender worked his way toward her, wiping the counter with a towel. He smiled. He was a big guy, probably no older than Jane, and had a vague look in his eyes.

Maybe he's loaded, she thought. Or naturally moronic. Or he might even be a brain. Jane had known brilliant people who appeared to go through life in a daze because their minds were always off on field trips.

'Hi,' she told the bartender. 'I'll have a beer. Do you have Budweiser?'

'Got any ID?'

Nodding, she opened her purse. She found her billfold and removed her driver's license from its clear plastic sheath. She showed it to the bartender.

He squinted at it. 'So, that'll make you twenty-six and legal.'

When he came back with her mug of beer, he said, 'Want me to run you a tab, Jane?'

'Yeah. Good idea, thanks. You picked up my name from the license, huh?'

He sniffed. 'Jane Marie Kerry.'

'What's your name?' she asked, and took a drink of beer. It was cold and good.

'Glen.'

'Nice to meet you, Glen. You wouldn't happen to know, would you, if maybe someone left an envelope here for me? It would have my name written on it.'

He shook his head, his heavy cheeks shimmying. 'You hang on a minute and I'll ask the help.' His gaze swayed away from Jane. He called out, 'Tango!'

Jane swiveled on her stool and saw the barmaid striding through the smoke. This had to be Tango. A pert blonde with pixie hair, dressed in half a T-shirt and short-short cutoff blue jeans. She walked behind a loaded tray.

Stopping alongside Jane, she slid the tray onto the counter. 'Yow,' she said to Glen.

Close up and out of the shadows, she stopped looking young and cute. She had to be at least forty-five. Her face looked long and horsy. She wore a hideous excess of eye makeup. Her lipstick had wandered past her lips. Her cheeks and chin were pitted and lumpy with old acne scars.

'What's up?' she asked Glen.

'Meet Jane Marie Kerry,' he said.

Tango slanted her eyes down at Jane. 'How's it hangin', Jane Marie Kerry?'

'Okay. And you?'

'Peachy, 'cept for I got me this fuckin' ingrown toenail givin' me hell.' She pointed down at her right sneaker. 'You ever get one a them ingrown toenail fuckers?'

'I've had 'em,' Jane said. 'Not in a long time, though.'

'Yer lucky.'

'Yeah, they hurt.'

'*Nasty* fuckers.'

'I keep telling you, honey,' Glen said. 'Let me at them with my pliers.'

Tango laughed and shook her head and snorted a few times. When she was done, she told Jane, 'Our Glen, he's a card. Him and his pliers.' She laughed a few more times, and sniffed. Then she asked, 'Ya lookin' for a fella?'

'Well, in a . . .'

'She's looking for an envelope,' Glen explained. 'Do you know anything about somebody leaving an envelope here for her?'

'It would have my name on it,' Jane said.

'Who'd they give it to?' Tango asked.

'I don't know.'

'But yer spose to get it?'

'Right.'

'Who's it from?'

Jane almost answered, 'Mog.' But that certainly wasn't the Master of Games's real name. It wouldn't mean anything to Tango or Glen. In fact, it would probably make them wonder about Jane. Mog sounded, more than anything, like the name for a creature from outer space.

Like something lumbering out of the fog in an old black-and-white monster movie.

Jane could hardly tell them, either, that she was expecting an envelope from the Master of Games. She would just have to explain that she didn't know who it was from.

Whoa!

'Babe,' she said. 'I got a message that I'm supposed to come here and get an envelope from Babe.'

Tango stepped back from the bar, turned sideways, and swung an arm high. 'Yow! Babe! Haul yer butt over here!'

One of the pool players nodded at her, said something to a friend, laughed, and handed away his cue. A few long-neck bottles of beer were lined up on the rail of the pool table. He grabbed one and swaggered forward.

Babe didn't look old enough to be legal. He hardly looked eighteen, much less twenty-one.

Maybe that's why they call him Babe, Jane thought.

He was tall and slim, with a handsome face. Sideburns grew down to his jaw. His dark hair was drawn straight back and swung behind him in a pony-tail. He wore an earring. His denim jacket hung open and its sleeves had been taken off. He didn't wear a shirt. He had tattoos on his chest and arms. Just below his navel, he wore a big brass belt buckle. His raggedy jeans hung so low they looked ready to drop. Their frayed cuffs brushed against black motorcycle boots with side-buckles.

His eyes roamed down Jane as he approached.

'You two met?' Tango asked.

Jane shook her head.

'This is Jane Marie Kerry,' Glen announced from behind her. 'She's looking for you, Babe.'

'Looking for me?' He took a pull at his beer. He glanced from Glen to Tango. 'She a cop?'

'I'm not a cop,' Jane said.

'She looks like a cop.'

'Whatcha worried about cops for?' Tango asked him.

'Ya better *not* be worried 'bout no cops.'

'I'm not, I'm not! Shit, get off my back!'

'I'll lay into ya.'

'I ain't done *anything*! Shit!' He was grimacing and breathing hard. 'I just thought she looked like a cop, that's all.'

'I'm not,' Jane said. 'Not even close. I'm a librarian.'

Babe smirked. 'You ain't no *librarian*.'

'I'm *the* librarian. I run the place. The Donnerville Public Library.' She raised her right hand. 'Scout's honor. So don't worry, I didn't come here to arrest you.'

'I didn't *do* nothing.' He cast a nervous glance at Tango. 'I swear to God, Mom.'

Tango made a hissing sound through her nose. 'Ya got somethin' for Jane?'

He narrowed his eyes. 'Like what, for instance?'

'The envelope,' Jane said. 'Somebody named Babe was supposed to give me an envelope.'

He frowned for a few moments.

Then he brightened. 'Oh! You're *that* Jane! Sure. I've got your envelope.' Nodding, he tilted back his head and finished his beer. 'Didn't wanta bring it in with me. Come on, let's go get it.' Reaching between Jane and Tango, he plonked the empty bottle down on the counter.

'Where's it at?' Tango asked him.

'Just out front. I forgot and left it in my saddlebag.'

'Just go out 'n' bring it on in.'

'No, that's fine,' Jane said. 'I'll go with him. I'm just here for the envelope. I'll get it and go.' She swiveled around, took a few quick swallows of beer, and set down the mug. 'What do I owe you, Glen?'

'You have to run off so soon?' he asked, sounding vaguely disappointed.

'Well, it's pretty late for me.' She took out her billfold.

'One fifty should cover it,' Glen said.

She slipped a five onto the counter. 'Keep it. And thanks. Thanks, both of you.' She smiled at Tango.

Tango smiled back, and gave Jane's arm a squeeze as she hopped off the barstool. 'Don't be a stranger, Janey.'

'So long,' she said, and hurried after Babe.

At the door, he waited for her. He held it open, and followed her outside. 'That's my Harley, over there.' He pointed at a big motorcycle on the other side of the street. They waited for a car to pass, then started across.

'How did you actually get the envelope?' Jane asked.

'What do you mean?'

'Was it mailed to you with instructions? Did somebody hand it to you?' She shrugged. 'The thing is, I don't have any idea who's sending them. If you met him, I'd sure like to know who he is, what he looks like . . .'

'I didn't meet him.'

They walked behind a couple of parked cars, and stopped beside Babe's Harley-Davidson. He patted its saddle. 'Ain't she a beaut?'

'She's a great looking machine.'

'I'm saving up, gonna get out there to Sturgis next month.'

'That sounds nice,' she said, though she didn't know what he meant.

'Ain't never been there. Spose to be about the best ol' time you can have, though. I aim to find out. You like motorcycles?'

She shrugged. 'I don't know much about them, really.'

'Wanta hop on with me?' He mounted up, grinned over his shoulder at Jane, and patted the seat behind him.

She shook her head. 'Thanks, I don't think so. It's

getting awfully late. I really need to get home.'

'Aw, come on.'

'No, really. Thanks, though. Not tonight.'

He hung his head for a minute, then climbed off his bike and faced her. 'What's going on with you and your envelope, anyhow?'

'What do you mean?'

'You come in the saloon saying I'm spose to have it, and all, but you don't know who it comes from. Do you know what's in it?'

She didn't like the sound of this. 'Do you?' she asked. 'Did you open it?'

'Nope.'

'May I please have it?'

He lowered his head. 'I reckon you're gonna call me a liar and go tell on me, but I honest-to-God don't know nothing at all about no envelope.'

'What?'

'I don't know nothing at all about . . .'

'You said you've *got* it.'

He raised his head and looked at her. 'You're the one said I had it. You told Tango and Glen how I'm spose to have this envelope of yours and how I'm spose to hand it over to you. Only thing is, it's news to me.'

'You don't have it?'

'I *never* had it.'

'But you said . . .'

'That was only just to stop Tango from figuring I ripped you off. Who you think she's gonna believe – you or me?'

Jane shrugged. 'If your own mother won't believe you . . .'

'Aw, Tango ain't my mother.'

'You called her Mom.'

'Well, it's just a thing I call her sometimes. She's my old lady.'

Old lady is right, Jane thought. Tango certainly looked old enough to be Babe's mother. And the way she'd talked to him, threatened him . . .

'She's your wife?' Jane asked.

'Might as well be.'

'Oh.'

'I ain't been in no real trouble in more than a year, but she's always got her eye on me, you know? And now you come along and I'm spose to have your envelope and I *claim* I ain't got it, she's gonna tear into me. She can get awful mean when she wants to. So the thing is, I'm hoping you won't tell on me.'

'This is . . . you don't *have* my envelope?'

'Nope.'

'You *never* had it?'

'Nope.'

He seemed sincere. And worried. And sorry.

'Cross your heart and hope to die?'

Nodding, he fingered a big X in the middle of his chest. 'Hope to die,' he said.

'If you're not the right Babe . . .' She grimaced. 'I don't want to make any trouble for you. Are you going to be in trouble?'

'I don't know. Maybe not, if you don't tell on me.'

'Come on.' She took hold of his arm and led him across the street. 'Do you know of anyone else named Babe? Maybe a regular customer, or something?'

'Just me.'

'There's a chance I might've come to the wrong place – chosen the wrong Paradise.'

'If your envelope turns up, I'll sure get it to you.'

'I'd appreciate that, but I think it went somewhere

135

else.' She pushed open the door and entered the Paradise Lounge with Babe at her side. She spotted Tango standing over a table, talking to a customer. 'Tango?'

Babe's old lady looked around and grinned. 'Howdy there, Janey.'

'Got it,' she called. 'Thanks a million for the help.' With Tango watching, she slapped Babe on the back a couple of times. Then she headed for the door.

Chapter Fourteen

Back to square one, Jane thought as she climbed into her car.

Not quite square one. We know it isn't the Paradise Lounge. At least it probably isn't. Just some sort of weird coincidence that there happened to be a guy named Babe at the place.

Or maybe not a coincidence, she told herself. Who the hell *knows* what's going on?

Anyway, Babe had seemed like a fairly decent guy. They'd all seemed like decent people. A little peculiar, but nice enough. Not at all the sort she would've expected to find in a grubby bar on Division Street.

Maybe I'll take Brace there some night, we'll sit at the bar and have a few beers and chat with Glen and Tango and Babe. Might be sort of a kick.

On the other hand, maybe not.

As nice and decent as those people had seemed, she was glad to be away from them. She could get along just fine if she never saw any of them again.

She suddenly realized that she felt uncomfortable sitting in her car this close to the Paradise Lounge. Someone might come out, come over to her . . .

She drove for two blocks, turned a corner, and parked under a streetlight. Reaching down between her legs, she found Brace's flashlight. She picked it up and tried it. With the new bulb she'd bought on her way to the library that morning, it worked fine.

Her purse was on the passenger seat. She swung it over to her lap, reached in and took out her notepad. She shone the flashlight on her brief list of paradises.

'So,' she whispered, 'which is it gonna be? The drive-in, the bowling alley, or the bone orchard?'

She sighed.

'Yeah. Just guess.'

Should've just gone to Paradise Gardens in the first place. We both knew that's where Mog was sending me. Brace knew it, I knew it. If I'd gone there, it'd probably be over with by now and I'd already be home.

Brace won't be waiting, she reminded herself. Home'll be lonely tonight.

'Just so long as Mog doesn't pay a visit,' she muttered.

Mog, she thought, is probably at the graveyard wondering what happened to me.

She switched off the flashlight and put away the list. After shifting her purse and flashlight onto the passenger seat, she checked the side mirror and swung out onto the road.

A U-turn headed her toward the cemetery.

My God. Going to a place like that at this time of night. Must be nuts.

'No big deal,' she said. 'It's not like they're gonna crawl out of their graves and come after me. Probably.'

She laughed once. It sounded a bit nervous.

She wished Brace was with her.

She turned the radio on. Garth Brooks was singing 'Friends in Low Places.'

How appropriate, she thought.

But it was a cheery, raucous song that she was always glad to hear. She turned the volume high.

By the time the song was over, she had left downtown Donnerville behind and was driving through a residential area west of town. The houses were small, close together, and dark. Not all of them were dark. A few had porch lights on. Here and there, dim light seeped through window curtains. Some windows shimmered with a glow that came from rooms where no lights were on, where a television kept away the night.

On her radio, the Traveling Wilburys were singing 'End of the Line.' She listened for Roy Orbison's clear, melancholy voice, but didn't hear it. Traveling Wilburys had recorded this song without him, she remembered. He'd died. In the music video, there was an empty chair to show that he was gone.

She turned the radio off.

The night seemed darker than before. Jane had driven beyond the last streetlight.

Out here, there weren't so many houses. Each stood by itself among trees and sheds. Each had at least one very bright light shining on the front yard or the driveway to discourage prowlers.

The last house before the cemetery didn't have any light at all.

It wouldn't, of course.

Jane had seen the old, two-story Victorian building a few times while driving this road in daylight. A decrepit ruin, it had obviously been abandoned many years ago.

No wonder they abandoned it, Jane thought. Who could stand living this close to all those graves? My God, you'd be afraid to look out your windows at night.

Unless you were a real weirdo.

An ideal home site for a necrophile, she thought, and smiled.

Leaving the old house behind, she took her foot off the

gas pedal. She gazed at the cemetery through the bars of its wrought-iron fence: gentle slopes of grass, tombstones, trees, crosses, shadows, monuments of saints and angels and children, vaults that stood here and there like small chapels.

She didn't like the looks of the place.

But at least nobody seemed to be wandering around.

I'm not really going in there, am I?

The hell I'm not. For eight hundred bucks, I'd swing naked on a vine over a pit full of rattlesnakes.

No, I wouldn't, she thought. But I'll do this.

She turned left at the corner, and followed the two-lane driveway to the main gates. They were wide, double gates of wrought iron beneath an archway of elaborate grillwork that read Paradise Gardens Memorial Park.

Once, Jane had been driving by and noticed a funeral procession entering.

Tonight, however, the gates were shut.

Shut, and probably locked.

What if I can't get in?

Fat chance, she thought. Mog wouldn't have sent me here if there wasn't a way in.

Not wanting to leave her car near the gates, she drove past them. When she spotted a thick stand of trees to the right, she eased off the road and steered into their shadows.

Her purse would be in the way, so she decided to leave it in the car. Her switchblade knife was in it, though. After shutting off the car, she found the knife. She dropped it into a pocket of her jeans, along with her keys. After climbing out, she tried to stuff the flashlight into her other pocket. It wouldn't fit. These jeans were tighter than those she'd worn to the bridge, and had much

140

smaller pockets. So she carried the flashlight as she crossed the street and hurried to the main gates of the cemetery.

Thinking that Mog might've arranged to leave the gates unlocked, she tugged at them. They rattled slightly. They felt heavy and very secure. They were locked, but not with a chain and padlock, like the gates of the fence surrounding Crazy Horse. After studying them for a few moments, Jane decided they could probably only be opened with a key or by remote control.

She wouldn't be getting in through the gates.

Maybe I don't need to get in.

She spent a few minutes searching the area near the entryway, but found no envelope.

Of course not, she thought. He wouldn't make it that easy for me.

Wants me to climb.

The gates, topped by the arch of grillwork spelling out the cemetery's name, would make a more difficult obstacle than the fence itself. But climbing the fence wouldn't be easy. Or safe. Each of the upright bars looked like an iron spear aimed at the sky.

Standing close to the fence, Jane could reach high enough to grab the uppermost crossbar. But the points were higher still. If she managed to find a perch on the crossbar – and then fell wrong – she might find herself impaled on eight inches of iron rod. Maybe in more places than one.

One could go straight up my butt. Or worse.

Which *would* be worse? she wondered.

Thinking about it made her legs ache.

I'm not going to chance finding out, she decided. Not for eight hundred bucks.

She began to walk through the grass and trees along

the outside of the fence, searching for a less hazardous way to get in.

Beyond the bars was a fairly large parking lot, dim and gray in the moonlight. No cars at all were parked there, not even a hearse. Which probably meant the grounds were deserted: no visitors, no caretakers, no grave diggers, no guards, nobody.

Great, if I can just get in.

Soon, she found the answer to her problem.

The tree branched out low and stretched a good thick limb over the tips of the fence.

Crouching near the trunk, Jane reached between two of the iron bars and set her flashlight down on the grass. Then she climbed. The tree, with its easy angles and rough surface and plenty of good places for her hands and feet, was a much easier climb than Crazy Horse. It gave her no trouble at all.

On her belly, clutching the limb between her thighs, she squirmed out beyond the spear points of the fence. When they were well behind her, she crawled to the underside of the limb, let go of it with her legs, dangled by her arms, and allowed herself to drop.

The ground jolted her, but not badly. She rolled with the impact and got to her feet. She came up with the back of her shirt wet and clinging, but the dew didn't soak through her jeans.

She looked at the fence and smiled.

Got over that hurdle without a scratch. I'm getting good at this stuff.

She hurried back to the fence and picked up the flashlight. Keeping it dark, she turned toward the cemetery.

Now, to find the envelope.

'Babe,' she whispered. 'Gotta find Babe.'

She wondered if Babe might refer to a monument – maybe a statue depicting an infant.

Might be a cupid, she thought.

Cupid? In a graveyard?

Who knows? It's possible.

She decided to keep her eyes open for statues of babies, but to concentrate on checking the names on headstones.

She hurried to the nearest grave. After a quick look around to make sure she was still alone, she shone her flashlight on the marble slab.

No Babe buried under this one.

Nor the next, nor the one after that.

This can't be right, she thought as she aimed her light at another tombstone. There must be more to the clue, or this is the wrong paradise, or something. Mog wouldn't make me go around and check every grave here. Doesn't make sense. It could take all night.

She kept at it, though.

This *had* to be the right paradise.

It won't take all night, she told herself. I'll just go row by row, take it one step at a time. Should be able to cover the whole place in a couple of hours.

She walked quickly from grave to grave, stopped in front of each, aimed her flashlight at every headstone, pushed the button to send a beam of light through the darkness, read the name of the deceased, killed the light and hurried on.

The grass was long and wet.

The beautiful, uncut hair of graves. Whitman? Had to be Whitman, *Leaves of Grass*.

The dew on the grass soaked through her shoes and socks.

The wet hair of graves.

She thought of the bodies underneath the ground. Bodies in coffins – some of the coffins maybe so old they'd fallen apart, some of the bodies nothing but bones, others in various stages of rot, some almost fresh – all around her. Nothing between her and them except a bit of dirt.

I'm walking on them.

Stepping on their faces, or maybe on their chests or bellies or . . .

Cut it out, she told herself.

And she wondered if they knew she was here.

They can't know.

She wondered if they could feel her footsteps.

Don't be ridiculous.

She wondered if they were lying there, motionless, listening to her approach, feeling her weight as she stepped on them, growling softly in the silence of their graves, hating her for walking on them and maybe hating her for being alive, maybe dreaming deadman dreams of dragging her down into the earth with them.

They're dead. They don't dream shit.

And maybe Jane would believe that, be certain of it, have total faith in it on a sunny afternoon, especially if she were with some good friends.

But this was the middle of the night in a graveyard, and she was alone, and she could *feel* them.

Feel them hating her, wanting her.

She knew it was ridiculous. The bodies beneath her feet were completely unaware of her presence. And they were mostly – probably – the bodies of nice, decent people. Friendly folks who'd left loved ones behind.

Not fiends.

So how come they feel like fiends?

Like fiends and trolls who can't wait to get their hands on me?

144

If I don't stop this, she thought, I'm going to scream and run and that'll be the end of Mog and his game.

She stopped in front of a grave, shivered, plucked the damp back of her shirt away from her skin, and shone her flashlight on the stone marker. This one, a thin slab, stood at a tilt in the tall grass. It was so old and weathered that the inscription had been worn down. Only shallow valleys remained of the words and dates that had once been chiseled deep.

With a marker like this, she thought, must be nothing at all left of the body.

The chances of this being Babe . . .

The chances will be excellent if it's the only headstone I can't read. It'll be sure to be the one if I skip it. That's how things work.

So she sank to a crouch in front of the tilted slab.

Holding the flashlight in her right hand, she reached out to the headstone with her left. She traced the first letter with her fingertip.

Might be a B. But more like a P.

Am I squatting right over his face? she wondered. What if he's not really six feet down? What if he's only a couple of inches under the dirt and . . .

The tombstone fell, knocking her hand away, pounding her left knee. She yelped with alarm and pain. As she fell backward, the stone *whumped* the ground.

Missed my toe.

She landed on her back.

Right on top of him!

Sprawled on her back, arms out, legs spread, she wanted to clutch her hurting knee. But she thought, This is when he gets me. Reaches up right out of the ground and grabs me . . . bites . . .

She flipped over, rolled, and scurried to her feet. After limping a few steps backward, she whirled around to make sure nobody was coming. The whirl saved her from colliding with the corner of a vault. Halting herself, she turned and gazed at the fallen headstone.

It was barely visible in the tall grass.

No cadaver was rising in front of it.

What did you expect?

Bending over, Jane rubbed her knee. It didn't hurt much, now. She supposed it would be black and blue tomorrow.

I shouldn't have touched that tombstone, she thought. Not the way it was leaning like that.

She wondered if she should set it back up.

I've got to, she thought. I'm the one who knocked it over.

Would've fallen down, anyway.

Sure, but it was me who made it fall tonight.

She muttered, 'Shit.'

She hurried to the stone, stepped behind it, crouched and leaned forward and grabbed it near the top with both hands. It felt cool and damp – a little bit slimy. Shifting her weight backward, she raised it. The slab was heavy, but manageable. She settled its base into the trench of loose soil from which it had been uprooted. When it was standing upright, she tested it by relaxing her hold. Each time she started to release it, the slab began to tip.

'Great,' she muttered.

What am I supposed to do, stay here forever?

Forever, or until morning – whichever comes first.

Being careful not to let it fall, she turned around. She sat down hard on top of the slab. It made soft noises in the soil. She raised herself and sat down again. Five times, she stood and sat, using her body to pound the slab deeper.

That seemed to be enough.

The tombstone remained upright as she made her way around it, stomping the earth to pack it firm.

She stepped back.

A job well done, she thought.

She rubbed her rump.

And she realized that she was probably standing directly on top of the buried corpse, but it didn't bother her. This grave, at least, no longer contained a fiend. In this one was the body of someone who'd needed help with a bad tombstone. He, she, whatever – almost felt like a friend.

Jane was a little winded, but her jitters were gone. She took a deep breath.

She turned around slowly, scanning the moonlit graveyard.

Though she was aware of having wandered quite far from the tree where she'd entered the cemetery, she was surprised to discover that the parking lot and fence were no longer in sight. She must've roamed quite a distance while studying the names on the tombstones.

Off to her left, through the trees, she could see a small part of the roof of the old, abandoned house by the edge of the graveyard.

Which meant that the parking lot and the front gate should be behind her. She turned around, and found herself looking at the slope of a low hillside.

What should I do? she wondered. Keep searching? Head back?

From the sweet, moist smell of the air, the night seemed very late.

She shone her light on her wristwatch.

Ten after two.

'Jeez,' she muttered.

She didn't need to be at the library until noon, though. She could sleep as late as eleven, if she had to.

Keep at it, she told herself. Babe's bound to be here someplace. Just a matter of being persistent.

She stepped to the next tombstone and shone her flashlight on it.

Somewhere not very far away, a car horn beeped.

Chapter Fifteen

From the top of the rise, Jane could see a pickup truck at a far corner of the cemetery's parking lot. It stood motionless and dark under the moonlight.

It hadn't been there before.

Jane shifted her gaze to the main gates. They were too far away and too dark; she couldn't see whether they were open or shut.

She started moving, keeping low, staying in shadows, ducking behind trees and tombstones, taking her time but steadily closing in on the pickup. Now and again, she halted and gazed at it.

Had it been there before? She was sure she hadn't noticed it. The way the small truck was tucked away in a corner, though, she might've simply failed to spot it.

It looked like one of those tiny little Japanese pickups, the kind that city people bought when they liked the rugged, man-of-the-earth image of driving a pickup truck, but had no real use for one.

It was the only vehicle in sight.

It's gotta be the one that honked.

Horns don't honk by themselves, she thought. Not usually. Which means somebody must've beeped it.

But why? Just for the hell of it? Honk in the graveyard, see if you can wake the dead?

Or was it meant to be a signal?

A signal for who?

Maybe somebody else has been here all along.

Or maybe it was meant for me.

Maybe Mog got tired of all my fooling around, looking for the envelope in all the wrong places, and he beeped to call me in.

I'll find out soon enough. Maybe.

Stopping, Jane peered around a tree trunk. Moonlight gleamed on the windshield of the pickup truck. She couldn't see into the cab.

Somebody has to be in there. Or nearby. The truck didn't get here by itself. It didn't honk by itself.

But she couldn't see inside, not even after sneaking almost to the edge of the parking lot and peering at the windshield from behind a bush no more than fifteen feet away. The moonlight still plated its glass with silver.

I can't see in, but he can see out.

Charming.

At least there can't be a whole gang inside, she told herself. No more than two people could fit in the cab. Two fairly small people.

She was tempted to stand up in plain sight and walk straight to the truck and get it over with.

That'd be a real smart move.

But what if I go in really low? she wondered.

If she squirmed on her belly, the driver's view of her would be obstructed by the hood.

Not at first.

For the first several feet, she would be in plain sight. If the driver happened to be looking in the right direction, he would probably spot her.

Once she'd made it closer to the pickup, though, she would be hidden.

Worth a try, she thought.

So she lowered herself flat onto the grass behind the bush. Dew soaked through the front of her shirt. Head up, she squirmed around the side of the bush and writhed her way toward the pickup. Dew made it through the front of her jeans. A few tips of grass tickled the bare skin of her chin and throat.

Her heart thudded.

She listened for the sound of a door opening.

If the door opens or the engine starts . . .

Then she was on the asphalt. It felt warm under her body, but hard. Bits of gravel scraped at her ribs and belly and forearms through the thin cloth of her shirt. The bra helped a little. The jeans gave her very good protection.

She remembered the denim jacket that Babe had been wearing. If she had a jacket like that . . .

BABE!

The front license plate of the pickup truck, level with her eyes, read BABE 13.

Tomorrow, when churchyards yawn, see the Babe.

YES!

She quit belly-crawling and studied the front of the pickup: its tires, bumper, grill, headlights. No sign of the envelope.

It had to be nearby, though.

It had to be somewhere on the pickup, or inside it.

Maybe under it.

The space beneath the pickup looked slim.

I won't go searching under there, she told herself, except as a last resort.

She squirmed toward the license plate, stopped just in front of the bumper, and pushed herself up. On hands and knees, she was almost high enough to peer over the hood. But she kept her head down and crawled to the left. Past the corner of the bumper. Past the tire. At the passenger door, she turned toward the pickup. Still on her knees, she reached up to the door. Hand braced against it, she raised herself.

She moved very slowly. Inched her head higher, higher.

No matter what you see in there, she warned herself, don't make a sound.

Just get ready to run like hell.

Though her eyes were still lower than the bottom of the window, she knew that the top of her head was exposed. Anyone watching the window was sure to see it. So she raised herself high enough to peer in.

And she could see straight through the cab and out the window beyond the driver's side.

Nobody!

Now, if nobody's hiding in back . . .

She stood up straight and looked past the rear of the cab. The pickup's bed was large enough to conceal two people lying side by side. Short people, anyway. And someone *could* be lying there, cloaked by the heavy shadows.

Jane raised her flashlight and shone it in.

Nobody there.

The bed of the pickup truck was empty except for a single board: a two-by-four about five feet long. She wondered why anyone would drive around with nothing but one board. No tool box, or . . .

Doesn't matter, she told herself. What matters is, nobody's hiding in there.

The coast is clear.

She took a deep breath and blew out, puffing her cheeks. She rubbed the back of her neck.

She brushed bits of gravel off the damp front of her shirt and jeans, then began to wander around the pickup, sweeping it with the beam of her flashlight, looking for the envelope.

The vehicle was bright red, and appeared to be brand new. Its make was announced in raised, white-painted letters on the tailgate: TOYOTA. Its rear plate, like the one in front, read BABE 13.

At the driver's door, Jane found a set of keys. One dangled from a ring while the other was stuck into the door's lock.

Fine, she thought. I can get in. But where's the envelope?

Inside. That's why he left me the keys.

Jane pinched the door key between her thumb and forefinger, turned it, saw the lock button pop up, and yelped and leaped back as a growling, snapping dog sprang out at her face.

Its muzzle slammed against the driver's window.

It hit with such force that it rocked the pickup.

'Jeez!' Jane gasped.

The dog rebounded off the window, then attacked again, pounding the glass, shoving at it, snarling, trying to bite it.

Six feet away, Jane aimed her flashlight at the dog.

It looked a lot like a German shepherd, but its muzzle seemed too broad, too stubby.

A Rottweiler? That's what it is.

Its fur was black, its teeth huge and white, its tongue pink. One eye, apparently blind, was the color of phlegm.

It lunged at the driver's window, wild and drooling, as if nothing else mattered but getting Jane.

She supposed it must've been down on the front seat, probably asleep, until she'd twisted the key. The sound of the door unlocking must've awakened it.

If the dog had delayed its attack for half a second

longer, she would've had the door wide open.

What's Mog doing, trying to kill me?

Booby-trapped the car with fucking Cujo!

Just my luck, she thought, the envelope's probably in there with the monster.

As she thought that, she spotted a rectangle above the steering wheel. On the windshield?

Please let it be on the outside! Please!

She hurried to the side of the pickup, leaned over its hood, shone her flashlight at the windshield and stared at the rectangle.

It seemed to be flush against the glass.

Through the glass, her named showed.

That's it!

Moving closer, she saw that the envelope was taped to the inside of the windshield. Just to make sure her eyes weren't betraying her, she ran her fingertips down the glass. Cool and slick.

'Terrific,' she muttered.

And her heart gave a kick as the dog hurled itself at her. The steering wheel stood in its way, but it shoved its head through the ring and barked and snapped.

The envelope was just beyond its teeth.

Jane stepped back, wanting some distance between herself and the dog. Then she stopped, gazed at the envelope, and wondered how to lay her hands on it.

Smash the windshield right where the thing's taped to it, she thought, and maybe I can grab it without getting myself chewed up.

She had never broken a car window, however, so she couldn't be sure how the glass might behave.

Obviously, it would break inward.

Which would obviously push the envelope closer to the dog. Not good. Worse, maybe the glass would crumble and drop the envelope to the pickup's floor. And worst of all, what if the glass *really* came apart when she broke it? Instead of making a hole the size of her hand, she might demolish it.

Making a way for the dog to get out and nail her.

'Yeah,' she muttered. 'Thanks anyway.'

Anyway, she told herself, it isn't my car. It's probably stolen, or something. God only knows how much it'd cost the owner to have his windshield replaced.

I'm not gonna wreck someone's car, not for eight hundred bucks.

So, she wondered, how do I get the envelope?

Wouldn't be any problem at all, except for the dog.

Normally, dogs liked Jane. Even if they gave a nervous growl or two at first, a few words from her would calm them down. Before you knew it, Jane would be squatting over them and they'd be swishing their tails, licking her hand, rolling onto their backs and squirming as she scratched their bellies.

She had a feeling this dog might be different.

I let it out, it'll rip me up one side and down the other.

Maybe not, she told herself. Maybe it's only acting so crazy because it's trapped in there.

Right. Sure.

She wondered, though.

She stepped close to the driver's window. The dog threw itself at her. It hit the glass, shaking the pickup. It barked and snapped. It rammed its paws against the window and worked them as if trying to dig a tunnel through the glass, claws clicking, clattering, squeaking.

'Hey, boy,' Jane said.

The dog stopped attacking the window. It looked at her and tilted its head sideways.

'Hi, there. Are you a good fella? Huh? You look like a

pretty good fella to me. What's your name?'

It bared its teeth and growled.

'Aw, that's no way to behave, is it? Not if you want me to let you out of there. Do you want me to let you out? Huh, boy?'

The dog quit snarling.

'What's your name, Cujo?'

It lunged and snapped, front teeth clashing against the window.

'Maybe not. How about Rin Tin Tin? You sort of look like a mutated Rinty, you know? God, you are a spooky looking thing. Real nice eye. You look like you *belong* in a bone orchard. Spook, the graveyard hound. Is that your name, Spook?'

The dog hurled itself at the window.

Jane wished she had food for it.

She had nothing on her that she cared for it to eat.

If she went back to her car . . . ?

No food in it. Except maybe some chewing gum in the glove compartment. Chewing gum wouldn't do the trick. What she needed was a package of bologna, or a slab of steak, or a hamburger: something good and meaty that she could throw and be certain the dog would chase if she opened the door.

Maybe I can lay my hands on a corpse around here someplace – cut off an arm or something for my pal Spook.

Course, I'd need a shovel.

She smirked at the thought, and shook her head.

What I could do, she realized, is go back to my car and drive into town and buy stuff.

There were several twenty-four-hour fast food joints and convenience stores. She could buy the dog an irresistible feast.

156

Only one problem with the idea; Jane didn't want to do it. Getting into the cemetery had been tough enough – physically and emotionally. To deal with the fence again and drive into town and buy the food and come back and deal with the fence again and come back to the pickup and throw the food and grab the envelope and deal with the fence again . . .

Too much. Way too much.

Besides, who could say that the pickup would still be here when she returned?

There's gotta be another way. Something quick and simple.

She stood there, watching the dog leap and snap and slobber on the window. Stood there thinking. Trying to free her mind and let it roam.

And she found a new idea.

She considered it for a while.

It *ought* to work.

Feeling a warm squirm of excitement in her belly, she twisted the key in the lock of the driver's door. The lock button sank down, then popped up when she turned the key the other way.

Unlocked.

She pulled the key out, then hurried around the front of the pickup to the passenger door. As she reached it, the dog slammed its snarling muzzle against the window.

'Oh, quit it,' she muttered.

The lock button appeared to be down. She pushed her key into the slot, twisted it, and watched the button jump up. She dropped the keys into a pocket of her jeans.

Too bad the door didn't have a real handle. She could just loop her belt through one like that . . .

This oughta work, though.

She stepped past the cab, aimed her flashlight at the

two-by-four in the bed of the truck, saw that the board was near enough to reach, then leaned in over the side and dragged it closer. She would need both hands to lift it out, so she switched off the flashlight and set it on the floor behind the cab.

She hoisted out the board. Propping it up against the truck, she took off her belt. She slipped one end of her belt through its buckle, then dropped the leather loop over the top of the two-by-four. She pulled until it was cinched loosely around the board a couple of inches from the top.

Then she braced the door shut, propping the board at an angle from the pavement to just below the handle. The dog yapped and crashed against the window as she worked the handle and unlatched the door.

She tugged the board and jammed its top end under the handle.

The door lurched as the dog hit it.

The two-by-four's lower end started to scoot away.

Jane grabbed the board with both hands, put her weight on it, and kept the door from flying open.

She stomped on the bottom end, hoping to make it more secure against the asphalt.

The next time the dog struck, the board didn't scoot.

Jane grabbed the dangling end of her belt. The brace continued to hold as she took a step backward. It still held as she climbed over the side of the pickup. Getting to her feet behind the cab, she saw the dog attacking the rear window. No wonder the brace worked so well: the dog had quit hitting the door.

She stood motionless for a few seconds, trying to catch her breath, wondering if she should go ahead with her plan.

If anything goes wrong, I'm dog food.

A little bit late for backing out, she thought.

Leaning out over the right side of the pickup, she jerked her belt. It yanked the end of the two-by-four out from under the handle of the passenger door, swung the board toward her, released it. As the loop of her belt jumped up, the board dropped toward the asphalt.

The clamor of its impact reached Jane as she bounded to the other side of the pickup and leaped. Landing, she whirled around and reached for the driver's door.

Through its window, she glimpsed the dark swish of a tail as the dog sprang out the passenger door.

How smart is it? How smart is it? What if it wheels around and jumps right back in . . .?

She heard the click of its toenails, the huff of its breath as it dashed around the rear of the pickup.

Atta boy!

Jane threw open the driver's door, leaped in behind the wheel and slammed the door shut. An instant later, the dog crashed against it.

She dropped across the passenger seat, reaching for the open door.

Couldn't reach it.

This wasn't how she had figured things.

She hadn't figured on the passenger door standing wide open, so wide that she'd have trouble shutting it fast.

Where's Spook?

Jane squirmed across the seat, reaching . . .

Reaching . . .

'Damn it!' she cried out.

Her fingertips caught the inside handle. She pulled. The door swung and thumped.

It didn't thump shut.

It thumped against the broad black head of the dog,

and the handle was torn from her fingers as the dog thrust its way in.

Jane was sprawled on her right side, her right arm pinned beneath her body, her left arm extended.

Immediately, she jerked her left arm to her face. She twisted onto her back and drew her knees up as the dog sprang on top of her. Though her upraised arm protected much of her face, a paw got through and jabbed her cheek. Others stomped on her shoulders and chest and belly. Toenails scratched her, dug into her.

Jane shoved her right hand down inside the pocket of her jeans and grabbed her switchblade knife.

The dog stood on her, front paws near her hips, chest against her belly, rear end high, hind paws on her shoulders, penis swinging above her face.

Jane pulled out her knife.

The dog's thick muzzle burrowed in between her thighs, snapping.

'Get outa there!' she yelled.

A paw tore at one of her upraised legs. The denim of her jeans wasn't thick enough to save her from the pain of the raking nails.

'Ow! Stop!'

She got the knife to her mouth. With her front teeth, she ripped at the rubber band she'd wrapped around it to keep the blade in. The band snapped, stinging her lips.

The dog sank its teeth into the crotch of her jeans. Jane felt them thrusting and chewing, trying to get at her through the denim.

She thumbed the button on the handle of her knife.

The blade sprang out and clicked.

She rammed it up into the dog's belly.

The animal yelped. Hot fluid spilled down onto Jane's chest and throat.

God, no, she thought. God, no.

But she stabbed the dog again, and then it twisted around and sprang off her. Sprawled on her back across the seats of the pickup truck, she heard it run away yipping and squealing.

Chapter Sixteen

She shut the passenger door, then stayed on her back, gasping for breath.

She felt as if she'd been beaten up by a thug.

The dog's paws had done more damage than its teeth. She could feel at least a dozen places where they'd probably left their marks. Only one place where the teeth had gotten her.

Damn good thing I'm not a guy, she thought.

She supposed she was bleeding here and there. Probably nothing very serious, though. It was the dog's blood, not Jane's, trickling down her face, coating her throat, pasting her shirt to her chest. The wetness at the crotch of her jeans was probably the dog's slobber. She hoped it wasn't more than that.

She wondered if she'd killed the thing.

It might not be dead yet. It soon would be, though. *I stabbed it. I stabbed it twice.*

She still held the knife in her hand. Its handle felt slick and sticky.

She wondered if she could find the dog and bring it back to the pickup and take it to a vet. With the right kind of medical treatment, it might pull through.

Why would I *want* it to pull through? she asked herself. So it can get well and attack me again? I'm lucky I stabbed it before it had time to *really* mess me up. The thing's a vicious monster. Maybe next time it'll go after a little kid. Maybe it'll kill somebody. I'd have to be nuts to try to save it.

If I want to be a good citizen, she thought, I oughta track it down and finish it off.

'Right,' she muttered. 'Give it another whack at me.'

Groaning, she swung her feet to the floor. She struggled to sit up, elbowing the seat, twisting, then grabbing the steering wheel and pulling at it. Finally, she sank into the driver's seat.

She shut her eyes and tried to catch her breath.

The blood made her skin feel itchy. She wanted to wash.

She wondered if there was a creek nearby. She hadn't noticed one, and she'd probably seen most of the cemetery during her search for Babe's tombstone.

Besides, the dog was out there. It might not be dead quite yet.

Just get home, she told herself.

Keeping the knife open, she set it on her lap. Then she wiped her right hand on the leg of her jeans, reached around the steering wheel and peeled the envelope off the windshield.

There better be eight hundred bucks in here. Went through all this. Killed a dog.

She wondered if eight hundred dollars was enough. It seemed like pretty meager pay for going through a night like this.

She ripped the envelope, spread it open, and pulled out the note. Wrapped inside the folded sheet of paper were quite a few bills. She pulled them out. In the moonlight coming in through the windshield, she saw that they were hundreds. She counted them. Eight.

She tilted the note toward the windshield. She could

see lines of scribbles, but there wasn't enough light for reading them.

She couldn't get to her flashlight without leaving the cab.

She reached for the door handle, figuring to open the door and activate the interior light. But she remembered that the door had just been open – both of them had been – and no light had come on.

'The hell with the note,' she said.

It could wait. She wrapped it around the money, tucked it all inside the envelope, then folded the envelope in half. When she shifted her body to slip the envelope into a seat pocket of her pants, she felt the knife slide and fall between her legs. She finished putting the envelope away, then bent down and searched the floor near her feet.

First, she found her belt. The belt came as a surprise. She'd lost track of it after whipping it off the two-by-four, but she must've kept hold of it until she got inside the cab. She brought the belt up, undid the loop, then wrapped it around her waist. After fastening the buckle, she bent down again and found the knife.

She wiped both sides of its blade on a leg of her jeans. With the hanging front of her shirt, she cleaned off the handle. Then she folded down the blade. No rubber bands to keep it safe, but the possibility of the blade flying open by accident didn't concern her. Not after everything that had happened.

She slipped the knife into a front pocket of her jeans, fumbled around down there and brought out the pickup's keys. She tried one of them in the ignition, and it fit. She turned it. The engine kicked into life.

She considered putting the headlights on, but decided against it.

After fooling with the controls for a few moments, she made the Toyota start moving in reverse. She backed toward the middle of the parking lot, stopped, shifted, and turned toward the main gates of the cemetery.

The gates appeared to be shut.

No problem.

She drove past them, over a low curb, and onto the grass. She steered alongside the fence and stopped.

Sure be easier, she thought, than hunting for a tree to climb.

This close to the fence, she wouldn't be able to open the driver's door more than a few inches. So she moved to the passenger seat. She reached for the handle, then hesitated.

She frowned at the glove compartment.

Could the registration slip be in there? What if this pickup isn't stolen – suppose it belongs to Mog and the registration gives his name, his address?

She reached out fast and opened the glove compartment.

A light came on inside it.

No registration slip.

Nothing.

Nothing except a stainless steel pistol.

'Whoa,' Jane said. 'What the . . . ?' She leaned closer.

The pistol had black grips and a small square of paper taped to its slide. On the paper was written, 'For you, my sweet. Interesting times await. Mog.'

He left it here for me.

To use on the dog?

She wondered if it was loaded and ready for action. From the size of the pistol, she supposed it must be a twenty-two. It looked like a smaller, less powerful version of her father's Colt .45 automatic. She'd never been strong enough to handle the .45, but she'd watched him with it. This weapon probably operated on similar principles.

She plucked off the note and stuffed it into a pocket of her jeans.

Keeping her finger away from the trigger, she held the pistol in the glow of the glove compartment's light. Tiny markings engraved in the steel informed her that it was a Smith & Wesson twenty-two. She tilted it and drew back its slide. Through the port, she saw a cartridge being retracted from the chamber.

He gave it to me loaded, ready for bear.

Ready for dog.

She let go of the slide, rechambering the round.

Very considerate of him.

Why the hell didn't he leave it out where I could see it?

At least I've got it now, she told herself.

She released the magazine. It felt heavy for something so small and slim. She could see cartridges through a slot in its side. Maybe five or six of them. To be sure how many, she would need to empty the magazine.

There didn't seem to be much point in that.

She slid the magazine up the handle and bumped it into place with the heel of her hand.

She located a thumb switch that was probably the safety. She flipped it up and down. The up position appeared to be what she wanted.

She shut the glove compartment. She scanned the darkness beyond the Toyota's windows. She saw nobody. She saw no dog.

It's black. It might be anywhere.

It's probably dead by now, she told herself.

Pistol in her right hand, she opened the door. She aimed at the dark grass, braced herself for the noise of a

166

bang, and squeezed the trigger. The trigger wouldn't budge.

Very good, she thought. Now we know about the safety.

She switched the safety off. Then she climbed out of the pickup, swung the door shut and stood motionless, listening and watching.

She heard only the twitter and hoot of night birds.

The parking lot looked empty. The gentle slopes of the cemetery looked crowded.

But nothing came at her.

She thumbed the safety on, then climbed into the bed of the pickup truck. She picked up Brace's flashlight. She stuffed the pistol into a seat pocket of her jeans. On the way in, it made the envelope crackle. It felt hard and snug against her buttock.

She knew the flashlight was too big for a pocket, so she lifted her shirt, sucked in her belly and started to push the thick cylinder down under her waistband. A tight fit. And if she fell wrong with it in there, she might hurt herself. So she pulled it out.

After giving the problem some thought, she realized the solution was the belt hanging slack around her waist. She tugged it, cinching in her shirt as tight as possible. Then she unfastened a button at her belly. She slipped the flashlight in. The belted shirt held it like a hammock.

As she shut the button, the corner of her eye caught a movement. She turned her head.

She groaned.

She felt her skin start to crawl.

The dog was coming.

Big and black against the gray of the grass, paws wobbling at the sky, head and tail hanging toward the ground and swaying slightly as the dog was carried through the graveyard high above the head of a man in tattered rags.

A tall, gawky man who staggered like a drunkard.

'Oh, Jesus,' Jane murmured. 'Oh, my God.'

She scurried onto the roof of the pickup's cab. From there, she took one large upward step and planted her left foot on the crossbar of the fence. She shoved off with her right, and kicked forward.

For a moment, she was poised on one foot above the spikes at the top of the fence.

Then she was dropping fast. Clear of the spikes. The fence to her back. The flashlight leaping straight up somehow between her breasts and out the top of her shirt and striking the underside of her chin.

An instant after the flashlight hit her, the ground slammed the bottoms of her feet. Her legs collapsed. She tumbled across dewy grass.

Getting to her knees, she could feel the pistol stiff against her rump. But the flashlight was gone from inside her shirt. She twisted around and spotted it on the ground, its cylinder shiny in the moonlight.

She crawled back for it.

On the other side of the fence, the Toyota blocked her view. She couldn't see the stranger lurching toward her with the dog, couldn't tell how far away they were – or how near.

She snatched up the flashlight and ran from them.

Ran for her hidden car.

After a quick sprint that took her past the main gates and across the road, she slowed to a trot and looked back.

The stranger had stopped short of the pickup truck. He was turning around and around, swinging the dog by its hind legs. Together, they whirled in the moonlight.

The dog seemed to stretch. Its forelegs reached out like the arms of a little Superhound about to take flight.

And then the man let go.

The dog flew high into the night, coming for Jane.

It almost made it over the fence.

The spikes at the top of the fence snagged it out of the sky.

Jane heard the ringing thunk it made. And quick wet ripping sounds.

And then the laughter of the man beyond the graveyard fence.

Chapter Seventeen

After a long, hot shower, Jane went into her bedroom. She took off her robe. The air felt cool after the steamy heat of the bathroom. She looked at herself in the mirror on her closet door.

Could've been a lot worse, she thought.

The dog's paws had scuffed and scratched her right cheek, her shoulders and chest, her sides, her belly, her hips, and her right thigh. But she could find only four places where the toenails had actually drawn blood. All above her waist.

The jeans had done a good job protecting her. Her thigh was red and striped with welts where the dog had raked it with a paw, but the skin was intact. The heavy denim had also blunted the dog's attack on her groin. Through her sparse coils of hair, she saw red marks, but the two deep dents made by the lower fangs were now only shallow dimples. Soon, they would probably be gone entirely.

She had brought cotton balls and a bottle of antiseptic with her from the bathroom. She dampened cotton balls and patted them against her wounds.

The clear liquid felt chilly except when it hit raw flesh and seemed to burn her. Mostly it felt good, though. Where it dribbled down her body, it felt like ice water.

I *am* losing more weight, she thought as she watched

herself. A little skin here, a little blood there – it adds up.

She made a grim smile.

Keep going with this, and I'll end up in great shape. What's left of me.

I'm a lot better off than the dog.

She felt a little sick again, thinking about what she'd done to the animal.

It attacked me, she told herself. It didn't have to do that.

But I didn't have to let it out of the pickup. I wanted the money. That's why the dog is dead.

And because Mog put it there to make life hard for me.

She was tired of thinking about it, tired of feeling the guilt. She'd gone over all of it in her mind, again and again, while driving home from the cemetery, while dealing with her bloody clothes, while taking her shower. She didn't want to think about it any more.

Done with the first aid, she put on her robe. She returned to the bathroom with the cotton balls and antiseptic, then went into the kitchen and poured herself a small glass of bourbon. In the living room, she sat on the sofa. She sipped her drink.

She stared at the money on the coffee table. She'd tossed it there, along with the note, after emptying the blood-smeared envelope. Leaning forward, she set down her glass and picked up the stack of bills. Then she reached into the side pocket of her robe and took out all the other money that she'd received from Mog since the start of the Game. She put both bunches together and counted.

Thirteen hundred, fifty dollars.

One thousand, three hundred and fifty bucks.

'Not bad,' she said. 'Not bad at all for three nights' work.'

Worth killing a dog for?

We weren't going to think about that, she reminded herself.

She started to remember how it had felt to shove the knife into the dog, so she muttered, 'Self defense,' and leaned forward and picked up her glass. She took a drink.

Self defense with Rale and his buddy, too. They would've messed me up good. And I saved Rale's life. And his pal got away with my two hundred bucks.

Was it Rale in the graveyard tonight? she wondered. Looked like a bum, the guy who threw the dog.

Looked like a goddamn zombie, is what he looked like.

But Rale had seen the note. He might've figured out where to go.

It wasn't Rale unless he'd shaved, she told herself. This guy had a face.

She'd seen it, a pale blur in the moonlight.

Creepy son-of-a-bitch. Why the hell'd he wanta do that with the dog?

It was dead, anyway.

Yeah, dead anyway. Thanks to me.

She took another drink. Then she dropped the stack of money onto the cushion beside her, reached past the arm of the sofa and lifted the telephone off the end table. She set it on her lap, reached again to the table and picked up Brace's business card.

Should I or shouldn't I? she wondered.

He did tell me to call him, she thought. And he didn't tell me not to call if it was after three in the morning.

Maybe he's wide awake, wondering how come I haven't phoned yet. Maybe he's really worried by now.

Holding the glass between her knees, she raised the handset to her ear, heard the dial tone, and punched

172

Brace's number. As she listened to the ringing, she began to think it had been a bad idea, phoning him at this hour. After the fifth ring, she hung up.

He must've fallen asleep, she thought.

His talk about staying awake to wait for the call had been nothing but talk.

The power of Jane's disappointment surprised her.

It's no big deal, she told herself. I should've known better than to call him this late.

But he promised to stay up!

The hell with it.

She lifted the glass from between her knees. It was almost to her mouth when the phone rang. Her flinch slopped bourbon over the rim of the glass. Liquor splashed her chin and spilled off it, dribbling onto her chest, running down all the way past her navel before it was stopped by the barrier of fabric where her robe was belted shut.

Jane squirmed, set her glass down, mopped with her robe at the wet trail down her front, and picked up the handset.

'Hello?' she asked.

'It's me.'

It was the voice she wanted to hear. A calm, comfortable feeling spread through her. And so did a shimmer of excitement. 'Hi there.'

'I hope that was you who just phoned,' Brace said.

'It was. Did I wake you?'

'I was reading. You hung up before I could get to the phone.'

'I let it ring *five* times. Is your place enormous, or something?'

'Just a one-bedroom apartment. Guess the first few rings didn't sink in. I should've warned you. When I'm reading, I don't always hear the phone. You might have to let it ring ten or twelve times.'

'Ah. Your deep powers of concentration.'

'My curse. Anyway, how'd it go?'

'Not bad.'

'Rale didn't show up, did he?'

She hesitated before answering, 'Nope.'

'You don't sound very sure.'

'Oh, I saw a creepy-looking guy over at the bone orchard, but it wasn't him. This guy didn't have a beard.'

'Did he hurt you?'

'Nope. He never got close enough.'

'You had to go to the cemetery, huh?'

'Yeah. You were right about that. I should've gone there in the first place. The Paradise Lounge was sort of interesting, though.' She told him about it, and he seemed both surprised and amused by the news that she'd found a Babe there – the wrong Babe. Then she told him about her foray into Paradise Gardens Memorial Park. As she spoke, she decided to skip the part about the dog.

Why bring it up? At best, Brace would be upset to hear that Jane had gotten herself into a dangerous situation and had been injured. At worst, he might despise her for killing the beast.

I'll have to make up a story to explain the scratches on my face. Maybe I tripped and hit something. And I'd better make sure to keep my clothes on till all the other places are healed.

'So just as I went to unlock the door,' she said, 'this huge mother of a dog leaps at me.'

I thought I wasn't gonna tell him.

'He left a *dog* in there?'

'Yeah. I think it was a Rottweiler. It was a monster. Blind in one eye . . .'

174

'The dirty bastard.'

'The dog?'

'Mog,' Brace said. 'What the hell is he trying to do to you?'

'Trying to keep the Game interesting, I guess.'

'The dirty bastard.'

'It's all right,' Jane told him. 'I got the envelope.'

'You *got* it?' He sounded astonished. 'How?'

'I let the dog out.'

'Oh, great.'

She explained about using the two-by-four to prop the door shut, how she'd climbed onto the truck, jerked the board free, then beaten the dog in a race to the driver's door.

'But after I got in,' she said, 'I couldn't shut the passenger side fast enough. So it jumped in on me.'

'Oh, Jesus. What'd it do to you?'

'Not much, but . . .'

'A Rottweiler?'

'I had to kill it.'

Only empty sounds came from Brace's end of the phone.

'I got it with my switchblade before it had a chance to bite me.'

'You're kidding.'

'It was so awful, Brace.' Her throat tightened. 'The way it squealed. I didn't want to hurt it.'

'You could've been torn to pieces.'

'But I wasn't. I'm okay, mostly. I just feel bad about the dog.'

After a few seconds of silence, Brace said, 'I don't like the way this is going.'

'*I'm* not exactly thrilled.'

'I mean, it's one thing when he's sending you to find

money in a book. But then he had you climbing up Crazy Horse – you bashed your head and almost fell.'

'That was my own fault.'

'You wouldn't have gone up there except for Mog and his damn Game. And then last night . . .'

'I don't think he put the bums there.'

'But he put *you* there. And he must've put the dog in the pickup tonight. It's getting worse and worse. He's escalating on you.'

'Well, the stakes are getting higher.'

'If he'll put a Rottweiler between you and your money, he might do anything. Maybe next time it'll be a nut with a chainsaw.'

Why'd I go and tell him about the dog? I knew better! Should've kept my mouth shut!

'Are you saying you think I should quit?' she asked.

'Do you think you shouldn't? How far do you want to go with this thing? You've already made over a thousand bucks . . .'

'Thirteen hundred and fifty.'

'That might seem like a pretty good bunch of money, but look what you've gone through to get it.'

'I know exactly what I've gone through.' She couldn't keep the annoyance out of her voice. She took a drink of bourbon.

'Look,' Brace said. 'Suppose someone offered you that much to go out and stab a stray dog? What if someone offered you *five* thousand dollars to stab a stray dog to death. Would you do it?'

'This was different. I didn't go out and murder the thing; it *attacked* me.'

'I'm not trying to condemn you for killing the dog, Jane.'

'Well, you could've fooled me.'

176

'It's just that you're being dragged by this guy into some very bad situations, and each one's getting worse. He's making you *do* things. And he's doing things *to* you. God knows why. But I don't like it. You've been lucky so far, but . . . I wish you'd quit before your luck runs out.'

She drank the rest of the bourbon. There was more in her glass than she'd expected, though. It made her eyes burn and water.

'Well,' she said. 'As it turns out, I don't need to quit.'

'What?' Brace asked.

She leaned toward the table, put down her glass and picked up Mog's most recent note.

'I would've told you earlier, but you started in on me, and . . . Anyway, listen to what his note says this time. "Dearest Jane, the fell hand of circumstance is waving farewell to your master, yours truly. I am compelled to fold my tents like the Arabs, as the saying goes. The Game is done. The rest is silence. Adieu, Mog." And then he's got a P.S. down here. Says, "It's been swell." So. I guess that's it. He isn't escalating the Game, he's calling it off.'

'Well, now,' Brace said.

'I can't say I'm delighted about it, but . . . I suppose it's just as well. Things *were* starting to get a little hairy.'

'Mog's calling it quits?' She could hear the relief in Brace's voice.

'That's what it sounds like. He must have to leave town, or something. "The fell hand of circumstance . . ." Maybe he lost his job, or got transferred . . . or the cops got after him about something? Who knows?'

'Maybe he ran out of money,' Brace suggested.

'Could be.'

'Well – whatever the reason, I'm glad it's over. The past two nights . . . Anyway, I'm sorry your bonanza has to end so abruptly, but better that than . . . whatever might've happened if the thing had kept going on.'

'I suppose so,' Jane said.

Brace said nothing.

She settled back against the sofa and put her feet on the coffee table. It felt good to stretch out her legs. She crossed her ankles.

'I'm going to miss working on the clues with you,' Brace said.

'Same here.'

'Maybe we can try collaborating on crossword puzzles.'

'Oh,' she said, 'we'll think of something to do.'

'How does tomorrow night sound?'

She moaned. 'That'd be nice, but . . . I'm feeling awfully worn out from all this chasing around. I've got to get some rest, or I'm gonna drop. What I need to do is come home tomorrow night and hit the sack early. So maybe we should wait till the weekend. How would that be? The library's closed Sunday and Monday, so . . . how about if we get together Sunday? We could make a day of it. By then, I'll be all rested up and ready for action.'

'Sunday?' He sounded disappointed.

'Is that all right?'

'It's a long time off.'

'I know. It is. I'm gonna miss you.'

'Will you?' he asked.

'I miss you right now.'

'Want me to come over?'

She closed her eyes and smiled, thinking how nice it would be to have him here. 'It'd be great,' she said, 'but you'd better not. As it is, I won't be getting enough sleep tonight. And what about you? Don't you have classes to teach in the morning?'

'Can't let a little thing like that get in the way.

Besides, my first class doesn't start till nine.'

'Nine *a.m.*?'

'No problem. I . . .'

'Jeez, I shouldn't have called. Go to bed.'

'You can't give me orders,' he said. 'We're not married.'

She could almost see his grin and the mischief in his eyes. 'Very funny,' she said.

'You aren't blushing, are you?' he asked.

'What do you think?'

'Definitely. I bet you're as red as a rose.'

He's almost right, she thought, staring down at the ruddy skin exposed by her open robe. 'If you think you know so much,' she said, 'what am I wearing right now?'

'Uh . . .'

'Give up?'

'Yeah. I'd better not, uh . . .'

'Just my telephone.'

From the other end, she didn't hear anything.

'You still there?' she asked.

'Uh. Yeah. You're kidding about the phone, right?'

Now who's doing the blushing?

'Wrong,' she said. 'I've got nothing on but the phone on my lap. Goodnight, now. See you Sunday morning, okay? But don't make it too early. Maybe ten or eleven.'

'Okay. If you're sure you want to wait that long.'

'I think it'd be a good idea.'

'Okay. Well . . . goodnight, Jane.'

'Sleep tight,' she said, and hung up.

Then she picked up the note from Mog. She had only read it twice before. She read it again.

Dearest Jane,

I do hope that you prevailed over the canine with little or no injury to yourself. I should hate to see

179

your ability to continue the Game impaired, or your loveliness diminished.

Did you find your gift in the glove compartment? Be sure to bring it with you.

Our usual time.

At the house at the edge of Paradise.

Your Master,
MOG

Chapter Eighteen

All day at the library, Jane kept expecting Brace to stop in. He was supposed to stay away from her until Sunday, but he was bound to show up. Just to say hi, maybe. Just to see her. Maybe he would ask her to supper.

And she would be glad to see him.

She might even tell him about the lie.

The lie gnawed at her. It had been a cowardly way to squirm out of arguing over the Game. She should've stood up to Brace, instead – explained that she appreciated his concern, but wouldn't quit until she was good and ready.

His response to that would've been well worth hearing. Maybe he would've lost his temper, raged, demanded obedience. Or he might've pouted. Or begged. Or simply dumped her. Or calmly accepted her decision.

The calm acceptance seemed to be Brace's style, but she'd been afraid to test him.

Afraid of getting the wrong response.

A wrong response would ruin things, so she'd avoided it by lying to him.

Stupid! Like committing suicide to avoid surgery.

During the course of the day, she made up her mind to confess.

When he shows up, she thought, I'll tell him all about

it, show him the note . . . It'll be his reward for coming over.

He will show up, she told herself. He has to.

He didn't.

Nor did she find him waiting when she returned home at nine-thirty that night.

Jane put a small, frozen pizza into the oven, then popped a can of Budweiser and went to her bedroom.

'What do you wear to a haunted house?' she muttered. 'Chains. Or a sheet.' She sipped her beer. 'No, that's ghost attire. I'm not the ghost, I'm the fearless treasure-hunting heroine. Right.' She set her beer can on the bureau and started to unfasten her denim skirt. 'Make that the brainless heroine going where she knows she shouldn't. What would be the proper . . . ? She laughed softly as she stepped out of her skirt. 'Running shoes.'

Then she thought, Why stop with the shoes?

She changed into the loose blue shorts and tank top that she used to wear when she went for morning runs with Ken, the filthy son-of-a-bitch, back in olden days when she was slim and fit.

The outfit felt light and cool.

She remembered how the running used to feel.

I'll start doing it again, she decided. Every morning. Get back into shape.

She stepped over to the mirror. Gazed at herself and grimaced. Not because she looked too husky; she was used to that, and the past few days had led to some major improvements. It was the condition of her skin that shocked her. In the skimpy, clingy shorts and top, a lot of it showed. Where it wasn't pallid, it was bruised or scratched. She'd looked a lot better after her shower last night, when her skin had been ruddy from the hot water and most of her injuries had been shades of red.

I can't go out looking like this, she thought. What if somebody sees me?

Who's going to see me? I'll be in my car the whole way, and then in a creepy old empty house.

Which may or may not be empty.

She imagined herself wandering through the dark rooms. Too much of her body bare and vulnerable in the running outfit. Too much skin available for sharp edges, splinters, odd debris, for dirt and webs and spiders, for mice and rats.

No way, she decided.

She would change into long pants and a long-sleeved shirt, but that could wait until it was almost time to leave.

Staying in her running clothes, she picked up her beer can and returned to the kitchen. She waited there until her pizza was ready. Then she took her meal into the living room and tried to watch television while she ate.

She spent a lot of time staring at the bruise on her thigh.

A swath of purple and red and blue and gray – lovely.

If Brace shows up, she thought, I'll run in quick and put on my robe. Can't let him see all this.

He won't show up. Not now. Not this late. He would've been here by now if he was coming over.

My own fault. I told him to get lost till Sunday, and that's what he plans to do. Probably figures it'd be a sign of weakness to come any sooner. He'll stay away just to keep his pride.

'Men,' she muttered.

Of their many faults, however, she supposed that pride wasn't as bad as most. It probably screwed things up as much as anything else, but at least it was an honorable flaw. And one that had some worthwhile sides.

He won't call me, Jane thought, but I could call him. Just tell him I changed my mind and I want to see him tonight. If he comes over right away, we'll have the better part of an hour together before it's time for me to go . . . and maybe he can stay here like he did when I went to the bridge . . .

She got up from the sofa and stepped to the end table. There, she found his business card. She picked up the handset and tapped in his phone number.

When he gets here, she told herself, I'll show him Mog's note, and explain. It'll make everything all right.

Sort of all right, anyway.

She listened to the ringing at his end of the line.

What if he asks me to stay home and forget about going for the envelope?

Depends on how he asks, she thought. Maybe if he asks in a very nice way . . .

Why isn't he answering his phone?

It must've rung eight or nine times by now. Could Brace be reading, not yet aware of his ringing telephone?

'Come on,' she said.

What if he's not there? It's Friday night. Maybe he went out.

Maybe he goes with someone, and just hasn't bothered to tell me . . .

A sickly warm feeling of jealousy spread through her.

No, she told herself. If he went out, he went out alone.

Yeah, right.

If he's like every other guy . . .

'Come on,' she said. 'Pick it up, Brace. Don't do this to me, okay?'

You've gotta be there!

She wondered if he might have an answering machine set to take messages after the fifteenth ring – or the twentieth.

Not that anyone would ever stay on long enough to hear it.

Besides, his phone must've rung at least twenty-five times by now.

More like thirty.

If he isn't there . . . If I don't at least leave a message, he won't know where I've gone.

She waited a while longer. Then she hung up.

She watched her phone. Last night, Brace had called back almost at once.

Tonight, the phone stayed silent.

For the next hour, Jane stared at the television and fidgeted. She felt abandoned and betrayed, though she knew she had no right to feel that way.

He'll call, she told herself again and again. Any second now, the phone will ring. Or the doorbell. The doorbell, that'd be great.

Right now, he's on his way over.

She hoped so, but she doubted it.

She pictured Brace in bed with a slim, gorgeous, eager woman – maybe one of his students.

Screwing the gal just to get back at Jane. Accused of it, he says, *You don't want to see me till Sunday, huh? Well, guess what, you're not the only fish in the sea.*

She imagined him eavesdropping on such thoughts, sneering, saying, *You sure must have a high opinion of yourself, thinking I'd nail some other babe just to make you jealous. Here's a news flash, Janey – you ain't that hot.*

Brace isn't like that, she told herself. He would never say things like that. Nobody but a filthy son-of-a-bitch

185

like Ken would ever say things like that.

And Traci might've been hot, but she had the personality of a weasel and the brains of a bug.

'Not to mention a tattoo on her ass,' Jane muttered.

A butterfly. A butterfly on her butt.

Jane tried to laugh, but then she couldn't stop herself from remembering Ken's mussed black hair down there between the butterfly and the mattress of his bed.

And wondered why the memories still caused her so much pain, why she remained so bitter. Ridiculous. Absolutely. Hell, she was lucky to be rid of Ken, the filthy son-of-a-bitch. What if she *hadn't* caught him with Traci? What if, God forbid, she'd married him?

I oughta be thanking Traci every day of my life for saving me from him.

Maybe years from tonight, she thought, I'll be thinking I should thank some other bitch for saving me from Brace.

She looked at her wristwatch.

Eleven thirty-two.

Mouth dry, heart pounding hard, she made another phone call to Brace. This time, she counted the rings. She counted them up to twenty, then lost track as she wondered if she might be disturbing his neighbors. After a few more rings, she hung up.

She glared at the phone. 'Where the hell are you?'

Time running short, she hurried into her bedroom. She threw off her shorts and tank top, and searched her closet until she found an old pair of corduroy trousers. They were too tight around the waist, but they would have to do; the pants from her previous adventures had been soaked to remove the stains, but she hadn't yet run them through the washer.

She put on a long-sleeved chamois shirt.

186

Dressing like it's winter.

I'll melt, she thought, but at least I'll be protected.

'Speaking of protection,' she said.

She went to her nightstand, pulled open its drawer, and took out the pistol. She slipped it into the right front pocket of her corduroys. Into the left front pocket, she dropped her switchblade knife.

'Ready for bear,' she said, heading into the hallway.

Her purse was on the dining room table. So was Brace's flashlight.

She hooked the strap of her purse over her shoulder, but left the flashlight on the table.

It had given her too much trouble.

And she kept feeling guilty for breaking it.

On her way to work that morning, she had bought another bulb for the thing, and had purchased a flashlight for herself.

The new flashlight was much like Brace's, but half the size. It should fit nicely into any of her pants pockets. For now, it was buried somewhere inside her purse.

On her way to the door, she stopped beside the end table.

Try to phone him one last time?

Why bother? He isn't home.

I'm going into that awful old house and Brace won't know anything about it. If something happens, he won't know where to look for me.

She thought about stopping by his apartment and leaving a note – maybe sliding it under his door. She could get his address off the business card. But then she'd have to hunt for the place.

But what if he turns out to be there? What if he's with someone?

Another glance at her wristwatch, and Jane decided

that she didn't have enough time, anyway, for a trip to Brace's apartment. She snatched up the note from Mog, folded it into a square, and slipped it into a pocket of her shirt on her way to the front door.

Chapter Nineteen

Jane stopped across the road from the old house and shut off her headlights. She could hardly believe that she actually intended to go inside.

Gray in the moonlight, it looked ancient and dead.

From the first time she had seen the place, there had always been something familiar about it. She'd assumed it reminded her of the Bates house in *Psycho*. But now she realized the memory it evoked was from a novel she'd read as a teenager. She couldn't recall the name of the book, or its author. But she would never forget the house.

It was located in a coastal town somewhere north of San Francisco. A weathered, grim Victorian structure with turrets and gables and a witch's cap, just like this one. Instead of an abandoned ruin, however, that house had been a wax museum. On display were grisly figures of men, women and children who had supposedly been ripped apart by some sort of monster. In the daytime, you could go safely through with guided tours. But people kept sneaking in at night. As Jane recalled, some pretty awful things had happened to most of them.

That was only a book, she told herself. This place won't have any monsters in it.

And it can't be any worse than the graveyard.

Oh, yes it can, she thought.

She turned her eyes to the cemetery and scanned it through the bars of the fence.

Sure, the boneyard was creepy because of all the graves and tombstones and things – you knew you were surrounded by the dead. But at least you were out in the open. You could see what was coming in time to run away.

Like that awful man who came after her with the dog and threw it . . .

God, I hope he isn't somewhere in the house.

If he is there, she thought, he'd better be careful he doesn't get shot.

She checked her wristwatch again.

Five till twelve.

Gotta get moving.

Though no other cars had come into sight since she'd left the town behind, Jane didn't like the idea of parking here. It was just too close to the house. Anyone driving by would be sure to see her car and guess where she'd gone.

No good cover nearby, either.

But a dirt track, overgrown with weeds and low bushes, led past the side of the house toward the tilted ruin of a garage in the rear.

Keeping her headlights off, Jane steered by moonlight onto the driveway. Gravel crushed by the tires made groaning sounds. Brittle limbs crackled and crunched as she rolled over them, while others scraped the undercarriage, squeaked against the sides of her car.

Hope I don't get a flat tire driving through this crap.

Should've let Brace know where I was going.

A little too late for that, now.

At the rear of the house, she shifted to reverse and swung her car tail-first off the driveway. The gravel noises ended, but the dry foliage of the desolate lawn was thick and loud.

When the house completely blocked her view of the road, she stopped. She killed her engine. For a moment, she left her key in the ignition; it would be good there in case she needed to make a fast getaway.

Then she changed her mind. Better to waste time fumbling with her keys than to come out in a big hurry and find that the key had been stolen.

Or the entire car.

She pulled the key, then removed the new flashlight from her purse. She tucked the purse underneath the driver's seat. After climbing out, she started to put the key case into the right front pocket of her cords. That's where she liked to keep it when she didn't carry her purse.

But the pistol was already there.

She wanted nothing in the way of getting to her handgun, so the key case went into her left front pocket where the switchblade was.

She eased the car door shut.

Considered locking it, but decided not to.

She might be in a very big hurry when it came time to leave.

Standing in the knee-high weeds beside her car, she wondered if she was forgetting anything.

Forgetting to be smart and get my butt out of here.

Yeah, sure. And pass up sixteen hundred bucks? Not to mention a chance at the next bundle – twice that. Three thousand, something. Over six, the time after that. If Mog comes through and if I can stick it out.

With the flashlight in her left hand, but dark, she

trudged through the weeds. They rubbed at her legs, snagged the fabric of her trousers, but gave way to the force of her strides.

At the back of the house, a flight of wooden stairs led up to a small, covered porch. Jane aimed her flashlight at the darkness under the porch roof. She switched it on. The beam shot out a narrow, bright path.

She saw the remains of a screen door. The hinged frame and pull handle were there. But the frame lacked a screen.

The solid interior door was either wide open or gone. Jane's light reached all the way into the darkness of the house.

The place is wide open.

Of course it is, she thought. Mog had to get in and hide the envelope.

But maybe it had been wide open for a long, long time.

God only knows what might be inside.

Probably not the wax dummies of mutilated murder victims. Certainly not a monster. Or ghosts or goblins or ghouls.

If anything, an ordinary horror like a mad dog or wino or druggie or rapist or serial killer or some other brand of fruitcake.

Any of which she would hate to run into.

With the gun, though, she ought to be fairly safe.

She pulled it out of her pocket. Keeping her finger away from the trigger, she started to climb the stairs. The old planks sagged a little under her weight – felt like thin ice on a river. They groaned and squeaked like ice, but much louder.

One of these is gonna bust, she thought.

Instead of continuing up the middle, she moved to the side where the treads should be less likely to give out.

Her left hip rubbed the banister as she finished the climb.

Then she stood with her rump against the railing. In front of her, on the other side of the porch, was the screenless door. She shone her light through it.

Nobody came lurching out at her.

Be ready for it, though, she told herself. Don't pitch a coronary when it happens. If. If it happens.

She couldn't see much through the doorway: a floor littered with broken glass that sparkled in the shine of her flashlight; chunks of plaster on the floor, and leaves and a dark rag and the tumbled sheet of a newspaper; across the floor and off a bit to the right, the ruin of an old refrigerator; straight ahead, a doorway with more littered floor beyond it – and the rest of the house.

I'd better get in and start looking, Jane thought. This might take a while.

She hesitated. She didn't want to go inside.

It's just an old house, she told herself. Nothing evil about it.

Somebody's in there.

Somebody or something.

You go in, and you're asking for it. Why do you think Mog gave you the gun? Because he thinks you'll need it, that's why.

If you go in, things will get ugly.

But the alternative was to back down, quit, go home, never get any more prize money, lose any chance of finding out who Mog was or why he'd chosen Jane to be his player or what the point of the Game was.

Screw that, she thought.

Then she called out, 'Ready or not, here I come.'

Real smart, she thought. Announce you're here.

Why not? Maybe it'll scare off . . .

What if I get an answer?

Only silence came from the house.

'I'm coming in!' she yelled.

Reaching out with one foot, she pushed at the porch floor.

It didn't feel especially solid.

If it'll hold for just a split second while I take just one step . . .

What if this is it? she thought. This might be like the dog last night – Mog's surprise for me. Maybe I'm supposed to try crossing, and the floor gives out and down I go. And maybe he's got a treat down there under the porch for me. Like broken bottles or spikes or a pitchfork.

He doesn't want me ruined, she reminded herself. It'd spoil the Game. He wants to test me, not break me.

Yeah. That's encouraging. But he can't control everything. Like how rotten the floor is.

She shoved at it again with her right foot. It didn't fall apart, so she took a deep breath and swung her left leg forward. The floor squawked. She stepped down close to the door frame, then hurried through.

'Thank you,' she whispered. 'Thank you, thank you.'

The hardwood floor beneath her feet felt good and sturdy as she took a few strides deeper into the house. Stopping, she swept the area with her flashlight. This was definitely the kitchen. It had cupboards, sinks, an old stove, and the refrigerator she'd seen from outside.

The refrigerator door was rusty, dented, and pocked with bullet holes.

Somebody had used it for target practice.

Wonderful, Jane thought.

Maybe they put someone in it, first.

That was an especially charming thought.

Why not open it up and find out?

There isn't a body inside, she told herself. I'd be able to smell it.

Depending on how long it's been there.

I'm not going to look. No way.

But what if that's where Mog put the envelope?

She stepped closer to the refrigerator. It was the primitive type that hadn't been made for ages – the kind that had a lever handle. They'd been outlawed. Kids used to get trapped inside and die.

A dreary, abandoned house like this might attract kids. The daring ones. It'd be a fine place for playing spooky games, especially hide and seek.

What if a kid came along and hid inside the refrigerator and his friends couldn't find him?

There'd been no reports of missing children since Jane had moved into town. But someone might've gotten trapped in the old refrigerator a year ago, two years ago, five . . .

Or it might happen tomorrow, Jane realized.

Somebody should've taken this door off its hinges.

To free a hand for opening it, she tucked the flashlight under her right arm. She pointed her pistol at the door, and turned her body slightly until the beam of light also pointed at it. Then, with her left hand, she gripped the handle.

Might be something pretty bad inside. Whatever it is, don't panic. Stay cool.

Just in case, she switched off her pistol's safety. She curled her forefinger across the trigger.

Then she tugged the handle. The door swung open, hinges growling.

Nothing leaped at her. Nothing tumbled out. Nothing

hideous or dangerous waited for her on any of the shelves or racks.

The refrigerator appeared to be empty except for a single white envelope hanging by a strip of tape from the edge of the center shelf. Handwritten on the envelope was her name.

The first place I looked!

Jane wanted to be elated. But she felt too nervous for that.

It can't be this easy.

With her left hand, she tore the envelope free. She liked the feel of its thickness and weight.

If this is really it, I can get out of here.

But she had doubts.

She backed away from the open refrigerator. When her rump met a counter, she stopped, switched the safety back on, then bent down and clamped the pistol between her knees. She kept the flashlight pinned beneath her arm. Using both hands, she tore open the envelope.

She took out the packet.

A sheet of notebook paper, as usual, was folded around the bills. She removed the bills and fanned them out. At the corner of each was a big 100.

She counted how many. Sixteen.

She felt a warm swelling of excitement in her chest.

This was easy, she thought. This was really easy. Good thing, too. Wouldn't have taken much at this point to make me quit. Maybe Mog sensed that, or something.

She folded the money in half and slipped it down inside a rear pocket of her corduroys. The seat of the pants was fairly tight. She could feel the stiff block of the cash against her buttock.

All mine. Incredible. All it took was a little guts.

She opened the note and held it up in front of her flashlight.

Dearest,
    The Game remains afoot, so carry on. Hotfoot it upstairs to the Master bedroom.
    You won't be sorry.

Love & kisses,
MOG

Chapter Twenty

Jane read the note again, her elation sinking.

Not a word about the Game being over for tonight and resuming tomorrow night at the usual time. Mog was clearly telling her that it was continuing right now.

'Terrific,' she muttered.

She didn't want to go upstairs, especially not to the master bedroom. She wanted to go home.

It's supposed to be over when I get the money!

Not necessarily, she thought. On the first night of the Game, she'd gotten three payments: the fifty at the circulation desk, the hundred inside *Look Homeward, Angel*, and the two hundred at the top of the Crazy Horse statue. Only on the second and third nights had she been given single tasks and payments. From that little pattern, she'd assumed it would remain one per night.

Shouldn't go assuming, she told herself.

Anyway, Mog's the Master of Games. Which probably means he can make up whatever rules he pleases. And change them when he likes.

Doesn't mean I have to go along with it. I can quit.

She looked again at the note.

The Game remains afoot, so carry on.

Which ought to mean, Jane realized, that another envelope would be waiting for her upstairs in the master bedroom.

So far, Mog had remained consistent about doubling the amount of money.

If I carry on, she thought, I'll get twice sixteen hundred dollars. Three thousand, something.

In her mind, she doubled the sixes. They added up to twelve, making two hundred after you carry the twelves one over for the three thousand. Giving a total sum of three thousand, two hundred dollars that should be somewhere upstairs in an envelope for her.

'Man,' she whispered.

She tucked the note into a pocket of her shirt, then shut the refrigerator door.

She started to turn away, then faced the refrigerator again.

I can't just leave it this way, she thought. Someone might come along.

In the morning, she could make a few phone calls – notify the authorities. They'd send people out to remove the door, cart the whole thing away, or whatever. But what if a kid should come along tonight and climb inside and . . .

'Fat chance,' Jane muttered.

Besides, nobody was likely to suffocate in there – not the way it was riddled with bullet holes.

Still . . .

She frowned. There must be a way to make the thing safe. She opened the door and studied its hinges.

I'm procrastinating, she realized. Anything to keep me from going upstairs.

But this is important. It might save a life.

Yeah. Maybe.

She didn't have the tools for removing the door from its hinges. She supposed she could *shoot* the hinges off. That'd be awfully noisy, though, and a waste of ammo.

She might be able to turn the refrigerator around, shove it door-first against the wall. Or tumble the thing forward onto its door.

Yeah, drop it onto me. Great plan.

Then she found an idea that seemed just fine. She spotted the old sheet of newspaper that she'd noticed earlier, picked it up, ripped it, crumpled it, and stuffed a thick wad into the refrigerator's latch hole. After making sure it was packed in tightly, she swung the door shut.

A soft bump, and the door swung back open again.

'Brilliant,' Jane whispered. 'If I was any smarter, I'd be a threat.' She laughed softly, then felt her bowels crawl.

Gotta go upstairs, now.

'Oh, man.'

Hey, she reminded herself, it's for three thousand, two hundred bucks. For money like that, I'd walk through Dracula's Castle blindfolded with a bloody nose and my period.

'Or maybe not,' she muttered.

Flashlight in her left hand, pistol in her right, she stepped out of the kitchen and entered an area that had probably been the dining room. Before going farther, she swept the room with her light.

She saw nothing capable of attacking her.

The room was empty of furniture. Wallpaper hung in tatters like shredded rags. In some places, the walls had been bashed and torn open. Glass from the shattered window was mixed on the floor with broken slabs of drywall and old boards of various sizes, some with nails jutting, points up. Odd pieces of clothing were strewn about: a sock here, a pair of pants there, a boot, a stiff wad of boxer shorts. She spotted a crushed cigarette pack, part of a potato chip bag.

Being careful what she stepped on, Jane walked across the room.

The air smelled like old, wet books.

What a charming place, she thought.

In the next room, she whispered, 'Ah, this one's furnished.'

The furniture consisted of one skinny, stained mattress over in a corner. On the floor near the mattress were smashed beer cans, broken liquor bottles, and dark mounds that Jane supposed were blankets and an assortment of clothing and rags.

This room smelled worse than the other. Mixed in with the musty aroma were scents of booze, urine and feces.

Jane felt an urge to gag, so she held her breath and quickened her pace.

As she rushed along, she kept her light and eyes on the dark mounds. They were probably just blankets or clothes or rags, but she worried that one of them might be covering things – things that might start to come at her.

Soon, they were behind her.

She found the foyer, the front door, and the foot of a stairway that led to the second floor. Still holding her breath, she shone her light at the top of the stairs.

Nothing coming down at her.

She turned around.

Nothing coming at her from behind.

She tested the first stair. It creaked, but felt good and solid. Those that she could see above her looked all right, so she climbed. When she reached the sixth stair, she let out her breath and filled her lungs.

The air didn't seem quite so bad, here.

She supposed that she would need to go back through

that horrible room on her way out, though.

Unless she could leave by the front door.

None of the house's doors or windows seemed to be boarded up.

I should be able to get out that way, she thought. Unless it's nailed shut, or something.

She wished she had tried to open it before starting up the stairs.

Find out soon enough, she thought.

She aimed her light again at the top of the stairway. *So far, so good.*

If I was in that horrible book, she thought, I'd have a monster bounding down at me. One of those slimy white ape-things with teeth in its cock.

It wouldn't take one of those to scare me witless, she thought. Wouldn't take much of anything at all.

But nothing appeared.

At the top of the stairway, she halted. She swung her flashlight this way and that, spotted no assailants coming at her from up or down the long corridor, but glimpsed plenty of shadows and debris.

What'm I doin' here? she thought.

We're here because we're here because we're here because we're here . . .

Three thousand, two hundred bucks, she reminded herself.

And more after that if the Game goes on.

If I don't drop dead.

I'm too young to drop dead.

Sure.

I've probably felt worse, she told herself.

She was having a difficult time catching enough breath. Her heart was slamming. Her mouth was parched. Her face dripped sweat. Her hair felt soaked. So did the sides

202

and back of her shirt, and the seat of her panties. Soaked and clinging to her skin.

This isn't so bad, she thought. At least I'm not getting hurt by some damn dog – or bums. Not yet, anyhow.

She just wished that she hadn't worn such heavy clothes. A long-sleeved shirt on a hot night like this? Not to mention corduroy pants?

They're cooking me.

Should've stayed in my running shorts.

But she would be grateful for the shielding clothes if things turned bad.

She glanced at the side of her pistol to make sure the safety was off. The red dot showed. All set. Keeping her forefinger straight out alongside the trigger guard, she began to search for the 'Master bedroom'.

Why did Mog use the upper case M? she wondered. He's so big on hints and clues, it must mean something.

Master is what he calls himself. Is he saying it's his bedroom?

What if he lives in this place?

She probed a bathroom with her flashlight beam, then backed away until she met the wall at the other side of the corridor. With the wall against her back, nothing could sneak up on her.

What if Mog lives here?

Maybe this is it, she thought.

She'd supposed from the start that Mog's scheme had a special purpose. She couldn't be sure what its purpose might be, but maybe the Game was designed to lead her, step by step, toward a particular destination – a place she would normally shun.

Such as a creepy old house by a graveyard.

Such as Mog's bedroom inside that house.

Envelopes of money like a trail of cheese for the rat to follow.

I'm not a rat, she told herself.

And then gasped as something scurried over the side of her neck, something with legs that tickled. Spider! Shuddering, going prickly with gooseflesh everywhere, she sprang away from the wall and swept at the creature with the head of her flashlight.

Got it!

But a moment later, she felt a tickle underneath her shirt, just below her collar bone.

God, no!

Fast as she could, she shoved the flashlight between her thighs. While she did that, the spider scampered downward onto her left breast.

She slapped it through her shirt.

Felt it crumble and squish.

After the sting from her slap faded, she could feel the body like the weight of a coin on her breast. It was stuck to her skin, mashed into the moisture of her sweat, glued there with its own juices.

The feel of it disgusted her.

She had to wipe it off. Fast.

So appalled she could hardly think straight, she tugged open the top of her shirt. She had to do it one-handed. It came undone, and a moment later a button clicked on the floor.

The barrel of her pistol would only smear the mess, so she jammed her hand down into her corduroys and brought out the switchblade knife. Tonight, she hadn't bothered with a rubber band to keep the blade shut. She'd decided to take her chances rather than slow things down – and snap her lips.

She thumbed the button and the blade sprang out.

She wished she could see what she was doing.

But the flashlight was between her legs, pointing into the bathroom. She could see nothing of her breast.

Maybe just as well, she thought. I don't want to see whatever's left of the damn spider.

Just be careful. Real careful.

Quickly, she lowered the edge of the blade until she felt it against her skin just above where the mess was. Then she scraped. One quick stroke as if shaving the top of her breast with a straight razor. She felt the small gob skid along in front of the blade, and hoped it wasn't leaving much of itself behind.

Bending at the waist, she gave the blade a flick.

That should've gotten most of it.

She wiped both sides of the blade on a leg of her trousers. Clamping the handle between her teeth, she lifted the untucked end of her shirt and scrubbed at the trail left by the spider.

Then she took the flashlight from between her legs and inspected the damage. Her flushed skin was landscaped with countless goosebumps. The knife, however, had left no visible mark. The spider had left no trail of juice or pieces; the blade or the vigorous wiping with her shirt had gotten it all.

Except that!

It looked like a thick black whisker.

Jane knew it was part of a spider leg.

She tucked her chin down and blew on it. The leg trembled slightly, but stayed. Wincing, she brushed it away with the edge of her gunhand.

She checked her breast once more with the flashlight.

It looked as if it had been dipped in ice water.

No traces remained of the spider, so she clamped the flashlight under her right arm and closed her shirt. She kept the flashlight where it was, and took the knife from her teeth.

She held on to the knife.

Let's find that envelope and get out of here, she thought. Before we meet another spider.

Turning, she followed the pale beam of light down the corridor toward another doorway.

One more spider and I'm gone. Rather face fifteen Rottweilers than . . .

The door was shut. Jane nudged it with her knee. Squalling on dry hinges, it swung open. Her light stretched into a large room.

She caught a whiff and quit breathing.

What the hell died in here?

Doesn't matter, she told herself. This is the place.

She would find the envelope here.

Inside the dirty coffin in the middle of the floor.

She stepped through the doorway. Twisting her torso, she swept the light from side to side. She saw no human or animal. The room seemed to be empty except for the coffin.

No hidden recesses. No other doors.

Two windows on the far wall exposed the night. Some of the night came in through them, tossing crooked grimy rectangles onto the floor.

Jane bent slightly at the waist to drop the angle of her light. She turned around slowly, inspecting the floor. It looked much the same as the floors downstairs: scattered with glass and plaster, broken boards bristling with nails, leaves and shreds of paper and plastic wrappers, rags, remnants of clothing.

The coffin had been dragged across the room from the doorway, scraping a path through the debris.

Jane stepped closer to it.

The coffin was constructed of wood. Pine, maybe. It looked like a good piece of furniture that had been left out in the weather for a few years.

Underground is more like it.

The top and sides were filthy with dried mud.

Terrific, Jane thought. He dug it up out of the neighbor's yard.

Or wants me to think so.

She started to ache from holding her breath, so she hurried toward one of the windows. As she neared it, she felt a warm breeze on her face. Shards of glass snapped and crunched under her shoes.

At the window, she leaned forward carefully, ready to stop if her head should meet trouble.

Bumping nothing, being stabbed by nothing, she eased her head outside and breathed deeply. The air smelled of summer and of deep night, but was not without a vague but revolting scent of rotten flesh. She could feel the breeze sliding inside the open front of her shirt. It felt very good in there on her hot, sweaty skin.

The window gave Jane a panoramic view of Paradise Gardens Memorial Park. From this height, she could see most of it.

She found herself searching the graveyard for the stranger who'd been there last night, who'd carried the dog overhead like a barbell and hurled it at her.

She spotted a few human shapes, but none that moved. They were probably statues.

Or one might be him, standing still. Maybe gazing up at her.

A whole new swarm of goosebumps raced up her skin. They were quick and cold. They stiffened the flesh at the back of her neck and squeezed her scalp and made her nipples rise hard and achy.

He's watching . . .

Jane started to duck away, but forced herself to stop.

Big deal if someone's down there staring at me. As long as he's down there and I'm up here.

Fighting her urge to get away from the window, she took time to scan the parking area, the main gates, and the section of fence near the gates.

The Toyota pickup was gone. So was the dog that she'd last seen skewered on top of the fence rods.

Bet I know where the dog is now, she thought.

Easing herself clear of the window, she turned around.

The flashlight beneath her arm swung its beam to the coffin.

Right in there, she thought.

I'm supposed to think Mog dug the coffin up, complete with corpse.

A real test of my willpower. Do I have the guts to open it and see how a person looks after being in the ground too long? Will I go that far for my three thousand, two hundred bucks?

'You betcha,' she whispered.

But she wouldn't be finding a dead person in there. She'd be finding the Rottweiler, a day old, torn open and stinky. That's where Mog put the thing. And that's where he put the envelope.

She stepped to the side of the casket, lifted her left foot and pounded her heel against the edge of the lid.

The lid wobbled.

Not fastened down.

Jane considered putting away the knife and pistol, placing the flashlight between her legs, bending over, and removing the lid with her hands. But she wanted to keep her weapons ready. And she certainly didn't want to have her face down there when the lid came off.

No way.

Unless, she amended, it turns out that none of the other ways will work.

Like kicking.

Bending her left leg slightly for balance, she lashed out with her right. The sole of her shoe caught the coffin lid, raised it, knocked it crooked, shoved it and dropped it. The lid skidded off the far edge of the coffin, then crashed to the floor.

Jane flinched at the noise it made.

She stared into the coffin, hardly able to believe her eyes.

No stinky, mutilated dog. No human cadaver.

She felt as if she'd been tricked, but she was relieved, almost delighted.

The coffin contained nothing dead or disgusting.

With its shiny blue satin lining and pillow, it looked almost inviting.

Her envelope had been placed on the pillow. She glanced at it, then turned her eyes to the flat box near the middle of the coffin. The box, about the size of a hardbound novel, was brightly wrapped in gold foil paper tied with a scarlet ribbon and bow that gleamed in the shine of her flashlight.

'Now he's leaving presents,' Jane whispered.

At the sound of her voice, she realized that she had been forgetting to hold her breath – probably ever since coming away from the window. Without thinking about it, she'd been taking shallow breaths through her mouth.

Now, she tried a small sniff. The stench hadn't gone away, but it seemed less horrible than earlier. She was growing accustomed to it. But the source of the foul odor was obviously somewhere other than inside the coffin.

Maybe a dead rat over in a corner, something like that.

The inside of the coffin *looked* as if it should smell like perfume.

As nice as a freshly made bed.

Mog's bed? she wondered. In the note, he'd called this the 'Master bedroom'. And he's the Master of Games.

Is he nuts enough to sleep in a coffin?

The satin lining and pillow case were smooth, without a wrinkle. Jane doubted that anyone had ever slept on them.

She began to feel very nervous.

Mog got his hands on an old, weathered coffin, she thought. Maybe by digging it out of the graveyard. He fixed it up with brand new upholstery.

What'd he do with the body?

Why'd he fix it up?

She swiveled around fast to make certain she was still alone in the room. Then she thumbed her safety on and slipped the pistol into her pocket. After changing the knife to her right hand, she bent over, reached into the coffin with her left, and picked up the envelope. She slit it open with her knife.

Pulled out the money wrapped in a note.

She counted the hundred-dollar bills. Thirty-two of them.

'Man,' she muttered. 'Man, oh man.'

Her heart was thudding. Her throat felt tight. Her stomach squirmed.

She felt very odd: elated, scared.

This plus the sixteen hundred – almost five thousand just tonight.

How much does this make altogether? she wondered.

She tried to calm herself so that she could remember and count.

No luck.

It's a lot. It's a real, real lot.

But she was afraid to read the note. Afraid of the gift-wrapped box. Afraid of who or what might be in the house, maybe watching her right now, maybe sneaking closer.

The note fluttered in her twitching hand as she held it in front of the flashlight.

My Dear,

I do believe I'm falling in love. Not only are you a vision of delight, but oh! such spunk to have come this far.

The gift is for you. Open it now. You'll be glad you did.

Kisses,
MOG

Chapter Twenty-one

Jane crouched over the coffin, set her knife on the satin-covered pad, and picked up the brightly wrapped box. Flashlight pinned between her right arm and ribs, she tore off the bow and ribbon and wrapping paper and let them fall to the floor.

Holding the bottom of the box steady on the edge of the coffin, she peeled off its top.

Inside, she found a kitchen timer, a negligee and a note.

The note was taped to the timer.

Darling,

You've labored long and hard, this night. You deserve a rest.

Slip into this dainty number, set the timer for half an hour, and ease yourself down onto satin comfort.

At the sound of the ding, you may rise, collect your prize, and be off.

Your Master,
MOG

Jane read the note three times.

More times than that, she thought, he's gotta be kidding.

She was shaking very badly. She had an odd, numb sensation behind her forehead. And a strange, buzzy feeling down inside as if a low-level electrical current might be humming through her bowels.

She placed the timer beside her knife at the bottom of the coffin.

Then she let the box fall to the floor as she stood up with a shoulder strap of the negligee pinched between her thumb and forefinger. The strap looked like a slim ribbon of silk. The garment swaying below it might just barely be long enough to reach from Jane's chest to her thighs.

The beam of her light passed through the gauzy red fabric.

A dainty number?

He actually wants me to strip and put this on, she thought. And then lie down in the coffin for half an hour.

'Oh, man,' she muttered. 'He's got the wrong gal.' In a loud voice, she said, 'You're out of your mind.'

No answer came.

Not that she expected one.

Mog never answered.

But he must be here, she told herself. He promised another 'prize' if I follow orders. He has to deliver it, doesn't he? And if he isn't watching, how will he even know whether I do what I'm supposed to do?

If he isn't watching, why does he *want* me to do it?

He's watching, all right. Maybe through a hole in the wall, something tricky like that.

Wants to pay me six thousand, four hundred bucks so he can play peeping Tom.

Peeping Tom in a dark room.

If I turn off the flashlight, she thought, he won't be able to see anything.

Besides, what is there that he hasn't already seen? He must've spied on me in the shower that night. And who knows how many other times he's seen me with nothing on? He comes and goes as he pleases like some sort of invisible man.

Maybe he *is* invisible, she thought. That would sure explain a lot.

Maybe he's a ghost.

'A rich spook,' she muttered, 'with a penchant for voyeurism.'

He's making *me* rich, she reminded herself. This could be the end of it, if I don't follow orders. Am I going to let a little modesty get in the way of six thousand, four hundred dollars? Plus all the money that might come my way later on if I don't back down?

Especially since he's already seen me naked?

And since he can sneak into my house – probably sneak just about anywhere just as if he *is* invisible even if he's not, and see or do just about anything that pops into his head?

I can do it, she told herself. No big deal.

Okay, but what about the coffin part?

I can do it. I can do anything. It's all in the state of mind.

Moving her flashlight slowly, she inspected the interior of the coffin. No sign at all of dirt or bugs. It appeared to be perfectly clean.

She wondered how the satin would feel against her skin. Probably slippery and cool.

She'd been tempted, at times, to buy satin sheets for her bed at home . . .

This isn't a bed.

No? I don't see any other furniture in here, and this is supposed to be the 'Master bedroom'.

Does Mog sleep right here inside the coffin? she wondered. Like a vampire?

Maybe *that's* what he is.

'Bull,' she whispered.

If he does sleep in the thing, she thought, that's his problem. It's clean now. It looks plenty clean enough for me.

She stepped on the back of a shoe, pulled her foot out, raised her leg over the side of the coffin and lowered her foot onto the padded bottom. Holding the negligee's strap between her teeth, she reached down with her empty hand and removed her other shoe.

She left both shoes on the floor.

Standing inside the coffin, she switched off her flashlight. She crouched and placed it near her feet. Then she stood up, took the strap from her mouth, and looked down at herself. All she saw was black and shades of dark gray.

In this sort of darkness, she could prance butt-naked through a crowded room and nobody would be the wiser.

Balancing on one foot, she raised the other and peeled off its sock.

She felt the satin under her bare foot.

Oh, my God, I'm doing it.

She felt shivery all over.

This can't be happening. I can't really be doing this.

But she didn't stop.

When her socks were off, she crouched, reached over the side of the coffin and tucked them into her shoes.

She slipped her pistol underneath the pillow.

Needing both hands, she returned the negligee's strap to her mouth. It was moist from being there before. It felt and tasted like a wet shoelace, and she found herself wondering when she had ever had a shoe lace, wet or otherwise, in her mouth.

Must've been when I was a kid, she thought.

Right now, it was hard to imagine she'd once been a kid. It even seemed strange to think there had been a time before coming into this house tonight.

I had a life before all this. I'll have a life after. This is just . . . a weird interlude.

Wary of the filth on her clothes, Jane rolled her shirt and corduroy pants into bundles, crouched and set them carefully on top of her shoes. Then she stood up. She raised her arms to slip the negligee down over her head, but changed her mind and lowered them.

Just give me a couple of seconds, she thought.

Her clothes had been heavy and hot and sticky with sweat. She was glad to have them off, and not yet ready to put on something else, not even such a scant and wispy bit as the gift from Mog. The night air felt like a soft breath stirring against her bare skin. She wished there was more of a breeze. She thought about taking off her panties.

They were snug and damp, and made her feel a little itchy.

She'd intended to leave them on. Mog's note, after all, had only told her to wear the nightie – not to strip naked. Keeping her panties on wouldn't be going against any specific orders.

I'm supposed to take them off, even if he didn't come right out and say so.

She pulled them down, stepped out of them, squatted and added them to the pile on the floor beside the coffin. For a while, she remained squatting, savoring the feel of the air where she was so very hot and moist.

She was shivering so much that even her lungs seemed

to tremble as she breathed in and out.

A feverish shiver.

It had nothing to do with cold. It had little to do, anymore, with fear. It had mostly to do with being naked and feeling the soft breeze, with knowing why she'd stripped, with knowing where she was.

Shaking badly, she forced herself to stand.

She looked down at her body.

She'd been wrong to think that the darkness would hide her.

Mog has to be watching, she thought.

I don't care.

She raised her arms high, arched her back, stretched and twisted, relishing the feel of her flexing muscles and how the air touched her.

Jane suddenly realized that she *wanted* Mog to be watching her.

Watching the show.

His watching made it more delicious, somehow.

What's he doing to me?

Hugging her breasts, Jane dropped to her knees.

She had a quick urge to get dressed and run from the house. And be done with it. Done with it forever.

But part of her mind wondered why.

Because he's making me do these things!

He isn't *making* me do anything. I'm doing all this because I want the money.

No no no no no.

I want the money. Of course I want the money. But it isn't just that. It's a lot more than that.

It's because I want to do these things.

Some of them, anyhow.

This, for instance.

Turned on like crazy. But not so frenzied now. Calmed

217

at least slightly by the shame of catching herself at it.

Let's just try to get down to business, she told herself – do what needs to be done, and go home.

Still on her knees, she slipped the negligee over her head. It drifted down her body, hardly touching her at all, gliding against her here and there with a tickle so soft and subtle that she had to squirm. As expected, it didn't reach down very far. Its edge brushed her high up on the thighs.

The breeze stirred the weightless nightie, caressed her with it. Trying to ignore the sensations, she searched the dark bottom of the coffin with her hands and she found the flashlight. She thumbed its switch, then squinted as the sudden brightness hurt her eyes. When she could see again, she took a quick look around.

He can see me, but I can't see him.

She looked down at herself.

The scanty garment didn't cover much of her. Except for the slim straps, she was bare to mid-chest. There, the negligee draped little more than her nipples, stiff and jutting and plainly visible underneath. The wispy fabric concealed nothing, but gave a red hue to her skin, her scratches and bruises from the dog last night, and the small, pale triangle of hair between her legs.

Jane could hardly believe she was wearing such a thing.

What *won't* I do? she wondered.

It's no big deal, she told herself. People wear nighties like this all the time.

Yeah. Only maybe not for pay, while they're kneeling in a coffin in a cruddy old ruin of a house at the edge of a graveyard – with a stranger watching.

Anyway, she thought, this is a lot better than last night.

So far.

And so what if the whole deal's got me a little hot? That's no crime.

She slipped the flashlight between her thighs, beam up. Holding the timer in the light, she twisted the dial until it pointed to thirty.

The ticking sounded very loud.

She placed the timer on the floor of the coffin where it would be near her feet. After sliding her knife aside, she took the flashlight into her hand, turned and sat down. She stretched out her legs, spreading them so that the timer was between her ankles, then started to ease herself down. When the top of her head rubbed against the end of the coffin, she scooted forward a bit. Then she continued going down until her back met the cushion and her head sank into the soft pillow.

The satin felt cool and slick.

This isn't half bad, she thought. Just don't think about how this is a coffin.

This is a coffin.

This is what it's like to be in a coffin. Except I'm alive. Someday, I'll be stretched out in a coffin, dead, and they'll put the lid on, and . . .

A sick feeling started swelling inside her.

No! Stop it! Who's to say I'll end up in a coffin? A lot of things can happen – I might get disintegrated in a nuclear explosion, or . . .

Quit it!

Think about something else!

Now I lay me down to sleep, with bags of peanuts at my feet. If I should die before I wake, you'll know it's from a belly ache.

Die before I wake. Wonderful.

Mog is doing this to me, wants me to think horrible

thoughts – that's why he's making me lie here.

She wondered how much time had passed.

No more than a minute or two, probably.

This half hour is going to take forever.

In a very quiet whisper, Jane began to sing, 'A hundred bottles of beer on the wall, a hundred bottles of beer, if one of those . . .'

She stopped, afraid her voice might hide the sound of Mog's approach. She wanted to hear him if he came.

He'll come, she told herself. He has to. It's only a question of when – and what he'll do when he gets here.

Silently set the envelope on her pile of clothes, and sneak away?

But what if this really *is* what it's all about? What if the whole point of the Game was to get me here? Here where nobody will hear my screams. Here in this coffin – Mog's bed? What if this whole thing is about raping me and torturing me and murdering me?

She suddenly remembered the pistol.

A gift from Mog himself. So lighten up, bucko. You're not here to get nailed. Not by Mog, at least.

Reaching under the pillow, she took hold of it and pulled it out.

The heavy, solid feel of the pistol made her feel safe.

Everything's just fine, she told herself.

Gun in hand, she straightened her arm down along her right side. She placed the flashlight by her left hip, searched nearby until she found her switchblade, then set the open knife onto her belly. Leaving it there so she could feel it and grab it quickly in an emergency, she lowered her left hand and gripped the flashlight.

Nothing to do now except wait.

Wait and listen to the ticking of the timer.

It didn't actually make a ticking sound. More of a tock-tock-tock.

It was the beating of his miserable heart!

Right, start thinking about Poe stories, why don't you? Wonderful idea.

Try 'The Premature Burial.' Yeah, great.

And what if Mog's idea of a good time is to sneak up while I'm in here and drop the lid on me and seal me in? Maybe there's an open grave just waiting in the neighbor's yard.

The one this coffin came out of, for instance.

He wouldn't do that to me, she told herself.

You hope.

Could she shoot him through the lid? Maybe. The pistol was loaded with .22 long rifle cartridges. They were capable of blowing a hole through an inch of wood. But a strong, hard wood might stop them. It'd all depend on the lid.

It won't come to that.

He won't do anything to me. This is just another step in the Game. The whole deal is to have me strip and put on the nightie and stay in the coffin for half an hour.

Only this and nothing more.

When the half hour is up, I'll get dressed and find an envelope full of money and go home.

Somewhere nearby, the floor creaked.

Chapter Twenty-two

The sound of the creaking board sent a shock of cold through Jane. Her body went stiff, heart slamming, hands tightening on her flashlight and pistol. She held her breath. She cursed the clock for its tock-tock-tock-tock that got in her ears and stopped them from hearing any slight disruption of the silence of the room.

Old houses make lots of sounds, she told herself. That one little noise doesn't mean someone's coming.

Wanta bet?

It's Mog, she thought. He's on his way. Maybe just to leave the envelope, or . . .

What if it isn't Mog!

What if it's Rale, or that creep from last night, or God only knows?

Shoot first and ask questions later.

Wonderful idea. And suppose it does turn out to be Mog? I've just blown away the goose that lays the golden egg. Or maybe some harmless kid or . . .

It's nobody at all, she told herself. The noise meant nothing. Nobody's here. Just relax. False alarm. God, you're so tense. When the timer goes off, you'll probably blow off a toe.

She thought about where the pistol was aimed, and figured that an accidental discharge wouldn't hit any of her toes. Instead, it would probably gouge the side of her calf, and maybe hit the knob of bone sticking out from her ankle. Not to mention scorching her thigh with powder burns.

She wondered if the safety was on.

Then she wondered how much longer before the timer would ding.

Then a brilliant light blinded her and she gasped and jerked rigid.

'Jane!'

No! Not Brace! Of all the people in the world . . . better anyone than Brace. But it had been his voice saying her name, Jane was certain of that. It was Brace, and nobody else, standing at the end of the coffin shining the light in her face.

'Damn it!' she cried out, and flung up her right arm. 'Don't shoot! It's me!'

What's he got, a headlight?

She used her upraised arm to shield her eyes. 'Get that light out of my face!'

It didn't move away, it moved down.

'Damn it, Brace!'

As she sat up, the strap fell off her left shoulder. That side of the negligee slipped down. Her breast was caught naked in Brace's beacon.

The light jumped away from it.

And came to a stop, as if by accident, aiming down at an angle between her parted legs.

Jane cried out, 'Damn it!' and threw her legs together and hunched forward, an arm across her breasts. 'Turn it off! Just turn it off!'

Instead of killing the light, he swept its beam away from her. She was no longer in its bright center, but still lit by the glow.

'How's that?' Brace asked.

'Turn it off!'

'Sorry, I can't.'

'What do you mean, you can't?'

'I mean I won't. Not in a place like this.'

'You didn't have it on when you were sneaking up on me.'

'That was different.'

'You bastard.'

'Get on up out of there, Jane,' he said, sounding very calm. 'We need to get out of here.'

'What're you *doing* here?'

'I was worried about you.'

'You followed me!'

'I know.'

'You followed me! You had no right! Damn you! What right do you think you had? You don't own me! Jesus! What the hell did you think you were doing? Just get out of here! Get the hell out! Go!'

'I don't think it's safe for you to be here.'

'So what!' Jane blurted. 'Just get out and leave me alone! This isn't any of your business!'

The beam swung back at her. She cringed and turned her face away. 'Get that off me!'

It stayed. 'I think we'd better leave,' Brace said.

'I think *you'd* better leave.'

'Not without you.'

'Ho! Not without me? Who the fuck do you think you are? Get out of here!'

'Look at yourself,' he said.

Jane didn't move. 'I know what I'm doing.'

'You do?'

'Yes!'

'You know where you are?'

'Yes!'

'You know what you're wearing?'

'Damn it, get that light off me!'

'Look what he's doing to you, Jane.'

'He isn't doing anything – except giving me a hell of a lot of money.'

'Sure looks like he's making you do a strip and sleep in a casket.'

'He isn't *making* me. I'm doing it because I want to. There's a big difference.'

'How much are you getting paid this time?'

'Maybe nothing, thanks to you.' Turning her head, she scowled at Brace through the glare of the light. 'What the hell possessed you, damn it?'

He moved the light a little so it no longer blazed straight into her eyes. 'I care about you,' he said.

'Great. I care about you, too. But what makes you think that gives you the right to screw around with my life?'

'It probably doesn't,' he admitted.

'Damn right, it doesn't! If I'd wanted you in on this, I would've told you so. I didn't *want* you in on this. That's how come I lied about the note.'

'I already figured that out,' he said.

'Obviously. But you just decided to go ahead and butt in, anyway, didn't you? God, I don't follow *you* around. I don't spy on *you*. You know why? Because I don't *do* that sort of shit. I respect people's privacy. Privacy. You know what that is? How would you like it if I did that to you? Huh? Snuck around and spied on you in the middle of the night? Do you think you'd like that?'

'I'm sorry you're upset,' Brace said. 'I'm not sorry I came here, though. Somebody . . .'

'I'll *bet* you're not. Got yourself a free show.'

225

'It wasn't something I expected.'

'Bet you watched, though. Didn't you!'

'Sure, I watched. Who wouldn't?'

'A lot of people.'

'Well, sorry. But I don't look away from things like that. I'm not a priest, and you're not an ugly cow. So I watched. But I can't say I enjoyed it much.'

'Oh, thanks.'

'For godsake, don't let *that* offend you. I was too damn shocked to appreciate the view. I couldn't believe you were really doing it.'

'Surprise, surprise.'

'I knew you were awfully eager to get as much money as you could from this guy, but . . . this is crazy. I never would've thought you'd stoop to it.'

'Sorry to disappoint you. But now you know. I'm nothing but a cheap slut. Nothing I won't "stoop to" for a buck.'

'I'm starting to wonder,' Brace said.

'Yeah, well, fuck you and the horse you rode in on.'

'Jane.'

'Get out of here, okay? Or haven't you insulted me enough yet? Or are you waiting around for another eyeful? God damn it, you weren't supposed to be here! You've ruined everything! Everything!'

'Someone has to watch out for you, Jane.'

'No! My God, what do you think I am – an invalid?'

'You're not an invalid,' he said softly.

'No, of course not. I'm a woman. Same difference, huh? I'm a woman, so I'm too damn stupid and emotional and weak to take care of myself. I need a big smart guy like you to make sure I stay out of trouble.'

'This isn't trouble?'

'No,' she said.

'You're dressed like a hooker and sitting in a casket with a gun in your hand.'

'So what?'

'Ah. This is normal behavior. I see.'

'There wasn't supposed to be an audience.'

'Ah. If nobody's watching, it isn't happening? Like the tree that falls in the woods . . .'

'Exactly,' Jane said.

'Ah. But what about Mog? He's watching, isn't he?'

'I don't know.'

'Of course he's watching. Do you honestly think anybody would pay you to do these things unless he wants to watch them happen?'

'I wouldn't know. I've never seen him. Have *you* seen him?'

'No.'

'Well, why the hell not?' she blurted, almost shouting. 'You've seen everything else!'

'Take it easy, Jane. You're getting upset again.'

'I've got a clue for you, buddy! I've never *stopped* being upset!'

'Look, let's just get out of here.'

'*You* get out of here.'

'Someone might show up. What if the police come along and find us?'

'Who cares?'

'What *do* you care about, Jane?'

'I used to care about you.'

Brace suddenly kicked the coffin so hard that it jumped and scooted. The blow jolted Jane. She gasped. She felt stunned, and shaken, almost ready to cry.

'Don't!'

'Game's over, honey. Get out of there. Right now, or I'll drag you out.'

'You've got no right!'

'Who cares?' he threw back at her. 'Out. Now.'

'You bastard.'

'I know.'

'How'm I gonna get my money if I leave?'

'You won't. At least I hope not. Learn to live on your salary like everyone else. You didn't know where to draw the line, so I'm drawing it for you.'

Her right hand, pressed against her breast, still held the pistol. In her mind, she saw herself swing her arm forward and aim the weapon at Brace; she heard herself order him to leave the house. But then something went wrong. He lurched for Jane. Her finger twitched. *Bam!* Brace slumped to the floor, a bullet hole in his forehead.

I could make it happen. I could shoot him.

The thoughts slammed through Jane.

Shocked her. Killed her rage and shame and her will to resist. Suddenly feeling very tired, she lowered the pistol to her side. She stood up, leaving it at the bottom of the coffin, along with her flashlight and knife and the ticking timer. She could feel the strap still dangling against her arm. She knew that her breast was bare, and that the negligee hid nothing even where it covered her.

She was on her feet, facing Brace, totally exposed to his gaze.

She didn't care at all. She felt weary and numb.

'You'd better get dressed,' Brace said.

'If you say so.' She slipped the negligee up her body and off, and let it fall.

'Jeez.' He sounded surprised and angry.

'You said I should get dressed,' she pointed out as the nightie settled softly across the tops of her feet. It felt light and ticklish like wisps of tissue paper. 'You're the boss,' she added.

228

Now who's the calm one? she thought. Just look how calm I am. Very easy to be calm when everything's ruined and nothing matters anymore.

Easy as pie.

'You don't have to act crazy,' Brace muttered as he hurried around to the side of the coffin.

'What's there to hide?' she said. 'You've already seen everything.'

'It wasn't supposed to be like this.'

'It never is.'

Crouching, he set his electric lantern on the floor and picked up Jane's panties. He held them out to her. 'Put these on.'

She felt the corners of her mouth curl up. 'Are you sure you don't want to fuck me first?' she asked.

'Of that I'm certain, my dear.'

She hit him very hard in the face with her fist. The blow made his head jerk a little sideways. But he turned back to Jane and gave her a terrible look of surprise and disappointment.

The timer went off just then, dinging like the bell at the end of a boxing round.

Jane burst into tears. She took the panties from Brace and bent over to step into them and lost her balance and he caught her by the shoulders and held her steady until she had her panties on. He held her again when she had trouble getting into her corduroys.

The bastard! Why doesn't he mind his own fucking business and let me fall!

She wished she could stop crying.

When she tried to stop, however, it only got worse. She was bawling out of control by the time she'd finished dressing.

With Brace's help, she gathered her belongings.

'What about that stuff?' Brace asked, shining his light at the negligee and timer still at the bottom of the coffin.

'They . . . aren't . . . mine,' she gasped out between sobs.

'Are you sure you don't want them?'

'Leave 'em.'

'Okay. Let's go, then.'

Brace led the way. Jane followed him out of the room and downstairs and out of the house. His car was parked on the rear lawn, next to hers.

'Will you be able to drive home all right?' he asked as he opened her car door.

Jane sniffled. She wiped her eyes. 'I'm not drunk,' she said.

'You're awfully upset.'

'You oughta know.'

'I'm sorry about all this.'

'Not as sorry as me.'

'Don't bet on it,' he said.

'Yeah. Right.' She dropped onto the driver's seat and tried to shut the door.

Brace held it open. 'I'll follow you home,' he said.

'Don't bother.'

'I just want to make sure you get there okay.'

'Swell. But don't . . . don't think I'm gonna . . . let you in. I never . . . never never never . . . wanta see you again.'

He let go of the door, and Jane slammed it shut.

Chapter Twenty-three

Still half-asleep the next morning, Jane rolled onto her side. The sheet beneath her body felt cool and slippery. Nice. But the mattress seemed strangely hard under her shoulder and hip. She tried to curl up. Her knees and heels bumped walls.

Uh-oh.

Her eyes sprang open. She flipped onto her back, glimpsed a stained and tattered ceiling, then snapped her head from side to side.

She was lying in the coffin.

'Oh,' she murmured.

Shoving at its padded bottom, she raised herself to her elbows. She muttered, 'Oh, my God,' at the sight of her negligee. She couldn't believe she was wearing such a thing. It had no more substance than mosquito netting. And it was twisted crooked, leaving her bare below the waist.

Through the transparent red material, Jane watched her skin darken to a deep shade of scarlet as she remembered that Brace had seen her dressed this way.

Worse. I even took it off.

The memories of last night began pouring into her. Though the morning air felt cool, she soon was dripping with sweat. Bad enough that Brace had found, *caught* her in the coffin with nothing on except this poor excuse for a nightgown. But the horrid things she'd said to him! How could she have said such things? And acted that way?

I even hit him!

What was I, nuts?

None of it would've happened, she told herself, if Brace had stayed away. It was really all his fault. He followed me, snuck up on me, looked at me. Shone that damn floodlight on me and saw everything, the dirty . . .

Saw all my wounds, too. And saw me before I could get back into decent shape.

Well, that's the last he'll ever see of me.

Pushing at the bottom of the coffin, she sat the rest of the way up. She looked around the room to make sure she had no visitors.

Nobody here.

Except maybe for Mog at a peephole or something – who knows with him?

The place was a mess. It looked a lot worse in daylight.

'What doesn't?' she muttered, casting a glance at her awful nightie and all it exposed of her scratches and bruises and places that clothing was normally meant to hide.

He never should've seen me in this, she thought.

I'm the one who put it on.

But he wasn't supposed to show up, damn him!

Forget it, she told herself. Doesn't matter. It's all over.

Leaning forward, she reached to the timer between her feet and picked it up. It was silent, the pointer on the zero.

Did I forget to set the thing? Jane wondered.

No. She could remember thinking, *Here we go again,*

while she'd turned the dial to the thirty.

I slept through the bell, that's all. Hardly surprising.

It had been after four in the morning by the time she'd set the timer for her second try. Four thirteen, to be exact; she could remember glancing at her wristwatch.

After being escorted home by Brace, she'd watched him drive away. Then she'd turned off the lights and waited just in case he was only pretending to leave.

Soon, she'd decided it was pointless to wait any longer. Even if Brace *was* keeping an eye on her, he probably wouldn't dare confront her again.

So she'd hurried out to her car and returned to the house, parked behind it like before, and rushed upstairs.

This time, there'd been no hesitation.

She'd hopped into the coffin, stripped, slipped into the negligee, sat down on the bottom of the coffin, set the timer for thirty minutes, then stretched out and shut her eyes.

She hadn't fallen asleep immediately.

She could remember thinking, I might be a lot of things, Brace old pal, but I'm no quitter.

And she was pretty sure that, just before falling asleep, she had called into the silence of the dark house, 'Hey, Mog, I'm back!'

Jane put the timer down. She looked at her wristwatch.

Nine thirty-five.

Fine. No problem. Plenty of time to drive home and shower and grab a bite to eat before going to work.

Now if I can find the envelope . . .

Jane got to her feet. Standing on the smooth satin pad, she stretched and moaned. Then she took off the negligee. She rolled it into a small bundle, planning to

233

take it home with her, certain that Mog meant for her to keep it.

She knew that Mog might be peering at her. She supposed it didn't matter, though.

Squatting, she set down the negligee. She reached under the pillow, found her pistol and put it on top of the gown. It mashed the bundle almost flat. Her flashlight was beside the pillow. She slid it closer to the other things.

Unable to spot her switchblade knife, she remembered that she'd left it in the pocket of her cords.

That's everything, she thought, and stood up.

Again, she yawned and stretched. She felt awfully good.

Muscles a little sore, but taut. The softness of the breeze.

I ought to be feeling miserable, she thought. All that with Brace . . . But I'm okay. I feel better than okay.

Maybe because I had the guts to come back. And it's a wonderful morning. And I'm free. And I'm about to lay my mitts on gobs of money.

Hands on hips, Jane turned slowly, scanning the room for the envelope.

'I came through for you, Mog,' she said. 'I hope you held up your end of the deal.'

A few moments later, she said, 'You're gonna make me search for it, huh?'

Kneeling, she reached over the side of the coffin. She gathered the piled clothes between her arms, lifted them, turned, and brought them in with her. As she lowered them, they brushed against her thighs.

And something scratched her skin.

For an instant, she wondered if her knife had once again sprung open on its own.

She placed the bundle of clothes in front of her knees, glimpsed the thin pale mark on one leg, then reached down and found a stiff point of something between her folded corduroy pants and her shirt.

Not the tip of her knife, at all.

The sharp corner of an envelope.

'All right!'

She slipped the envelope out. And there was her handwritten name.

This envelope felt twice as thick as the last one.

Jane tore it open and pulled out a thick stack of bills wrapped in a single sheet of lined paper.

She ignored the note.

All the bills were hundreds. She counted them.

Sixty-four!

Jane let out a whoop of joy. Which sounded horribly loud, and made her cringe.

She glanced at the two windows overlooking the graveyard. The panes of both were shattered, of course.

Her delighted shout could've carried down to the cemetery.

What if a grounds keeper had heard it? Or grave diggers?

What if a graveside funeral service is going on down there and *everyone* heard it?

Fast as she could, she slipped into her shoes. She leaped from the coffin and ran for the nearest window. Wary of being spotted, she hunkered down at the last moment. Then she straightened up, raising her head above the sill.

Nobody seemed to be down there.

But she wanted to make sure, so she stayed at the window and kept on looking. She could almost *feel* someone down there.

Maybe the creep who threw the dog . . .

It's probably just my imagination, she told herself. From this height, she could see the entire cemetery. The distant parking lot was empty. Nobody was mowing the grass, or tending to flowers, or visiting the grave of a loved one. Nobody was there at all, unless they were hidden from view behind a monument or vault or bush or tree.

Or hiding at the bottom of that hole way over there by the corner of the fence.

Not a hole, Jane thought, a *grave*. An open grave. Which must mean somebody's getting buried today.

I've gotta haul my butt outa here!

She hurried back to the coffin. She didn't step in, this time, but stood beside it and ducked down to pick up her clothes. When she was dressed, she stuffed the pockets of her corduroys with the pistol, flashlight, and thick wad of cash.

Six thousand, four hundred bucks, she thought. Incredible.

Next time, it'll be twelve thousand, eight hundred.

God knows what he'll make me do for that kind of money.

Reaching into the coffin, she picked up the note and the empty envelope. She had already decided not to read Mog's message until she got home.

Whatever it might say, she wasn't ready for it.

She slipped the note and envelope into a pocket of her shirt.

Then she reached into the coffin and took out the negligee.

A souvenir of my most humiliating experience, she thought.

A souvenir of the night I lost Brace.

She was halfway down the stairs when she suddenly unfurled the garment and, making whimpery noises and grunts, tore it to shreds.

Chapter Twenty-four

Dearest Jane,

 You're far better off without the insufferable lout. Who needs him? Am I right?

 We have each other.

 We have the Game.

 Who could ask for anything more?

 I will be in touch. In the meantime, rest and heal.

Love,
MOG

P.S. I kissed you as you slept, my sweet,
   In the casket in my lair.
   I kissed you here, I kissed you there –
   I kissed you almost everywhere.

She had planned to save the note and read it after her bath. Pulling out the envelope while emptying her pockets in the bedroom, however, she had changed her mind.

 Stunned, she read it twice.

 She thought, I can't handle this. Huh-uh. No way.

 She dropped the note and it drifted to the floor.

 Then she took a bath. Sprawled in the hot water, she rubbed herself thoroughly with a bar of soap.

 Did he really do it? she wondered. Kiss me? Here and

there and almost everywhere? Maybe he's just kidding about that. But he sure had the opportunity. He did sneak over to the coffin while I was asleep. That's how the envelope got there. So maybe he really kissed me. Here and there and almost everywhere. While I was zoned, dead to the world.

What else did he do to me!

Probably nothing else, or he would've bragged about that, too.

But it sickened her to think that a stranger's mouth had been on her while she slept.

You sure Mog counts as a stranger? she wondered. We've never met, but we've sure been in touch . . .

He's been in touch with *me*.

And touched me, unless he's kidding about that.

So we aren't exactly strangers.

Sure. Right. He's been kissing me all over the place and I don't even know what he looks like. I don't know if he's handsome or repulsive. For all I know, he might be a skulking horror with rotten teeth and runny sores.

And even if he's the best-looking, most wonderful specimen of man to ever stride the Earth, he's got no business messing with someone who's asleep.

Sick. Perverted.

Perverted? Give me a break, bucko! This is the guy who set a Rottweiler on you and made you stretch out damn near naked in a coffin that looked a hell of a lot like a USED coffin and it's coming as some sort of big surprise to you that he might be a bit of a pervert? Get real. If you're very lucky, maybe he did nothing worse than stick his tongue in you.

And I asked for it, she told herself. What does that say about me?

Says I'm either stupid or crazy.

Brace was right – I didn't know where to draw the line. Which still didn't give him any right to interfere.

'You really blew it,' she muttered.

Done with her bath, Jane considered phoning Don to tell him she was too sick to make it in for work today. This being Saturday, with the library closed on Sunday and Monday, she would be giving herself a three-day weekend.

Three whole days for doing only what she wanted.

She wanted only to go to bed and stay there.

Wanted to sleep and forget about everything that had happened with Brace and with the dog and with the bums by the creek – sleep and stop worrying that the Game might be over.

The note had said, 'I'll be in touch.' Sounded a lot like a brush-off. Maybe Mog ran out of money, Jane thought. Or maybe he got tired of playing . . . or tired of me.

Or the Game simply ended – ran its course, whatever that might've been, and came to its natural conclusion.

If it's over, why didn't he just say so?

Who knows?

It probably isn't over. 'We have each other. We have the Game. Who could ask for anything more?' That doesn't sound like a guy calling the Game off.

This is just an intermission.

He wants to give me a night or two off, that's all.

Knows I've been through a lot. Knows I need to rest and heal.

I can use it, she thought. I can really use it.

Since Mog apparently wouldn't be sending her on a mission tonight, Jane decided against calling in sick. She would go to work as usual, then come straight home after closing the library, and hit the sack, and not have to be back at work until noon on Tuesday.

She still had time for a meal before getting dressed and heading for work, so she went into the kitchen. She planned to make coffee, bacon and eggs, and toast.

She made only the coffee and two slices of toast.

The rest seemed like too much effort.

After buttering her toast, she didn't even feel up to bothering with jelly.

Without jelly, the crusts were too dry. She ate only the centers of her toast. They were soggy with butter and tasted very good.

Jane's day at the Donnerville Public Library was marked by all that didn't happen.

She didn't pull out of the daze that made her feel dull in the head and body.

A surprise envelope from Mog didn't appear.

She didn't get any sleep, even though she tried during her lunch hour, shutting the office door and closing the blinds and putting her head down on her desk.

Brace didn't phone her.

She didn't eat.

Brace didn't show up.

She didn't phone him.

She didn't ask Don to keep her company when it came time to go upstairs and close the stacks.

All alone in the gloom of the stacks, she didn't feel afraid.

On her way home from work, Jane stopped at the drive-up window of the Jack in the Box and ordered three tacos.

When she got home, Brace wasn't there.

She searched her house, looking for an envelope from Mog.

She changed into her robe, took a beer out of the refrigerator, and sat down on the living room sofa to watch TV and eat her tacos.

She could only eat one taco. It seemed dry and tasteless, and she had trouble swallowing it at all.

She doubted very much that it was the taco's fault.

She took the two remaining tacos into the kitchen and put them in the refrigerator. While there, she grabbed herself another beer.

She drank a total of four beers, and woke up to find herself sprawled on the sofa, all the lights on, a movie on the TV that she recognized as *The White Zombie* with Bela Lugosi, her neck stiff, her head splitting, her blood vessels buzzing, her bladder feeling huge and about to burst.

The way her bladder was, she couldn't stand up straight. She could hardly walk.

But she made it to the bathroom, finally, in time to save herself.

When she finished on the toilet, she found herself to be wide awake. She looked at her wristwatch as she staggered to the sink.

This time last night, she'd already been caught by Brace and was on her way home.

She wondered what Brace was doing right now.

Probably sleeping, if he's got any sense.

Maybe Mog is sleeping, too. That could be the real reason he called a stop to the Game – he needs some rest, himself. Even God rested on the seventh day.

On the other hand, this *is* Saturday night. Well, Sunday morning by now. Maybe the fellas are out on the town with dates, or something.

'Both my guys,' she said to herself in the mirror, and shook her head. 'Former guys,' she corrected. 'Brace and Moggie, gone with the fucking wind.'

She washed her face. She brushed her teeth. She swallowed two Excedrin PM tablets with a fizzy glassful of Alka-Seltzer, then made the rounds of the house to turn off the TV and lights.

Can't make a habit of this crap, she told herself as she headed for her bedroom. I'll turn into a drunken old sow.

So who cares, anyhow?

She flicked off her bedroom light. Halfway across the dark floor, she shrugged off her robe and let it fall. She crawled onto her bed and clawed the covers down.

Between the sheets, she sighed.

'Ain't life grand,' she muttered.

But she had to admit that it was good to be back in her own bed. It had no satin sheets, but it wasn't a coffin.

She woke up Sunday morning sprawled on top of the sheets with sunlight shining on her from the window beside her bed, and a breeze caressing her like feathers. She had no headache. She felt very fine until she remembered about Brace.

This was the day she and Brace had planned to spend together.

Would he do anything about it? Phone, or maybe come over?

He might.

He probably will. He'll apologize and I'll forgive him, and we'll take it from there. Maybe we'll go on a picnic.

Feeling good again, Jane got out of bed.

Her robe lay in a heap on the floor. She picked it up, put it on, then checked its pockets in the hope of finding an envelope from Mog. The pockets were empty.

So she searched through the house.

She started in her bedroom, then went out into the hallway and checked the closets and bathroom before heading into the living room. She crouched, stood on tiptoes, searched on shelves and cupboards. Looked for an envelope from Mog in the very same sorts of places where, as a child an hour's drive from here, she had searched on Easter Sundays for the treats hidden about the house by the Easter bunny.

She never failed to find loads and loads of candy eggs and bunnies.

This morning, she had no success at all in finding an envelope left by Mog.

Probably because he didn't leave one, Jane thought.

Still hopeful, she went outside. The sun felt hot, but a nice breeze was blowing and it made her robe slide softly against her skin. She hadn't put on shoes. The concrete stoop and driveway were hot under her feet. The grass was cool and still wet from last night's dew.

She walked completely around her house. Twice.

No envelope.

Back inside, she felt sad and lonely. She placed a phone call to her parents. As she listened to the ringing, she remembered that they'd planned a trip to Lake Tahoe for this weekend.

She hung up.

She stared at the phone.

Call Brace?

I can't. It's up to him. He's the one who screwed up, so he's gotta be the one to make the next move. Besides, maybe he doesn't want to see me again.

Yeah, and maybe I don't want to see him, either.

She wondered how she would feel if she had to face him.

We'll find out, she told herself. We'll probably find out pretty soon, too.

Jane spent all day waiting for Brace to call or show up at her house.

While she waited, she went about her business. She ate, did a load of laundry, read a book, watched television, vacuumed the floor. She thought about phoning some of her friends in Mill Valley, but didn't want to tie up the phone in case Brace should call. She thought about taking a walk, or driving to the mall or the video rental store, but didn't want to leave the house.

The day passed very slowly.

Night came.

By nine o'clock, Jane had lost all hope that Brace would call or arrive.

I was kidding myself, she thought, to think he might. It's over with him.

At least I've still got the Game, she told herself.

'Oh, yeah?'

I *will* still have the game, if Mog ever gets over this stupid idea of giving me a rest period. If that's really what's even going on.

'It'll be okay,' she said, nodding at the television. 'He'll come through for me. He won't let me down like certain dirty creeps I could mention.'

I've just gotta figure out how to kill the time till he gets back to me.

At midnight, she left the house.

She had no mission from Mog. She carried no purse or flashlight or weapons.

She left the house dressed in her tank top, gym shorts, crew socks and running shoes. She wore her wristwatch.

A key to her house was tucked inside the top of one sock.

She walked briskly along the street for a while, loosening up, getting used to the notion of being out on her own at this time of the night with nowhere special to go.

No envelope full of money waiting somewhere up ahead. No bizarre or dangerous task, either.

Which doesn't mean I have to stay home, she told herself. Just because Mog hasn't got a mission for me, I don't have to sit home and rot.

Leaning forward slightly, she picked up her knees and began to run. She ran slowly at first, then quickened her pace, pumping her arms, swinging her legs out longer and faster until she was sprinting along the roadside. It felt wonderful. The speed, the mild night air blowing against her, the smooth feel of her muscles at work.

Too soon, the fine feelings turned to misery. Her lungs burned. Her muscles grew sore and tight and heavy. Sweat stung her eyes. The sweet night air became the breath of an oven.

She quit running and walked – grimacing, huffing, drenched with sweat.

Gradually, her body recovered. She found herself ready to run again. Instead of sprinting, however, she tried a moderate jogging pace. It lacked the thrill of an all-out dash, but it didn't demolish her. She was able to maintain a good, steady pace for a long time before succumbing again.

She hadn't started out with a destination in mind.

The idea was simply to run in the night. To run as hard and as far as she could.

Slowing down for a breather, however, she saw that she was just across the street from the university campus.

* * *

The gates of the chainlink enclosure were secured with a new chain. This chain seemed to have no broken links. So Jane climbed the high fence, dangled from its top, and dropped to the other side.

Within the enclosure were vague, dim shapes in the moonlight and darkness. Familiar shapes: the Porta-potties, the tractor mower, the bird bath, the statue of David, the maze of Doric columns off in the corner. They looked just the same as they had looked on Tuesday night when she had been here with Brace.

But there was a big difference, too.

Nothing seemed menacing or strange or dangerous.

It was a familiar, comfortable place to be.

Jane climbed the statue of Crazy Horse and sat behind the chief on the stiff shelf of his unfurled loincloth. She leaned forward against his back. Her hands held him by the sides. Her knees pressed against his hips. The bronze was hard and cool against her.

Chapter Twenty-five

Monday was easier for Jane.

Since Brace hadn't gotten in touch with her yesterday, a day they'd set aside for being together, the chances of a call or visit from him today were slim.

Worse than slim.

So she didn't wait around for him. After getting up late in the morning, she skipped breakfast and went to the Donnerville Fashion Mall.

As she wandered from shop to shop, it dawned on her that she could afford to buy *anything* she saw. I really could, she thought. There was probably nothing in the entire mall that cost as much as $12,550 – her take, so far, from the Game. She hadn't brought that much with her, of course. She'd brought five hundred of it, and left the rest hidden at home.

The five hundred dollars in her purse felt like a fortune.

What'll I do with it? she wondered.

Buy a wheelchair, maybe.

Oh, it's not quite that bad. Almost, but not quite.

With every step, Jane's body ached. The aches came from muscles that had been worked hard. They reminded her of the running. They reminded her that she was becoming stronger, slimmer.

In a sporting goods shop, she bought new running

shoes, a pair of shiny blue shorts, and a gray tank top. She also bought two iron weights that looked like miniature barbells and weighed twelve pounds each.

She carried her purchases out to the parking lot, shut them in the trunk of her car, and returned to the mall.

She bought two blouses, one skirt, pajamas that were royal blue and shiny like satin, three pairs of panties that were very sexy and expensive and that she doubted anyone but her would ever see, and a bikini that she intended to wear nowhere except inside her fenced back yard.

She hurried on to the bookstore, and helped herself to eight paperbacks she'd put off buying for several weeks.

It's great to have money, she thought.

At the food court, she ate cashew chicken.

Then she left the mall and drove across the road to the Cineplex. She bought a ticket, but she avoided the refreshment stand.

By the time the movie ended, she was eager to get home.

It came as a disappointment, but no surprise, that Brace wasn't at the house waiting for her.

The mail had arrived. It didn't include a letter from Mog.

Without an answering machine, she didn't know whether Brace had called. She doubted it, though.

'Ask me if I care,' she muttered.

She wandered about the house, looking here and there just to make sure Mog hadn't left a new envelope for her. It was a casual search, however; she didn't really expect to find one.

A glance out the kitchen window showed sunlight on the patio. Jane picked the book she was most eager to start, then snipped the tags off her new bikini. She changed in her bedroom. And stared at her image in the mirror.

She supposed she had always wanted a bikini like this. Never dared, though. Afraid someone might see her in it.

After the negligee from Mog, this thing seemed downright modest. The shiny blue fabric didn't cover much, but at least it hid the little that it covered.

She wondered if she would ever have the guts to wear it to the beach.

Not till I've lost three scabs, fifteen bruises and ten more pounds.

Not even then, she admitted.

In the bathroom, she rubbed sunblock over her skin. Then she washed the goo off her hands, grabbed an old blanket, put on her sunglasses, picked up her paperback, and went out the back door.

She spread her blanket on the grass and stretched out on it. Propped up on her elbows, she tried to read. But her mind refused to stay on the story. After a while, she set the book aside, sank down against the blanket and folded her arms beneath her face.

The heat of the sun seemed to melt the soreness out of her muscles. She thought about reaching back to untie her bikini top, but she couldn't bring herself to move. She felt too comfortable and lazy.

Oughta, she told herself. Better yet, take it off – Brace'd be *sure* to show up, then. The guy has a talent for catching me without my clothes on. I try a little nude sun-bathing, and he'll be johnny-on-the-spot.

Last thing I need. Shocked him once too often, already. Guy thinks I'm nuts and about half a rung up from being a whore.

Thanks a heap, Mog.

Hey, don't blame Mog. He didn't force me into that coffin. Or into that nightie.

Brace's fault. He should've stayed away.

Comes when he's supposed to stay away, stays away when he's supposed to come.

Like now.

The hell with him. The hell with him, anyway. If he cared about me at all, he would've come over yesterday.

Anyway, who needs him? Nobody, that's who.

Then she imagined Brace climbing over the gate at the side of her house and coming into the back yard and seeing her there on the blanket, stretched out shiny in the sunlight. She saw his smile and the look in his eyes.

'I had to come,' he says. 'I've missed you so much, Jane. I couldn't stay away any longer, I just couldn't.'

'I've been waiting for you,' she tells him.

Kneeling over her, he kisses the nape of her neck. Then he unties her bikini top and begins to massage her bare shoulders and back. His hands slide on her slippery skin.

Jane woke up. The weight of the sun seemed to be pressing her against the blanket. She was drenched with sweat. The sweat slid and ran as she rolled over and flopped onto her back.

Shouldn't fall asleep again, she warned herself. Don't wanta burn.

She tried to sit up, but felt as if all her energy had been sucked out.

In her mind, she was sprawled on a beach, the sky pale blue overhead, gulls swooping and squawking, combers washing ashore with a steady, hushed easiness. She heard the song, 'Surfer Girl.'

She woke up feeling renewed. Roasted and basted, but full of energy. She sat up, spilling sweat down her body.

The dribbles made her itch. She wiped them off with slippery hands, then scurried into the house.

In the bathroom, she dried herself with a towel. Her hair was a jumble of wet coils, her skin flushed, her bikini dark with moisture and clinging.

Jane liked the way she looked.

Wild surfer girl.

It's only a start, she told herself. A couple more weeks, and there'll *really* be a difference. Brace won't even recognize me.

Forget him, will you? Just forget him.

I'm doing this for myself, not for Brace.

With the towel draped over her shoulders, she went to the living room and picked up her new weights. She carried them outside. Standing in a shaded area close to the side of the house, she began to work with them.

She'd had no training, so she used her imagination and lifted them in every way that popped into her head. By the time she finished, she was breathless, again dripping sweat, and her muscles ached all over her arms and shoulders and neck and chest and armpits.

She set the weights down, and returned to the blanket. It was still moist. She lay on it and began doing sit-ups and toe touches and leg lifts. As with the weights, she improvised.

When she was done, she couldn't move for a while.

Finally, she struggled to her feet. She wiped herself all over with the towel, then hung the towel and blanket on a line to dry.

In the shower, she kept her bikini on for a while. Then she peeled it off, wrung it out and draped it over the top of the shower doors. Her skin was slightly rosy except where the skimpy garment had kept the sun away. The pale areas looked stark. And a little sickly, she thought.

No big deal, she told herself. Who's gonna notice?

Besides, most of the color wouldn't last. It would fade, and so would the rather startling contrast.

After her shower, Jane made herself a tall vodka and tonic loaded with ice. She sat on the sofa and swung her legs up. Drink in one hand, book in the other, she boarded The Busted Flush with Travis McGee.

Who's McGee gonna nurse back to physical and emotional health this time? she wondered.

Poor bird. Whoever she is, she's bound to end up dead.

At midnight, wearing her new running shoes, shorts and top, Jane left her house.

She walked with long, quick strides. The muscles in her legs and buttocks felt stiff and sore. With every step, they seemed to bunch and slide underneath her skin.

Then she tried to run.

After a few strides, she gasped, 'Oh my God,' and stopped. No more running tonight; her legs and arms couldn't stand it.

At least I can still walk, she told herself.

Where to?

Doesn't matter.

No orders from Mog, so it's my choice. All up to me. Free to go where I wish.

She could think of nowhere she wanted to go, but decided that she didn't need a destination. It was enough to be outside and on the move, getting exercise, wearing off calories, enjoying the sweetness and mysteries of the night.

Only now and then did a car go by. Most of the houses along the street were dark except for porch lights. She supposed that people were asleep inside – or trying to sleep. From many of the houses came the noisy hum of air conditioning units. From a few, she heard music or voices.

People were in houses all around her.

Most sleeping. A few awake. Probably all of them strangers.

If any look out and see me passing by, she thought, they'll wonder who I am and where I'm going. Some are sure to think I'm crazy to be out alone at this time of night. Or up to no good. Some will probably envy me and wish they were doing it, too.

They might like to be out, but they stay safe in their homes.

And watch me go by. And wonder.

And know they're not as free as me.

This is so great, she thought. Why haven't I been going out every night like this?

Wouldn't have dreamed of it before Mog.

Back when I was sensible – and afraid of so much.

Look at all I was missing!

Then she heard the quick smack of footfalls coming at her from behind.

Jeez, I'm gonna get nailed! So much for a whole new life featuring midnight walks.

The rushing footsteps bore down on her. Someone running, panting.

Just a jogger?

Look and see. Maybe it's Brace.

Yeah, right, sure. More likely Rale or some other brand of demented creep. Maybe with a knife he's eager to plant in my back.

All the more reason to look.

Jane swiveled and twisted her head. The man, only a few strides away, was young and shirtless, dressed in shorts and running shoes, apparently nothing worse than a jogger. He gasped, 'Hi.'

'Hi,' she told him, and stepped off the sidewalk to make room for him to pass.

But he didn't pass. He stopped and faced her. 'Warm night,' he said. Huffing for air, he put his hands on his hips, lowered his head, and shook one of his legs. Then he raised and shook the other leg. He met Jane's eyes. 'You're the librarian, aren't you?'

Great. He knows me.

'That's right,' she said.

'Thought so. You live near here?'

He sounded friendly, but Jane didn't trust him. 'Not very far away. How about you?'

'Over on Plymouth. By the way, I'm Scott.'

'I'm Jane.'

'I've seen you at the library.'

Have I seen him? she wondered. He looked somewhat familiar, but she supposed there must be plenty of men in town with a similar appearance: average height, slim build, neatly trimmed dark hair, and a face that was pleasant but hardly memorable.

'You sure don't look much like a librarian,' he said.

'Ah, well . . .'

'Bet you get that a lot, don't you?'

'On occasion.'

'Are you going anywhere special?'

Jane shrugged.

'Well, what-say we team up for a while? Do you mind?'

'I'm not running,' she said.

'That's okay. I'll walk with you.'

She shrugged. She didn't want him walking with her, wanted to be rid of him, wanted her solitude back. But she couldn't bring herself to refuse. 'All right,' she said. 'We can walk for a while, I guess.'

She stepped onto the walkway and started out.

'You set the pace,' Scott said, matching her stride.

'Thanks.'

'You do this much?' he asked.

'Do what?'

'Go for walks. This time of night.'

Wonderful, she thought. He's hoping we can make it a regular thing. Just what I'd need.

'No,' she said. 'I'm usually asleep by now.'

'Not me. I'm a real night hawk.'

He means 'night owl,' Jane thought, but decided not to correct him.

'You don't need to be at a job in the morning?' she asked.

'Not me.'

'Oh? What do you do?'

'Sleep in.'

'Ah,' she said. Let it drop, she told herself. If he wants to be coy about his employment, if any, that's fine with me. 'So,' she said, 'I take it you're a bank robber.'

Oh, well. What the hell.

He laughed.

The sort of laugh that seemed to say, 'I did notice the attempt at humor, babe, but it dropped well short of the mark. Nevertheless, I'm quite the sport. I give you credit for the try.'

'Guess again,' he said.

'I'll pass.'

'Aren't you the least bit curious?'

'I'd be happy to hear what you do for a living, if you want to tell me. But it doesn't matter. You can let it drop, no big deal.'

He grinned. 'As a matter of fact, I don't work at all. I'm a man of leisure.'

'Ah.'

'Fabulously wealthy.'

'No fooling?'

'I kid you not.'

'Are you sure you're not a used car salesman?'

That laugh again.

'Trust me,' he said, 'I'm fabulously wealthy.'

Jane grinned at him. 'Do you know what? It's been proven by scientific studies that ninety-nine point nine per cent of the time, the words "trust me" precede a bald-faced lie.'

Scott grinned back at her. 'Are you calling me a liar?'

'No, of course not. Trust me.'

'I bet you get into a lot of trouble with that mouth of yours.'

'Oh, on occasion.'

'But do you know what? I like a girl with spirit. How would you like to come over to my place? We'll kick back and sip a little *vino*, get to know each other . . .'

'Are you serious?'

'A ten-minute walk from here . . .'

'Well, thanks anyway. But A, I hardly know you; B, it's after midnight; C, I don't go into stranger's houses.' That's a good one, she thought. 'D, all of the above.'

E, I don't like you much.

'I'm not just some fellow trying to pick you up, you know.'

'Ah.'

'I wish you wouldn't say that so often.'

'What?'

'Ah.'

'Ah.'

'It's . . . condescending.'

'I see. But what about that "spirit" of mine you like so much?'

'I don't enjoy being mocked.'

'Ah.'

'Or called a liar.'

'I never called you a liar. What I did, I mocked you for saying, "Trust me." You may very well be so rich you've got money coming out your wazoo, but "trust me" is a very annoying thing to say. I kid you not.'

'You're beginning to wear a bit thin.'

'Then you won't want me coming over to your place, will you?'

'I didn't say that. The offer stands.'

'If you don't like being mocked . . .'

'You can be trained.'

'Oh. I like the sound of that. Are you talking about whips?'

'Gentler arts of persuasion.'

'Ah. What do you do, troll the streets at night looking for gals to take home?'

'This is a first.'

'Oh, sure.'

'What do you say?'

'Not interested. Thanks, anyway.'

'I'll pay you.'

The words kicked away Jane's bluster. She stopped walking. She gaped at him. He grinned back at her.

'You'll pay me?' she asked, hardly able to lift her voice above a whisper.

'That's what I said.'

'Oh, my God.'

'Cash money. A lot of it.'

'Who are you?'

He raised his eyebrows.

'Are you him?'

'Who?'

'Mog?'

His grin stretched. 'Let's go to my house and talk about it.'

He took hold of Jane's arm, but she jerked it away. 'Not so damn fast, sport. *Are* you Mog, or aren't you?'

'That all depends, doesn't it?'

'Knock off the games.'

'Okay, I admit it. I'm him. Of course I'm him. Now, let's walk over to my . . .'

'What does Mog stand for?'

'Truth, justice, and the American way?'

'M-O-G.'

Without a moment of hesitation, he said, 'Man of God.'

Is he joking around, she wondered, or doesn't he know?

'Memories of Grandeur?' he suggested. 'Multiple Orgasms Granted? Meal of Guts?'

'Okay, cut it out.'

'Master of . . . Gonads?'

'If you're him, tell me. Tell me, or I'm leaving right now.'

'I already told you,' he said.

'Make me believe.'

He smirked. 'Forget it. If you want to leave, fine. Nobody's stopping you. I just thought you might want to come with me and have a good time and make yourself a little spending cash, okay?'

'Why me?' she asked.

'Why not?'

'Why?'

'Because you're here,' he said. 'And I like the looks of you.'

'That's all?'

'Is there supposed to be more?'

'Yeah.'

'I like your spirit,' he reminded her.

'Only not very much,' she pointed out.

'I bet you're fierce in bed. A tiger.'

'You'll never find out.'

'Five hundred dollars says I will.'

'You'll pay me five hundred dollars to sleep with you?'

'Sleep isn't exactly what I have in mind.'

'Ah.'

'Five hundred smackaroos.'

'I thought you were supposed to be fabulously wealthy.'

'Five hundred's a lot of money.'

'Not nearly enough.'

'You think you're worth more than that?'

'I'd say so.'

'You're dreaming.' He laughed at her, and jogged away.

Chapter Twenty-six

Stunned, Jane watched him run down the sidewalk. Her throat was tight and she had tears in her eyes.

'Bastard,' she muttered.

How could he say that to me? *You're dreaming*.

Bastard was cut from the same cloth as that filthy son-of-a-bitch, Ken.

As he turned the corner at the end of the block, his head swung toward Jane and he raised his arm and jabbed his middle finger at the sky.

Same to you, bud, she thought.

A moment later, he vanished down the sidestreet.

'Good riddance to bad rubbish,' she said.

She considered turning around and heading for home.

If I do that, she told herself, I'm nothing but a quitter. Why should I let a creep like him ruin my night?

So she wiped her eyes, then continued with her walk.

How come he offered me money in the first place? she wondered. Does it show? Have I got it scribbled on my forehead, 'This gal does weird stuff for cash?'

I won't do *anything*, though, will I? Guess I proved that.

Hey, Brace, there *are* some limits after all, huh? Some lines I won't cross?

But a small voice in Jane's head whispered, Maybe, or maybe the guy just didn't make the offer tempting enough.

Five hundred is a pretty meager sum when you've got more than twelve thousand at home. Suppose he'd gone to a thousand? Or ten thousand?

We'll never know.

We'll never know because I'm not worth any more than five hundred bucks. I'm *dreaming* if I think I'm worth any more than that.

'What a piece of scum,' she said.

Soon, Jane found herself across the street from the university. She was tempted to head for Crazy Horse.

Not tonight, she told herself. Do it again tonight, and next thing you know, you'll be going there every night.

Why not? It's so nice and safe inside the fence, and it's wonderful to be up there high on the statue. It's like having a special tree to climb and hide in. But the statue feels so much better than a tree. It's cool and smooth.

And it's where I went with Brace.

Our special place.

All the more reason *not* to go there.

She didn't cross. Instead, she walked straight ahead, leaving the campus behind, and two blocks later came to Standhope Street.

She gazed up at the sign.

She suddenly felt shaky.

So this is where Standhope is, she thought.

As if you didn't know.

I didn't know. I had an idea it might be over here in this general vicinity, but I didn't know. And I for sure don't remember Brace's address. It's not like I came out on purpose to look for where he lives.

I'm not an idiot. I would've brought his card along. Or at least made an effort to memorize the address.

She turned her head, looking both ways. Just down

the street to her right was the business district. Brace wasn't likely to reside in that direction. To her left, the street was mostly bordered by apartment buildings.

Closer to the university, too.

Jane chose that direction, crossed the road, and began wandering along Standhope.

This is nuts, she thought. What if I *do* find where he lives?

Don't worry. Not much chance of that.

Anyway, I'm not *trying* to find it. I'm just out for a little exercise and fresh air, and I happen to be strolling down Standhope Street.

I don't even *want* to find it.

Who cares where he lives?

In this section of town, there seemed to be a lot of activity in spite of the late hour. Cars went by. Quite a few young men and women were out walking. Loud music thumped from many of the apartment windows. She heard laughter and shouts.

If Brace lives in the middle of all this, she thought, how does he ever get any sleep?

How does anybody?

She checked her wristwatch. Five after one.

What time do things settle down around here, anyway?

She stepped aside to make way for an approaching threesome: a girl supported by two fellows. They were swaying, stumbling, laughing. Jane supposed they must be drunk.

The girl in the middle, arms around the shoulders of the boys, wore a big floppy hat and earrings that were peace symbols. Her T-shirt read 'SAVE A TREE, EAT A BEAVER.' The shirt was pocked with gaping holes that showed her skin. It ended halfway down her belly. Her denim mini-skirt hung very low on her hips. She wore fishnet stockings and white cowgirl boots.

The boys under her arms didn't look nearly so flamboyant. One wore a white polo shirt and matching shorts and shoes. The other was shirtless, jeans hanging, the white waistband of his underwear on display.

'Top of the evening to you!' the girl greeted Jane.

'And to you. Could I ask you something?'

The trio halted and swiveled. 'We are at your service,' said the girl. 'Ask, and ye shall receive.'

They *aren't* drunk, Jane realized, now that she could see their faces in the lights from the apartment building. They looked too alert to be drunk or stoned. Just kids goofing around.

'I'm looking for a friend,' Jane said.

'We'll be your friends,' the girl announced.

'Join in,' said the shirtless guy, offering his empty arm.

'Thanks, but that isn't . . . I have a friend who's a student and I know she lives on Standhope, but I lost her address. I didn't think I'd have any trouble finding her place, but now that I'm here . . .' She shook her head. 'I was over at her place last month, but things look so different at night.'

'They do,' the girl agreed. '*Everything* looks different at night.'

'Especially the sky,' said the guy in the polo shirt.

'The sky, my eye,' the girl said. '*Most* especially, the face of reality.'

'I'm just having trouble with these apartment buildings,' Jane interrupted. 'Maybe you can tell me which one she's in. If you know her.'

'What's her name?' asked the shirtless guy.

Jane hadn't gotten to the point of thinking up a name

for her non-existent friend. So she said, 'Jane. Jane Masters.'

The girl frowned. 'Masters, Masters.'

'Jane Masters.'

'I know a Jean Masterson,' offered the shirtless guy.

'This is Jane Masters.'

The girl turned her head from side to side, asking, 'Bill? Steve?' Both of her friends looked puzzled and shook their heads. She faced Jane. 'Afraid we don't know anyone by that name.'

'Well, thanks for . . . hey!' Jane blurted. 'I just thought of something. Last time I was there, she introduced me to a member of the faculty who lives in the same building. A guy. An English teacher, I think. He had a name like . . . Patton, or maybe . . .' She shook her head.

'Paxton?' the girl asked.

'That might be it! Paxton?'

'Light brown hair? Semi-gorgeous?'

'Sounds like him. His place was right next to Jane's, so if you . . .'

'I just happen to know exactly where he lives,' the girl said. 'Followed him home a couple of times. Such a cute butt.'

Steve in the polo shirt scowled. 'Men do *not* have cute butts.'

'Disgusting,' agreed Bill.

'Appalling,' added Steve.

'Wrong,' said Jane.

'Three blocks straight ahead,' the girl said. 'I can't give you the address, but the place is called the Royal Gardens. Sort of a fancy-ass name, but what're you gonna do? My name's Splendor, can't get much more fancy-ass than that.'

'What's in a name?' Jane said.

'Precisely.'

'Splendor is a splendid name,' said Steve.

'Well,' Jane said, 'thanks for the help.'

'The pleasure was ours,' Splendor said. 'Delighted we could be of service.'

'Hope you find your friend,' Bill said.

'Thanks.' She stepped around them. 'Have fun.'

'We do,' Splendor told her.

Jane smiled as she watched the trio skip off down the sidewalk. And she laughed softly when they began to sing, 'We Three Kings.'

Christmas carols in June, she thought.

Youth.

As she started walking away and heard the singing voices fade, her amusement changed to a gentle feeling of sadness. She didn't know why. Maybe because Splendor and her friends had seemed so free and happy. Maybe because she knew they would only have a few such nights.

She wondered if they knew how special it was to be skipping along the sidewalk in the hours after midnight, arm in arm with true pals or lovers, talking nonsense and singing.

I could've gone with them, she thought.

Yeah, but I would've been an outsider. It's six or eight years too late for me to be playing the wild and goofy co-ed.

Truth be known, it wasn't all that great at the time.

Oh, it was pretty great.

But the past always looks better after you've left it far behind. Even the crummy stuff.

A few years from now, she thought, I might look back on tonight as being magic and wonderful.

Especially if things go nicely at Brace's place.

Just within the lighted entryway of the Royal Gardens, Jane found the name Paxton on the mail box for apartment #12. She opened the wrought iron gate, walked through the passageway and found herself in a courtyard that had a fairly large swimming pool.

She heard air conditioners, and music, and voices. Nothing loud, though.

All but a few of the windows were dark.

Nobody was wandering about the pool's concrete apron or the second-story balcony.

Nobody seemed to be in the pool. Its lights were out. Much of the surface glinted with reflections of the lights from the surrounding apartments. Somebody might be hiding in one of the dark places, but . . .

No big deal, she told herself. Who cares if I get seen? I'm not here to burglarize the joint.

Or murder anyone.

But why *am* I here? she wondered. There must be a reason. I sure went to a lot of trouble to find the place.

Curiosity. That's all. I just want to know where he lives. See the building and see his door and his window and maybe catch a glimpse of him.

That's all.

Is it?

Who the hell knows?

In a corner of the courtyard near the deep end of the pool, she found a 12 on a door. The curtains of the large picture window glowed with light.

He's up! Oh, my God!

Probably reading. He stays up till all hours reading, doesn't he? He's probably stretched out on his sofa with *Youngblood Hawke* on his lap.

In the very middle of the window was a vertical strip

of light where the curtains didn't quite meet. Spotting it, Jane moaned. She gritted her teeth and pressed her legs together and rubbed her arms.

You don't do this sort of thing, she told herself. You don't peek in at somebody. Just go to the door and knock.

That's what I want, anyway. To have him open the door and see that I've come to him, and watch his face, and then step in and feel him take me into his arms and kiss me.

But what if he's asleep?

So what if he's asleep?

He'll think he's dreaming when he comes to the door and there I am.

Quietly, slowly, Jane stepped to the door of Brace's apartment. She stared at it. She grimaced.

Just do it! she told herself.

And raised her fist to knock.

What if he hates me?

He doesn't. Probably takes me for a money-grabbing idiot who'll do anything for a buck, but . . . He's the one who screwed up. Followed me around, *spied* on me as if I was some sort of a criminal.

Lowering her arm, she looked over at the narrow space between the curtains.

Why not? she thought. Why the hell not? Turn-about's fair play. It'd serve him right.

She crept over to the window. The gap revealed very little as she approached it. Not until she stopped and leaned forward, brow to the glass, did the opening give her a good view into the apartment.

Her heart gave a rough lurch when she spotted him – sitting on the sofa, naked, his back toward her . . .

No, that's not . . .

What *is* that?

268

And then she knew what she was seeing. The naked back belonged to a woman, a short-haired blonde kneeling on the sofa, sitting on Brace's lap, her legs wide apart and Brace's bare legs between them, Brace's thick shiny cock sticking straight up and disappearing into her, all of it vanishing as she sank down on him, then showing again as she raised herself.

Jane felt as if she'd been clubbed in the belly.

This is what I get. Never should've looked. This is what I get.

The dirty rotten filthy fucking bastard!

She wanted to run away.

But she stayed.

Let's just see what the bitch looks like. Come on, turn around. Let's get a look at you.

Maybe it's someone I know.

That didn't seem likely. Except for patrons of the library, Jane hadn't met very many people. All her friends had been left behind when she moved here to take the job.

Never *should've* come here, she thought.

Who is she? Who is this miserable damn slut . . . ?

Probably one of Brace's students. I'd bet on it. A dirty thing to do, fuck your students. Happens all the time, though. And what the hell, he's a guy. It's the sort of thing guys do. They're all so horny they'd fuck the crack of dawn.

Why should Brace be different.

But I thought he was.

Yeah? Well, watch him in action – giving one of his English majors a private lesson.

Come on, bitch, turn around. Let's see what you've got, huh?

Are you prettier? You got bigger tits?

269

Obviously, she was slimmer. She didn't need to turn around for that to be apparent. Jane could see the way her back tapered down to a slender waist before flaring out around the hips and rump.

She's not *all* that much thinner than me, Jane told herself. And I bet I'm stronger.

Yeah, she's skin and bones. Looks almost frail.

The cock came all the way out of her. Nobody reached down to do anything about it. The girl kept hold of Brace's shoulders, and his hands stayed out of sight — probably playing with her tits. The engorged head of his cock prodded her a few times, then found its way in and she sank down, taking all its length and thickness into her.

Jane groaned.

Stop watching! Stop it!

No. I've gotta see what she looks like from the front. See what's so special.

Try knocking on the window, Jane thought. She'll be sure to look around, if I give it a few good sharp raps.

Why not? Why the hell not?

They'll catch me, and they'll know I was watching, and . . .

So what? What's Brace gonna do about it, dump me?

Go on, do it!

No. That'd be crazy.

Suddenly, Jane heard voices from the other end of the courtyard. She scurried backward away from the window and looked toward the gate. Nobody there. Not yet. But she still heard the voices.

Male and female.

Probably another prof bringing home a student to screw.

Oh my God, I can't be caught here!

270

She twisted this way and that, looking for a place to hide. And spotted a lounge chair she might duck behind. But it was at the far side of the pool. No chance of getting to it in time.

Nowhere else to hide.

Nowhere close enough to reach in time.

Except for the pool, only a few paces away.

Jane rushed to it, sat down quickly and lowered her legs into the chilly water. She scooted forward until the edge of the poolside pressed into her rump. Then, hanging on to the edge, she eased herself down. The water climbed her body, wrapping it with cold.

When the water reached her waist, she turned herself around so she faced the wall. She lowered herself to the chin, took a deep breath and let go of the side. She went under. Motionless and limp, she waited. After a few moments, the water began to lift her. So she blew out some of her air and stopped rising.

Her lungs began to ache.

She wondered if it would be safe to rise.

They're probably inside an apartment by now, she told herself. But even if they haven't gone in, they aren't likely to spot me over in the corner here. Probably so dark here they wouldn't see me even if they looked.

But she decided to wait.

How about half a minute? Can I hang on for half a minute?

In her mind, she started counting slowly toward thirty.

By the count of ten, her lungs felt as if they were being squeezed by vices while fires blazed inside them.

At thirteen, she came up for air. She sucked in a deep breath with a gasp.

Hope nobody heard that!

Blinking water out of her eyes, she tried to breathe

more quietly as she scanned the courtyard.

No sign of the intruders.

Curling her fingertips over the edge of the pool to hold herself high enough, she peered at Brace's window.

Just as well I had to run for cover, she thought. Otherwise, I'd still be standing there.

You can't go back, she told herself. Not without making puddles and footprints on the concrete. You sure don't want to leave tell-tale signs like that at his window.

What I'll have to do is climb out of the pool at the other end – put my trail as far from Brace's rooms as I can.

Screw it.

She boosted herself up, water sluicing down her body and splashing into the pool, then pattering on the concrete. Her shorts had been tugged halfway down her rump by the pool's suction as she popped out, so she pulled them up.

Her shoes made squelching noises with each step as she walked toward the window.

She thought, Who cares?

Why am I doing this? I know better!

She stopped just in front of the window and leaned forward until her dripping forehead touched the glass.

Guess I won't need to knock, she thought.

Because the girl was facing her – off the sofa and striding straight toward her, filling her view.

All Jane could see was the girl.

Tall and slender, wet coils of hair clinging to her brow and temples, sweat speckling her face, her skin ruddy around her mouth from too much kissing, blotches on her neck and shoulders and breasts from the suck of a mouth – Brace's mouth.

It isn't her face that got him, Jane thought. I'm a lot prettier.

Has to be her boobs.

Twice the size of mine.

They bounced and swung as she walked.

Gimme a break.

She reached up and grabbed the edges of the curtain, and started to pull them together, and happened to look straight forward – straight at Jane.

Who mashed her face against the glass and bared her teeth.

The girl's eyes bulged. Her mouth leaped open.

Jane listened to the muffled shriek as she sprinted alongside the pool.

Glancing every which way, she saw nobody look out any windows at her, no doors swing open.

If I'm quick enough . . .

Then she was hidden in the passageway.

Made it!

She opened the gate, stepped out, eased it shut, then dashed across the street and ducked behind a parked car. From there, she watched the front of the Royal Gardens. Nobody came rushing out.

She started walking. As she hurried away, she kept an eye on the gate of the apartment building. So far, so good.

At the first cross-street, she headed to the right.

Got away with it!

She let out a laugh.

'Did you hear that bitch scream?' she asked herself. 'Got her! Man, did I get her!' She laughed again.

Brace might figure out it was me, she thought.

So what? He can't *do* anything about it. And who gives a shit what he thinks of me, the filthy son-of-a-bitch? And I hope I scared the piss out of his hot little teeny-bopper slut.

Then Jane was crying, bawling as she walked along.

Don't be a twit, she told herself.

She kicked an empty beer can. It tumbled and skidded along the sidewalk. 'Hope his fuckin' dick drops off,' she muttered. After a sniffle, she added, 'Probably will, too. Asshole never heard of a rubber?'

Chapter Twenty-seven

Jane woke up, saw that she was in her own bedroom and the morning looked sunny outside her window. A beautiful day, she thought. But a cold, hollow feeling in her belly told her that the day was about to turn foul. Something really ugly had happened, and as soon as she could remember . . .

Oh.

Brace.

The sudden memory of what she'd seen through Brace's window made her groan and roll onto her side and hug her belly and bring her knees up.

Her clothing didn't feel right.

Looking down, she found herself wearing her tank-top and running shorts.

She frowned.

What'd I do, just flop into bed last night without . . . ?

That's what I did, all right.

She could remember it now: staggering into the house, breathless and crying, half-blinded by her tears, stumbling along until she came to her bed, then flopping on it face-down and burying her face in the pillow.

Ah, yes.

Didn't even so much as take a shower.

Should've at least brushed my teeth, she thought.

She ran her tongue across her teeth. They felt scuzzy.

'Great,' she muttered.

Groaning, she crawled out of bed. When she tried to stand, muscles everywhere rebelled. She groaned again. And groaned with each step as she hobbled, bent over, toward the bathroom.

The first thing I'll do when I get there – if I get there – is brush my teeth. Next comes peeing. Or should that be first? No, gotta brush my teeth first – they're disgusting and they're in my mouth.

Brush, then pee, then shower, then scoot into the kitchen and get the coffee started.

Or do the coffee first, so it'll be ready . . . ?

No no no. It can wait.

In the bathroom, Jane made her way to the medicine cabinet, then forced herself to stand up straight. She gazed at her reflection in the mirror as she scrubbed her teeth.

Hair a tangle, eyes dazed, cheeks hollow, still a dim yellow bruise on one cheek where the dog had stepped on her face.

A vision of loveliness, she thought.

And spit a mouthful of foam into the sink.

Then studied her face some more as she resumed brushing.

On my worst day (and this might be it), I look better than that pony-faced whore of Brace's.

Done with her teeth, she put the brush away and bent over the sink to rinse her mouth. As she cupped up water with her hand, she saw her cleavage in the mirror.

Okay, so she's got bigger boobs than me. Doesn't mean hers are any *better*.

Jane shook her shoulders, and watched how her breasts shimmied a little inside the drooping front of her shirt.

'Oh, well,' she said.

She laughed once, then turned away from the mirror. Stepping toward the toilet, she peeled the tank-top over her head. She tossed it into a corner.

Her back to the toilet, she hooked her thumbs under the elastic waistband of her running shorts. As she was about to give the shorts a pull, she looked down.

'Huh?' she murmured. Not troubled, at first. Just confused, disoriented.

Whatever the things might be, maybe she wasn't seeing them quite right. Maybe they were something *normal*.

But she didn't think so.

What they looked like were rows of black marks across her skin between the bottoms of her breasts and the waist-band of her shorts.

Small black squiggles mixed in with tangles of horizontal and vertical lines.

She bent lower. Pressing her breasts closer to her chest, she peered over the backs of her hands.

'Oh, my God,' she muttered.

Handwriting.

Someone had scribbled a message across her skin. With a felt-tipped pen, from the looks of it.

But Jane couldn't read the message.

Even though she was viewing it upside-down, that wasn't the problem; from time to time, she had practiced reading things upside-down.

This looked like gibberish.

A foreign language? she wondered. No. That's not . . .

It's backward writing!

Just like the letters you see on the front of an ambulance when you aren't looking at them through the rear-view mirror of your car.

Jane hobbled over to the medicine cabinet. In its mirror, the jumble of black marks became letters, words . . .

My Dear,

On the tablet
of your body and soul
we script the book
of

Of what?
She tugged her shorts down.

Jane

Chapter Twenty-eight

At first, Jane felt sickened by the knowledge that Mog had come to her bedroom during the night while she was fast asleep. He'd done that sort of thing before, of course.

And left his little verse about kissing her.

Almost everywhere.

This time, he had penned his poetry (if it could be called that) on her very skin.

How could he do that without waking me up? she wondered.

A delicate touch, maybe.

What else did he do?

'Anything he wanted,' she muttered.

She stared at the message and pictured Mog crouching on the mattress, lifting her tank top, starting with 'My Dear' just below her breasts and working his way downward, line by line, the pen's felt tip sliding on her skin, the 'of' fitting in nicely between her navel and the waist of her shorts.

Ran out of room on purpose, she supposed.

Because that's how he'd wanted to finish his weird little note: by scrawling her name down where she would read it through the wispy coils of her pubic hair.

Mog's idea of a little humor, she supposed.

Or maybe he'd done it that way figuring it had some sort of major significance.

This is Jane – her essence, her center.

Or what I am to Mog, she thought.

Maybe it's just his way of calling me a pussy. Or worse.

Could be a lot of things, she supposed. It might be nothing more than his way of showing he was there.

Mog and his bizarre little ways.

Like writing the stuff backward. How the hell did he do that, anyway? Using a mirror? Better yet, why? Just to make things even stranger than usual? Trying to freak me out?

Suppose he did it just so I could read the thing in my mirror? Wanted to make it easy for me.

Maybe.

Maybe maybe maybe.

Why does he do anything?

The pervert gets a charge out of messing with me, that's why.

Tilting back her head, Jane called out, 'Hey, Mog. If you're gonna drop in and screw around and write on me and everything, how about dropping off some of that money you're so famous for? I'd appreciate it.'

Then she smirked at herself in the mirror, and gave her head a shake.

'Do you find me amusing, Mog?' she asked.

At least *he* hasn't deserted me, she thought. I oughta be grateful for that. *He* hasn't dumped me.

Faithful and rich, what more could a gal want in a fella?

Sanity, perhaps?

Laughing softly, Jane left the bathroom. She went to the kitchen and started a pot of coffee. By the telephone, she picked up a notepad and pen. In the bathroom again, she stood in front of the mirror and copied the message.

Then she read it off the note pad.

My Dear,

On the tablet
of your body and soul
we script the book
of

Jane

'Right,' she muttered.

Then she studied it, wondering if there might be hidden clues about where and when she might go off to seek another envelope.

She couldn't find anything of the sort.

Which didn't surprise her. This just didn't *seem* like that kind of message.

Not an instruction. More of a commentary.

Which, she supposed, would explain why it hadn't been accompanied by a payment.

Who says there wasn't a payment?

I'll have to look around, she told herself. Shouldn't just assume he didn't leave a bunch of money for me somewhere.

The search, however, could wait till after her shower.

Before heading for the shower, she double-checked her note against the mirror's reflection of the writing on her skin, found no errors, and set the pad aside.

She started to turn away.

What if he wrote on my back?

She whirled around and peered over her shoulder at the mirror.

Her back was slightly pink from yesterday's time in

the sun. The bikini ties had left a thin, pale line across it. On her buttocks was a pale triangle with stripes that reached to her hips.

Nobody had used her back as stationery.

'Oh, well.'

She supposed she ought to be glad about that, but all she felt was mild annoyance and disappointment.

She took a long, hot shower.

The writing did not come off easily. She scrubbed at it with a soapy washcloth, rinsed, found a dim ghost of the message lingering on her skin, and had to scour it two more times before washing away every trace of ink.

After her shower, she roamed casually through the house, searching for more money but not expecting to find any.

None turned up.

So she ate breakfast, put on her work clothes and drove to the library. She arrived a little early, and got busy.

It helped, being busy.

Whenever her mind strayed to Brace or his teeny-bopper, she felt like yelling in rage. Or weeping.

Though it was awfully funny, the look on that gal's face when she saw me in the window. That was damn near worth the price of admission.

What price, a broken heart?

Sometimes, Jane smiled or chuckled quietly when she thought about how she'd shocked the girl. But her amusement never lasted long before it twisted and dropped and left her feeling ruined.

Thinking about Mog, at least, didn't cause her any pain.

It only confused her, worried her, made her blush with shame, filled her mind with countless questions, frightened her, excited her.

Like I've got a phantom lover, she thought.

That night, she thought about doing exercises or lifting weights.

But she was too tired for that, and her muscles ached too much.

What about a walk?

Yeah, she thought. Right. A, I'm way too tired. B, what if I run into that creep from last night, Scott? C, if I go out I'll probably sneak over to Brace's place, or something, and make more trouble for myself.

D, all the above.

She wanted to do nothing except go to bed.

She put on her new pajamas. They were royal blue, shiny as satin, and felt slidy against her skin. In front of her bedroom mirror, she unfastened the top button. Then she brushed her hair.

Don't forget your lipstick, honey.

Yeah, right, she told herself. This hasn't got anything to do with Mog. If it was for him, I'd put on a see-through nightie or nothing at all. And I always brush my hair at night so it won't be knotty in the morning.

Like hell you do.

I do when I think about it!

She left her bedroom window open and lay on her bed with the covers down. Hands folded beneath her head, she closed her eyes.

She wondered what time Mog would come.

Late. Very late, probably.

Maybe I should try to stay awake, she thought.

I'd never make it. Way too tired.

What if I set my alarm to wake me at midnight?

She considered it. With a couple of hours of sleep, she

could probably stay awake for hours. Play possum and wait for him. Be wide awake when he arrives.

It seemed like a good idea.

But she didn't have the energy to roll over and reach out to set her alarm clock.

In the morning, she woke up feeling wonderful. She was sprawled on her back, uncovered, arms and legs out as if she'd awakened from a dream of floating on the warm surface of a lake.

She heard birds twittering, the sputter of someone's lawnmower, the faraway sound of Garth Brooks singing 'Unanswered Prayers.' The air smelled sweet. She could feel it blowing softly across her from the window.

A great morning.

But then a shadow of unease began creeping toward her.

Brace.

Don't think about him, she warned herself. He's history. Nothing but a filthy . . .

The way the breeze felt, she suddenly realized her pajama shirt was open.

Mog came!

Shoving her elbows at the mattress, she raised her head and gazed down her body.

Except for her arms and shoulders, still covered by the shirt, she was bare to the waist.

Her skin was still slightly pink where the sun had been on it. The bruises were vague yellow-green patches, nearly gone. Little remained of the scratches.

Nobody had left a message on her chest or belly.

Sitting up fast, she popped open the snap at the waist of her pajama pants.

But found no writing.

She flung off her shirt and stood up. The pants dropped around her ankles. She stepped out of them and hurried to the full-length mirror.

She inspected her front. Turning around, she gazed over her shoulder at the reflection of her back. She even stood on one leg at a time to check the bottoms of her bare feet.

She found no writing anywhere on her body.

She found no sign of any kind that Mog had visited her overnight.

It's all right, she told herself. Maybe he had other things to do.

But she couldn't help feeling just a bit abandoned.

Done with breakfast, Jane still had a couple of hours before it was time to leave for work. She put on her bikini, took her book outside, spread her blanket on the grass, and read in the sunlight. Then she exercised and lifted the weights until she ached all over. After that, she took a shower, got dressed, and drove to work.

She tried not to think about Brace or Mog.

But she thought about them a lot.

She supposed it was partly her fault that things hadn't worked out with Brace. He'd wanted her to quit the Game, and she'd lied to him, then gone on a rampage against him when he showed up at the creephouse.

Bastard sure was quick to find himself a replacement.

We might've patched things up . . .

Still could.

Yeah, right. Forget it. Not after what I saw him doing to that bitch.

He's gone, *kaput*, outa here.

Good riddance to bad rubbish.

But what the hell happened to Mog? she wondered.

Has he dropped me, too? Maybe he pulled Brace's stunt and found himself a new gal to play with.

Then where'll I be?

Alone.

Big deal. I've been alone before. I can handle it. I can get along quite nicely, thank you, by myself.

After work that night, Jane changed her clothes and went running. She ran *away* from downtown, *away* from the campus. Her muscles ached a little, but she felt stronger than ever. She poured on the speed, pumping her arms, swinging her legs out with long quick strides, feeling the caress of her shorts and top, feeling the warm breath of summer blowing against her bare skin, filling herself with the sights and aromas of the night, the freedom of fast moving.

She ran until she couldn't run any more.

Then she walked home.

She took a long, cool shower.

In her pajamas, she carried a glass of ice water into the living room and flopped on the couch. She stretched out her legs, bare feet on the coffee table. Pointing the remote control through the space between her feet, she thumbed the TV on.

The clock on the VCR showed 11:12.

Why am I even bothering? she wondered. Everything's already started.

She was sure to find movies on the higher channels, though. There would be something she'd already seen, an old film she could watch for a while until she'd fully recovered from the running and was ready to turn in.

As she made her way up the channels, she stopped at every station to take a brief look.

When she saw the front of a B. Dalton bookstore on the screen, she quit changing channels.

It looked like the one at the Donnerville Fashion Mall.

They all pretty much look alike, she thought. But it might be . . .

'. . . seen Monday night when she left her job as a sales clerk at this bookstore. Young Gail Maxwell never made it home.' The view of the bookstore was replaced by a photograph of the missing woman. A brunette, probably no older than Jane. The photo stayed on the screen as the newswoman kept on talking. 'Her car, a white Toyota, was found abandoned early yesterday only two miles from the mall where she worked.'

'She's a gonner,' Jane muttered.

And quickly left that channel behind.

I was *at* that bookstore on Monday. If that's the one at the Donnerville Mall.

Probably isn't.

But . . . No, the face in the photo hadn't looked familiar.

Hope to God it *wasn't* Donnerville. That's just what we'd need, some sort of maniac out there . . .

Jane flipped back to the station that had carried the story, but now there was footage of a protest march, the Rev. Jesse Jackson in the front row walking arm-in-arm with activists for some cause or other.

She shut off the television.

And wished she hadn't turned it on in the first place.

Switching channels at any time of the day or night, you could hardly fail to bump into a news broadcast, and the damn reporters were *always* eager to fill you in on something that you'd rather not know about.

Maybe I'd better quit running at night, she thought.

Screw that. I'll just start carrying my gun. Anybody tries to put the snatch on me, I'll blow their brains out.

Yeah, sure.

She turned off the living room lights. She made a stop in the bathroom to pee and brush her teeth. Then she went into the kitchen. She opened the 'junk drawer' where she kept a collection of rubber bands, tape, glue, paper clips, small tools, string and writing implements. After a quick search, she located her blue, felt-tipped marking pen.

She carried the pen into her bedroom.

She took off her pajama shirt, tossed it onto the bed, and stood in front of her mirror.

Carefully, glancing from the mirror to her own body, she drew a broad M underneath her right breast.

In the mirror, it appeared to be under her left.

Confusing.

While considering her plan earlier in the evening, Jane had wondered whether or not to write her message backward. Maybe Mog could only read things spelled out that way. An eye disorder, some sort of dyslexia, who knows?

But Mog most likely had a normal ability to read.

She'd made her decision to write from right to left, not reversing the letters, so her message would be legible to someone looking straight down at her while she slept.

She no sooner started to write than she discovered that the trick was to avoid looking at the mirror, keep her eyes on herself, concentrate on how the letters should look upside-down, and watch her hand guide the pen over her skin.

After finishing, she clamped the pen between her teeth and pushed in her breasts and bent down and tried to proof-read her message.

It seemed okay, but . . .

She raised her eyes to the mirror and saw crooked lines of gibberish.

Then an idea struck her.

She fetched a hand-mirror from the top of her dresser. Twisting herself and adjusting angles, she managed to find the big mirror's image of her torso in the glass of the small mirror.

Reversed twice, the message she'd scrawled on her skin was crooked and sloppy but legible.

MOG,

Please come back
and tell me
what you want
me to do.
I'm ready.

She'd had to lower her pajama pants just slightly to fit in 'I'm ready.' There'd been no room for adding her name.

I could write it where he wrote it, she thought.

No. That would be going too far.

And this isn't?

Anyway, it doesn't need to be signed. Mog is fairly sure to know who wrote this.

She decided not to bother putting her shirt back on.

She turned off the lights and went to bed. She lay on her back, arms up, hands under her pillow, and stared at the ceiling. She felt edgy, excited.

A very long time passed before she was able to fall asleep.

In the morning, she hurried to the mirror and found Mog's answer written on her back:

> My Dear,
> I am delighted
> by your eagerness
> and taste.
> The Game will resume.
> Not yet, butt

> Soon   Soon

Mog had penned one 'soon' on each of her buttocks.
'Real cute,' Jane muttered.
And what's that about being delighted by my taste? she wondered.
Face it, the guy definitely has a crude side to him. But at least he came through. He answered. And he says we'll get back to the Game soon soon.

That night before going to bed, Jane wrote on the clean slate of the skin:

> MOG,
> When ? ? ?

In the morning, she found written beneath her navel:

> EAGER

She tugged her pajama pants down to find the other half of his message:

When she saw that, she muttered, 'Asshole.'

Though not really expecting to find any more remarks from Mog, she turned her back to the mirror and looked over her shoulder.

The message there began between her shoulder blades and worked its way down:

> Honey
> Sweetness
> Light of my life
> Guess who is the
> **MASTER**
> around here
>
> ME   MOG

'Guess we can add surliness,' she muttered, 'to your list of sterling qualities.'

When she went out to the driveway that morning, she found an envelope taped to the windshield of her car.

He came through!

But why did he have to put it there, of all places?

No doubt because he finds it amusing to remind me of the dog attack and how I murdered the thing.

'You're a real creep, Mog,' she said.

Bending down, she peered into the window on the driver's side. Then she sidestepped and looked through the back window.

She saw nothing inside her car that shouldn't be there.

She glanced up and down the street in front of her house, scanned the sidewalks and the neighboring houses.

Nobody seemed to be approaching or spying on her. Nothing seemed out of the ordinary.

She took a few steps backward, then got to her knees and looked underneath the car.

Nothing there.

So she opened the trunk.

No surprises there, either.

She unlocked the door on the driver's side and stepped backward again as she pulled the door open wide. Standing motionless, she waited and watched and listened.

He *must've* booby-trapped the car somehow, she thought. That's how he operates. Wouldn't be any fun if he couldn't pull a stunt on me.

She half expected to see some small, unpleasant creature crawling on the seat or floor.

Or squirming.

She listened for rattlesnakes.

Nothing.

As a final precaution, she opened the back door and inspected the rear seats and floor.

Okay, she thought. Maybe this time he *didn't* leave me a nasty surprise.

Leaning into the driver's side, she reached over the steering wheel and dug her fingernails under the tape at the top edge of the envelope.

The envelope was *fat*.

'Oh, man,' she whispered.

She tore it from the windshield.

It seemed like a very long time since she had held an envelope from Mog in her hand.

Not since the coffin.

Stepping back a safe distance from her car, she ripped open the envelope. Inside, two sheets of lined paper were wrapped around a thick stack of bills.

She pulled out the bills.

All hundreds.

She began to count them, but her mind strayed and she lost track somewhere in the sixties. She thought about starting over.

No need to bother, she told herself.

She knew how many there would be. God knows, she had thought about it often enough during the past few days – and wondered if Mog would ever come through with it.

One hundred and twenty-eight hundred-dollar bills.

Which added up to $12,800.

Taking so much money to the library didn't seem like a good idea, so Jane went back inside her house. She put it with the rest.

For a grand total so far of $25,350.

Minus what she'd spent at the mall on Monday.

Still, a lot of money. One hell of a lot of money.

'Now let's see what the catch is,' she muttered. With a mixture of fear and excitement, she unfolded the two sheets of paper. She read the one on top.

Surprise!
You're invited to a party, Jane!

Where: 482 Chestnut Street
When: tonight, 9:30 p.m.
Why: just because.
B.Y.O.B. (Bring Your Own Body)
R.S.V.P. Not applicable. I have every
confidence that you'll be there.
Special Instructions: At the door, present
your host with the enclosed note.

Jane read the enclosed note, shook her head, and muttered, 'What the hell are you trying to do to me?'

Chapter Twenty-nine

Parked in her car half a block from the party house, Jane once again read the note she was supposed to present to her host:

> My Friend,
>   I will never be able to thank you properly for what you've done. Please greet my servant, Jane.
>   She is yours to use as you please until midnight. Your wish is her command.
>   I have already seen to her payment.
>   Enjoy.
>
> Gratefully yours,
MOG

She folded the note and dropped it onto her lap.

All day, she'd wondered if she would have the nerve to follow through. She'd never really doubted it, though.

Not much I won't do, comes right down to it.

Not with more than twenty-five thousand dollars at stake.

When I get that, I'll have over fifty thousand bucks. *Fifty thousand.*

She took a deep breath. She was shaking badly. Otherwise, she felt all right: alert and strong.

This won't be so bad, she told herself. Whatever

happens between now and midnight, it can't be much worse than what I've gone through before.

Anyway, she thought, nothing happens without my say-so.

Reaching into her purse, she found her pistol.

Before leaving for the library that morning, she had inspected the weapon to make sure it hadn't been tampered with: looked it over carefully, unloaded it and dry-fired it. It had seemed fine. The ammo had seemed okay, too.

Just to be on the safe side, however, she'd stopped by a gun shop on the way to work and bought a fresh box of ammunition. She'd emptied the magazine and refilled it with brand new cartridges.

The pistol went nicely into the big, loose pocket on the right front of her culottes.

She dropped her switchblade knife and car keys into the left front pocket.

After tucking her purse under the passenger seat, she picked up Mog's note and climbed out of the car. She locked the door before shutting it. Then she walked slowly up the street until she came to the house at 482 Chestnut Street.

It came as no great surprise that the place wasn't brightly lit, noisy with music and laughter, and swarming with merry-makers.

This, after all, was a party devised by Mog.

A surprise party?

With probably no one being more taken by surprise than its host.

Don't be so sure about *that*, Jane thought. The host may be none other than the Master of Games, himself.

She walked slowly toward the lighted porch.

That'd be perfect, she thought. He sends me to himself with a note like this.

But would Mog live in such a place? It looked like the modest home of a middle-income family, maybe two or three bedrooms, nicely kept up, but hardly a mansion. Not the sort of place where someone really wealthy would choose to live.

And Mog had to be filthy rich, or he wouldn't be throwing around so much money for the sake of his Game.

You never know, Jane told herself. Mog *might* live in a place like this. Or he might even live in a place like the creephouse by the cemetery – in his poem about kissing me, he called *that* miserable ruin his 'lair.'

I kissed you here, I kissed you there . . .

Shaking her head, Jane jabbed the doorbell button.

Her heart suddenly began to hammer.

Everything'll be all right, she told herself. Everything'll be fine. Whatever goes on, it'll be over by midnight and I'll get twenty-five grand.

She flinched when the front door swung open.

A man gazed out at her through the screen door.

Of course, a man. She'd hoped, all day, that she might find a nice, pleasant young woman living at 482 Chestnut. But she'd known that Mog would never make things that easy for her.

This guy doesn't look too bad, Jane thought.

Though barefoot, he wore an old pair of blue jeans and a plain white T-shirt that looked almost new. He was probably only a few years older than Jane, and had a fairly ordinary appearance. Though not especially handsome, he was certainly not the sort of drooling, hideous creature Jane had half expected.

Maybe this'll turn out okay, she thought.

His expression as he stared out at her showed pleasant surprise.

'May I help you?' he asked.

Jane fluttered the sheet of paper at the screen. 'I'm supposed to give this to you.'

'Oh?' He raised his eyebrows. Then he unlocked the screen door and swung it open.

Jane handed the note to him.

The door swung back and bumped against his shoulder. He stayed where he was, keeping it half open as he read the note. After a few seconds, he frowned at Jane.

'Who's this from?' he asked, looking curious but untroubled.

'I don't know. It's signed M-O-G.'

'Hmm. I don't know anyone by that name. Funny name, too.'

'I think it's his initials.'

'Oh. You're probably right.' His frown deepened. Apparently, he liked to frown while he concentrated. 'I can't think of anyone with those initials, either. This isn't a joke of some kind, is it?'

'I don't think so. He paid me good money to come here and be your servant till midnight.'

'Well then, you might as well come on in.' He pushed the screen door open wide for her.

It swung shut after she was inside.

The man closed the main door.

Wonderful, she thought.

'Would you rather I leave it open?' the man asked.

'It's up to you.'

'The air conditioning's on,' he explained.

'That's fine.'

'You look worried.'

'I'm okay.'

'I could open it if you want.'

'Well . . .'

He reached for the handle, then hesitated and looked at her. 'You don't have accomplices out there, do you?'

Whoever he is, he's a little worried, too. He doesn't know what's going on.

Unless it's an act.

'Nobody's with me,' Jane said. 'It's just what the note says. I'm here to be your servant until midnight.'

He looked at his wristwatch. 'That gives us . . . just shy of two-and-a-half hours.'

'What would you like me to do?'

'Sit down.'

They entered the living room. Jane sat on the sofa, but the man chose an easy chair off to the side. He reread the note from Mog, then looked at her. 'You're Jane, I take it.'

'I'm Jane.'

'Do you know who I am?'

She shook her head.

'I'm Clay. Clay Sheridan.'

'Nice to meet you.'

'Would you care for a drink?'

'It's up to you. I'll have a drink if that's what you want.'

'I see.' He stared at her as if she were a strange animal that had wandered to his door.

Jane looked away. The room was cluttered, but didn't seem to be dirty. It had a rather comfortable, almost rustic feel to it. On the walls were several paintings of woods and mountains. She found no evidence of anyone trying to feminize Clay's surroundings.

What do you think, Mog would send you like this to a married guy?

And I suppose there's no chance he's gay, either.

'Do you live alone?' Jane asked.

'I'm not sure if I should answer that.'

'You don't have to worry,' she said. 'I'm not here to case the joint.'

'I hope not.'

'I'm not a criminal.'

'What are you?' he asked.

Good question, she thought. He probably figures I'm a prostitute.

'Your servant,' she told him.

'Uh-huh. According to the note here, this person feels that he's indebted to me for some reason, and he sent you to me by way of appreciation?'

'Right.'

'Very thoughtful of him.'

She shrugged one shoulder. 'I guess so.'

'The thing is, I've got no idea who this guy is and I can't think of anyone who might feel particularly indebted to me. I've helped people from time to time, but . . . I sure can't think of anything I did to warrant . . . such an extravagant display of gratitude. It's puzzling, you know?'

'I know.'

She thought about telling him, *It doesn't matter why I'm here. You'll never figure it out, anyway, so don't waste your time. Just go along with things.*

Then she realized how stupid it would be to talk him out of questioning the situation. The more time he spent at that, the less time he would have left for making use of his 'servant.'

'You honestly don't know who sent you here?' Clay asked.

'No. He mailed that note to me in an envelope with my instructions and payment.'

'So, here you are.'

'That's right.'

'Have you done this sort of thing before?'

For a few moments, she thought about how to answer. Then she said, 'I've done errands for him. Never anything like this, though. He's never sent me anyplace to be someone's servant.'

Clay fidgeted and shrugged. 'I hope you won't take offense at this, but . . .'

'I'm not a prostitute.'

'Oh? Okay. I couldn't help but wonder. This is really . . . out of the ordinary. Women just don't pop in on me every night like this and . . . You're definitely not a prostitute?'

'No.'

'But you've been sent here to have sex with me.'

So far, Jane had managed to stay calm, fairly detached. Now, she felt a hot blush spread over her skin.

'That isn't what the note says,' she explained.

'Not in so many words.'

'Not in *any* words.'

He laughed softly. 'Well, I suppose you're right about that. But the implication is there. You're mine to *use* as I please? My wish is your command? It sounds pretty obvious what he's getting at.'

'I don't think *he's* getting at anything. He's offering you my services, not telling you how to use me. That part is up to you.'

'And you've never done this before?'

'Never.'

'Has he ever . . . ordered you to have sex with anyone?'

'No. And he isn't doing that now, either.'

'But my wish is your command.'

'That's what the note says.'

'You'll do *anything* I ask?'

'Ask and find out.'

He sighed. Staring at Jane, he rubbed his chin. 'This is very strange.'

'I know.'

'If I just knew who sent you, maybe . . .'

'Knowing who sent me won't change anything.'

'Well, I'd sure feel better if I found out it was some friend behind all this – especially if he's the sort who enjoys a good prank . . .'

'If I were you, I wouldn't consider this a prank.'

'What would you consider it?'

She shrugged. 'I'm not sure. An opportunity? A challenge? If nothing else, you're about to learn quite a lot about yourself.'

'That's a pretty good bet, I guess.' Settling back in his chair, he smiled at Jane and raised his eyebrows. 'How does Clay Sheridan, who thinks of himself as a good and decent fellow, behave when offered a gorgeous young woman to use as he pleases?'

Gorgeous. He just called me gorgeous.

Hmmm.

'Are you a cop?' he asked.

She couldn't help but laugh a little at that one. 'If I am, I don't suppose I'd be likely to admit it.'

'Good point. I suppose I could search you.'

Oh, no.

'If I *am* a cop, which I'm not, do you think I'd bring along my badge for something like this?'

'I don't know. I bet you'd bring a gun, though.'

Oh, shit.

'Maybe I'd better have a look,' he said. 'Would that be all right?'

She tried to smile. 'I'm your servant. If that's what you want to do . . .'

'This isn't one of those deals where I just get one wish, is it? Or three, or something?'

'There's only the time limit.'

'Okay. Good. 'Cause if we're counting wishes, I'd hate to throw one away by asking to search you.' He got to his feet. 'Why don't you stand up and come around to the other side of the table?' As Jane followed his orders, he said, 'I feel kind of awkward about this. I'd like to be able to trust you. You seem like a very nice person, and everything. But all this is so odd.'

'I know. I understand.'

She thought, I could pull the gun now and keep him covered till midnight.

But I'm supposed to do what he wants.

If I go against him, Mog'll probably know it.

For all I know, this guy is Mog.

As Clay approached, she raised both her arms.

He let out a nervous laugh. 'I'm new at this. Guess I was supposed to say, "Stick 'em up."'

'This is a first for me, too,' Jane said. 'I've never been searched before.'

He stopped in front of her. He grimaced a little. His hands patted the legs of his jeans a few times. Then he moved his gaze slowly down Jane's body, and up again. 'Well . . .'

'Well?' she asked.

'What've you got in your pockets there?'

'You're *asking*?'

'I don't want to put my hands in your pockets.'

'I don't bite.'

'All the same. Just tell me, all right?'

'You trust me to tell the truth?'

303

'Let's give it a try,' he said.

'Okay. I've got my keys, a switchblade knife and a pistol.'

'A knife and a *gun*?'

'Just in case of trouble. Do you want to see them?'

He shook his head. 'I'll take your word for it. Do you have a billfold?'

'In my car.'

'So you don't have any ID at all with you?'

'Not on me.'

'Are you wearing a wire?'

She let out a laugh. 'You've gotta be kidding. You've seen too many movies.'

'I like movies.'

'So do I. But this *isn't* one. A wire. Really.'

He looked a little sheepish. 'I'm just trying to find out what's going on, that's all. For all I know, you might've been sent in here to set me up for something.'

'I don't think so,' Jane said. 'And I know I didn't come in here with a hidden microphone. Or camera. But go ahead and search me.'

'I'm *not* going to search you. You can go ahead and put your arms down.'

She lowered her arms.

Clay stood facing her, looking into her eyes and not moving. He seemed very uneasy.

'So,' Jane said, 'what now?'

'I don't know. What do *you* want to do?'

'Don't ask me, I'm the servant. You're the one who's supposed to give the orders around here.'

'You don't have any suggestions?' he asked.

She shook her head.

'Well, I have an idea.'

Oh God, here we go. What's it gonna be? Something

sick. Mog knows what he's doing; he wouldn't send me to a nice, normal, decent sort of guy. Where would the fun be in that?

'Let's call it a night,' Clay said.

'What?'

'Look, it's been very interesting and I'm glad we had this chance to meet, but I don't have any real use for a servant tonight.'

'You're kidding, right?'

'No. Why don't you just go on home, now, and I'll go to bed, and that'll be the end of it? That way, neither one of us will wake up in the morning with something to regret.'

Jane couldn't believe at. 'You mean to say you don't want to . . . have me?'

'Not tonight.'

'What's that supposed to mean?'

'I don't know. It just wouldn't be right.' With a smile, he added, 'I don't do servants.'

'You're kidding,' she said again.

'Sorry. You're very . . . attractive, but . . . I'll have to pass.'

'Oh, man. So . . . that's it? I'm supposed to leave now?' Jane checked her wristwatch. 'It isn't even ten yet. I don't know about this. I'm supposed to be here till midnight. I *can't* leave. If I leave now, I could lose a . . . a *lot* of money.'

Clay looked concerned. 'Really?'

'Really.'

'Well, in that case, you can stay. And if you're staying, you might as well go ahead and be my servant. Come with me, and I'll give you some orders.'

He led her into the kitchen.

Jane tried to follow his orders, but didn't know where

anything was, so they worked together.

When they were done, Clay carried the glasses of Pepsi into the living room and Jane carried the big plastic bowl of popcorn. He said, 'Wait, don't sit down yet.'

Jane stood by the sofa.

Clay brought her a VCR tape. 'Do you know how to load this?'

'Sure.'

'What are you standing around for! Do it! *Schnell!*'

She laughed and said, *'Ja wohl.'* She took the tape from him, hurried to the TV, crouched, and inserted it into the VCR.

Then they sat down beside each other on the sofa, munched popcorn, drank their sodas, and watched the video tape – a John Candy movie called *The Great Outdoors.*

Jane had already seen it three times before, but she didn't mention that to Clay. It was one of her favorite movies. She was glad to watch it again.

During the movie, they laughed. Occasionally, they made comments. Jane held the remote control. She used it to rewind a few times at Clay's command – particularly so they could take more time reading the subtitles that translated the awful things the raccoons were saying.

Clay never touched her.

At the end of the movie, he announced, 'We still have some fifteen minutes.'

'Why don't we take this stuff into the kitchen and clean up?' Jane suggested.

'Are you telling me what to do, servant?'

She smiled. 'So sorry.'

'Anyway,' he said, 'there isn't much. I'll take care of it after you're gone.'

'So. What would you like to do for the next fifteen minutes?'

He turned toward Jane and stretched his arm across the back of the sofa. 'I've got a great idea.'

'Shoot.'

'Tell me what's really going on.'

'What do you mean?'

'My wish is your command, right? So here's my command: tell me the truth.'

She wondered if she should.

Then she said, 'Okay. It's like a game, I guess. M-O-G stands for Master of Games. He's pays me money to go places and do things. I don't know who he is, or why he's doing it, or why he chose me to be his player. I just know that each time I follow his instructions, I end up with a new batch of money and a new set of instructions. So I keep on doing it. Why not? It's a lot of money. And I have my weapons in case anything gets out of hand.'

'Have you had to use them?'

'I had to stab a dog that attacked me. That's the only time.'

'What sort of things does he have you do?'

'Things like come here tonight.'

'What else?'

'I don't want to get into any of that. Okay? We hardly know each other. The thing is – as far as you're concerned – I don't know why he picked you for this deal tonight. Maybe he had a special reason, or maybe he just picked you at random. Or maybe you're him.'

Clay grinned. 'Mog? You think I might be Mog?'

'Are you?'

'No.'

'Can you prove it?' Jane asked.

'Can you prove I *am*?'

'If you *are* Mog, I'd sure like to know.'

'I already told you I'm not.'

'But why should I believe you?'

'Why shouldn't you?'

'Okay.'

'Anyway,' Clay said, 'I think he must be a real jerk.'

'He gives me a lot of money.'

'Only a jerk would send a young woman like you to a man's house with a note like that. Either he doesn't care what happens to you, or he's *trying* to get you into trouble. Either way, he's a jerk.'

'And am I a jerk,' Jane asked, 'for playing along with him?'

'You're not a jerk.'

'Are you sure?'

'You can't be a jerk. I like you, and I don't like jerks.'

'Thanks.'

Clay looked at his wristwatch. 'Five after. I guess it's okay for you to go now. You've been a fine servant.'

'Thanks. You've been an excellent master. And you make good popcorn.'

She followed Clay to the front door, and he opened it for her. She turned and face him. 'I was awfully worried about all this,' she said.

'You had every reason to be.'

'The chances were about one in a million that I'd actually run into a man who didn't want to ... mess with me – or worse. Especially with Mog picking the guy.'

'He might've sent you here without knowing anything about who's in the house.'

'Maybe.'

'And I don't think it's as bad as one in a million.'

'I do. Anyway, I sure am glad he sent me to you.'

'Me, too,' Clay said.

308

'Hey, maybe he did know what he was doing.'

'Sent you here because he knew you'd be safe with me?'

'Yeah.'

'Don't bet on it. He couldn't know me that well. *I* don't know myself that well. I probably shouldn't tell you this, but it was never a sure thing. When you raised your arms like that for me to search you . . .' He shook his head. 'Plenty of other times, too . . . It was close. It might've gone the other way.'

'But it didn't.'

'Guess I'm a wonder of self-control,' he said, then smiled. 'You should see yourself blushing.'

'It's nice to know . . . that I wasn't easy to resist.'

'Incredibly difficult.'

'Good.' Looking into his eyes, she stepped toward him.

He gripped her upper arms and stopped her. 'You'd better go,' he said.

'What's wrong?'

'Nothing. Just . . . Come back some time after you've finished your game with Mog. If you want to.'

'After it's *finished*?'

'Yeah.'

'But that might not be for . . . I don't know, weeks, months. Who knows?'

'It'll only go on as long as you're willing to play.'

My God, she thought, he sounds exactly like Brace.

'The game's crazy,' Clay said. 'But you've already figured that out, I think.'

'Maybe. It might be crazy, but it's lucrative. And it gives me something to do.'

'Well, *I* don't want anything else to do with it.'

'Including me?'

'I'm afraid so. The way I see it, you're playing Russian

309

Roulette and this Mog fellow – he's the gun. I don't want to fall for you any more than I have already and then stick around while you blow your brains out.'

'It's not like that,' Jane said.

'Well, that's sort of how it looks. Anyway, you know where to find me.'

'Okay.'

'Be careful, all right?'

'Okay.' She offered her hand. 'You can shake, can't you?'

'Sure.'

He took her hand gently, and shook it.

Jane murmured, 'See you.' Then she hurried away.

That wasn't so bad, she told herself. It really *couldn't* have gone any better. What the hell was Mog thinking, sending me to a guy like Clay?

Probably a mistake. He probably goofed with the address, or something.

Don't cry!

She could feel it coming.

Don't!

Maybe *that's* his game, trying to make me cry. Well, I'm not going to do it. Not this time. He threw me against Clay just to show me what I'm missing out on. I'm not falling for it.

Anyway, Clay's probably a bastard underneath it all. He can't be as nice as he seems. Nobody is.

Brace sure proved that.

'Who needs either one of 'em,' she muttered.

When she opened her car door, she found an envelope on the driver's seat.

'Thank you, thank you,' she said, picking it up.

She sat down and locked her door, then turned on the overhead light and tore open the envelope. The stack of hundred dollar bills seemed twice as thick as the bunch she'd received that morning.

She figured there should be two hundred and fifty-six of them.

Not bad pay for two-and-a-half hours entertaining a fellow who didn't really want anything out of you except maybe some companionship. Better than ten thousand bucks per hour.

If Mog keeps this up, she thought, I'll be able to spend my old age in the lap of luxury.

Might be the only lap I get.

'Ha ha,' she muttered, and drove away without reading Mog's note.

Chapter Thirty

My beauty,

Tomorrow night, 901 Mayr Heights for a gala time.

In the meantime, don't feel lonely. You have me. I shall come to you tonight.

No need to wait up.

> Love to my lovely
> hot wet wench,
> MOG

Hot wet wench. Why did he have to be crude like that?

He wouldn't be Mog, she told herself, if he weren't such a crude, nasty creep.

Part of his charm.

Yeah, right.

She'd first read the note after returning to her house, just before hiding the money. Now, in her pajamas and sitting on the edge of her bed, she read it again.

Not only crude, she thought, but arrogant. Like he's under the impression that I just can't wait for him to show up.

'I've got a secret for you, Mog,' she said. 'It's no big deal to me whether you show up or not. You know what I mean? I never get to see you, anyway, so who cares?'

Maybe this time, she thought, I really should try to stay awake for him.

Won't work. The guy's like Santa. He won't come while I'm awake.

Why don't I try leaving him a message again?

Her heart beat quicker.

I shouldn't make a habit of this, she thought.

She slipped off her pajama top and went to the dresser where she'd left her marking pen. She stepped close to the mirror. On the stretch of lightly tanned skin below her breasts and above the waistband of her pajama pants, she wrote:

WAKE ME
SHOW YOURSELF
PLEASE

In the morning, Jane found written on her back:

GREAT TIME
TOO BAD YOU SLEPT
THROUGH IT ALL

'Right,' she muttered. 'What's your idea of a great time, Mog? Practicing your penmanship?'

If it'd been much more than that, she told herself, I wouldn't have slept through it.

Don't be so sure. It might've been a lot more than that.

So what else is new? she thought. He can do whatever he wants – and probably has been doing exactly that. No way to stop him.

Not that I've tried.

Pretty much the opposite, comes right down to it.

Tipping back her head, she said to the bedroom ceiling,

'The least you could do, Mog, is wake me up next time.'

Mog, of course, didn't answer.

Jane dropped her pajama pants and inspected herself carefully. The writing on her back seemed to be the only evidence of Mog's visit.

After starting her coffee, Jane took a shower to wash off the messages. As usual, they needed a lot of scrubbing. When she was done, she put on her bikini. She carried a cup of coffee and her book outside to enjoy the morning sunlight for a while.

She drank two cups of coffee. Then she brought her weights out of the house, took them to her blanket on the grass and worked out until she was dripping sweat, huffing for breath, and worn out.

Back in the house, she took another shower. Near the end, she made the water chilly and stood beneath it, rigid, her teeth clenched. She didn't stay in the shower for long. Time was getting short, and she didn't want to be late for work.

Still dripping, she hurried out of the bathroom with her towel. She was mostly dry by the time she reached her bedroom.

As she stepped into her panties, she decided to go ahead and wear her denim culottes and a good, short-sleeved blouse – the sort of outfit she usually wore to the library – and go straight to the Mayr Heights address after work.

It's probably a house, she thought.

Mog had written about a 'gala time.' Which might mean there would be a party.

Right, a party of two like last night.

On the other hand, suppose he means it this time?

The 'Heights' in the name of the street sounded ritzy.

What if this turned out to be a fancy section of town, and she was expected to participate in an actual party of some sort?

Not awfully likely.

The place might just as easily turn out to be a filthy old ruin like the creephouse by the boneyard.

It might be just about anything.

So I ought to be ready for anything, she told herself.

Ten minutes later, dressed and groomed and ready to go, Jane left the house with a paper sack in each hand. Stuffed into one were blue jeans, a chamois shirt, and a pair of running shoes. In the other sack was a pair of blue pumps and a neatly folded evening dress that the filthy son-of-a-bitch Ken had bought for her to wear to a dance at his parents' country club.

Two weeks ago, the gown wouldn't have fit her.

But she'd tried it on quickly before putting it into the sack, and the fit had been fine.

In the mirror, she'd looked smashing.

Hard to believe, though, that she had actually gone to a dance wearing a garment like this. Elegant, but terribly clingy and revealing. Of course, Ken had insisted.

He was always insisting on something.

She could remember protesting, 'I can't wear this. My God, everybody'll *stare* at me.' To which Ken had replied, 'I *want* 'em staring at you, babe. I want 'em *drooling*. What's the point in having you if I can't show you off?'

And I'm going to take this with me tonight? she'd asked herself.

Why the hell not? I look great in it.

Besides, it's my only good gown. And the chances of having to wear it are slim to none.

As she carried the two sacks out to the driveway, her purse swung by her hip. It was heavy with her flashlight, knife, pistol, and box of ammunition.

She put the sacks into the trunk of her car, then drove to work.

A dead end?

'Great,' Jane muttered, and slowed down as she drove past the sign.

The last address she'd been able to spot, some distance back, had been in the seven hundreds. Now, all of a sudden, Mayr Heights was planning to pull a disappearing act?

What the hell happened to 901?

The road seemed to continue for a while, though. Maybe she would find 901 before it ended.

No such luck.

The road curved to the left, and her headlights illuminated the barricade. She drove closer to it, wondering if this might mark an interruption, not an end.

Off beyond the barricade, the hillside seemed to drop away.

She reached for the map on the passenger seat, then changed her mind. There was no need to check. What did it matter if the road resumed somewhere else? This was the section where 901 should be.

She must've simply missed it.

She'd seen no houses at all on Mayr Heights. Apparently, they were hidden on the wooded hillside and you could only find them by venturing onto those awful little driveways. She'd seen plenty such driveways – if that's what they were. Narrow lanes, paved but dark, bordered by thick bushes and trees. Often, they'd seemed to be unmarked. No visible mailbox or address. No clue at all as to where the things might lead.

One of them, she supposed, must go to 901. I probably drove right past it.

'Terrific,' she muttered.

She made a U-turn near the barricade, and drove slowly back the way she'd come.

From the few addresses she'd been able to find on the way up, she at least knew that the odd numbers were over to her right. The house she wanted would be uphill. At the top of one of those nasty little driveways.

But which one?

Check them all. Stop and get out and look.

The third time she climbed out of her car to study a small, paved gap in the roadside foliage, she found a redwood mailbox buried in the bushes. Carved into the side of the box was the address, 901, and a name, S. Savile.

'Yes!' she gasped.

She shone her flashlight up the driveway.

The concrete was cracked, crumbling in places, with small weeds growing out of the fissures. Bushes pressed in close on both sides, so that the lane resembled a very narrow tunnel – a tunnel up an awfully steep grade. Near the far reach of her flashlight, where her beam faded to a hazy glow, the driveway curved out of sight.

'Yuck,' Jane muttered.

Sure I'm gonna drive up that thing. When I get done, I'll try walking blindfolded up some rollercoaster tracks.

She felt a little cowardly as she headed back to her car.

Driving up there would be stupid, she told herself. Forget how creepy the thing looks, it's *one way*. What if I run into another car on my way up?

Better yet, what if I run into one on my way down?

I'm not gonna let myself get trapped. No way.

317

S. Savile might be a perfectly nice fellow – like Clay last night. But he might not be. The way Mog is into word games, it's probably significant that name has 'vile' in it.

Back at the car, she climbed into the driver's seat. She moved the car a good distance past the driveway entrance, then pulled as far off the road as possible.

Now that she faced a hike to the top of the steep driveway, she knew for sure that she wouldn't be wearing the party gown. She considered her jeans and chamois shirt. Protective clothes, but heavy. And hot. She would be a lot more comfortable if she stayed in her culottes and light blouse.

But who knows what's at the top? she thought. Maybe I'd rather cook in my jeans and shirt than end up having bare arms and legs in a bad place.

She hurried to the trunk and opened it. No cars were coming. No house was in sight. From all she could see and hear, nobody seemed to be nearby. So she undressed at the rear of her car and quickly got into her jeans, running shoes, and chamois shirt.

She shut the trunk.

Standing by the driver's door, she took what she needed from her purse. She slipped the keys and knife into the front left pocket of her jeans. The pistol went into the pocket on the right. She opened the box of ammunition, filled her hand with cartridges, dumped them into the right front pocket of her shirt, then returned the box to her purse. She clamped the flashlight under her left arm.

Then she tucked her purse under the passenger seat, locked and shut the door.

She headed for the driveway.

As she walked, she felt the weight of the extra

ammo dragging at her pocket, swinging under her breast.

It had surprised her a bit when she'd decided to take more ammunition. She hadn't *planned* to do that. She'd briefly considered it earlier in the day, but hadn't made up her mind.

The business of Mog's about a 'gala time,' that's what had made her think of it in the first place.

He isn't sending me to any party.

In the library that afternoon, a bit of poetry had crossed her mind: 'Lo, 'tis a gala night.' And then it had crossed again and again. She hadn't been able to get rid of it.

The opening of 'The Conqueror Worm,' by Poe.

She knew the poem well. Too well. Back in junior high school, she'd memorized it for a Halloween presentation. She could still recite it – and often did, usually late at night, usually half drunk, and always to the annoyance of her friends. Oh God, how the language slithered and rolled off her tongue! 'It wriiiiithes! It wriiiiithes with mortal pangs! The mimes become its food!'

What a fabulous, gross poem.

But it wasn't something you wanted in your head when you were planning to visit a stranger's house late at night.

Vermin fangs, in human gore imbued.

Charming stuff.

Mog's 'gala time' had snapped it all into her mind and kept it there. And made her think that extra precautions might be in order.

Maybe take along a few more bullets?

And then to see that the resident of 901 Mayr Heights was someone by the name of Savile.

Change one letter, you've got 'So vile.'

I'm probably just going paranoid in my old age, she thought.

Better safe than sorry.

If I really think I might need the gun – much less a pocketful of extra ammo – I shouldn't be going up there at all.

The same old tune, she thought. A tune that doesn't mean a whole lot, anymore, now that the stakes are up to fifty thousand bucks.

More like fifty-one thousand, something, she corrected.

She began to trudge up the driveway. She couldn't see much of it: a strip of gray speckled only here and there by moonlight, with darkness on both sides. Though she held the flashlight in her right hand, she kept it off. Better to stumble along in the dark than to make herself conspicuous with the light.

Her leg muscles, still a little stiff and sore, ached at first. Soon, the aching faded.

In spite of the many curves in the driveway, the climb was steep, and hard work.

Gasping for air, drenched with sweat, she stopped to rest.

No sign, yet, of an end to the driveway.

What if it goes on for miles?

It won't, she told herself.

She fluttered the front of her shirt, and felt cooler air from the outside come in and buffet her hot skin. The back of the shirt was clinging to her. So was the seat of her panties.

Hope the house has air conditioning, she thought. Or a pool. Wouldn't it be great to leap into a cold swimming pool about now!

She fluttered her shirt again, took a very deep breath, then resumed her trek.

And suddenly found herself at the top of the driveway.

The dim strip of moonlit pavement stretched across an open field to the garage of the house at 901 Mayr Heights. There were a few lamps on posts along the sides of the driveway. They looked like old-fashioned gas lamps. Not one was lighted, though.

The front porch of the old, two-story house was dark. So were all the windows.

Well, Jane thought, obviously there isn't a party going on.

That was a relief. She wouldn't have to hike back down for her gown. Nobody would have to see her in it. She wouldn't need to talk her way in to the party, or mingle with strangers or try to fend off the advances of pushy, obnoxious men.

Odd, though, that *all* the lights were off.

Mog hasn't sent me to another abandoned house, has he?

Chapter Thirty-one

Instead of walking straight up the driveway, in plain sight of anyone who might be watching from one of the dark front windows, Jane stayed among the trees and bushes beyond the edge of the lawn and made her way around to the side.

Only a few yards of open space separated her from the wall of the garage.

She dashed across it.

Cupping her hands against the garage window, she peered in. Blackness. So she took the risk of turning on her flashlight. Its beam hit the dirty glass, went through, and formed a bright disk no larger than the lid of a small mustard jar.

Jane scowled.

After a few moments of studying the odd phenomenon, she realized that her light was being blocked, just inside the window, by thick, black fabric.

The fabric covered the entire window.

This is a wonderful sign, she thought. Someone wants to make sure nobody can see in.

Or maybe it's just to keep out the sunlight.

Terrific. A vampire lives in the garage.

Jane laughed quietly, nervously.

Screw vampires, I wanta know if there's a *car* in there.

Break the window?

That'd be a great move, particularly if somebody's in the house (or garage) and hears it.

Besides, she told herself, cars or no cars in the garage, you couldn't be completely sure whether someone's in the house.

Giving up on the window, Jane slipped along the side of the garage and gazed around its corner. The rear grounds were dark, just as she'd expected. She took a few strides until she could see the back of the house.

Dark, everything dark.

She was tempted to explore the area back here: it looked lush and extravagant. Trees, benches, walkways, statues, a gazebo off in the distance. She wouldn't be surprised to find brooks and waterfalls, and maybe even a fabulous swimming pool.

If everything turns out okay, she told herself, I'll take a look later. Right now, I'd better concentrate on getting into the house and laying my hands on the envelope.

Wherever the hell it might be.

She hurried to the front of the house, climbed over the railing at the end of the veranda, and crept as quietly as she could toward the front door. The huge window beside her looked black. She ached to shine her light on it, but didn't dare take the risk.

No sounds came from the house.

She tried to make no sounds herself as she crossed the veranda, but its old floorboards sometime squawked under her weight, and once she walked into something that bumped her belly an instant before she struck it with her knee. She stifled her gasp, but the thing – whatever it was – scooted loudly and thudded.

Moments later, she found it with her hand.

A chair. She felt its wicker back under her fingers.

After that, she walked more carefully and encountered no more furniture.

Turning, she faced the front door.

She took a few deep breaths. She lifted the front of her shirt and mopped the sweat off her face. Then she opened the screen door and tried the handle.

The solid oak door was locked.

She had pretty much expected that.

Now what? she wondered.

Without pausing to think, she jabbed her fingertip into the doorbell button. She listened for the sound of ringing from inside the house, but heard nothing.

Great, she thought. How am I supposed to know if the damn thing works?

She waited. She listened hard, but heard no one approaching.

So she poked the button a few more times.

Nothing.

A, she thought, nobody's home. B, the bell doesn't work. C, whoever's in the house is asleep, or doesn't hear the bell for some other reason. Or D, somebody is hearing it just fine, but *choosing* not to come to the door.

'Swell,' she whispered.

Let's at least eliminate B as a factor.

She knocked hard on the door, pounded it until her knuckles hurt. And waited some more.

Okay, she thought as she backed away from the door. Now what?

Two choices: either break in, or go home.

Midway between the front door and other end of the veranda, she found a window that looked just right for smashing; double-hung with a screen on the lower half, and low enough to climb through.

She stared at it.

Her stomach hurt.

I shouldn't do this, she thought. I should just go home. If I do this, I'm nothing better than a criminal.

It's my fifty-one thousand dollars inside!

It *will* be mine, she corrected herself, if I have the guts to go in and find it.

But this isn't an abandoned old ruin by the edge of a graveyard – this is a house where people actually live. They might be away right now, but this is still their property, their home.

If I go in, I'm a house-breaker. An intruder. They'd even have a right to shoot me.

Nobody's going to shoot me. Nobody's home.

What if there's an alarm, or something? What if the cops show up? They might shoot me. Or at the very least, I could end up in jail.

If they catch me.

She shut her eyes and muttered, 'My God, Mog, what are you trying to do to me?'

Then she bashed a hole in the upper window with the butt of her flashlight. The clamor of bursting glass made her cringe and clench her teeth. After the glass stopped falling, she waited – ready to run.

Nothing happened.

She reached through the hole and unlocked the window. With her switchblade, she cut the screen out of its frame. Then she slid the window up.

She stared into blackness.

Let's just see what the hell . . .

She switched her flashlight on.

And its beam was abruptly stopped by a heavy black shroud.

Oh, boy.

Jane killed her light. She was holding her knife in her

right hand. With that hand, she reached forward. She pushed her knuckles gently against the fabric. It had the scratchy feel of a thick, wool blanket. It had very little give. Instead of hanging like a curtain, it seemed to be drawn taut across the window.

Somebody likes a lot of privacy. Or darkness. Or something.

Definitely queer.

Jane pierced the fabric with the tip of her knife. She slipped the blade in a bit farther, then drew it downward, carving a four-inch slit. A faint thread of light came through the cut.

Jane switched her flashlight off. She stuffed it into the left front pocket of her jeans to free her hand, then spread the slit apart and peered in.

The room looked like it might be a den or a study, but she couldn't see it very well. The only light came through its doorway from a hall.

She ripped the gap wide and stuck her head in and looked all around. Nobody. She listened. No voices, no music, no sound whatsoever to suggest that anyone might be home.

Great, she thought. Now what?

Shit or get off the commode, that's what.

But I don't wanta break into someone's house! It's illegal! It's wrong! It's in a whole different ballpark than the other stuff. If I do this, I'm really really crossing the line.

But it's *my* money I need to go in and get. I won't be stealing anything of theirs.

And hell, I've already busted the window. The job's half done: I've done the breaking, now all that's left is the entering.

When I find the money from Mog, I'll leave them a

couple of hundred to pay for the damage.

She liked that idea. Pay for the damage. Maybe even leave them a decent chunk. If she left them quite a lot, they might even be *glad* she broke in.

How about giving them a thousand bucks?

Before she could do that, however, she would need to locate Mog's envelope.

Feeling somewhat less like a criminal than before, Jane split the fabric all the way down to the window sill and climbed into the room.

Then she stood motionless, barely breathing. It was strange to be in someone else's house without permission. It made her feel powerful, but very exposed and vulnerable.

It would be great, she thought, if you could do this sort of thing without any fear of being caught.

She wondered if that's how it was for Mog. He seemed to be capable, somehow, of coming and going wherever he pleased, never showing himself . . .

Quit dinking around, she thought. Nobody's home. But they might come tooling up the driveway any second, so you'd better get on with it and get the hell outa here.

She hurried to a lamp and turned it on.

Should've brought gloves, she thought.

Never figured I'd have to worry about leaving fingerprints. Jeez!

Just watch what you touch.

Quickly, she scanned the room: bookshelves, lamps, a desk, a couple of small tables, an easy chair, a familiar painting on one wall – a print of the Goya that has a giant about to bite off someone's head.

So-vile living up to his name.

But she was looking for her envelope, not for clues to the character traits of S. Savile.

And she saw no envelope here.

This could take forever, she thought.

Holding the knife in her teeth, she slipped Mog's note out of her shirt pocket and unfolded it. She read it slowly, wondering if she might've missed a clue during the previous readings.

My beauty,

Tomorrow night, 901 Mayr Heights for a gala time.

In the meantime, don't feel lonely. You have me. I shall come to you tonight.

No need to wait up.

Love to my lovely,
hot wet wench,
Mog

Only the first part seemed at all relevant to tonight. 'Tomorrow night, 901 Mayr Heights' was there to tell her when and where. Could there be a clue in 'My beauty'?

It brought to mind *Beauty and the Beast*. Maybe Mog hinting that he's a beast. But what could that have to do with the location on the envelope?

Maybe a lot, she decided. Keep it in mind.

'My beauty' also made Jane think of *Sleeping Beauty*.

Interesting. A couple of fairy tales. Are they both from the Brothers Grimm? she wondered. She wasn't sure. But she did know that many different versions of the old tales had been published, and that Disney had made animated feature movies of both stories.

Maybe the envelope's inside a book of fairy tales. Or in a Disney book. Maybe it's hidden in a Walt Disney section of Savile's home video collection, if he's got such a thing.

Keep an eye out, she told herself.

Now, what about 'a gala time?' Maybe the guy has a Poe book. Hey, maybe this big old house has a ballroom or a dance floor.

Anything else in the note?

Nothing that seemed to pertain to tonight.

She returned the note to her shirt pocket, took the knife from her mouth and hurried over to the bookshelves. As fast as possible, she scanned the titles.

No book of fairy tales. Nothing about Disney. None by Poe, or any that appeared likely to contain poetry. Most of the books were nonfiction works and they seemed to cover only two subjects: police procedures and true crime.

'A real good sign,' Jane muttered. 'Splendid.'

She turned off the lamp. At the doorway, she leaned out and glanced up and down the hall. Nobody there. She stepped forward. To her left were a few doorways. But she could see the foyer and the foot of a stairway to her right, so that's the direction she chose.

Where would Mog put that envelope?

He wants me to find it, so he probably hid it somewhere fairly obvious. But he wants to make me work for it.

Upstairs.

Upstairs in a bedroom. That's where he made me go in the creephouse. And it'd tie in with *Sleeping Beauty.* And that's where he'd like to put me, up where I'll have a hard time escaping in case S. Savile comes home.

Hell, maybe he's got a coffin waiting for me.

The foyer was lighted by a rustic chandelier made from a wagon wheel. The candle-shaped bulbs gave off a weak, yellow glow so murky that Jane felt as if she were viewing the front door through a pool of cider. For a moment, she couldn't find the windows. She knew they should be there: long, narrow windows on both sides of the door. She'd seen them from outside, but . . .

Oh.

Masking the windows, on this side, were black rectangles framed like works of art and nailed in place.

Somebody went to a lot of trouble, Jane thought. This is looking worse and worse.

But she noticed a good sign – the guard chain for the front door hung from its mount. Normally, if people were home at night, they would secure that sort of chain.

They probably *aren't* home, she told herself.

Maybe S. Savile took his wife to the movies. If there is a Mrs Savile. Which Jane was beginning to doubt. Like Scott's place last night, S. Savile's home showed no signs (so far) of a female influence.

So maybe he went out for a night on the town by himself. Or with a significant other of the male persuasion.

Maybe he went on a business trip. That's something to hope for. Gone, not due back for days.

Unless he's back already, just now steering his way up the driveway.

Jane opened the door, mostly to see if she could.

It opened easily.

She looked out toward the area where the driveway slanted down out of sight.

I oughta get out of here right now, she thought. Any second, there might be headlights and it'll be too late.

Sure, boogie right outa here and kiss fifty-one thousand bucks goodbye. What I'd better do, instead, is find out where the back door is. That way, if I need to make a quick exit . . .

What I'd better do is go upstairs and find the envelope and haul my butt outa here!

330

She shut the door, turned around and gazed up the stairway. There were no lights on at the top. She grimaced.

Maybe I'd better look around down here for a . . .

Just do it. Get it done!

She slipped her right hand into the front pocket of her jeans and wrapped it around the grips of her pistol. She started to pull the weapon out.

And just who am I planning to shoot, the owners of the house?

Terrific.

She left the gun inside her pocket. As she began to climb the stairs, she thought about putting her knife away, too. She shouldn't have a knife in her hand if the man of the house suddenly appears at the top of the stairs.

But she couldn't bear the thought of having no weapon ready.

Reaching behind her with both hands, she lifted the tail of her shirt and slid the blade down between her belt and the back of her jeans.

By the time she'd finished doing that, she was almost to the top of the stairs. She thought about taking out her flashlight.

No, better to sneak through the darkness.

She was one stair from the top when a woman screamed.

Chapter Thirty-two

A quiet, muffled scream that came from somewhere nearby and felt to Jane like an icicle stabbing her low and deep.

Oh, Jesus! Oh-my-God-oh-Jesus, what was THAT?

When the scream ended, Jane unfroze and climbed the final stair and hurried to the right. She knew she was making too much noise. Someone was in the house, after all – a woman in enough trouble or pain to make her scream like that – and Jane wanted to be silent but she needed to hurry and her shoes thumped on the carpet of the upstairs hall – *Christ, I sound like a stampede!* – and she threw open the first door that she found.

The skinny young woman sitting in the middle of the bed looked up and grinned. Her lips and chin were bloody. A finger pointed at Jane from between her teeth. On the plate on her lap was the rest of the hand.

A right hand.

Her right wrist was a bandaged stump.

So was her right thigh.

She wore a sleeveless T-shirt. It had an arrow pointing to the left and read, 'I'M WITH STUPID.' It was spattered with dried brown blood and wet red blood. She didn't have on any pants. The plate with the severed hand covered her groin.

Jane could only stare at her, shocked.

With her remaining hand, the woman took the finger from between her teeth and nibbled skin off its side.

Jane gagged and looked away.

'Hi,' the woman said. 'I'm Linda. Who are you?'

She sounded cheery.

'Jane.'

'Haven't seen you around here before.' She dropped the finger onto her plate. It made a bad sound landing. 'Show me your arm?'

'What for?'

'Just because.'

Jane unbuttoned the cuff and slid the right sleeve of her chamois shirt up her forearm. When her fingers touched her arm, they felt like ice.

'Mmmm,' Linda said. 'You've got meat on you.'

Jane took a step backward, swallowed hard, and said, 'What's going on here?'

Linda grinned. Her front teeth were bloody. 'I'm eating myself, what does it look like?'

'Why?'

She shrugged and smirked. 'They let me.'

'They *let* you?'

'Yeah. They wouldn't let me eat nothing, you know? Just kept me here and fucked around with me and wouldn't give me nothing to eat. I got hungry. I got *real* hungry. I begged and begged for something to eat. So finally, Steve goes, "Okay, I'll get you some food. And what'll you have?" he asks me. So then I go, "Anything, anything." So then he cuts off my right foot and lets me eat that. Not much to a foot, but it was better than nothing.'

Jane took a deep breath. It didn't feel deep enough.

Her heart seemed to be pounding too hard to let her breathe properly.

'I only just wish I hadn't of gone on my diet last year. You wanta stay away from diets, Janey. I dropped *thirty* pounds and wasn't I proud of myself! Biggest mistake I ever made. Shoot, I was only just skin 'n' bones when I got here, and things've gone downhill ever since. You're lucky you've got some meat on you. Take off your shirt for me, will you?'

Jane shook her head. 'No thanks.'

'Oh, come on.' She grinned.

'Look, I'll help you get out of here.'

'Oh, really? Do you really think so? Whoo! You'd better think again, Janey. Nobody gets out of here.'

'Are there others?'

'Why, sure. Me and Marjorie and Sue . . . woops, no more Sue. Poor girl just dwindled down to nothing.' Linda laughed. 'There's the new girl, too. She's a skinny thing already, and hasn't been here more'n a few days. I danced with her last night, 'n' I could feel her rib bones poking me.'

'Danced?' Jane heard herself murmur.

'Why, sure. The boys throw dances for us all the time. Steve plays himself a killer fiddle, and . . .'

'But your leg . . .?'

She laughed. 'I get around real good for a crip. Just lift up your shirt, okay? All I wanta do is get a look at how much meat you got on you.'

'Forget it. Who else is here? You, Marjorie, and the new girl.'

'Gail.'

'And Gail.'

'Not *and*. Gail, she's the new girl.'

The name suddenly pounded her.

334

A gala time.

'Where's Gail?' Jane asked.

'Where do you think?'

'Hey, come on.'

Linda batted her eyelids. 'You know what I want.'

'Okay, okay.' Jane lifted the bottom of her shirt, baring her midriff.

'Nice. You look good 'n' firm. You been working out?'

'Tell me where Gail is. Come on.'

'Higher.'

'Hey.'

'Do you wanta know where she is?'

Jane did as she was told.

Linda said, 'Oooo, nice. Come here so I can feel.' She reached out her hand.

Jane didn't move.

'Okay, be that way. Wanta see mine? I already had one of 'em, but . . .' She pulled up her T-shirt to show Jane.

Jane looked away fast and jerked her own shirt down so hard it made a soft *whap* as it went taut.

'Mighty tasty, but Sue's was better. Not that I got enough of it. They're all such a bunch of pigs around here, and poor Sue didn't have that much to go around in the first place, if you know what I mean.'

Jane whirled around and ran for the door.

'Don't you wanta know where Gail is?' Linda called.

Jane staggered into the hallway. She glanced both ways. Nobody.

As she ran toward the next door, she dug into her pocket and pulled out her pistol. She thumbed the safety off. With her left hand, she flung open the door.

This had to be Marjorie on the bed.

Apparently, Marjorie had been here longer than Linda.

Too much was missing. She had leather harnesses holding her up.

'Heh-lowwww,' Marjorie greeted her. 'Come in, come in.'

Jane shook her head. Then she threw up.

'Well,' Marjorie said as Jane vomited, 'Isn't this a fine how-do-you-do? All that wonderful grub going to waste on the floor. How am I supposed to get to it? Tell me that?'

This can't be happening. This just cannot be happening.

When her stomach was done erupting, she turned away from Marjorie's door. She stumbled down the hall.

'Bring me some in a cup!' Marjorie suggested, and giggled.

Jane stopped at the next door. She grabbed the knob, but hesitated.

This can't be as bad, she told herself. Gail's new.

She opened the door.

The woman flat on her back looked very pregnant. She still had both of her legs. They were spread wide apart and tied at the ankles to the corners of the bed frame. She suddenly sat up. She still had both her arms.

Nothing of this woman seemed to be missing. But she was naked and she looked as if she'd been worked on by people trying to make her scream.

'You've gotta get me out of here!' she blurted. 'They want my baby! They want my baby!'

'Are you the one who screamed?'

She nodded.

'Are you . . . starting labor?'

'Huh-uh, no.'

'That isn't why you . . .?'

'They wanta eat my baby.'

336

'Nobody's going to eat your baby.'

'Promise?'

'Yes. Are you Gail?'

'I'm Sandra.'

'Where's Gail?'

'You've gotta help me!'

'Shhh. I'm looking for Gail.'

'Please.'

'Don't worry. I'll get you out of here. Where's Gail?'

Sandra nodded her head to the left.

Jane rushed down the hall to the next room and threw open the door. The woman standing against the wall by the bed gazed at Jane with bulging eyes. She had a broad strip of duct tape across her mouth. Though her dark hair was a tangled mess and she looked haggard and terrified, she didn't appear to be badly hurt. A few bruises, many minor wounds that trickled blood – but none of her body parts had been removed. She stood with legs apart and arms outstretched, a human X fixed to the wall by tight strands of barbed wire. The blood came from places where the barbs had pierced her skin.

Wires crossed her ankles, her thighs, her waist, her ribcage, her breasts, her neck and forehead. They looped across her raised upper arms, and they looked very tight where they crossed her wrists. Thin streamers of blood from her wrists ran down her arms and armpits and sides all the way down past her hips.

Jane glanced around to make sure nobody else was there. Then she scanned the room more carefully, looking for the envelope.

This is Gail's room. The place to have a 'gala time.' This might just be where Mog put the envelope.

Jane suddenly wondered how she could even *think* about the envelope at a time like this.

Fifty-one thousand bucks, that's how.

Right, and what about self-preservation? I've gotta get out of here! I've gotta get these poor wrecked women out of here before these fucking lunatics come along and catch me and . . .

I'll shoot myself, she thought, before I'll let them do this shit to me.

Don't shoot yourself, shoot them.

'It's gonna be all right,' she said. 'I'll get you out of here.'

As she stepped closer, she could see that the woman was standing rigid, trying not to move, but having trouble breathing through her nostrils. Each time she inhaled, her breasts, her ribcage and her flat belly pressed against strands, sinking half a dozen barbs into raw bloody holes already there.

Jane walked up close to her and stopped. She glanced over her shoulder.

So far, so good.

She switched the pistol to her left hand, and used her right to rip the tape away from the woman's mouth. The mouth sprang open and the woman gasped – and whimpered as her wild breathing drove barbs into her skin.

'Take it easy,' Jane whispered. 'Easy. You're hurting yourself.'

The woman shut her eyes. Tears spilled down her face.

'Just take it easy and I'll get these wires off you.'

Jane studied the hook-up. Each strand seemed to be attached at both ends to swivel eyes in brass plates screwed into the wooden wall. This was no make-shift rig that had been thrown together in a few minutes. Each plate took four screws.

'Was this already here?' Jane asked.

'Uh. The things here in the wall?' Her voice sounded high and shaky. 'Yeah.'

Jane started to untwist one end of the wire that crossed the woman's breasts. 'Are you Gail?'

'Yes.'

'You're in a lot better shape than the others.'

'They . . . they only got me . . . Monday.'

Monday. Gail.

Jane looked at her face. It did seem a little familiar. Was this the face she'd seen on the TV news? 'You're the one from the mall.'

'They got me . . . on the way home.'

With a final twist, the wire loosened its grip on the brass eye. Jane pulled it through and shoved it aside. She started to work on the strand across Gail's ribcage. 'Who's doing this stuff?'

'I don't know . . . who.'

'How many?'

'Three? Maybe more but . . . I've only seen three . . . together. When they got me. And at the dances. There could be more. I don't know. They have masks they wear.'

'Where are they now?'

'I don't know.'

She got the second wire loose, drew it out through the brass eye, let it swing away, and started on the strand across Gail's waist. 'Did they leave the house?'

'I don't know.'

'Did they drive away? Did you hear a car?'

'No. I don't know where they are. They don't tell me what they're doing. They don't tell me much. They just come in and do things and go.'

'What things?'

'A lot of stuff.'

'Do they come in very often?'

'It seems like . . . all the time.'

Jane finished the wire at Gail's waist, started on the one across the girl's left thigh, then decided it would be better to free her arms before starting on the legs. That way, maybe Gail could lend a hand. She wished she'd thought of that earlier.

Straightening up, Jane started to untwist the wire beneath Gail's upper arm.

'What about tonight?' she asked. 'Have you seen any of these guys tonight?'

'One came in a while ago.'

'How long ago?'

'I don't know. Maybe an hour. He's the one . . . He put me here with the wires. He raped me on the bed, and then he made me stand here and he wired me and then he raped me again. He did it really rough that time, and made the wires stab me. It really hurt, and that's when I bit him. So then he taped my mouth.'

'You bit him, huh? Good for you.'

'But I couldn't breathe. I thought I was gonna suffocate.'

'You'll be fine.' Jane reached high and began to work on the wire under Gail's wrist. 'I'll have you out of here in just a minute.'

'Who are you?'

'Jane.'

'Are you with the police?'

'No.'

'I don't . . . how come you're here?'

'A very long story.'

'You saw the others, didn't you?'

'How many are there? All together?'

'Four. Including me. That I know of, anyway.'

'I saw the other three,' Jane said.

'They're really fucked up.'

'Yeah. So I noticed. Except Sandra. She's pretty much okay and she isn't nuts like the others. Maybe because they haven't started cutting her up yet. What sort of asylum is this, anyhow?'

She freed the wrist, and Gail lowered her arm.

'I'll get your legs,' Jane said, crouching. 'You get the wires up there. And keep an eye on the door. Anyone shows up, yell.'

'They . . . maybe they're in the show room?'

'What?' Jane looked up at her. Gail was unwinding an end of the wire across her throat.

'They've got a special room downstairs. It's like a movie theater. They've got one of those giant-screen TVs in there. They took us in and we watched *Saturday Night Fever* last night before the dance.'

'Downstairs?'

Jane thought about all the noise she'd made at the front of the house: ringing the doorbell, pounding the door, breaking the window.

What if they'd heard her and come to the door and let her in and pretended to be friendly and then had taken her by surprise and brought her to one of these rooms and . . . ?

Didn't happen. Don't think about it.

I could've ended up like . . .

Don't!

She finished with the wire across Gail's left thigh, then reached down for the ankle wire.

'Is it soundproof?' she asked.

'What?'

'That viewing room downstairs. Is it soundproof?'

'I don't know. Maybe.'

'Must be. If that's where they are.'

'It might be where they are,' Gail said.

'It would explain why nobody's shown up yet,' Jane said. 'Unless they went somewhere. God, I hope they went somewhere. If we can just get out of here before they come back . . .'

'Just the two of us?' Gail asked.

'No, we'll take Sandra.' Finished with the ankle, Jane shifted sideways and started to unfasten the wire at Gail's right thigh.

'She's awfully pregnant.'

'All the more reason to take her,' Jane said.

'She'll slow us down.'

'I'm not going to leave her.' Glancing up, she saw that Gail was done with the wire across her forehead and was busy with the one pinning her right wrist to the wall. 'You don't have to help.'

'That's okay. I'm sticking with you. Whatever you want.'

'Thanks.' Jane worked at the ankle. 'We'll have to leave the other two. I don't see how we could take them with us.'

'Anyway, they're crazy.'

'Yeah,' Jane said. 'Maybe it makes you crazy when you eat yourself. What we'll do, we'll try to make it to my car and we'll go somewhere and call the cops.'

'Let's call them from here.'

'If we have to. It'd be better to get away first. The sooner we're out of here, the better.' She drew the ankle wire out through the brass eye and looked up in time to see Gail shove the arm wire aside.

'That's it?' she asked, rising.

'That's it.' Gail stepped away from the wall and suddenly wrapped her arms around Jane and squeezed

342

her hard and began to sob. Jane kept her gun hand down. She put her other hand on Gail's back and stroked her gently. The skin of Gail's back felt slippery.

'It's all right,' she whispered. 'It's all right.'

'You . . . you saved me. I'll never forget . . . Oh, God, you'll never know . . .'

'We aren't out of here yet, Gail. Come on.' She eased Gail away from her. 'We've still gotta get Sandra.'

'I can't leave like this.' Sniffling, she wiped her eyes.

'Where're your clothes?'

'I don't know.'

'Just grab a sheet.'

Gail sniffed and nodded and stepped toward the bed. Where she'd been standing a moment ago, Jane saw the rough, body-shaped outline of the brass plates on the wall, the strands of barbed wire sticking out every which way.

Midway between the two brass plates that had held the wire across Gail's ribcage, a thick white envelope was tacked to the wall.

The sweat from Gail's back had smeared the ink of Jane's name.

Chapter Thirty-three

Jane tore the envelope from the wall. It felt soggy. She plucked the thumb-tacks out of each end, and tossed them aside.

'What's that?' Gail asked, wrapping a bedsheet around her shoulders. 'I felt something back there . . .'

'It's what I came for.'

The envelope was sealed, and seemed at least two inches thick.

'What's in it?'

Jane shook her head. Clamping the pistol between her knees, she folded the envelope to make a tight package around the money. Then she reached up beneath the hanging front of her shirt and shoved the envelope down the front pocket of her jeans.

Taking the pistol in her right hand, she rushed for the door. She crouched before peeking out.

The hallway looked clear.

'Let's go.' She walked quickly, watching the hall ahead, twisting around to check the rear.

Gail hurried along behind Jane. The bedsheet was wrapped around her shoulders, held together in front with both hands and trailing behind her like the train of a child's makeshift wedding gown. She had a very frightened look on her face, but she tried to smile when Jane glanced at her.

Sandra was braced up on her elbows when they entered her room. She gazed at them over the huge mound of her belly.

'We're getting out of here,' Jane said.

Sandra started to cry.

'What should I do?' Gail asked.

'Watch the hall,' Jane said. On her way to the bed, she switched the pistol to her left hand. With her right hand, she reached under the back of her shirt and pulled the knife from her belt.

She slipped the blade underneath the rope that stretched from Sandra's right ankle to the bed frame. Her hand was shaking very badly. The blade of her knife jittered under the taut rope.

'Anyone coming?' she asked.

'Not yet,' Gail said from the doorway.

Jane tried to sever the rope with a single quick upward tug. The rope jumped and jerked Sandra's foot off the mattress, then slipped off the tip of the knife and dropped Sandra's foot.

Jane saw the shallow cut and muttered, 'Shit.'

She started sawing at the rope.

She pictured herself a long-time prisoner here, a ruin like Linda, eating herself and wondering how it ever came to this. *It came to this because I didn't sharpen my knife. I could've done it so easily, too. If only I'd bothered.*

The rope parted. She leaped sideways and started on the other rope.

'Just a few more seconds,' she said.

'It's okay here,' Gail told her.

As she sawed at the rope, she looked up at Sandra. 'Will you be able to walk?'

'I don't know.' Sandra snuffled. 'My legs . . . I can't feel them.'

'They look okay – probably just asleep. Once you're up and moving, you'll be fine.'

Sandra bobbed her head. Her eyes were red and shiny, her face dripping. She had stopped crying, though. 'What about Marjorie and Linda?'

'We'll have to leave them.'

'Good.'

'Good?'

'They're so horrible.' She took a deep breath, making a high whiny noise that trembled. 'They're after my baby. They call out at night and say . . . awful things about eating it, like which parts they . . .'

'Got it!' Jane blurted as her knife popped up through the top of the rope. 'Let's move, let's go!'

Sandra pushed at the mattress. She sat up and stared at her legs. Then her lips stretched thin and twitched at the corners. 'I can't move them!'

'Don't worry.' Jane said. She called over her shoulder, 'Give us a hand.'

Gail nodded and hurried over.

Quickly, Jane slipped her knife under the belt at the back of her jeans. She set her pistol on the mattress by Sandra's right foot. She scowled at it. She hated not having it in her hand.

Gail had to let go of her sheet, and she let out a quiet little whimper as it slipped off her body.

They each took hold of an ankle.

Together, they swung Sandra's legs sideways and off the bed and lowered her feet to the floor. Then they took her by the upper arms and hauled her up. After she'd been standing for a few seconds, Jane said to Gail, 'You got her?'

'Yeah.'

'Right back.' She let go and hurried to the end of the

bed. With Gail and Sandra both watching over their shoulders, she picked up the fallen sheet, took out her knife again, and cut a straight, two-foot slash in its center.

'Neat idea,' Gail said.

'You want one, Sandra?'

'I guess. My legs are starting to . . . Oooo . . . Pins and needles . . . ow!'

Jane yanked the sheet off the bed and cut a slit for Sandra's head. She put her knife away, picked up her pistol, and carried the sheets to the women. One-handed, she helped Sandra and Gail into the garments.

With Sandra in the middle, her arms across the shoulders of Gail and Jane, they hurried across the room and into the hallway. Jane had taken the right side to keep her gun hand free, but now she regretted it; she was nearest the bedroom doors.

Though she kept her eyes forward, her peripheral vision saw into Marjorie's room, saw the remnants of the woman swaying in her harness above the bed.

'Hey!' Marjorie yelled, suddenly twisting and lurching.

'We'll send help for you,' Jane called. And took one more step that put Marjorie out of view.

'No! You can't take 'em! Hey! Sandra! Sandra, you get back to your room! Gail! Come back!' Then she shrieked, *They're getting away!*

With every shout from Marjorie, Sandra flinched rigid against Jane's side as if she were being lashed.

'It's okay,' Jane whispered.

Help! They're getting away!

'Make her be quiet!' Sandra begged.

Sure thing, Jane thought. 'We'll be out of here in a minute,' she said.

Linda! They're getting away!

347

Linda, at least, was staying quiet so far.

That's all we'd need, Jane thought – both of them yelling like a couple of maniacs.

At Linda's doorway, Jane looked in.

The bed was empty except for the plate and the gnawed hand. Jane swiveled her head to scan the room as she hurried by with Sandra and Gail. She saw no Linda.

'Where'd Linda go?' Gail asked.

'Who knows? At least she isn't yelling.'

Jane realized that Marjorie had stopped yelling. From the room down the hall came growls and snarls of rage, mixed in with squeaks and creaks and groans from the leather harness, and buckle sounds that clinked and jingled.

'Marjorie's going ape-shit,' she muttered.

Sandra gave her a quick, frantic grin, then looked back and yelled, 'You won't get my baby now, you crazy bitch!'

'That's what you think!'

Sandra faced front. She quickened her pace, rushing Jane and Gail along with her outstretched arms. In an odd, very high-pitched voice, she said, 'Shit?' as if asking a question.

'Should've kept your mouth shut,' Gail told her.

Realizing that Sandra had recovered the use of her legs, Jane said, 'I'll go first.' She dropped her arm from across Sandra's back, slipped free and hurried ahead.

The two seemed to get along fine without her.

At the top of the stairs, she studied the area below. She saw the foyer and the front door, dimly lighted by the wagon wheel chandelier.

She saw nobody.

She considered a quick dash down the stairs and out

348

the door. Such speed would be noisy, though. In spite of all the noise so far, she wanted silence now.

Besides, Sandra was enormously pregnant. Even with her legs recovered, she wouldn't be capable of much speed.

So Jane made her way slowly down the stairs, treading lightly, sometimes glancing back. Sandra and Gail, just behind her, seemed to be doing fine. In their bedsheets, they looked like overgrown urchins dressed as angels for some sort of skid-row Christmas pageant. Battered, wingless angels who were sweaty and haggard and scared.

And I'm leading them to safety, Jane thought.

Did Mog send me here to save them?

Nobody's saved yet.

At the bottom of the stairs, Jane hurried to the door and opened it and looked outside. The grounds looked the same as before: dark and empty.

She stepped back, swinging the door wide for Gail and Sandra. Then she followed them out onto the veranda and eased the door shut. 'My car's all the way at the bottom of the driveway,' she whispered. 'It's pretty far away. We'd better hurry. You go first, I'll cover the rear.'

She waited, watching them climb down the veranda stairs.

Hurry!

At any moment, headlights might push a pale glow into the darkness at the top of the driveway. Or the door might be flung open behind them.

Who knows where the bastards might come from!

And chase us down.

And take us back inside.

And oh God I don't want to think about it – just let us please make it to my car and get out of here – don't let 'em

*get us, please, please – as if God gives a rat's ass anyhow
or He wouldn't let scum like these filthy bastards ever get
born in the first place to do these things to people – or if
they have to get born at least He should stop them and
save all the poor innocent . . .*

'Wait,' she said, and stopped at the bottom of the
veranda stairs.

Gail and Sandra looked back.

With her left hand, Jane dug into the front pocket of
her jeans. She brought out her car keys. 'Catch.' She
tossed them to Gail. 'You two go on ahead. But watch out
and hide if a car comes along. Get off the driveway fast.
Hide in the trees. You'll be all right as long as you aren't
seen. My car's off to the right when you get to the bottom
of the driveway. A Dodge Dart. Get in and wait for me,
but if somebody else comes along, just take off – then get
the cops out here as fast as you can. I shouldn't be more
than five minutes, though.'

'What're you *doing*?' Gail asked.

'I lost my necklace.' She touched her neck. 'I think I
know where it happened.'

'Forget it,' Gail said. 'Don't go back in there.'

'Not for a necklace,' Sandra added. 'They might get
you if you go back in.'

'My name's engraved on it.'

Gail moaned. 'I'll come with you.'

'No. Do like I said, okay?'

'I think they're in there,' Gail said. 'Their movie might
be ending any second . . .'

'Then we'd all better hurry. Get going.' Jane turned
away. At the top of the veranda stairs, she looked back
and saw the sheeted women heading for the driveway.
She hurried to the front door.

Locked.

Of course.

So she entered the house through the window she'd used before. There was no longer a need for silence. She wanted to be quick about this, get it done and catch up with Gail and Sandra.

Either they're here or they're not.

She raced through the ground level of the house, checking doors.

In the living room, she found a black door to left of the fireplace. She turned its knob, eased the door wide enough to see the darkness on the other side, then opened it a bit wider and slipped in and gently shut it.

She stood with her back against the door.

She wished her heart would slow down. She wished she could get a big enough breath. Gasping for air, she used a sleeve to wipe the sweat out of her eyes. This room seemed even hotter than the rest of the house.

On the giant-screen TV at the end of the room, Barbra Streisand was belting out a song in a movie that looked like it might be *Funny Girl*. The volume was terribly high, the voice blasting.

No wonder the guys hadn't heard anything. Whether or not the room was soundproofed, the noise from their show would've been sufficient to overwhelm every other sound in the house.

Jane saw the silhouettes of three heads above the seat-backs of the front row.

Hail hail, the gang's all here.

They took up the center three seats of the first row, leaving an empty seat at each end. Jane counted six rows. Seating for an audience of thirty.

But the Show Room appeared to be empty except for these three.

So-vile and his buddies, she supposed.

In the light from the TV screen, Jane could see that the heads were facing the front. They had short hair.

Clean-cut fellas.

None turned around as she walked down the aisle.

When she got closer, she saw that their shoulders were bare.

No wonder, it's so damn hot in here.

She entered the second row of seats and crept in. From here, she had a fairly good side view of the three. They looked young, not much older than twenty. They looked ordinary. Though she could only see the left side of each face, she was fairly sure that she didn't know any of these men.

Each had a can of soda, and they took turns reaching into a big bowl of popcorn on the lap of the man in middle.

She shot the middle one first, the muzzle of her pistol an inch from the back of his head.

The shot came at a quiet place in the movie.

The heads of the two other men started to swing around.

She shot one in the temple. She aimed for the temple of the other but his head was still turning and her bullet punched through his left eye.

It was over very fast.

The one in the middle was still pitching forward by the time Jane finished her third shot. He wasn't wearing any pants. His soda can rolled toward the TV, flinging sudsy fluid. Somehow, the popcorn bowl positioned itself just right, so the top of his head jammed into it and he stayed that way on his knees with his butt in the air and his head in the bowl.

The one who'd taken the bullet in his temple simply slumped sideways as if to lean on an invisible companion in the neighboring seat. His can, up-ended on his lap, burbled soda onto his half-erect penis.

The one who'd been shot in the eye fell to the floor and landed on his side next to his friend. He looked as if he might be down there for a special perspective on his friend's stunt with the popcorn bowl. He still held onto his drink. He suddenly spasmed, crushing the can so it shot out a gush of soda.

Jane was pretty sure that all three men were dead.

She shot each of them one more time, to make sure.

Then she thumbed the release and slid the thin black magazine out of her pistol. She clamped the pistol between her thighs. With the empty magazine in her left hand, she used her right hand to scoop cartridges out of the pocket of her shirt.

Both of her hands felt cold and tingly. So did her face.

She tried to thumb a fresh cartridge into the top of the magazine. She dropped it, and tried with another. This one slipped from between her thumb and forefinger, and she jabbed her thumb on a sharp metal corner of the magazine.

'Ow!' She stuck the thumb in her mouth.

Forget it. They're all dead, anyway. I don't need the gun.

So she dumped the ammo into her pocket, the .22s tumbling against her breast and dropping to click against the others at the bottom of the pocket.

She took a last look at the three men.

Did I really do that?

Then she said, 'Fucking perverts,' turned away from them and walked to the aisle. There, she broke into a trot. She hadn't been very long at this. She might be able to overtake Gail and Sandra before they could reach her car.

At the rear of the Show Room, she shouldered the door open. While wiping the knobs on both sides with the loose front of her shirt, she wondered if there were other places where she had left fingerprints.

Probably.

My prints aren't on file, anyway.

What about hairs and threads and . . . ?

The only sure way to destroy every bit of physical evidence would be to burn the place.

No way, she told herself.

Finished with the door knobs, she rushed toward the foyer.

Burning the house might be a great idea, but she'd need to take Marjorie and Linda outside first, and she never wanted to *see* either of those women again, much less touch them, try to carry them . . .

And then she *did* see Linda.

Linda stood on her one leg, her back to the front door, and grinned at Jane. In her only hand, she held a big, shiny meat cleaver. 'Hi-dee ho,' she said.

Jane stopped. 'What's going on?'

'I've got the hungries.'

'It's all over, Linda. I'll be sending help for you and Marjorie as soon as . . .'

'We don't need no help, Janey. We get along jusssst fine. Fact is, I was about to help *myself* to Marjorie, but she's slim pickins at this stage, so . . . *HAPPY TRAILS!!!'*

As she shouted, she bumped her way off the door with her bare rump and lunged at Jane, hopping, hoisting the meat cleaver high.

Jane aimed the pistol at her face. *'FREEZE!'*

Though Linda couldn't know the gun was empty, she squealed with delight. She kept hopping forward on her single leg, bouncing closer and closer to Jane, swinging her cleaver in circles overhead, flapping her arm stump up and down, kicking her leg stump back and forth, giggling as she hopped, her one breast bobbing and swinging under her grimy 'I'M WITH STUPID' T-shirt.

Jane threw her pistol at Linda.

It seemed like such a dumb move. In every shoot-out she had ever seen on the screen, the bad guy who runs out of bullets throws his gun at the hero. The hurled weapon sails by. Or bounces harmlessly off the hero's shoulder.

Jane's pistol smacked Linda in the face. The blow knocked her head sideways and gashed her cheekbone. As the gun caromed off her face, her giggle changed to a cry of pain and she went backward – hopped a couple of times, waving her arm and swiping at the air with her stump. Then she slammed the floor with her back.

Jane leaped across her body and kicked her hand. The cleaver skidded away.

Linda flopped over onto her belly. She started to push herself up.

Jane kicked the arm out from under her.

Linda dropped hard, face striking the floor.

'Stay put!' Jane shouted.

Linda lay sprawled on the foyer floor, gasping and sobbing. Jane snatched up her pistol, then ran to the front door and jerked it open. As she used her shirt to wipe the inside knob, she said, 'I'll send help.'

She shut the door, wiped its outside handle, and raced for the driveway.

Chapter Thirty-four

She was huffing and sweaty by the time she reached her car. She found Gail behind the steering wheel and Sandra stretched out across the back seat. Gail swung the door open for her, then scooted over. Jane climbed in. The pistol in her back pocket pushed hard against her buttock, but she didn't feel up to doing anything about it. She fluttered the front of her shirt to stir some air against her hot skin.

'How'd it go?' Gail asked.

The engine was quietly idling. She shifted, and swung onto the road before answering. 'Okay.'

'You found it all right?'

Found what? she wondered. Ah! My non-existent necklace. 'Yeah. It was where I thought it'd be.'

'Did you run into anyone?' Sandra asked from the back seat. She sounded nervous.

'No. Thank God. Maybe the guys went out to a movie, or something. This *is* Saturday night.'

'Date night,' Sandra muttered. She sounded bitter.

'Like those bastards needed dates,' Gail said. 'They had a houseful of fucking slaves. You gonna turn your headlights on?'

'Oh.' Jane put them on. 'If we see a car come along, you'd better duck out of sight.'

'Don't let 'em get us again,' Sandra said.

'I won't.'

'They wanted my baby. That's why they took me. They were gonna dig a fire pit in the yard and do it like a pig – like . . .' She sobbed. 'Like a . . . Hawaiian thing . . . a luau. Steve . . . that's what he wanted to do, and Linda said she knew how, she'd lived on Maui and . . .' Then Sandra gave up trying to talk.

Jane glanced back at her, but quickly returned her gaze to the road. 'I never heard any news reports about you.'

'They grabbed her in Reno,' Gail said. 'That's why. It didn't make the news out here. They got Linda in Oregon and Marjorie in New Mexico.'

'You're the only local gal?' Jane asked.

'Yeah. One of them got the hots for me. He used to watch me at the store, he said. The B. Dalton at the mall?'

'Yeah.'

'He said that's why they picked me.'

'Are you all right back there, Sandra?'

The high, uncertain voice answered, 'Yeah.'

To Gail, she said, 'Where do you want me to take you?'

'Home?'

'Where do you live?'

'On Standhope.'

Brace's street.

She was vaguely surprised to find that she could feel pain and loss through the heavy daze that seemed to muffle her mind.

'Do you know where that is?' Gail asked.

'Yeah. I used to have a friend . . . Maybe I should take you to the hospital. You could both use some medical care.'

'I don't want a hospital,' she said.

357

'I wanta go home, too,' Sandra said.

'Do you have people in Reno?'

'My . . . husband.' She resumed crying hard.

Gail looked around at her. 'You can phone him from my place, if you want.'

'Phone the police first,' Jane told Gail. 'They've gotta get up to the house for Linda and Marjorie. Do you know the address?'

Gail shook her head. 'You can call the cops, okay? You'll come in with us . . .'

'I can't.'

'What?'

'I'm going to drop you two off and disappear. I can't get mixed up with cops and stuff.'

'You can't? How come?'

'Any sort of attention, and I'm . . . I ran away from my husband a few months ago. He used to . . . do terrible things to me. He'll kill me if he finds me. And I know he's looking. He even has private investigators searching for me. They check the newspapers . . . even a general description of me, and they'll figure it's a lead and come looking. If they have any idea where I am, they'll tell him and . . . God only knows what he'll do to me. I might be better off with Savile and his pals.'

'No, you wouldn't,' Gail said.

'I have to be kept out of this.'

'You saved our lives.'

'Looks that way.'

'I'll never do anything to hurt you.'

'Me neither,' Sandra said from the back seat, and snuffled.

'Why don't you say it was a guy who saved you?' Jane suggested.

'If that's what you want.'

'Sure,' Sandra said.

'But why were you there?' Gail asked. 'Why, really?'

'I went in to find the envelope. It has money in it. I was just after the money. I had no idea about any of the other things.'

'You didn't know we were there?'

'Nope.'

'So . . . you just found us by accident?'

'I'm not sure how much of an accident it was,' Jane said, 'on the part of whoever put the envelope there. You didn't see who put it there?'

'I felt it behind me, that's all. I didn't see it until you showed it to me.'

'The guy who wired you to the wall must've known it was there,' Jane said.

Or put it there, himself.

'Guess so.'

She suddenly wondered if Mog was one of the men she'd shot. She had always suspected that a mission would eventually bring her face-to-face with him, but . . .

If one of those guys was Mog, what was he doing butt-naked in the Show Room with his buddies watching a Streisand movie and stuffing his face with popcorn when he knew I'd be coming?

That didn't make any sense.

But the envelope had been in plain sight on the wall. The guy who wired up Gail couldn't possibly have missed it.

He had to be Mog.

No, not necessarily. The guy who put it there might've been following Mog's instructions.

But he might've been Mog.

'What did he look like?' Jane asked.

Gail shook her head. 'He wore a mask. One of those

359

leather masks with zippers. Red leather. It covered his whole head. It made him look like . . . an executioner.'

'What about the rest of him?'

'He was big. He was awfully big. Maybe six-four. And he was all muscles. His . . . he had a huge *thing*. I mean, it was terrible. It was way too big, but he . . . he managed.' Gail turned her head away and stared out the window.

'Are you sure about his size?'

'Are you kidding?'

Jane felt an odd tightness in her throat.

Even though she hadn't seen any of them standing up, she was certain that none of the three guys in the Show Room had been over six feet tall.

The man who'd fixed Gail to the wall with barbed wire was nobody Jane had shot.

I do believe that I'm about to scream.

Cut it out, she told herself. Whoever he was, wherever he might've been, you're away from him now. You're safe. We're all safe. No call for panic, here.

She stopped for a red light, and realized she was only a block or two away from Standhope Street. She looked over at Gail. 'Was there anything else about him? Tattoos, a birthmark, any sort of scars . . . ?'

Gail nodded.

'What?'

She looked at Jane and frowned. 'He didn't have any tan at all. None. A guy like that, you'd figure him for a sun-worshipper, you know? But he was white all over. It gave me the creeps.'

From the back seat, Sandra said, 'I never saw a guy like that.'

'I didn't either till tonight,' Gail said.

'He wasn't at the dances?' Jane asked.

'No, he sure wasn't. Or if he was, he must've been somewhere out of sight. I never laid eyes on him till he came into my room . . . a couple of hours before you showed up.'

'Man,' Jane muttered. 'He's *gotta* be the one who put the envelope there.'

'I just hope to God I never see him again.'

Slowing as she approached Standhope, she asked, 'Which way?'

'Go right.'

Right. Away from Brace's apartment. Thank God.

'It'll be a few more blocks,' Gail told her.

'Do you live with somebody?'

'My folks. They're probably out of their minds. They probably think I'm dead. Look, couldn't you come in and meet them? I mean, you saved my life. They'll really want to meet you.'

'Not tonight. The fewer people who see me . . . Maybe I'll get in touch with you sometime after all this has blown over.'

'That'd be great.'

'Remember about saying I'm a man, okay?'

'I won't forget,' Gail said.

'Me neither,' Sandra said.

'And don't tell what kind of car I drive. Say it's some other kind. How about a Jeep Cherokee?'

'That sounds good. What color?'

'Black.'

'Okay.'

From the back seat, Jane heard, 'A black Jeep Cherokee.'

'Do we know your name?' Gail asked.

'No. The fewer things you need to lie about, the better. The cops'll ask you what I look like, so maybe you should just describe me the way I am – except turn me into a male.'

The sound of a small laugh came from Gail. 'That's pretty good. Do you do this sort of thing a lot?'

'Not really.' Jane slowed and turned a corner.

'Hey.'

'I know.' She swung to a curb in front of a dark house and killed her headlights. 'I want to let you off here.'

'We're still two blocks . . . Oh. Yeah. I get it. This'll be fine.'

'I'd like to drop you off at your door, but . . .'

'No, this is great.' She turned toward Jane. 'I think . . . I'd like us to be friends. It isn't just what you did. There's something about you that . . . hell, you're gonna start thinking I'm a lesbian or something . . .'

'Not that there's anything wrong with it.'

Gail laughed. 'Right. But I'm not. But I really like you. I sort of feel like we might have a lot in common, or . . . I don't know.'

'I know. And I think you're right.'

'So . . . is there a way for me to get in touch?'

'I'll get in touch with you. Don't worry, I know your name and where you work. And almost where you live.'

'Okay, then.'

'Okay.'

Gail reached over and squeezed Jane's wrist. 'Take care.'

'You, too.' She looked over her shoulder. 'You too, Sandra.'

'Thanks. And thanks for getting me out of there.'

Gail climbed out of the car and opened a rear door. As she helped Sandra out, Jane said, 'Remember to lie for me, gals.'

'You bet,' Gail said.

'Yeah,' said Sandra. 'And thanks again.'

'My regards to the hubby.'

Sandra laughed in a way that sounded almost happy. Then Gail shut the door.

As they started across the street, Jane swung away from the curb. She watched them in the side mirror. In the white bedsheets, they looked like a couple of overgrown trick-or-treaters out in ghost costumes on the wrong night.

Chapter Thirty-five

Back on Standhope, she drove in the direction of the Royal Gardens apartment complex.

I won't even stop, she told herself. I'll just take a look at the place, just to . . . Why? Just to torture myself? Just to rub it in how I lost him and now when I really need someone – not *someone*, Brace – now when I need him, I can't go to him?

I don't need him. Hope he rots, the filthy son-of-a-bitch. Him and his cute little teeny-bopper slut.

As she drove along, she realized that her right buttock hurt from the imprint of the pistol. Shifting her weight, she reached back, pulled the weapon out of her pocket, and sighed. She tucked it between her thighs.

Could always reload and pay them a visit, she thought. Blow 'em both away. No big deal, just running up the score a bit.

It made her feel sick to think about it, even in a joking way. *I don't want to shoot anybody! It was bad enough shooting those three . . .*

A block from the Royal Gardens, she turned off Standhope and headed for home.

She supposed she ought to get rid of the gun. If she kept it, she might end up using it again. Besides, she was in danger from the law as long as she had the murder weapon in her possession. *The Godfather* movie had taught her that. And the lesson had been reinforced by plenty of other movies, and scads of crime novels. It was a physical link to the shootings. Being caught with it could mean real trouble.

But what if I need it?

I won't need it, she told herself.

So how do I get rid of it? she wondered. Throw it off the bridge? Right, so Rale or Swimp or some kid can fish it out of the creek and use it on someone? Toss it in a dumpster? Bury it? Gotta think of a way to dispose of the thing so nobody'll have a chance of ever finding it.

Best way to make sure nobody gets their hands on it, she thought, is to keep it myself.

I don't want it! What if I use it again?

I won't, she told herself. I'd just better keep it. That way, I'll know who has it.

Besides, no telling how Mog got the pistol in the first place. What if he went to a gun shop and bought it under my name? Could he do that? Hell, why not? He gets into my locked house and writes on me whenever he gets the urge, shouldn't be any big trick putting my name on a few government forms.

I'd damn well *better* hang on to the thing.

If I get rid of the ammo . . .

Up the street, a car was parked at the curb in front of her house. It looked very much like Brace's old Ford.

Even before she spotted Brace, she knew that it *was* his car. It had to be his. He'd come to see her, and she was about to face him and she suddenly felt squirmy and hot deep down.

I don't need this. Oh, God. What does he want? Why tonight? I don't need this. I don't!

As she steered into the driveway, her headlights swept across Brace. He was sitting on the front stairs, leaning way back with his elbows on the stoop.

Jane moaned.

To find Brace here seemed almost more strange and dream-like than what had happened back at the house on Mayr Heights.

She climbed out of her car and approached him. She felt sick with despair and hope. Brace stood up as she walked toward him.

'What do you want?' she heard herself ask as she stopped in front of him. Her voice sounded far away and cold. She felt as if her whole body were trembling, inside and out.

Brace stepped forward and put his hands on her upper arms. His touch made Jane flinch.

'Don't,' she said.

Instead of letting go, he held her and moved up close against her.

'Damn it!' She shoved him away.

This time, he did let go. He took a step backward and frowned at her. 'I don't care about your game,' he said, his voice soft. 'You can run around chasing Mog's envelopes from now till hell freezes over, I'll go along with it. I'll worry like crazy every time you step out of the house for one of your missions, but I won't get in your way. I won't let it come between us. The past week has been . . . I was fine before I met you, but . . .' He shook his head. 'I can't get along without you – not now, not any more.'

They were the sort of words she would've longed to hear – before watching Brace with the girl. Now, they seemed like a mockery.

'You looked like you were doing just fine Monday night,' she said.

He looked confused.

'You and your cute little teeny-bopper slut.'

'What?'

'You're not the only one who can sneak around and spy on people.'

As he shook his head, a corner of his mouth turned up. 'You spied on me, huh? Well, I suppose I deserved it. But what is it that you saw?'

'You know damn well what I saw.'

'Me and my "cute little teeny-bopper slut"?'

'You got it, pal.'

'When was this?'

'Oh, come on. You don't remember? What is it, an everyday occurrence, slipping it to your students?'

'Is that what you think you saw?'

'It's what I did see.'

'I don't see how.'

'It was easy. You should've been more careful about closing your curtains.'

Brace's jaw suddenly dropped.

'Ah. You do remember.'

'This was Monday night, around one or two in the morning?'

'Now you've got it.'

'*You're* the one she saw in the window.'

Jane sneered. 'Yeah, me.'

'You scared the hell out of half the people in the building. You're lucky the cops didn't get you.'

'You called the cops?'

'I didn't, personally. Dennis made the call.'

'Dennis?'

'Lois's husband.'

'Lois?'

'The one who saw you. You *really* gave her a scare. I went down to their place just after it happened, and she

367

was hysterical. She thought you were a guy, for one thing. And she said you looked insane.'

Jane shook her head. 'What're you trying to . . . ?

'They were . . . actually going at it when you looked? No wonder she was so upset. But how could you mistake Dennis for me? We might be about the same size, but the resemblance sure stops there.'

'You trying to say it wasn't you?'

'Of course it wasn't me. You didn't see what you thought you saw, Jane.' He smiled slightly. 'So you thought it was me "slipping it" to Lois. That's what you get for spying.'

'I saw you.'

'Not my face, obviously. Or if you did, your mind must've been playing tricks on you.'

Jane gazed at him. 'I know it was you,' she said. She *had* seen his face. True, the girl's back had been in the way most of the time, but . . .

'They *were* in my old apartment. We traded when they got married, so they could be down by the pool.'

'You traded?'

'It was all on the up and up.'

Jane blinked.

What is going on? she wondered. What is this? Has everything gone crazy?

'Oh, man,' Brace said. 'I gave you that business card, didn't I? It still shows me living in number twelve, so that's where you . . . I'm in twenty-two now. I'm directly above twelve. It never occurred to me that you might come over on your own, especially not after you'd dumped me.'

She heard herself say, 'What about your mail boxes?'

'What about them?'

'Did you trade mail boxes?'

He frowned and tilted his head a bit like a curious dog. 'You were going by the mail boxes. Ah. Well. We thought it'd be a lot easier all around if we just kept our same mail boxes. We didn't feel like getting into that whole change-of-address hassle . . .' Brace's smile returned. 'See what happens when you go sneaking around and you don't really know what's going on?'

'I'm supposed to believe this?'

'Yes.'

'Why?'

'Because I would never lie to you.'

'How do I know that?'

'Take my word for it.'

'Yeah. Sure.'

'Let's take a little drive. I'll introduce you to Lois and Dennis.'

'Are you kidding?'

'Or you could just look in the window at them.'

'Very funny.'

He checked his wristwatch. 'They're probably still up. Let's give them a call on the phone.'

'Okay.'

Brace followed her to the front door. She unlocked it and entered. As she let him in, she thought, Why bother calling? I didn't see his face. It happened the way he said, and I know it.

But she led the way to the end table and stood by the phone.

He picked it up and dialed for directory assistance.

'You mean you didn't trade phone numbers while you were at it?' she asked.

Boy, I can be such a bitch.

Yeah, and you should see me with a gun.

369

'Donnerville,' he said into the phone, and smiled at Jane.

'I'd like a number for a Dennis Dickens.' He nodded, then punched the cut-off button and dialed. 'Hope I don't catch him in the middle of "slipping it" to her.'

Jane snarled.

Brace chuckled. 'Hi! Dennis! . . . Yeah. Hey, sorry to bother you at this hour . . . Good. Look, remember your peeping maniac a few nights ago? . . . Wanta talk to her?'

'No!' Jane blurted.

'No,' Brace said into the phone, 'I'm not kidding. Remember when I was telling you about Jane? . . . Yeah, the librarian . . . No, I'm not kidding. She thought she was spying on me. And she's been mighty upset to think that whatever you were doing to Lois was what I was doing.'

How can he be telling all this to some guy I don't even know?

Because he doesn't lie, that's how.

'Would you talk to her?' Brace nodded and grinned and reached toward Jane with the handset.

She shook her head wildly from side to side.

Into the phone, Brace said, 'She's pretty embarrassed about all this.'

'Give it to me,' she muttered, and snatched away the handset. 'Hello?'

'So you're the one who caused all the excitement, huh?' The voice of Dennis sounded amused.

'I guess so. I'm awfully sorry.'

'Well, it sure perked things up around here.'

Things were mighty perky before I got there, she thought.

And she felt herself blush, remembering what she'd seen through the window.

370

That was this guy.

This guy, not Brace.

Apparently.

'What apartment number *are* you in?' she asked.

'Twelve. I used to be upstairs, and Brace had this place. He sort of traded with me for a wedding present.'

'How long have you lived there?'

'Still checking up on him, huh?'

'I guess so.'

'Don't bother. The guy is crazy about you. He's been a basket case for the last week. If you've got any sense, you'll get back together with him.'

'What're you, his PR man?'

'I know him, that's all. He's such a good guy it makes the rest of us look like shit, if you'll pardon the expression.'

'So, how long *have* you been living in apartment twelve?'

'It'll be exactly a month, tomorrow.'

'Would you tell me . . . I'm sorry, but . . . I've been through so much weirdness lately, I just hardly know what's going on any more.'

'I'll help any way I can. You know, I wanta see Brace happy, and . . .'

'What was going on in your place when I looked in the window?'

He hesitated. 'For starters, we were bare-ass naked. We'd been . . . fooling around, you know. And we no sooner got done than Lois realized the curtains weren't shut all the way. That's when she got up to pull them shut. She was right up there at the window and there you were . . . It was you, huh?'

'Yeah. I'm afraid so.'

'She said you snarled like a maniac.'

'I was pretty upset. I'm awfully sorry, though.

Will you tell her how sorry I am?'

'Want to talk to her?'

'No, that's all right. Thanks. I've gotta go, now. Goodnight.' She hung up.

Brace raised his eyebrows. 'Well?'

'How do I know you didn't coach him?'

'It's possible. Anything's possible. Didn't you once say something like, "When anything's possible, nothing makes sense?"'

'Did I?'

'I believe so. But the thing is, I had no idea the Peeping Tom might be you.'

'Maybe you saw me.'

He shook his head. 'I didn't see you. I had no idea who it was until you told me about it a few minutes ago – which didn't give me much of an opportunity to coach Dennis.'

Jane stepped away from him. She slumped on the couch, kicked off her shoes, and put her feet on the coffee table. She rubbed her face. 'I'm so wasted,' she muttered.

'Maybe I should leave, now – give you some time by yourself to figure things out. You can give me a call later, if you want . . . or drop by and see exactly who is living where.'

Still rubbing her face, she said, 'No. Don't go.' She raised her head. 'Everything's . . . don't leave me. Okay?'

He sat down beside her and reached an arm across her shoulders.

'I'm such a mess,' she muttered. 'It's good to have you back, though.'

'I *am* back?'

'As far as I'm concerned.'

He gently squeezed her shoulder. 'So what else has

been going on? You're still playing along with Mog?'

She reached into the front pocket of her jeans, clutched the thick block of paper and pulled. It was in there very tight against her thigh, but she felt it move a bit. Slowly, she was able to drag it out.

'Is that money?'

'I think so.' She unfolded the envelope and tore it open, revealing a small brick of bills wrapped in a sheet of paper. She tossed the paper aside. With her thumb, she riffled the bills.

'Good Lord,' Brace said.

'More than fifty thousand bucks,' Jane told him.

'What'd you have to do for it?'

She hesitated, then said, 'Break into a house.'

'An abandoned place like . . . ?'

'No. A big expensive place up on Mayr Heights.' She watched him. 'Do you know where that is?'

'Mayr Heights? Yeah. The head of the English department lives up there.'

'His name isn't Savile, is it?'

'Ketchum.'

'Well, that's where I had to go tonight. To a house up there. But I didn't think anyone was home. I rang the doorbell, and knocked, and everything. Nobody heard any of that – luckiest thing that ever happened to me, probably. Anyhow, I had to break in through a window. I planned to pay for it, leave a few hundred bucks behind to make everything all right.'

She saw the look on Brace's face.

'I know, I know, the money wouldn't have *really* made everything all right. But at least it would've paid for having the window fixed.'

'True. So what happened next?'

'If you're bothered by a little matter like breaking a

window, I'd better stop right there.'

'It gets worse?'

'I'd say so, yeah.'

He looked into her eyes as if studying them. Then he said, 'You don't have to tell me.'

'I don't think I can. Not right now. Is that all right?'

'It's fine,' he said, rubbing her shoulder.

'The thing is, I'm done with it all. It went . . . way too far. So you won't have to worry about me going out to strange places in the middle of the night. Never again.' She stuffed the thick stack of bills back inside the envelope and tossed the envelope onto the coffee table. It landed near her feet with a solid *whop*.

'Let's just find out,' she said, 'where I *won't* be going.' She picked up the note, spread it open, and held it over to her right so that Brace could see it, too.

She started to read it.

And felt heat rush through her body.

I must be nuts letting Brace read this!

My dear Jane,

No pain, no gain, as the body-builders say. Your body, I must say, is coming along splendidly.

I can think of some sweeties who would give an arm and a leg to be in your condition. Ho ho ho ho ho.

Please don't think too unkindly of their keepers. Boys will be boys, you know.

Hope you get out of here in one piece.

Tomorrow night, take a refreshing dip in John's pool. You'll feel like a new woman.

Love and kisses
and licks
MOG

She smashed it into a tight, hard ball and hurled it across the room.

'What's this stuff about women with keepers?' Brace asked.

Jane shook her head. 'I just don't feel up to . . . it'll probably be in the papers, tomorrow. And on the radio and TV news . . . the whole nine yards. Why don't we wait and talk about it then? Okay? I'm just too wasted. I'd probably go haywire if I had to talk about it tonight. But it's over. It went too far. There's not enough money in the world to make me go to that pool tomorrow night. Wherever it is.'

A corner of Brace's mouth curled upward. 'Bet I know where it is.'

'Well, don't tell me. It'll make it easier not to go there if I don't know where I'm supposed to go.'

Brace laughed softly. 'I won't tell.'

'Good.' She swung her legs off the coffee table and leaned forward, elbows on her thighs. 'I'd better get out of these,' she mumbled, and let her head droop. 'A nice shower.'

She felt Brace's hand roaming over her back, rubbing her gently through the heavy fabric of her shirt. Then he was rubbing the nape of her neck. She moaned.

'In a little while,' she mumbled.

Feeling almost too weary and comfortable to move, she turned sideways and lifted her legs onto the sofa and sank backward. Head on Brace's lap, she stretched out her legs.

'Were you . . . going somewhere?' she managed to ask.

'No,' he said. 'It's all right. You're fine right here. Just rest.'

Jane woke up and tried to scream, but her mouth wouldn't

open. The scream became a siren muffled inside her head as she searched the black night with eyes sealed shut, as she writhed on her back unable to move her arms or legs, as she felt the blade slicing her, the blood spilling.

What's happening? What's happening?

Where am I?

Where's Brace?

Why isn't he stopping this?

Maybe he's the one doing it!

She willed herself to stop screaming. And fought to suck in air through her nostrils. And tried not to think about the blade carving trails of raw pain in the space between her ribcage and navel.

Chapter Thirty-six

'JANE!' The agonized bellow startled Jane awake. She opened her eyes. The bedside lamp was on. Squinting against its brightness, she saw Brace rush toward her.

She had never seen him looking so terrified.

It scared her.

He stopped beside the bed and gazed at her, gazed at the area below her chest where she felt strangely stiff and burning. He was shaking his head. His hands were raised in front of him. He looked like a guy who had just dropped a priceless vase, watched it explode on the floor, and couldn't come close to believing he'd been so clumsy and lost so much.

Wanting to see how bad it was, Jane propped herself up with her elbows.

And joined Brace in staring at her body.

It came as no surprise that she was naked. But she'd expected to find her torso coated with blood. The cutter had obviously mopped up after himself; her skin was clean except for the handprints and the word.

He must've dipped his hands in her blood, then placed them on her breasts and hips and thighs – being careful to leave clear, unsmeared prints. They were extremely large hands.

The word across her midriff was no longer bleeding.

Its four big letters were made of slits that looked juicy inside but not very deep. The only letters she recognized at first were those at each end – the Y beneath her right breast and the O beneath her left.

Her mind reversed all four letters, and she understood Mog's message.

She almost told Brace that he needed to turn the letters around in his head. If she told him, though, he might figure out that she'd learned the trick by studying previous messages. She didn't want him to know about any of that.

'What does it say?' she muttered.

Brace, frowning, shook his head. 'I don't . . . I can't think. This is . . . Who *did* this to you?'

'Mog. It has to be Mog.'

'God!' he cried out.

'Take it easy, okay?' She tried to smile. '*I'm* the one who got cut up around here.'

'The bastard!'

'Shhh.' She frowned down at her word. 'It looks sort of . . . backwards.'

'We've gotta call the cops.' Glancing about the room, Brace muttered, 'Do you have a phone in here?'

'No cops,' Jane said.

'We *gotta* call the cops.'

'No, we don't.'

'He butchered you! The bastard butchered you!'

'I'm not butchered. I'll be all right. This was just a warning . . . whatever it says.'

Brace stepped out of the way as Jane sat up and swung her legs off the bed. She felt shaky. She walked slowly past him until she was standing in front of the full-length mirror. The first thing she noticed was the blood on her neck and face. More prints from Mog. Her stomach gave a nasty little twist. These weren't fingerprints.

Mog must've kissed her a dozen times with lips that he'd dipped in her blood.

Brace came to her side and she saw him looking at her reflection. She turned her own eyes to the word carved across her midsection:

OBEY

Brace was looking at the word, but also shifting his gaze up and down.

He's checking me out, she thought.

Don't be an idiot, he's inspecting the damage.

In the mirror, she saw that his shirt was untucked. It draped the front of his gray trousers. She quickly lifted her gaze to his face.

It was slack, flushed.

Is he shocked or turned on? she wondered. Or maybe both.

'How could he do this?' Brace asked, his voice husky and quiet.

'I'm sure he enjoyed it.'

'But I was just in the other room. I never heard anything.'

'I screamed.'

He shook his head. 'I didn't hear you. God, I'm sorry. If I hadn't fallen asleep . . .'

'That's okay,' Jane said. 'It wasn't much of a scream.' She turned away from the mirror. Bloodstains on the sheet formed a general outline of her body. Off to one side were a couple of wadded silvery clumps. 'Duct tape,' she said. 'My mouth and eyes were taped shut. My hands and feet must've been tied – I couldn't move them.' The only foreign articles on the mattress were the wads of duct tape. She looked at her wrists. No sign of having been bound.

Walking slowly around the bed, she looked for other indications of what might've happened.

She found no ropes, no cords, nothing that might've been used to bind her.

She did find her royal blue pajamas on the floor at the far side of the bed. She picked them up. The buttons were missing from the front of the shirt. From the neatly sliced appearance of the thread clusters, she guessed that buttons had been shaved off – no doubt by the same blade that had scribed OBEY on her skin.

As she slipped into the shirt, she asked, 'Was I wearing these pajamas?'

Brace shook his head. 'I don't know.'

'Must've been. But I thought I fell asleep on the sofa.'

'Yeah. You zonked right out. But then you woke up at about two o'clock and went to your room. You were still in your jeans and that big heavy shirt when you left.'

Stepping into her pajama pants, she tried to remember. Couldn't. 'What else happened?'

'You were really out of it,' Brace said. 'You know, disoriented. Like you didn't know what you were doing on the sofa. You don't remember?'

'Not really.'

'Actually, I thought you were planning to come back. You mumbled something about getting comfortable, and went staggering off. I stayed on the sofa. I heard your bedroom door shut. But I kept thinking you'd come back in a few minutes. Then I must've dozed off, myself.'

'And you didn't hear anything at all?'

'No,' he said. He looked miserable. 'God. I slept right through it.'

Jane felt herself grimace. 'I slept through some of it, myself. I guess the pain when he started cutting woke me up. I couldn't move. I could hardly breathe.' She found herself gasping now, as if the memories were robbing her of air.

Brace came around the bed and put his arms around her. He pulled her gently toward him. Jane wrapped her arms around him. They embraced, his body pressing solid and warm against her, but not quite touching the sore area where Mog had sliced his command. Jane pressed her face into the curve of his neck. She felt his hands glide slowly up and down the back of her pajama shirt.

After a long time, he murmured, 'I'll never let anyone touch you again.'

She knew he meant it. But she doubted that Brace – or anyone else – would be able to protect her from Mog.

'Don't think about it,' she whispered.

'You could've been killed.'

'I wasn't. He just wanted to hurt me.'

'He doesn't want you to quit the game.'

'No shit, Sherlock.'

Brace laughed softly, blowing a few small puffs of breath through her hair. She kissed the side of his neck.

'Maybe you'd better do what he wants,' Brace said.

'No. It has to end.'

'But he'll keep at you. He won't stop at this. If he's nuts enough to sneak into your room and cut *words* into your skin, he's . . . he'll keep at you until you cave in and do what he wants.'

Jane eased backward a bit and looked up into Brace's eyes. 'I've got news for Mog,' she said. 'I don't cave. The Game's over.' In a loud voice, she said, 'Do you hear that, Mog? The Game's over. You can whittle on me from now till Hell freezes over – I'm done with following your orders.'

'Do you think he can hear you?' Brace asked.

'Wouldn't surprise me. The way he comes and goes.'

Narrowing his eyes, Brace stared past the top of Jane's head as if studying the far corners of the ceiling. 'We'd better call the cops,' he said. 'Maybe they can find him.'

'No.'

'Yes. Look what he's done to you, Jane. It was different when he was just sneaking around and giving you money . . . he's committed a real crime now. It's gotta be at least assault with a deadly weapon. They can put him away for that.'

'They can put me away for murder,' Jane said, and watched Brace's eyes react.

They might look the same way if she suddenly shoved her switchblade into his belly.

She stepped away from him. 'But go ahead and call the cops, if that's what you want. I have to take a shower.'

He stood there, stiff and hunched over slightly, and watched her walk out of the bedroom.

The strong hot spray of the shower made her cuts burn, but it felt wonderful everywhere else. With a bar of soap, she scrubbed away the bloody handprints and rubbed her face to take off the marks put there by Mog's lips.

She wondered if Brace would call the police.

She doubted it.

Such a damn straight arrow, though, he just might do it.

She could hear him now. *As much as I care for you,*

Jane, I can't condone murder. You left me no choice but to turn you in.

Her back to the spray, she blinked water out of her eyes and looked down. The scratches and bruises from the dog attack had finally gone away, just in time to leave her skin unblemished for Mog's assault with the blade. She saw, however, that she'd gotten all the handprints off. Her skin looked shiny and clean except for the raw, carved letters.

I look pretty good, she thought. *Pretty* good? Better than ever. Thanks to all that exercise and some sunlight – and several days with almost no appetite at all thanks to Mog and Brace.

She supposed she had been thinner, years ago, but she had never been in such good shape.

Now, if Mog'll just quit cutting on me . . .

She set the bar of soap in the small tray by the side of the tub, then took a step, bent down, and reached for her plastic bottle of shampoo. As she wrapped her fingers around the slippery sides of the bottle, the door behind her skidded open.

She gasped. Letting go of the shampoo, she straightened up fast and turned around.

Brace stepped halfway into the tub. He looked at her and raised his eyebrows. 'Just say the word, and I'll leave.'

Jane didn't say the word.

He brought his other leg into the tub and slid the glass door shut. His body blocked the spray.

Jane went to him.

She halted when her belly met his erection.

His hands cupped her shoulders, and a smile fluttered at the corners of his mouth. 'I decided it wouldn't be wise to let you out of my sight. No telling where the enemy might be lurking.'

'Did you hear what I told you?' she asked.

'You killed someone,' Brace said.

'Aren't you going to turn me in for it?'

'Not a chance.' He put his hands on her breasts.

She took a quick, shuddery breath.

'I know you,' he said. 'If you did it, it was the only thing to do.'

'Oh, God.' She moved in, feeling him prod her and slide upward. She winced as one of her cuts was rubbed – part of the E, she guessed – but she didn't back away. She pressed herself more tightly against Brace. In spite of the slight pain from the pressure against her slit skin, she liked how she could feel the whole length of him straight up against her belly and know that he was this hard and this thick because of her.

Then she had the hot spray in her face and Brace was crouched, hands everywhere on her buttocks and the backs of her legs while he kissed and licked and sucked her breasts.

She pushed her fingers through his hair. She squirmed.

At the end, he had her back pinned to the slick tile wall and only the tips of her toes were touching the bottom of the tub. He was all up inside her. His thrusting jolted her, lifted her off her toes. The tiles slid up and down against her back and rump.

When they climbed out of the tub, Brace spread a towel over the bathmat and helped her to lie down on it.

OBEY was bleeding.

Parts of it had been bleeding for quite a while. A few times, Brace had gasped, 'We'd better stop,' and, 'We'd better take care of that.'

But she'd told him, 'It's all right.' She hadn't wanted

anything to be stopped, or even interrupted.

She supposed she must've said, 'It's all right,' about one thing or another ten or twelve times while they'd been in the tub.

Now, he said, 'Is it okay to use the washcloth?'

And she said, 'It's all right.'

Up on her elbows, she watched Brace spread a white washcloth across OBEY. He was squatting by her side, naked and dripping. On the cloth, specks of blood began to appear.

Brace shook his head. 'The washcloth'll probably be ruined.' Water falling off his chin tapped Jane near the hip.

'It's all right,' she said. She smiled.

Brace met her eyes and smiled. 'Is that all you know how to say?'

She nodded.

'We should've stopped. It's my fault you're bleeding again.'

'It's all right.'

He returned his gaze to the washcloth. 'I don't know what got into me,' he said.

'I know what got into *me*.'

'Funny.'

'That's me.'

'Not to mention I didn't . . . use anything.'

'It's all right,' she said.

'That's what you kept telling me.'

'It's still true.'

'You don't believe in . . . practicing safe sex?'

'I haven't been practicing *any* sex.'

'Well, that makes two of us.'

'So,' she said, 'the worst that can happen is we get a baby.'

'A baby?'

'You know. One of those little people.'

'Oh.'

'It's not terribly likely, though. I think we're safe . . . for now.'

She looked down at the washcloth. The specks had grown into bright red dots, but the dots formed only small bits of lines and curves.

'Doesn't look like you're in any danger of bleeding to death,' Brace said. He peeled off the washcloth and studied the wounds. 'We ought to put some disinfectant on here. And bandage you.'

'In the medicine cabinet,' she told him.

The hydrogen peroxide felt chilly when he poured it on her middle. It gave her goosebumps. It went white and fizzy wherever it touched her cuts.

She sent Brace into her bedroom for the bandage. He came back with a big red bandanna from her dresser drawer. Folded lengthwise into thirds, it formed a pad that completely covered OBEY. Brace fixed it in place with long strips of adhesive tape.

By the time they left the bathroom, the sun was up. Jane gave her robe to Brace. It fit him fine. She wore a big, loose T-shirt. They made coffee, and took their mugs into the living room. They sat on the sofa, close enough together so that their sides touched.

'I guess I'd better tell you about last night,' she said.

'If you want to.'

'You want to know about it, don't you?'

'I want to know *everything* about you.'

'My favorite color?'

'Everything.'

'Right now, I'd better stick with the stuff about last night.'

She began to tell him about it. When she came to the part about the women, he went pale and stopped drinking his coffee and kept turning his head to look at her. Finally, she told about sneaking into the Show Room and shooting the three men.

Brace gave her thigh a gentle squeeze. He kept his hand there, caressing her. 'I don't know how you could do something like that.'

'It was easy.'

'Jane, the jury.'

'Yeah. Me and Mike Hammer. But I had to do it. I had to make sure they wouldn't come after us. That was part of it. And it was partly to protect the two we had to leave behind. Once the guys knew there'd been an escape, no telling what they might've done to Linda and Marjorie. Anyway, they didn't deserve to live. Not after what they'd done.'

'I don't know,' Brace said. 'I'm just awfully sorry you had to do it.'

'You and me both. But if I'd just left . . . everything would've been my fault from then on. You know? They would've gotten away, I'm sure of it. And it would've all been on me, everybody they hurt or killed from then on.'

'I hope you really believe that,' Brace said.

'I do.'

'Because it's a big thing, killing someone. Maybe it's the biggest thing there is. To carry with you.'

'Have you done it?'

'No. I'm not sure if I could.'

'You could.'

'Probably.'

'I bet you would've killed Mog if you'd caught him carving on me last night.'

'I bet I sure would've tried.' His hand tightened on her thigh. 'We've got to figure out how to protect you tonight.'

'Yeah. I know. Are you hungry?'

'Are you kidding?'

Chapter Thirty-seven

Together in the kitchen, they made themselves breakfast. While bacon sizzled in the skillet, they leaned against counters across from each other and sipped coffee. Sunlight coming in through the window above the sink cast a glare on the linoleum floor and lit Brace to the knees. Where the sunlight touched him, it made his hair glint golden. Most of his left leg showed because of how the robe hung away from it. But only the bottom part was sunlit.

Jane stared at his legs as she drank coffee and told about how Linda had attacked her on the way out of the house last night.

'My God, you saved her and she did that!'

'I think she's warped in the head. Who wouldn't be, you know?'

'What do you think she did after you left?' Brace asked, and sipped his coffee. The kitchen smelled wonderful because of the bacon.

'I don't know. I suppose the police have her, now. She's probably been hospitalized, don't you suppose? She and Marjorie?'

'If she didn't . . . do something to Marjorie.'

'I know.'

'You thought about that?'

'It's crossed my mind. I didn't want to kill her, though.

If she went back upstairs for Marjorie . . . I hope she didn't, but . . . I don't know. I just don't know.' She turned away and checked the bacon. It looked ready, so she lifted the skillet off the stove and carried it over to the counter by Brace and forked out each strip of bacon onto a paper towel.

Waiting for the bacon grease to cool down, she helped Brace get started with the toast. Then she put him in charge of it. She took four eggs out or the refrigerator and cracked them on the edge of the skillet. None of the yolks broke. The clear jell surrounding the yolks grew white and solid quickly from the bottom upward without a crisp brown rim forming around the edges, so she knew the grease was right. She stood over the eggs, using her spatula to flip grease over their tops until the yolks turned creamy yellow and nothing on the whites looked like phlegm anymore.

By the time the eggs were done, Brace had finished with the toast. Two buttered slices on each plate.

Jane slipped an egg on top of each slab of toast. Brace added the bacon strips.

They carried their plates to a small round table at the end of the kitchen. Then they scurried about, gathering utensils and napkins, salt and pepper. With fresh mugs of coffee, they sat at the table.

They ate for a while without talking.

When half his breakfast was gone, Brace said, 'This is great.'

'Yeah,' Jane said.

'It doesn't get any better than this.'

'Are you talking about the bacon and eggs?'

'Yeah. And the toast and coffee. And how you look. And what we did in the shower. And just being here with you like this on a Sunday morning. I wish it

390

could be like this every morning.'

'We'd get a terrible cholesterol problem.'

'Yeah. I suppose.'

She smiled. 'We could do it once a week, though.'

'A Sunday morning ritual.'

'Let's just leave out the blood sacrifice.'

'Good idea,' Brace said.

'Do you think it'll leave scars?'

'No. I doubt it.'

'It isn't very deep,' Jane said.

'It won't leave much. Probably nothing.'

'It'll be a long time before it goes away, though.'

'I'll be able to read you like a book – Madame Librarian.'

'Shut up and eat.'

Brace laughed.

They stared at each other as they ate the rest of their breakfast. Afterwards, they cleaned off the table.

'I'll wash and you dry,' Brace said.

'I can take care of the dishes, if you want to go in the living room and relax.'

'I'd rather stay right here.' He filled the sink with sudsy hot water and began to scrub a plate with a sponge.

'I'll find a towel,' Jane said. She walked away from him. By the breakfast table, she took off her T-shirt. She draped it over the back of a chair, and crept toward Brace. When she stepped on the sunny place, the floor was hot on the bottoms of her feet.

She eased herself lightly against Brace's back. He must've expected her, because he didn't seem startled. He wiggled, the robe sliding cool against Jane. She could feel the heat of his back and rump through the thin fabric.

Reaching around him, she spread the robe apart. She

roamed his bare skin with her hands.

'You're destroying my focus,' he said.

'How much focus does it take to wash a few dishes?'

'Plenty. Maybe I should take a break.'

'No, no, you're doing fine. Let's see you do them all. Let's see if you've got what it takes. It'll be a test of your willpower.'

Though squirming and moaning, Brace worked his way through the plates and coffee mugs and silverware and spatula. But as he lowered the skillet into the sink, Jane squatted and reached under the back of the robe. She came up with one hand between his legs. As she grasped him from below with that hand, her other took him from the front, lightly encircling him and sliding downward.

'No fair!' he cried out.

Then he was on his back on the kitchen floor, Jane straddling him in the warm brightness of the sunlight that came through the window.

After that, they got dressed. Together, they removed the sheets from Jane's bed. She put the bloody bottom-sheet into a tub in the utility room to soak. Then they made the bed with fresh sheets.

When the bed was done, Brace sat on it. He looked up at Jane.

She stepped between his knees and caressed the sides of his face. 'Shall we give it a try?'

'What?'

'The bed, the bed.'

'Nope,' Brace told her.

'What do you mean, nope?'

'It's time for you to pack.'

'Pack?'

'A suitcase. Then we'll stop by my place and I'll grab a few things. Then we'll take off.'

'Where to?'

'The walls have ears.'

'Ah.'

'We'll decide along the way. The thing is, we'll pull a little disappearing act. See how good Mog is at cutting orders on you when he can't find you.'

'I hope he can't.'

'We'll find out.'

'How long will we be gone? I have to be at work on Tuesday. *You've* got classes to teach tomorrow.'

'I'll get someone to take them for me. Just bring enough for a couple of nights. We should know very fast whether or not it works.'

'By tomorrow morning,' Jane said.

'Probably.'

'It's worth a try.'

Brace sat on the bed and watched Jane while she hurried about her room, gathering clothes for the trip. He stayed with her when she went into the bathroom to stock her toilet kit. Smiling over her shoulder, she said, 'What if I need to use the john?'

'I'm looking forward to it.'

'Hey! '

With a quiet laugh, he stepped into the hallway and pulled the door shut. 'Yell if you need me,' he said.

When Jane came out of the bathroom, she had to search for Brace. She found him on the living room sofa, the *Donnerville Morning Times* in his hands. A coldness spread through her stomach. 'Terrific,' she said. 'The paper came.'

'Better take a look,' Brace said.

She sat down beside him. He passed the newspaper to
her. The headline stunned her.

INFERNO CONSUMES HOUSE OF HORRORS

'Oh, my God,' she muttered. She read the first few
lines of the story. 'It *burnt*!'
'You didn't know?'
'Somebody must've started it after I left. Linda, maybe.
Or the big guy.'
'Big guy?'
Jane took a deep breath. She was trembling. 'Gail
said there was a big guy,' she explained. 'Six-four. He
was the one who wired her to the wall. But nobody I
shot was that size. I never saw him. He might've been
Mog, I don't know. But if somebody started a fire on
purpose . . .' Shaking her head, she began to read the
story.

> Fire units, last night, arrived to find the Mayr
> Heights home of Steve Savile engulfed in flames,
> even as bookstore clerk Gail Maxwell, missing since
> Monday night, phoned the police emergency
> operator with a tale of escape from the Savile
> house, where she and several other women had
> allegedly been kept as prisoners.
> Ms Maxwell's ordeal, the details of which have
> not yet been fully disclosed, came to an end last
> night when she and a second female captive, Sandra
> Briggs of Reno, were rescued by an unnamed young
> man. The rescuer is believed to be an intruder who
> entered the house to commit burglary, but happened
> by chance upon the prisoners and chose to set them
> free.

'Nice touch,' Jane said. 'A burglar.'

'They took you for a guy. Were they blinded by their ordeal?'

'That was my idea. They really came through for me.' Jane returned to the news story.

> According to police sources, two other women, as yet to be identified, were also being held against their will at the time of the rescue. Subjected to severe abuse by their captors, however, they'd been rendered incapable of escape. It is now feared that they may have perished in the blaze.

'Are you okay?' Brace asked.

Jane grimaced. 'Just . . . My God.' She pictured Marjorie writhing and screaming in her harness as fire climbed her bed. 'Can you imagine being a multiple amputee in a burning house? *God*. It sounds like the punchline for a really sick joke.'

Brace nodded. 'What's worse than sliding down a banister that turns into a razor blade?'

'Yeah. Exactly.'

'Maybe they got out.'

'Maybe Linda. Not Marjorie, though. I should've taken her out when I had the chance. It's just . . . I thought she'd be okay. I mean, I'd killed the guys. And I didn't know about number four. So I thought she'd be okay. Unless Linda did something, but . . .'

'Don't blame yourself,' Brace said. 'You did what you thought was right. You saved two of them. If you'd tried to take out Marjorie, there's no telling what might've happened. Maybe *none* of you would've made it. You just never know.'

'It's so awful,' Jane said. 'She was just supposed to be

left there for a while, you know? Till the cops could show up and take care of things. I thought she'd be all right.'

'Things happen,' Brace said.

'Yeah,' Jane muttered, and went back to reading the story.

The four women, and possibly others, are said to have been abducted from various western states during the past year by three or more male Caucasians in their early twenties. The identities of the alleged kidnappers are unknown at this time. However, authorities suspect that the ring-leader may have been Steve Savile, present owner of the house where the victims were being held.

Steve Savile inherited the property four years ago following the brutal slaying of his parents, Dr and Mrs Harold Savile, and the rape and murder of his two sisters. Steve, away from home at the time of the crimes, was initially considered a suspect. No charges were filed, however, and the matter has remained a mystery to this day.

At this time, authorities believe that the captors may have fled the house upon detecting the escape of two of their prisoners. An all-points bulletin has been issued for Steve Savile.

Police indicate that the women, while held prisoner, were subjected to starvation, torture, numerous sexual assaults and other forms of abuse.

No information has been made available concerning the cause of the fire that totally consumed the Savile residence. Arson, however, is suspected and investigation is pending.

Police are hoping to identify and locate the young man who freed Ms Maxwell and Mrs Briggs from captivity, in hopes that he may be able to shed some light on the events of last night.

'Yeah, I can shed some light,' she muttered. 'Try looking in the ashes.' She folded the paper and tossed it onto the coffee table.

Before leaving the house, Jane dropped her switchblade knife into a pocket of her culottes. She reloaded the pistol and put it into her purse, along with the box of ammunition and five thousand dollars of the money she'd gotten from Mog.

They left her car in the driveway, and took Brace's car over to the Royal Gardens. He parked on the street in front of the building.

'Maybe I should wait here,' Jane said.

'It'd be better if we stay together. Besides, don't you want to see whether or not I live in apartment twelve?'

'I believe you. But I'll come.'

'It's not even nine o'clock, so I don't think you need to worry about running into Lois or Dennis. Or anybody else, for that matter. This place is dead on Sunday mornings.'

Side by side, they went to the front gate. Brace opened and shut it slowly, so that it made little noise. They walked toward the swimming pool. A bright plastic beach ball floated in one corner.

Jane saw nobody.

She heard nothing from the surrounding apartments except for the hum of a few window air-conditioning units. The only other sounds came from birds.

Brace led the way upstairs and along a balcony. They both walked quietly. Near the end of the balcony, Brace stopped in front of a door marked twenty-two. He unlocked it, eased it open, and gestured for Jane to follow him inside.

He stepped around to the front of the sofa, bent down and lifted a thick book off the coffee table. Showing it to Jane, he raised his eyebrows. The book was *Youngblood Hawke*.

'I believe you,' Jane whispered.

'No need to whisper,' Brace whispered.

Laughing softly, she turned around. The walls of the room were hidden behind heavily loaded bookshelves. Books, magazines, file folders and scattered papers littered every table in sight, and half the sofa. Only the easy chair in the corner was free of junk.

'You're sort of a slob,' Jane said.

'Oh, you'll probably cure me of that.'

'Not unlikely.'

'Maybe you should wait here,' he said.

'No no no – we'd better stick together.'

He made a grumbly noise, then led the way to his bedroom. Apparently, his bedroom doubled as a study. His desk, facing the only window, held a computer and pounds of written material. Bookshelves stood against two of the walls. A few shoes were scattered about the carpet in odd places, as if they'd been kicked in the dark. But Jane saw no dirty clothes on the floor or furniture. Brace's bed was unmade, but the sheets looked reasonably clean.

She sat on the edge of the bed.

Brace gave her a crooked smile.

'It's not so bad,' she said.

'You're very kind.'

She laughed, and Brace stepped up to her. She tipped back her head. He kissed her on the mouth. Reaching up, she caressed the sides of his face. Reaching down, he cupped and rubbed her breasts through her blouse.

Soon, he whispered against her mouth, 'We'd better quit.'

Jane whispered back, 'Quitters never prosper.'

'We've gotta get out of here.'

'I know.'

'There'll be plenty of time later.'

'I hope so,' Jane said.

He released her and stepped away. She sank down on his bed, sighed and closed her eyes.

Plenty of time later. Sure.

It's nothing, she told herself. It's not as if he's abandoned me. He's being practical, that's all. It's only because he's worried about me and wants to take me somewhere far away and safe.

But it hurt. It hurt anyway, even though she knew it shouldn't.

Don't be an ass. This is the best I ever had it.

She sat up. Brace swung a suitcase onto the bed and opened it beside her.

'It's weird, isn't it?' she said. 'That this is all because of Mog.'

'Yeah.'

'We wouldn't even know each other if he hadn't started the Game that night. You wouldn't have run into me in the stairwell . . .'

'Maybe not,' Brace said, looking over his shoulder as he opened a drawer of his dresser. 'We might've met, anyway. In fact, I'm sure of it. But his little game is what got us together. No way around it.'

'Do you suppose he *meant* it to be this way?'

'No.' Brace turned around and came back to the bed with socks and underwear. He tossed them into his suitcase. Then he met Jane's eyes. 'I think Mog is a very sharp and tricky guy, with maybe a bit of Houdini in his blood. But he's not invisible. He's not superhuman. He doesn't have any Big Plan. He never intended for the Game to bring you and me together – that was just an accident. And it's an accident that probably doesn't please him at all.'

'But a lot of good things have come out of all this,' Jane said. 'If he hadn't sent me to that house last night, Gail and Sandra would still be there . . .'

And Linda and Marjorie might still be alive, she thought.

But I saved the ones who were savable.

Yeah, sure.

'He might've sent you there,' Brace said, 'hoping that *you'd* be taken prisoner. Don't go and give him altruistic motives for any of this. He's using you, that's all. The Game is nothing but a gimmick for manipulating you. And now that you won't go for his bribes, he'll do whatever it takes to make you obey.'

'I don't know if he'll do *whatever* it takes.'

'If he'll cut words in your skin, he'll do anything.'

Jane sat silent, thinking. 'I don't know,' she finally said.

'You don't know what?'

'Maybe I oughta just go ahead and do what he wants. You know? The money . . . should be more than a hundred thousand. And whatever happens, it can't be worse than at Savile's house last night. And it might be a *lot* better than what he'll do to me if I refuse.'

'It's up to you,' Brace said. 'I'll stand by you, either way.'

She felt a corner of her mouth turn up. 'Of course, I threw away the instructions. I wouldn't know where to go, even if . . .'

'"Take a refreshing dip in John's pool. You'll feel like a new woman."'

'So I have to find a guy named John with a swimming pool?'

'I might be wrong, but my guess is that he wants you at the Calvary Baptist Church.'

'Ah,' Jane said, 'John the Baptist. A dip in the pool. Baptists practice immersion, don't they? And baptism supposedly changes you into a new person, so I'd "feel like a new woman." Very good, Brace. So where *is* this church?'

'Over on Park Lane. You can see it from Mill Creek Bridge.'

She met Brace's worried eyes. 'Why would Mog be sending me to a Baptist church?'

'Maybe he wants to see you do the Dance of the Seven Veils.'

'Think he'll bring me a head on a platter?'

'What do you think?' Brace asked.

'I ain't goin' to no Calvary Baptist Church at midnight, honey. No way.'

Chapter Thirty-eight

In the living room of his apartment, Brace searched the shelves and pulled out a telephone directory. He sat down and opened it on his lap.

'I don't need the address of the church,' Jane said.

'I had an idea. It'll take a few minutes, though. Do you want a drink or something?'

'No, thanks. What's your idea?'

'We're taking a taxi.'

'Huh?'

Smiling, he held up a hand. Then he made the call. After he'd hung up, Jane said, 'Why are we taking a taxi?'

'Mog probably knows my car. And he's rich and nuts. For all we know, he might have access to some sort of high-tech equipment.'

'Ah. Like homing devices.'

'Yep.'

'Good thinking.'

'We'll take the taxi to a rent-a-car outfit.'

'Excellent. Make things tough for the son-of-a-bitch.'

'If we *really* wanted to make it tough for him, we'd steal a car. Anything short of that, there'll be a paper trail he can follow. But . . . I'd like to get through this without breaking any laws.'

'Oh, you're such a stick in the mud.'

He grinned. 'That's me.'

'Hell, *I'll* steal a car. Laws mean nothing to me.'

He laughed and shook his head.

'I'm a regular Bonnie Parker.'

'I think renting a car should be enough to throw him off our track. We'll save your criminal talents for emergencies. Who knows, we might need to stick up a bank.'

'Are you kidding?' Jane said. 'I *am* a bank.'

Less than forty-five minutes later, Brace stopped the Mazda rental car at the exit of the agency parking lot. 'Which way?' he asked.

'Right's the quickest way out of town,' Jane said.

'Right it is.'

He made the turn.

Jane studied the road behind them. The only approaching car swung to the curb two blocks away. As she watched, the female driver climbed out and hurried across the street.

'The coast looks clear in the rear,' Jane said.

'Mog never got as far as the rent-a-car place. If he'd been trying to follow the cab, we would've spotted him.'

'Yeah. The guy pulling five Us behind us.'

'Five?'

'Something like that. The cabbie was having a ball. He should've tipped *us*.'

'I might try a few Uies myself.'

'Don't bother unless there's another car in sight.'

Two hours later, Brace swung onto the gravel shoulder of a two-lane road. On both sides, onion fields stretched into the distance.

Turning her face to her open window, Jane took a

deep breath. 'Smells great, doesn't it? Makes me want a hamburger.'

'We'll have to stop for lunch in a while.'

'Why are we stopped now?'

'Mostly, I want to see what comes along.'

Jane stared forward, then back. 'Nothing's coming.'

'We'll see.'

They waited.

After a few minutes, Jane climbed out of the car. She stretched, sniffed the scented air, tilted back her head to feel the sun on her face. The sky was cloudless. She heard nothing except birds and the soft hiss of the breeze.

Turning to the car, she ducked and said into the window, 'No sign of any helicopters. He might have some sort of high-altitude spy plane, though. What do you think?'

'I think we're probably safe.'

Jane's stomach suddenly fell as she heard the faint, distant grumble of an engine.

Down the road, something dark came around a curve.

'Someone's coming,' she said.

'Maybe you'd better . . .'

'Climb in?' she asked, swinging the door open. 'Good idea.' She dropped onto the passenger seat and shut the door. Looking over her shoulder, she saw that the approaching vehicle was a black pickup truck.

The driver wore a western hat. He had a thick red face and white eyebrows.

He slowed his truck. He stopped it beside them on the road. He leaned toward the passenger window and rolled it down. He wore an old, plaid shirt. Around his neck was tied a red bandanna just like the one taped across OBEY beneath Jane's shirt.

'You folks got trouble?' he called through the window.

'We're fine, thanks,' Brace told him. 'Just stopped to rest and switch drivers.'

'Well, that's all right, then.'

'Thanks for asking,' Brace said.

'No trouble. You folks have yourself a good day, now, y'hear?'

'You, too.'

'Thank you,' Jane called out. The old man smiled at her and touched a finger to the brim of his hat. Then he drove away.

'I don't suppose that was Mog,' Brace said.

Shortly after four o'clock that afternoon, they came upon a roadside sign that pointed to the right and read, Emerald Pines, 32 mi.

'What do you think?' Brace asked.

'I've never heard of Emerald Pines.'

'Neither have I. Sounds like just the place.'

'If they have a motel.'

'Every town has a motel.'

'You think so?' Jane asked.

'Maybe not *every* town.'

'Let's give it a try.'

The narrow, bumpy road to Emerald Pines took them into an evergreen forest where trees crowded the edges of the pavement. The shadowed road was very dark. Now and then, gaps in the trees allowed sunlight to reach down – long, slanting pillars of dusty gold.

Jane had her elbow out the window. The afternoon air blew against her arm and up inside the short sleeve of her blouse, hot and dry. It rubbed her face and tossed her short hair. It smelled rich and sweet and made her think of Christmases when she was very young.

'It's wonderful in here,' she said.

'Maybe we should've brought camping gear.'

'Not that wonderful.'

'Do you want to stop and look around?' Brace asked.

'I'd rather come back some time when all the bad stuff is over – when we don't have to think about Mog,'

As she spoke, she felt a cold little tremor.

This might be the only time we get.

Jane waited for Brace in the car. After a few minutes, he came out of the office of the Lucky Logger Inn and smiled at her. 'All set,' he said as he climbed in behind the wheel. 'We're in lucky number twelve.' He drove to the end of the gravel parking lot, and parked in front of the door to their room.

They went in together.

'Twin beds?' Jane asked.

'It's all they had.'

'Do you think we can both fit on one?'

'We'll have to stack up,' Brace said. Grinning, he swayed sideways and bumped against her. 'Not a bad room, though.'

'It's fine.'

The room looked very rustic: pine walls, beams across the ceiling, several framed paintings of woodland scenery. The lamp on the stand between the beds sported beavers on its shade.

Beavers.

The sight of the animals triggered a flutter in Jane's stomach.

EAGER BEAVER

Penned on her skin by Mog in the good old days when he'd done his writing with a marking pen instead of a blade. And what'll he write on me tonight? she wondered.

Nothing.

He won't find me tonight. Not here.

No way.

Everything will be fine. At least till we have to go back home.

Please.

They dined that evening on a pitcher of beer and a Winky's Special pizza at a saloon called Winky's that had sawdust on the floor and Randy Travis on the jukebox. The beer was so cold it made Jane's teeth ache until she got used to it. The Special had a thin, crunchy crust. It dripped grease and loops of melted cheese down their fingers and chins. They went through a small stack of napkins.

By the time they left Winky's, the sun had gone down behind the forest. Everything was tinted gray. The town had no sidewalk, so they walked along the road on ground that changed with every few steps: sometimes solid dirt, sometimes gravel, occasionally shin-high weeds, grass now and then, and areas of pavement. It made for tricky walking, especially in the dusk. Brace held Jane's hand.

'Are you going to let me up?' Brace asked.

'No,' Jane said.

He was pinned beneath her on the narrow bed.

Earlier, she had been hunched over him, clutching his shoulders, gasping and sweating, squirming on him and sliding herself up and down while he caressed and squeezed her breasts. That had been a while ago. Afterwards, she had eased herself down and stretched herself out on top of him.

They were bare against each other except where the

pad of Jane's bandage made a soft, moist barrier between their bellies. He was hot and slippery under her.

Jane wasn't gasping, now. Neither was Brace. His heart no longer pounded so hard against her chest. But he was still big and hard and buried deep inside her.

'I'm never going to let you get up,' she said. 'I'm gonna keep you right where you are.' She tightened herself around him. 'I've always wanted one of these things – now I've got one.'

His hands glided down her back and gently rubbed her buttocks.

'My "lucky log,"' she said.

He laughed. The laughing bounced her. She felt him twitch inside her. And grow.

'What's happening?' she asked.

'You.'

'Aren't you worn out yet?'

'Pooped,' he said.

'Me, too. I don't think I can move.'

'That's okay,' he said. 'Just lie still.'

Kneading her rump, he writhed under her. He eased up against her, lifting her slightly. He delved from side to side. Then he was pushing up harder at her, then harder, thrusting, twisting, shoving, bucking, clutching at Jane to keep her from being thrown off.

She stayed limp, letting it happen, not trying to hold on or help, savoring every sensation of the strange, wild ride.

Before it ended, he threw her onto her back. She started to fall off the bed, but he caught her behind the shoulder and swept her to the center of the mattress. Obviously not wanting to bear down on her wounds, he propped himself above her as if doing a push-up. Jane flung out her arms. She spread her legs as wide as she could.

They touched nowhere.

Nowhere except at the center where he pounded and plunged.

'I don't want to hurt you,' Brace said.

'It'll be all right.' She pulled at his arms. 'Please.'

So he lowered himself onto her, but she could feel that he was holding himself up enough to keep most of his weight off her body.

'Relax,' she said.

'I don't want to mash you.'

'You won't mash me.'

'Your cuts . . .'

'Obey,' she said.

'All right,' he said. 'But just for a minute.'

She felt him sink heavily onto her. The weight of him pushed her into the mattress, and felt good and safe. It made her feel sore where he pressed against the cuts, but that was fine. It was the rest of it that mattered.

She could feel his hot wet face against her cheek. His whiskers felt scratchy. His breath tickled her ear. She could feel the thudding of his heart, and how his torso seemed to swell every time he inhaled. His penis lay against the side of her thigh, heavy and sticky.

After a while, Jane flexed her leg muscles beneath it, 'Is it dead?' she whispered.

'Comatose.'

She laughed. Then she wrapped her arms around his back and hugged him as hard as she could.

Brace groaned.

When she relaxed her hold, he said, 'What was that, your bear hug?'

'I'm pretty strong, huh?'

'Superwoman.'

'I've been working out a little.'

'I know.'

She raised her eyebrows. 'You been spying on me again?'

'Nope. I can just tell. It's how you look and feel.'

'How do I feel?'

'Firm and smooth. And I know I've gotta be crushing you.' He started to rise.

'No, come on.'

He kissed her softly on the mouth, then pushed himself up and crawled backward. Jane lifted her head.

Brace, kneeling between her legs, was frowning at her mid-section.

OBEY was bare. The bandanna bandage hung at her side, dangling by a single strip of tape. She wondered at what stage of things the bandage had come unstuck.

The letters of the word were thin, red slits. Only the leg of the Y seemed to be bleeding at all.

'Guess you need to be repatched,' Brace said. 'Lie still, I'll take care of it.'

He climbed off the bed and headed for the bathroom. He walked unsteadily, limping a little.

After he shut the door, Jane shut her eyes. She stretched and moaned. The sheet beneath her body was damp. In places, it felt cool and sticky. She thought about trying to scoot away from the gooey areas. But she felt too lazy and good to move, and she decided she liked being on them.

Soon, Brace returned with Jane's bottle of hydrogen peroxide, her spool of tape, and a neatly folded white handkerchief that didn't look familiar.

'Your hanky?' she asked.

He nodded. 'It's clean.'

'It'll be ruined.'

He shook his head and grinned. 'Improved.'

'Right. So what does that make you, a hopeless romantic or a vampire?'

'A guy without much use for handkerchiefs.'

'Ah. That's begging for a quip, but I'm not gonna be sucked in.'

'Afraid you'll blow it?'

'Oh, oh!'

'Were you considering a barb about the way I keep my nose clean?' He trickled the cool antiseptic onto her wounds. She flinched. 'Or how I stick it into other people's business?'

'It's not your nose you've been sticking in.'

'It's not?'

''s not.'

'A few more days like today,' Brace said, 'and we might have to resort to it.'

'Maybe,' Jane grinned. 'Who knows?'

Shaking his head and laughing softly, Brace spread his folded handkerchief across OBEY. Jane felt it stick to the moisture there.

Brace came out of the bathroom wearing faded blue gym shorts. Jane, already washed and in bed, lifted a side of her sheet for him. She wore a fresh white T-shirt that hung low enough to cover the panties that she'd bought at the mall on Monday.

'Join me?' she asked.

'You gotta be kidding.'

She grinned. 'Just to sleep.'

He came to her, but didn't climb into bed. Instead, he bent down and kissed her. Reaching up, she stroked his

411

chest. His kiss seemed too brief.

'I think I'll stay up for a while,' Brace said.

'Aren't you *tired*?'

'Never too tired to read.'

He went to his suitcase, which was open on the dresser, and lifted out *Youngblood Hawke*.

The book he'd chosen the night they met.

The night the messages from Mog had started.

And Brace hadn't finished reading it yet. His bookmark, a small crescent of white paper, jutted out like a torn banner a quarter inch from the back of the book.

When was it due? Jane wondered.

A two-weeker.

He hasn't renewed it, so the thing must be way overdue by now. Wait. No.

My God, she thought. It isn't due till Tuesday. Day after tomorrow.

Not even two weeks since all this started!

It seemed incredible that so much could've happened in such a short span of time.

Jane rolled onto her side. Propping herself up with an elbow, she watched Brace walk past the other bed, set the book on the table by the curtained window, and turn on the nearby lamp.

'Are you going to be done by Tuesday?' Jane asked.

'With the book? I'll probably finish it tonight.'

'Well, we can always renew it for you. But I'm surprised you're not done with it by now.'

'I'm no speed-reader. And there've been a few interruptions.'

'You're not including me, are you?'

He turned up a corner of his mouth. 'I had a bad time for a few days. I was too screwed up to read. Couldn't concentrate on the words.'

'I thought your concentration was supposed to be all-powerful.'

'It kept straying to you.'

Jane felt her throat tighten.

Instead of sitting down to read, Brace lifted her purse off the table. 'I'd like to borrow your gun,' he said.

'Oh, God,' she muttered, feeling a little sickened by the reminder that Mog might be coming for her.

'I'm sure he won't find us here, but . . .'

'Yeah. You must be *real* sure, since you want my gun.'

'Just a precaution.'

'I know. I know.'

'May I?'

'Help yourself.'

He spread the purse open wide and peered in. Then his hand went inside and he came out with the pistol.

'Do you know how to use it?' Jane asked.

'I'm a guy, am I not? It's in my genes.'

She laughed, then saw him drop the magazine, look it over, knock it back into place with the heel of his hand, draw back the slide far enough for a glimpse of the round being retracted from the chamber, and let the slide snap forward.

'In your genes, my eye.'

He flashed her a grin. 'I am a man of many parts.' He set the pistol down on the table beside his book, then sat down.

'You're planning to stay up all night, aren't you?'

'Yep.'

'I should be the one who stays up,' she said. 'You should sleep.'

'Why is that?'

'Suppose he *does* show up? You're planning to shoot him, aren't you?'

'If I have to.'

'I don't want you killing someone for me, Brace. You said yourself, it's the biggest thing there is. I don't want you to have it on your conscience. If shooting needs to be done around here, I should be the one to do it.'

'No.'

'Hey, I already shot three guys dead in cold blood. What's one more?'

Even though the length of the room separated Jane from Brace, she could see how his eyes narrowed and went cold. 'Mog got you into this,' he said, his voice hard. 'He made you do things. He *cut* you. So this killing's on me.'

Jane felt an icy swarm of goosebumps racing up her skin.

After a few moments, the look of Brace softened. 'Anyway,' he said, 'Mog won't find us here. This is just in case. Okay?'

'Okay,' Jane said. She reached out to the nightstand, picked up her glass of water, and took a sip. The ice had melted, but the water was still very cold. She drank it all, then set down the glass.

'Would you like a refill?' Brace asked.

'No, that's all right. I don't want any more. I'm going to sleep.'

'Okay. Goodnight, honey.'

'Night.' Jane slid her elbow out from under her and settled down in the bed. She tucked her arm under the pillow. She watched Brace.

He picked up the book, crossed one leg over the other, and rested the thick volume against his upraised knee. He opened it to the bookmark. Then he looked up at Jane. 'Does my light bother you?' he asked.

'How would you read in the dark?'

'It wouldn't be easy. But I don't have to read.'

'Yes, you do. The thing's due day after tomorrow.'

'But I've got an "in" with the librarian.'

'That you do.'

'I'll turn off the light.'

'No. Don't. The light's fine. I want it to stay on. I want to be able to see you if I wake up.'

'I'll leave it on,' he said.

'Thanks.'

But the room was dark when Jane woke up.

Chapter Thirty-nine

Her heart slammed like a door kicked shut.

Flinging herself sideways, she shoved herself up on an elbow and stretched her other arm up through the darkness. Her hand bumped the lamp. She fumbled, found the switch, and thumbed it. The light came on.

Brace was gone from his chair. The book and pistol lay side by side on top of the small, round table. The other bed was empty, its covers smooth.

'Brace?'

Her voice sounded choked.

She tried again. 'Brace?'

No answer.

He wouldn't just leave!

She swung herself sideways, pushed at the mattress and stood up. And looked down at her front because something felt oddly stiff there.

Her T-shirt hung loose past her groin. A little wrinkled. But not bloody. It looked fine. And she could feel that she still had her panties on.

Quickly, she lifted the T-shirt up to her chin.

She hadn't been written on. She hadn't been cut. Everything seemed fine. Brace's folded handkerchief was still taped in place across her OBEY. It drooped a little near the middle, but still looked secure. It showed no traces of blood.

Nothing's happened, she told herself, and lowered her shirt.

False alarm.

She stepped past the end of her bed, turned to her left, and walked toward her reflection in the mirror over the sink. A section of wall stretched along the far side of her bed. Moving past it, she saw a strip of light along the floor to her left. The light came from under the bathroom door.

It's *all* a false alarm.

He's just in there using the john. Maybe Winky's Special pizza hadn't agreed with him.

With one knuckle, Jane lightly rapped on the door.

From behind it, she heard the hum of the ventilation fan.

'You okay?' she called softly.

He didn't say anything.

'Brace?' She knocked harder. 'Are you all right in there?'

She waited.

Heart thumping hard again, she grabbed the knob and turned it and pushed the door open.

Brace wasn't sitting on the toilet.

He wouldn't be taking a bath at this hour! Not when he's supposed to be guarding me!

The tub, off to the right, was hidden by the open door. Jane pushed the door out of her way. As it swung back toward the wall, she saw bright red spatters on the tile floor. They led toward the bathtub. The shower curtain was shut, and hanging inside the tub. Jane couldn't see through its heavy white plastic.

But she knew . . . *knew* . . . what she would find on the other side of the curtain, sprawled at the bottom of the tub.

Whimpering, she ran for the tub.

Her feet skated on the blood.

She flapped her arms. Her rump slammed the floor. The blow sent a shockwave up her spine and into her head. She slid, falling backward, and skidded on her back until the bottoms of her bare feet slapped softly against the side of the tub.

She flipped herself over. Got to her knees. Scurried to the tub and flung the curtain aside.

Brace's dead, mutilated body was not sprawled in the tub.

The tub was empty, and looked clean – but its bottom was wet.

Where is he?

Maybe he's okay, she told herself.

Maybe this doesn't have anything to do with Mog.

Like hell! Like fucking hell!

Sobbing, she held the edge of the tub and started to get up. She raised her right knee; planted her foot on the slippery tiles, leaned forward to put weight on it, and heard a crackly, papery sound.

It came from where the top of her thigh was pressed against her body – pressing the front of her T-shirt against the right side of the bandage covering OBEY.

And what's that stiff feeling in there?

Paper?

Swinging herself around, Jane sat on the cool enamel of the tub's edge. Her T-shirt was pasted to her back with the blood from the floor. She peeled it off and dropped it into the tub.

The makeshift bandage of Brace's handkerchief was fixed to her midsection with criss-crossing strips of tape.

She started to pick at them with her fingernails.

They stuck tightly to her skin. Finally, gritting her

teeth and growling, she ripped them away.

The bandage came off with them.

So did the long, white envelope that had been sandwiched between the bandage and her skin. The envelope fell away from Brace's handkerchief and dropped onto her lap.

Hanging the mass of cloth and tape across one thigh, she picked up the envelope.

It had her name on it.

She tore it open.

When she pulled the folded sheet of loose-leaf paper out of the envelope, she knew it contained something. Not a stack of money, but something.

Something that had leaked a few spots of blood.

She didn't want to think about what it might be – something gross, for sure. But she didn't quite suspect a body part.

The ear fell out when she unfolded the paper.

Yelping, she clamped her legs shut to catch it. She didn't want to let it hit the floor. The tiles were bloody and dirty and it was Brace's ear – had to be Brace's, didn't it?

It landed on the bit of gauzy black fabric at her groin, slid down the slope there, and was halted by her shut legs. She could feel its weight.

She picked it up carefully by the rim.

With hands that shook very badly, she wrapped it in Brace's handkerchief.

A guy without much use for handkerchiefs.

Till now, Jane thought.

Her crying got worse.

Holding the wrapped ear gently against her chest, she stood up. She slid her feet over the tiles. Outside the bathroom, the carpet felt safe. She knew she was leaving prints on it, but she didn't care.

She hurried over to the table and started to put Brace's ear into her purse.

What good is it? she wondered.

Well, shit, I'm not gonna throw it away.

Maybe it can be reattached.

Gotta put it on ice, she thought.

She ran toward the ice bucket. She could see it at the far end of the room, next to the sink. And she could see the tear-blurred image of herself running toward it. She looked like a madwoman in the mirror: hair wet and stringy, wild eyes spilling tears down her face, breasts bobbing and jumping, the slits of OBEY just above where her hands were cupping the hanky-wrapped ear.

She stopped at the sink. With one hand, she reached for the ice bucket.

Instead of ice, the plastic container held a few inches of water. Jane dipped her fingers in the water. It was still chilly, but not ice-cold. She dumped it into the sink.

'Gotta have ice,' she sobbed. 'Gotta . . .'

It all began to seem a little absurd as she hurried into her robe and found the room key and lurched into the night (the rental car still parked in front of the door) and raced barefoot down the motel's walkway toward the ice machine, the plastic bucket clutched to her belly, the cloth-wrapped ear sliding around the bottom of it.

Trying to save Brace's ear when, for all she knew, the rest of him might already be dead.

No!

Or she might not be able to find him for hours — or for days.

Or the ear might already be ruined.

She knew almost nothing about what was required for putting someone together again. Only that it could be done if the conditions were right, and you needed to keep the severed part on ice until you got it to the surgeons.

So maybe it's absurd, she thought. Maybe it's a waste of time. But I've gotta try, at least.

Earlier, she'd been to the ice machine with Brace. She knew where to find it. She knew how to use it.

As she ran, the belt of her robe loosened. She used one hand to hold the robe shut, though she saw nobody anywhere and supposed that everyone at the motel must be asleep.

At the ice machine, she took the ear out of the bucket. She set the bucket onto a grate beneath the dispenser's spout, held a red button down with her thumb, and waited while chunks of ice rumbled down like a tiny avalanche.

When the bucket was full, she didn't know what to do.

Unwrap the ear? Though the handkerchief seemed protective, it might increase the risk of contamination, or something. She just didn't know. She hated the idea of putting Brace's ear into the ice bare.

But that seemed like the right way to go.

She scooped out some ice, removed the ear from Brace's hanky, and gently set it down in the depression.

A small grave.

It's not a grave!

Sobbing, she covered the ear with chunks of frosty white ice.

Then she ran with it back to the room.

She set the ice bucket on the table.

Rubbing her eyes, she sniffed. 'Everything'll be fine,' she muttered. 'Everything . . . fine.'

But now what?

Gotta figure out how to find Brace, that's what.

She remembered the sheet of paper that had been wrapped around the ear.

Probably a note from Mog.

But she didn't have the note with her. She couldn't remember what had happened to it after the ear fell out.

So she hurried back to the bathroom and spotted it on the floor by the tub – a pale rectangle through the blur of her tears.

Heading for it, she slipped on blood-smeared tiles. This time, she managed to stay on her feet. It had been close, though. Too close. She didn't want to fall and hurt herself again. And a fall onto the blood would ruin her robe.

She took off the robe. A towel bar was within reach. She tucked the garment securely over the bar, out of harm's way. Then she lowered herself slowly to the floor and crawled the rest of the way to the note.

On her knees, she spread it open. She wiped her eyes again, and began to read.

Friends, Romans and Jane,

Guess who should've played along. Does the word OBEY mean anything to you? Which part of OBEY don't you understand?

In case you might be wondering, the ear belongs to your dear one. I hope you appreciate my kindness in sparing your favorite part – for now.

The rest of him will be waiting for you, intact until midnight. I have every confidence that you will not fail him . . . or moi.

Any further disobedience from you will be rewarded with an additional part. Perhaps you'll be able to rebuild him one piece at a time, but I doubt it.

Until midnight in the pool . . .

Yours forever,
whether you like it or not,
MOG

Chapter Forty

On her hands and knees, Jane scrubbed the bathroom floor. She used her T-shirt, since it had been ruined anyway by her slide through the blood. When the tiles looked clean, she did the best she could to clean the stains out of the carpet. Only her first few steps had made footprints of any consequence. She was able to scour away most of the blood.

Done with the floors, she tossed her T-shirt and panties into the wastebasket. She pulled her robe off the towel bar and looked at it closely. It had a few minor stains inside from when she'd worn it on her trip to the ice machine. It looked salvageable, though.

She took the robe into the shower with her and scrubbed its stains with soap and a washcloth. She lifted it close to the nozzle to rinse it. Then she turned and reached up to drape it over the shower curtain rod—and felt a stir of cool air against her back.

Looking over her left shoulder, she saw the window. She knew that she must've seen it before; it hadn't *grown* there. She couldn't recall it, though.

The sill was level with her chin. There was no screen.

She approached it, walking carefully toward the back of the slippery tub.

The window, with side hinges, had been cranked wide

open. She couldn't see its frosted pane until she peered out into the darkness.

A voyeur could have a field day, she thought.

She took hold of the crank and started to turn it.

And stopped.

And gazed at the tall, narrow opening.

A tight fit, but even a big man could probably squeeze through if he really worked at it – came in on his side . . .

That's how!

Mog squirmed his way in and waited in the tub. Probably with the shower curtain shut.

The curtain had been open when Jane had used the toilet just before going to bed.

Mog must've climbed in later, while she was sleeping and Brace was reading the book. Climbed in and waited in the tub. Eventually, Brace had set down his book, left it on the table with the pistol, and paid a visit to the john. That's when Mog jumped him. Subdued him somehow – very fast and silently. Then cut off his ear. And paid his visit to Jane.

Leaning forward against the cool tiles of the wall, she gazed out the window.

She could make out a clearing back there. Vague, black shapes of trees not far away.

What if he's out there now? she wondered.

He couldn't have taken Brace out through the window.

Don't count on it. How the hell do I know what Mog can't do?

Unlikely, though. He probably carried Brace out the front door. Stopped the bleeding first, then hauled him through and took him outside and drove him away.

Except maybe they *haven't* left yet. Mog might want

to stick around and watch the fun.

Jane scanned the darkness beyond the window.

He's probably out there right now, she thought. Looking back at me.

He's always watching, isn't he?

Suddenly, Jane's heart was slamming. She cranked the window. It swung toward her, its frosted glass shutting out the night.

Shutting her away from Mog's sight.

If he's out there.

If he's out there, hasn't left yet . . .

Brace!

Maybe locked in a car trunk, or . . .

She snatched her robe down off the curtain rod and whipped the curtain aside. Water spilling off her body, she slipped and slid her way across the bathroom. When she had carpet under her bare feet, she ran. She struggled into her robe. At the table, she grabbed the room key and pistol.

Then she stepped outside.

Here we go again, she thought.

She hurried along the walkway – the same route that she'd taken to the ice machine – lighted doors and dark windows to her right, the fronts of parked vehicles to her left.

What am I even looking for?

Mog.

A big guy, six-foot-four.

He was probably around back till I shut the window and wrecked his view. Might be coming around the corner of the building any time now.

Yeah, sure. He isn't going to let me see him. I've *never* seen him.

Not likely to see Brace, either. He's probably hidden

426

away in a car or something.

At the ice machine, she stopped. Her back to the machine, she turned her head and studied the vehicles in the motel lot. Most were lined up in spaces adjacent to the rooms where their owners were apparently spending the night.

As she peered at them, she fought to catch her breath. Her wet robe felt like a clinging layer of clammy skin. Water dribbled down between her legs, tickling – and making a puddle on the pavement. She rubbed her legs together.

Where do I even start? she wondered.

She could look them all over, one at a time, but getting into their trunks would be a pretty good trick.

And Brace might *not* be in a trunk. He might be in one of the motel rooms.

Start with the cars, she decided.

The nearest car was an MG.

Mog with an MG?

But both the front seats were empty, and a full-sized person wouldn't fit anywhere else in the vehicle. Jane walked past the rear of it. The trunk looked big enough, maybe, to hold half a man.

On the other side of the MG was an old Jeep Wagoneer. It had no trunk, but plenty of room inside. Jane stepped close to its rear window, bent over, and cupped her hands to the glass.

The cargo space wasn't empty.

Along one side, she saw a dark, bulky shape – a man covered by a blanket?

About the right size for that, but . . .

Jane heard an engine.

She whirled around.

The car rolled slowly toward her, headlights off, as if

sneaking past the rear-ends of those that were parked for the night. It looked very big and very black.

When she saw it was a hearse, her bowels went icy.

She stood rigid at the back of the Wagoneer, struggling to breathe.

As the hearse kept coming, she eased her right arm backward slightly and pressed the pistol against the side of her buttock. She thumbed the safety off.

It won't run me over, she told herself. Not unless it suddenly swerves.

It didn't swerve.

When the passenger door was directly in front of Jane and no more than one large stride away, the hearse stopped.

Oh Jesus! Oh sweet Jesus! What's he DOING!

She heard a quiet buzz as the window slid down.

Bending her knees, leaning forward, Jane looked in.

She saw the driver.

He was blackness, huge in his seat, topped with a cap like a chauffeur.

'Care for a lift?' he asked, his voice no more than a whisper.

Jane wanted to run.

She felt frozen.

He's got Brace.

'Care for a lift?' he asked again.

'Yes.'

'Try wearing high heels,' he said, and chuckled, and stepped on the gas. The tires whirred, spinning, throwing up smoke and gravel.

In the instant before they caught hold and hurled the hearse forward, Jane dived through the open window. She made it past her waist. Then the car clubbed her left hip and she cried out. Her shoulder punched the cushion

428

of a seatback. Her head jerked quick and hard. As she rebounded off the cushion, the momentum released her. She dropped. The windowsill rammed her. She folded, head dropping toward the empty seat.

With her left arm, she shoved at the seat.

She raised her right arm. Tried to lift her head, but couldn't. But knew where the driver was, didn't need to see him. Pointed her pistol. Cried out and dropped the pistol and wondered if her hand was broken and wondered why she had pulled such a stupid stunt in the first place as to dive through the window.

Ain't the movies, stupid.

Now I'm gonna be sorry.

She didn't think her wrist could bend any further, but it did. She hissed and shuddered with the pain.

'I like your guts, honey,' the driver whispered. 'You're not always so smart, but you've got spunk. Yer chock full o' spunk.' He chuckled.

Releasing her hand, he grabbed the nape of her neck. He thrust her down, pushing her forehead into the car seat.

'Yes,' he hissed. 'Your dear one is here in the hearse with us. All but his ear. Doing his Van Gogh routine in our coffin.'

Our coffin? The one she'd used in the old house by the graveyard?

'And yes, you will keep your rendezvous at midnight as planned. Yes?'

'Yes,' Jane grunted.

'For now,' he said, 'enjoy the ride.'

Keeping her head shoved down with one hand while he apparently steered with the other, he made a quick turn that hurled her legs sideways. The force threatened to fling her out of the hearse. She gasped with alarm – then with pain as the fingers dug into her neck.

When the turn ended, she felt as if she'd been released from a tug-o-war. Her legs fell against the side of the door. They swayed as the hearse sped along.

Where is everyone?

Someone has to be up!

Someone has to notice if a goddamn hearse is tooling through town with half of me sticking out its window!

But the town didn't last long.

Jane knew when they had left it behind; the seat cushion went dark under her eyes and somebody seemed to turn up the volume on the night-time wilderness soundtrack of bird and bug noises.

In spite of her discomfort and terror, she noticed the strong, piney aroma of the trees. The slipstream flapping her robe felt cool and moist where it rushed over her bare skin.

'Are you enjoying the ride so far?'

'Fuck you,' she said.

'How rude,' the driver said, sounding amused.

He slowed almost to a stop and turned right. The tires made crunching sounds. Then the engine noise swelled and the hearse lunged forward.

Not on pavement, anymore.

On a rutted, pitted gravel road.

The windowsill pounded Jane. She bounced on it, slid on it, bumped against one side then the other as her face was shoved harder into the seat. Her legs, hanging outside, crashed against the door and flew up and about, thrown every which way by the bounding hearse. Sometimes, they were hit by bits of rock spit backward by the front tire. Bushes or saplings growing close to the roadside jabbed her and whipped her.

'Midnight, darling. Be there or be square.'

The hand clutching the nape of her neck let go.

Chapter Forty-one

Jane woke up.

Her head ached. She felt a little nauseous.

High above her, leafy green branches were motionless against the blue of the sky. Beneath her, most places felt springy and soft but she could also feel hard knobs and pointy things.

It took her a few moments to remember about the hearse.

Midnight, darling. Be there or be square.

An instant later, the back of her head had crashed against something – the top of the door? – and out she'd gone. She had a vague memory of the falling, the impact, the tumbling down a rough slope. She might've been knocked out, but she didn't think so. She thought she could recall trying to stand up afterward, but feeling too tired and ruined for such nonsense, and sinking back down to the ground.

Couldn't have been very long ago.

A couple of hours?

From the look of the sky and the feel of the air, she guessed that this was early morning. Maybe seven?

Got till midnight to get to the church.

Jane raised her head, groaning as the pain swelled. She propped herself up with her elbows.

She hadn't lost her robe, but the right sleeve was torn

432

so it drooped off her shoulder, and the front was wide open. Her legs had caught the worst of things: they were cross-hatched with patterns of welts and scratches, gouged and bloody in a few places, scuffed with abrasions, filthy. She had a few pine needles in her pubic hair. Her midsection, though better off than her legs, was mottled with blood and dirt, battered and scratched so that she couldn't find more than a few traces of OBEY. Her breasts were dirty, but looked okay except for a thin scratch on the top of her right breast. It was two inches long, and ended at the edge of her nipple. It didn't look as if it had bled much.

On the tablet of your skin, we write the book of Jane.
Is that how it went? Close.
Then she thought about Brace's ear.
My fault. All my fault.
And now Mog's got him in a coffin, *our* coffin.
I was in it and wearing that nightie, and Brace found me in it and got so upset, and now he's in it himself. Except for his ear.
Doing his Van Gogh routine.
She didn't want to think about such things.
Stop thinking, she told herself. Just stop it and get moving.

She sat up, wincing and groaning as the pain in her head swelled. Her neck felt almost too sore to hold her head up. She ached everywhere.

Yeah, she thought, and what else is new? Been a wreck ever since Mog started in on me. Bumped my head on Crazy Horse's hair, that was the first . . . no, that wasn't the first. The first was when my switchblade popped open on the library stairs and caught me in the boob.

Been a damn pain-fest from the get-go.

As she struggled to stand, she squeezed her eyes shut. She felt herself swaying slightly. And felt a heavy weight swinging the right side of her robe.

Her hand went into the pocket.

And lifted out the pistol.

He gave it back to me?

Checking her other pocket, Jane found the key to her room at the Lucky Logger Inn.

Must've come down here after he threw me out . . .

She staggered over to a tree. Leaning back against it, she eased back the pistol's slide for a glance at the chambered round. It hadn't been removed. She checked the magazine. Still fully loaded.

Should've shot while I was diving in at him, she thought. Leaped and started pulling the trigger.

He who hesitates is fucked.

'Next time,' she muttered. 'Just wait till next time.'

Talking made her head hurt worse.

She slipped the pistol back into her pocket, then closed her robe and tied its cloth belt. With a thrust of her rump, she shoved herself away from the tree. She took a few slow, wobbly strides, then began to trudge up the slope.

On her way up, she found plenty of evidence that this had been her route to the bottom: furrows in the ground cover of dead pine needles; saplings with fractured limbs, white inside; moist, dark pits of various sizes where her passage had uprooted rocks.

At the top, she found the narrow, rutted lane.

Gotta follow it, she told herself. But which way?

To the left? Of course. I went out the passenger window and ended up on this side, so the hearse was heading to my right. I want to go back the way we came, so . . .

Left, it is.

She walked and walked. She longed for aspirin to soothe the tight, cold pounding in her head. She longed for a hot bath to ease the stiff soreness of her muscles. And she longed for shoes. With every step, she seemed to land a foot on something either hard or sharp that made her gasp and hobble.

Often, she found her mind straying to thoughts of Brace.

In the coffin in the hearse.

His ear in the ice bucket in the motel room.

Had the ice melted yet?

It'll be all right, she told herself. Everything'll be all right. Well, maybe not the ear. But we can get by without his ear – he can grow his hair long . . . The ear won't matter. It's the rest of him that counts. I'll go to that Baptist church tonight and do whatever Mog wants, and he'll give Brace back to me and everything will be all right except maybe the ear.

How long *is* this road?

At last, she staggered around a bend and saw two lanes of smooth, dark asphalt in the shadows ahead.

When she was standing on the asphalt, she balanced on one leg at a time and brushed the clinging gravel and twigs and pine needles off the bottoms of her feet. She found a few minor cuts. Patches of sticky sap. And a large black spider mashed against her right heel.

She wrinkled her nose at that.

Said, 'Yuck.'

It looked awfully fresh, though flat. She must've nailed the thing with the last step she took, or it would've rubbed off.

She found a twig and scraped the crushed body away.

A single black leg remained, clinging to her heel like a stray whisker.

Just like the spider at the old house by the grave-yard. It, too, had left a leg on her as a token of its death.

Jane rubbed her heel against the asphalt.

Looked again.

'Gotcha,' she muttered.

And heard a feeble, whinnying sound. A car engine?

She tensed.

Thought about making a dash for cover.

'Screw that,' she said. Instead of trying to hide, she stepped to the edge of the road, checked her robe to make sure it was shut, and slipped her hand into the pocket. She held her pistol, but didn't take it out.

Around the bend came an old VW bug being driven by a teenaged girl. The VW was a convertible. The girl's long, blonde hair blew behind her.

No passengers.

Leaving the pistol in her pocket, Jane waved.

The girl looked worried.

Can't blame her, Jane thought. I must look like I wandered away from a lunatic asylum.

Before reaching her, the car stopped. Jane didn't move.

Careful, she told herself, or this gal's gonna pull a Uie and head for the hills and I'll have a long and painful hike back to the motel.

'My boyfriend beat me up last night,' she called to the girl. 'He threw me out of the car and beat the crap out of me and left me in the woods. "Let's see if your feet work as good as your mouth, you damn bitch." That's what he said.'

'Golly,' the girl said. She didn't look worried any more. She looked, instead, rather befuddled. 'What'd you do to him?' she asked.

'I called him a name.'

'Yeah? What'd you call him?'

'Shit-for-brains.'

The girl smiled. 'How come you wanted to call him that?'

'He tried to run over a dog last night. It was crossing the road, you know? And he swerved and tried to hit it, but it got out of the way in time. That's when I called him shit-for-brains. I hate it when somebody pulls cruel stuff like that.'

'What sort of a dog was it?'

'A Rottweiler.'

'No fooling? I had me a Rottweiler once.'

Oh God, Jane thought. Don't tell me . . .

'Name of Randy, but it bit my kid sister's face and so my daddy beat it to death with a shovel.'

'Anyway, my friend – Roy? – he tried to run down that dog last night, so I yelled at him. Then he pounded me and left me out here.'

The girl wrinkled her face. She had a very pretty face when she wasn't busy contorting it, but mostly she kept it looking crooked and a little freakish. 'You want a ride, or something?' she asked.

'That'd be great,' Jane told her. 'I need to get back to my motel. The Lucky Logger?'

'Sure. That ain't far.'

Jane expected the girl to drive closer, but the car stayed put. So she limped toward it. The girl watched her approach, studying her, wide-eyed and mouth drooping.

Jane opened the passenger door. She sank onto the

437

seat, and sighed at the good feel of being off her feet. She pulled the door shut.

'This is awfully nice of you,' she said.

'Yeah.' The girl started to turn her car around.

'My name's Jane.'

'How come you're out here in your robe?'

How come *you're* in a long-sleeved sweatshirt and jeans? Jane wondered. Must be baking inside all that.

'It's what I had on,' she said. 'Roy wanted me to go with him in the car. I'd just taken a shower, and all of a sudden he wanted me to go with him for a drive in the woods.'

The girl made a huffing sound. 'That's a guy for you.' Done changing direction, she stepped on the gas. She shifted into higher gears as the car picked up speed. 'Won't take long now,' she said.

'I sure do appreciate this.'

'Bet you do.'

'What's your name?' Jane asked.

'Rhonda.'

'Rhonda. That's a nice name.'

'It's kind of frippy. Mostly, I just go by Ron, least with my friends. My daddy hates it – Ron. He says if he wanted himself a Ron he would of had a son. And I tell him how they shouldn't of stuck me with such a frippy name. Which goes over like a lead balloon, seeing as how they named me after Grandma. Grandma Rhonda. I call her The Old Vick. That's 'cause she smells like Vick's Vapo-Rub.'

'Sounds like you've got an interesting family,' Jane said.

'Yeah, they're all a bunch of losers.' She glanced over at Jane. 'Speaking of losers, whatcha gonna do about yours?'

438

'Huh?'

'Your guy. What's his name?'

Jane had to think for a moment. 'Roy?'

'Yeah, him. He staying at the Logger with you?'

'He was.'

'You gonna dump him, or what?'

'I don't know.'

'Better make up your mind, 'cause here we are.'

Looking forward, Jane saw the Lucky Logger Inn just ahead. Most of the spaces in front of the rooms were empty, now. The rental car in front of room twelve looked like an old friend. 'I think everything will be fine,' she said.

'Yeah?' Rhonda swung into the motel's parking lot. 'Where do I go?'

'Right up here by the gray Mazda, that'd be fine.'

'That's your car?'

'Yeah.'

'Spose Roy's in the room?'

'Guess so.'

Nodding, Rhonda swung her VW sideways and stopped it beside the Mazda.

Jane opened the door. 'Thanks a lot for the ride. I really needed it.'

'Sure.'

She climbed out. As she swung her door shut, Rhonda swung her door open. Then the girl stepped out of the car and smiled. The smile made her look a bit moronic.

Jane smiled back at her.

Oh, boy.

'I can come in, can't I?' Rhonda asked.

What is going on, now?

'Might not be a good idea,' Jane said, making her way slowly toward the door to her room – Rhonda coming after her. 'Roy's probably inside, and . . .

'Wanta meet him.'

'What on earth for?'

Rhonda made a lopsided smile and shrugged. 'Just because,' she said.

'Because why?'

'Gonna lick him for you.'

Jane put her back to the door and tried to keep her smile. 'You want to beat him up?' she said.

'Sure. Betcha I can, too. I can lick most anybody.'

'Well,' Jane said. 'That really doesn't sound like . . .'

Off to the right, a door opened and an elderly man stepped out, a suitcase in one hand.

Quickly, Jane dug out her key. She unlocked the door, threw it open and hurried inside.

Rhonda followed, and shut the door.

Oh, boy.

She's probably not dangerous, Jane told herself.

Look who's talking.

'Where is he?' Rhonda asked.

'Roy!' Jane called. 'Roy, you here?'

No answer. As expected.

Jane shook her head and tried to look perplexed.

'Where y'spose he went to?' Rhonda asked.

'I don't know.'

'I'll pound him till he can't see straight. You just watch and see if I don't. I got scars. I got scars all over me. Fellas, they been at me with knives and busted bottles and everything else. You just name it. But they're the ones who get whipped. This Roy of yours, I'll whip his ass. Teach him to go around whacking on you.'

'Well . . .'

Rhonda headed across the room.

'He must've gone away,' Jane said.

Ignoring her, Rhonda kept walking. She called, 'Roy, you in there? I'm talking to you, fella. You deaf?'

Deaf!

Jane jerked her gaze to the left – to the ice bucket on the table beside her. Brace's ear was submerged, but plainly visible beneath the clear water and floating bits of ice.

Almost to the sink, Rhonda called, 'You hiding in the toidy, Roy? Come on outa there.' She stepped out of sight.

Jane's left hand splashed into the icy water. She snatched out the ear and plunged her dripping hand into the pocket of her robe.

A moment later, Rhonda reappeared. She came back toward Jane, shaking her head.

'Too bad,' Jane told her. 'I would've enjoyed watching you whip his ass.'

'That's okay, I'll just wait. He's bound to come along.'

'I have to pack up and get going,' Jane said.

'That's okay. Don't mind me.'

Jane opened the door and stood beside it, holding the knob. 'I really think you'd better go, now, Rhonda. If you stay, I'm afraid somebody might get hurt.'

'And I know who. Roy, that's who.'

'Would you like a hundred dollars?' Jane asked.

Rhonda narrowed an eye. 'What do I gotta do for it?'

'Nothing. Just go on ahead wherever you were going before you stopped and picked me up – and forget about fighting Roy. I don't want you getting hurt.'

Rhonda waved a hand. 'Oh, I sorta *like* that part.'

'Getting hurt?'

'Sure. Don't you?'

'No. Not really.'

Rhonda smirked. 'Yeah. Right.'

Jane picked up her purse. Holding it to her belly, she walked past Rhonda, reached in, fingered her stack of money, and pulled out a bill.

She took it to Rhonda. 'It's all yours.'

'That's a *hundred*!'

'Yeah.'

'Holy smoking Judas!' She plucked the bill from Jane's fingers. She held it close to her face. 'It is real?'

'It's real, all right.'

'Never seen me a *hundred*.'

'Well . . . Thanks for the help.'

'How about I give you a hand with your packing?'

Jane sighed. 'I need you to leave, now. Okay? I have a lot of things to do, but I've got to be alone. Please?'

Rhonda folded the bill in half and shoved it down the front pocket of her jeans. Then she rubbed her nose. 'Tell you what. You're an okay gal in my book. Any time you need me, just give a holler. My daddy's in the phone book, name of Dodge. Ed Dodge. You call, and I'll come running.'

'I appreciate it. You're okay in my book, too, Ron.'

Rhonda stuck out her hand.

Jane shook it.

'*Adios amigo*,' Rhonda said. '*Via con Dios*.'

'You, too. And thanks again for the ride.'

Chapter Forty-two

Jane drove away from the Lucky Logger just before its ten o'clock checkout time.

She wore culottes and a fresh, white blouse. In the front pockets of the culottes were her pistol and switchblade knife. On the floor in front of the passenger seat – where she could keep an eye on it – was the plastic bucket from the motel, full of fresh ice and Brace's ear.

She'd left a ten-dollar bill in the room to pay for the bucket, though she doubted it was worth more than about eighty-nine cents.

She didn't want anyone taking her for a thief.

Driving along, she felt very strange.

The opening of *A Tale of Two Cities* ran through her mind: 'It was the best of times, it was the worst of times.'

The strange part was that she felt so good.

The woods were lovely; the warm morning breeze felt good; she was clean from her shower; her car seat was comfortable; her nicks and scrapes and bruises and sore muscles didn't bother her very much; aspirin had vanquished her headache; she was acutely aware that she loved Brace and that she intended to spend the rest of her life with him; she was on her way to rescue him.

'Or die trying,' she said. Then, in a low and somber voice intended to mimic some old Indian chief about to go into battle (though not Crazy Horse, she was pretty sure), she intoned, 'It is a good day to die.'

Her Indian chief, she decided, sounded a lot like Bela Lugosi.

So she tried, 'I vahnt to suck your blood.'

'Horrible,' she said, and softly laughed.

And glanced at Brace's ear, and felt guilty.

It didn't seem right to feel good, considering the circumstances.

This sort of thing had happened to her before, though.

Maybe it's a gift, she thought. Nature or God or whatever tosses some nice stuff your way – like sunlight or a good smell of trees or a bit of silliness – to help you get through the really bad stuff. Maybe because without it you'd just crumple and quit.

Throw in some love and hope, too. You gotta have those.

You don't gotta, she thought.

You can probably get by on how a forest looks, a good song on the radio, the taste of fried eggs with bacon and buttery toast . . .

Which made her think about the breakfast she'd had with Brace in the sunny kitchen of her house.

Which made her start to cry.

She'd eaten nothing since her Winky's Special pizza last night. Though she had an empty feeling inside, she had no appetite. She didn't *want* to eat.

By one o'clock in the afternoon, however, she was beginning to get a sickish feeling.

At a gas station, she filled the car and bought a can of Pepsi and a long brown stick of Teryaki jerky and a cellophane package containing a dozen orange-colored crackers, each pair pasted together by a thin tan layer of peanut butter.

She drank and ate as she drove.

The meal was delicious. It made her feel, at first, as if she were on a holiday trip. But then she glanced at the empty passenger seat, and she went hollow inside. She looked down at the ear, and the food went tasteless.

Everything will be okay, she told herself. I'll do whatever Mog wants me to do, and he'll let me have Brace back.

Until next time I disobey.

'Like fuck I'll do what he wants,' she muttered.

I'll take Brace back, and blow that bastard to Kingdom Come.

'I'll kill his ass,' she said, and smiled.

What remained of her Pepsi and jerky and peanut crackers suddenly tasted a lot better.

She plotted.

I'm supposed to be at the church at midnight, she thought. In the baptismal pool, or whatever they call it. Brace'll probably be somewhere close by.

It's all a question of how to rescue Brace.

And nail Mog.

Gotta do both.

What about calling the cops? Have them go in with a SWAT team. They'll need to know everything. That'd be okay, though. Better if they don't know anything at all about any of this – especially about killing those guys at Savile's house – but if that's part of the price for saving Brace . . .

Who says they'll save him?

They'll go into that church thinking Mog's just some everyday scumbag. Doesn't matter what I tell them.

They'll figure I'm a nut case if I start in on how it's almost supernatural the way Mog can operate.

They'll underestimate him.

And some of them might die, and Brace might die.

Nobody knows Mog like me. It'll take me to take him down.

Alone?

'The big stuff,' she said, 'you always do alone.'

And she grinned.

She wondered if she'd picked up that one from Hemingway. It sounded like Hemingway . . . or Mickey Spillane.

Tough talk, but not necessarily true. You don't always have to do the big stuff alone. Sometimes, you can use help.

So, how about going back to that town and finding Rhonda? Take her with me tonight. She'd love it – and hell, according to her, she can lick near anyone.

And how about Babe, the motorcycle boy from the Paradise Lounge? He acts tough and he owes me one. He'd probably be glad to help, too.

Maybe take along that Clay fellow who was so nice to me the other night – all we did was eat popcorn and watch *The Great Outdoors* and he didn't try to bang me. I bet he'd help, if I asked him.

Gail would probably do anything I asked, too. Hell, I rescued her from Savile and those other lunatics. And she probably has family and friends we could bring in.

We could throw together quite a gang.

Storm the church . . .

But Jane knew that she didn't have time to return for Rhonda. Even if she did have the time, she wouldn't do it. She wouldn't ask any of these people for help.

Brace had gotten involved, and look what had happened to him.

'It's just me,' she said. 'Li'l ol' me.'

She smiled. 'Me and Travis McGee,' she added. 'Me and Mike Hammer. Me and Steve Carella and Bert and Cotton and Meyer Meyer. Me and Matt Scudder. Just me with a little help from my friends.'

How would they handle a situation like this?

Splendidly.

'A,' Jane said, 'show up early. B, have some surprises up your sleeve. C, don't play fair. D, all of the above.'

Jane stopped at a convenience store and bought a bag of ice. A few minutes later, she pulled off the road and stopped beside a tree. She went behind the tree with the bag of ice and the plastic bucket. There, she plucked Brace's ear out of the nippy water.

It was looking a bit gray.

This isn't going to work, she thought. This thing's a gonner.

She couldn't simply toss it away, though. Brace might still want it.

And if he doesn't, I do.

So she dumped the bucket of cold water on the ground behind the tree, filled it with clumps of frosty ice, and gingerly added Brace's ear.

Half the bag of ice remained.

She placed the bucket on the floor in front of the passenger seat, the bag of spare ice on the floor behind it.

Later in the afternoon – having plotted until she was weary of plotting, and not wanting to think anymore about anything – she turned on the car radio.

Music played for a while. Then news came on. The woman read with a mild, pleasant voice. Jane didn't pay attention to the first story or two. Then she heard this:

In a shocking new development, a total of eleven bodies, including . . . uh . . . including several partial bodies, have now been removed from the Donnerville home of Steve Savile, which burned to the ground late Saturday night.

The bodies, charred beyond recognition, are believed to include those of Savile and possibly two other men suspected of abducting and committing brutal atrocities against an unknown number of women whom they held captive prior to the fire.

Authorities fear that a total of eight . . . that's eight . . . of the bodies found in the rubble may belong to victims of the three men.

Due to the intense heat of the fire, autopsies will be required in order to determine the causes of death – and even the genders – of all eleven bodies. Identification, if possible, will be based on dental and medical records.

On a happier note, Senator Ellis Jones is expected to make a full recovery from the gunshot wounds he received Sunday morning . . .

Jane turned the radio off.
Eleven bodies!
She couldn't believe it. The three she'd shot in the Show Room, plus Linda and Marjorie, only made five. Where had the other six come from?

If Gail and Sandra had known about other prisoners, they would've mentioned them. Wouldn't they? Of course.

Maybe the six had been kept separate from the others.

Maybe they'd already been dead.

Who knows? Who the hell knows?

Probably Mog.

I'll never find out, Jane thought. If Mog's the one with the answers, they'll stay in him because I'm not gonna ask him any questions. I'm gonna kill his miserable ass the first chance I get, so help me God.

By the time she reached the city limits of Donnerville, much of the ice was melted, water sloshing about in the bucket. But she wasn't ready to return home. Not quite yet. So she pulled off the road.

By the side of the car, she scooped out Brace's ear and dumped most of the water on the ground. A fair amount of ice remained. And she found several good unmelted chunks in the bag she'd stowed behind the seat. She added those, then added the ear.

Then she went to the mall.

She glanced into the B. Dalton book store as she walked by, but didn't spot Gail. Maybe Gail was taking time off to recover from her ordeal. She hadn't come to the mall, however, for a visit with her friend.

She paid a visit to the sporting goods store.

At the mall's food court, she had a supper of cashew chicken and fried rice.

Then she drove over to Division Street. Babe's Harley-Davidson was parked in front of the Paradise Lounge, so she knew he wouldn't be hard to find.

She was right.

Babe seemed very glad to see her, and eager to help.

Shortly before eight o'clock that night, Jane arrived home. On her first trip in from the car, she carried the ice bucket. She took it into the kitchen, plucked out

449

Brace's ear, shook off the excess water into the sink, gave the ear a little sniff (not bad), then sealed it inside a small, pink Tupperware bowl and placed it on a shelf in the freezer compartment of her refrigerator.

Then she set about making her final preparations.

Chapter Forty-three

There was something creepy about being in an empty church at night.

Every deserted building, Jane supposed, was creepy at night. Simply because of the silence and darkness. And you know that nobody should be there, but you're never quite sure what might lurk in the dark with you or who might be sneaking toward you, unseen.

This place seemed worse than others.

Because it was a church, she guessed. God's house, if there is a God. (Sometimes she doubted it; other times, she couldn't help but believe.) Maybe He didn't appreciate trespassers in his house.

Especially armed trespassers hoping to kill someone.

But regardless of what God might or might not appreciate, Jane didn't enjoy being in a place where people came every Sunday to hear sermons about such matters as death and Heaven and the eternal punishments waiting for sinners in Hell. Not to mention that an occasional funeral service was probably held in here.

And especially not to mention the cross.

The enormous wooden cross hung from the ceiling by chains directly above the baptism pool.

It looked ready for action.

Jane had been in Catholic churches. Catholics had

451

Jesus hanging on their crosses, looking miserable and bloody and pretty gross for Jane's taste. At least this cross here didn't have *that*.

Thank God, she thought.

And smiled.

And looked up at the cross looming above her head. It was a dim, vague shape in the darkness – lit only by whatever moonlight and street lights might be coming in through the stained glass windows.

It'd be *really* freaky with a body hanging on it.

Well, maybe not.

Maybe as long as you're sure it's only Jesus . . .

Might even be nice, in a way.

A little company.

Sure hope that thing doesn't fall on me.

At least I don't need to worry about vampires.

She looked at her wristwatch, but couldn't read its face in the dark. She knew better than to turn on her flashlight; that'd give away the whole deal.

Why haven't they shown up yet? she wondered.

It must be at least eleven, by now.

She'd arrived at nine, which *had* to be at least two hours ago. And Mog was bound to come early. He would need time to set up, wouldn't he?

Put the envelope somewhere interesting?

She wondered if there would be $102,400 in it. But more than that, she wondered if Mog would bring Brace here to the church.

She knew that part of the note by heart: 'The rest of him will be waiting for you, intact until midnight.'

Which seemed to mean he would be here.

This better be the right place, she thought – and remembered that it was Brace who'd put the clues together and said to come here.

Hope you weren't wrong.

This has to be the right place, she told herself.

Even if it is, the note didn't actually say he would be here. Just that he would be waiting for me. Maybe waiting somewhere else.

She might need another note to tell her where to find him.

Or maybe ten more notes.

Maybe I'd better *not* shoot Mog, she thought. At least not till I've found Brace.

Not that he'll give me a chance to plug him, anyway. He's too slick for that.

Yeah? We'll see.

Come on, Mog, where are you?

Might be anywhere.

After arriving, Jane had made a thorough search of the church. The parking lot outside had been empty, but that was no guarantee that someone wasn't inside. She, herself, had parked more than a block away and walked back. The main doors at the front of the church had been locked – a good sign. But she'd found a side door that opened easily – leading her to think that Mog might've arrived ahead of her.

Her search had turned up nothing, though.

By the time she'd finished roaming every corridor, searching every room, looking into every nook and under every pew – looking *everywhere* – she'd been sure that nobody else was in the church. Fairly sure.

You could never be completely sure.

Especially with Mog in the Game.

But Jane had gotten to the church *three hours* early, which certainly ought to be early enough to beat Mog.

For quite a while now, she had been sitting on the tiles

at the back edge of the baptism pool. Waiting and keeping watch.

If Brace was right about the message, this was where she belonged. At the pool.

But it also seemed like a very good place to be.

With a wall at her back, nobody could sneak up behind her. The wall had a large, stained glass window that let in a dim mist of moonlight – not much, but enough to let her see if anyone was sneaking toward her.

Elevated at the rear of the sanctuary, the pool gave her a height from which to look down at the back of the pulpit, the altar, and beyond to the nave with its row upon row of dark pews.

Only the choir loft, at the far end of the nave, provided a higher vantage point than Jane's place by the pool. The loft had drawbacks, though. The way its balcony jutted out, you couldn't see what might be going on underneath it. And for the best view, you had to be in the front row. If you kept watch from there, your back was vulnerable because of entryways at the rear of the loft. Someone could sneak up on you. Throw you over the railing . . .

Here by the pool was a much better place to be.

But her rump was starting to go numb from sitting on the hard tile edge.

Uncrossing her legs, Jane scooted forward. She eased herself down into the water. It was lukewarm, and deep enough to soak through the underside of her bikini top. Leaning back, she pressed her elbows against the top of the ledge and let her legs rise.

She would want to have the water warmer if this were a spa.

It's *not* a spa. Don't be sacrilegious.

A lot *like* a spa, though, she had to admit. But spas were usually round or square, whereas this was fairly long and narrow, with stairs at both ends.

A short distance beyond each set of stairs was a door. Like stage doors, they led into a network of corridors and small rooms. Dressing rooms, Jane supposed. Some of them, anyway. Where you'd go to change into whatever you wear to get baptised in.

Probably not a bikini, she thought.

Unless maybe you wear something over it, like a choir robe.

Those doors had her a little worried.

She looked at them now. They were way off to the sides, so she had to turn her head as if looking both ways before crossing a street. She could only see one door at a time.

When Mog comes, she thought, he'll probably come through one or the other of them.

They were several yards away, though.

They both had hinges that squeaked.

I'll have a second or two, at least . . .

Jane gasped as a door swung open.

Not one of the side doors, though. This was farther away – and straight ahead. It swung with a *whoosh* that was probably very quiet, but swept like a hollow gust through the stillness of the church.

Jane snapped her gaze straight forward.

She couldn't see the double-doors at the end of the center aisle; they were shrouded by the black shadow of the overhanging choir loft. But she was almost sure that one of those must be the door she had heard swing open.

Lowering her feet to the bottom of the pool, she stood up.

Out from the choir loft's shadow lumbered a black thing that didn't look like a man.

A bulky, cross-shaped oddity that walked on two legs.

Coming down the aisle toward Jane.

What the hell is it?

It *is* a man, she realized as it strode closer. A big man, a monster of a man, carrying someone across his shoulders.

Carrying Brace?

That *must* be Brace.

Jane ached to grab her flashlight and shine it on them – see Mog's face, at last – and make sure this was truly Brace. But she didn't move. Didn't go for the flashlight.

Gotta take him by surprise. My only chance.

She bent her knees slightly, lowering herself until her eyes were just high enough to see over the front side of the pool. Her shoulders were submerged. She felt warm water licking her under the chin.

Better, she thought. Nothing for him to see but the top of my head. And its very dark here. He probably won't see me.

As he came closer, Jane had an urge to submerge.

Disappear from sight.

But she had to keep watching.

A low railing stretched across the front of the sanctuary.

He stepped over it, took a few more steps, halted, swung the body off his shoulders and dumped it onto the altar.

The meaty sound of the impact was followed quickly by a grunt.

He's alive! Brace is alive!

You hear one grunt and you know it's Brace?

Yes! Damn straight! I'd know that grunt anywhere.

She heard a click. And had to squint as a lighter suddenly flared in the darkness. For an instant, she couldn't see anything except a shock of brightness.

Then she could see just fine.

The fire, the size of a candle flame, cast a glow like a golden mist.

Brace was stretched out on the altar.

He lay on his back. The eye that Jane could see – his right – was open. That side of his head looked dark and messy. It was where he had lost his ear. A silver patch of duct tape sealed his mouth. His arms appeared to be strapped down straight against his sides with duct tape that encircled his body. One band of tape crossed his chest. Another crossed him at the hips. His shorts were gone. His pubic hair shimmered in the firelight. His penis hung limp against his left thigh. More duct tape wrapped him around the thighs and ankles, strapping his legs tight together.

From what Jane could see of Brace, he looked unharmed except for the side of his head where his ear should've been.

The other man peeled a small strip of tape off the bottom of his lighter. The flame died. But the darkness didn't last long. When it came back, he was taping down the thumb-tab at the top of the lighter.

He pushed the bottom of the lighter into the crack between Brace's legs.

To free his hands, Jane realized.

Nothing more ominous than that.

With both hands, he took hold of straps at his shoulders.

He was wearing a backpack.

As he removed it, Jane studied him. She supposed that he must be at least six-four, just as Gail had described him. Not only tall, but powerfully built. His leathers, skin-tight and shiny bright red, encased a body that was packed with mounds and slabs of muscle.

There were many zippers on the outfit – mostly at odd angles, some in places where zippers didn't belong. They might have been put there to relieve strains on the outfit in case he should bulge too much.

The zippers looked like shiny scars.

Made him look like some sort of Frankenstein monster/ outlaw biker/sado-masochistic freak.

And executioner.

The sort of executioner who used to wear a hood over his head.

This wasn't a hood, though. This was a red leather mask. It covered his entire head. His eyes, hidden behind round holes, caught specks of light from the flame. A red flap protruded, pushed outward by his nose. His mouth was out of sight behind a three-inch zipper. The zipper was straight, but higher at one end. The pull tab dangled at the high end, gleaming in the light.

He swung the pack off his back. Holding it by one strap, he bent down. Jane couldn't see much of him. Just the zippered back of his red mask and the leather stretched taut across his back.

Certain that she couldn't be seen by him, she slowly turned around. The water rubbed her softly. It made some quiet, slurpy sounds, but nothing loud.

From the tile floor near where she'd sat before entering the pool, she picked up her flashlight and her .22-caliber pistol.

She knew the pistol would work.

Aware that it had been in Mog's possession after he'd thrown her out of the hearse, she hadn't trusted it. So she had checked it carefully before leaving home tonight. And she'd replaced the ammo in the magazine with fresh rounds. She had even tested it, taking it into the back yard and firing it once into the ground.

The pistol in her right hand, the flashlight in her left, she turned herself around.

A black candle now stood on the altar just above Brace's left shoulder.

Black.

What are you, Mog – a Satanist?

He lit another black candle on the flame of the lighter between Brace's legs, and placed this one above Brace's other shoulder. Then he lit two more. He stood them upright by Brace's ankles, then retrieved his lighter, killed its flame, and bent down again.

To put it in his pack, Jane supposed.

The four candles made things very bright.

Jane hoped she was beyond the reach of their glow. She slipped forward a bit, and lowered both hands to the cool tiles in front of the pool.

Realizing that her pistol might be pointed straight at Brace, she turned its muzzle to the left.

She thought, Why don't I just go ahead and shoot when he stands up? We're not here to play by Mog's rules. Don't need to wait for midnight. Just go ahead and . . .

But he came up holding a thick, white envelope. It made a soft *whop* as he slapped it against Brace's chest. He let go of it. It was tilted, lifted slightly at one end by the slope of Brace's left pectoral muscle.

It didn't look thick enough to be holding a hundred and two thousand, four hundred dollars.

Not in hundreds, anyway.

Maybe Mog's switched to thousand-dollar bills.

Or maybe he . . .

He rammed the ice pick down very fast.

It was on its way down before Jane even noticed he had it.

'NO!' she yelled.

As she jerked her pistol up to take aim, the shiny steel spike of the ice pick jabbed through the envelope and plunged into Brace.

Chapter Forty-four

Jane fired.

Brace jerked.

Mog whirled and dropped, falling as Jane snapped off two more shots. Through the ringing in her ears, she heard him crash to the floor.

Out of sight.

Brace and the altar in the way.

She hurled herself out of the pool, scurried on knees and knuckles, leaped to her feet and raced for the altar.

Brace's head turned to watch her.

She skidded to a stop against the altar, against Brace's arm, leaned over him and aimed down past him at the floor . . .

Nothing there but the backpack.

She thumbed her flashlight switch. Caught a shape of fleeing red leather halfway down the center aisle. Fired but he didn't fall or even flinch. Took careful aim and fired fast, emptying the pistol at his back.

But he didn't go down.

He smashed through the double doors at the rear of the nave.

And was gone.

She cried out, 'Shit!'

Then she realized that she could feel Brace's arm against the wet skin below her navel.

She set her pistol and flashlight on his belly.

'You'll be all right,' she whispered. 'You'll be fine. Everything'll be fine.'

Pressing her left hand gently against the envelope on his chest, she squeezed the shaft of the ice pick between her middle and index fingers. With her right hand, she gripped the wooden handle of the weapon. She pulled straight upward. Brace flinched and made a quick sniffing noise. The steel spike slid up out of him, warm where it was caught between her fingers.

She pushed the envelope away and grabbed her flashlight.

The wound was bleeding, but not much.

She shoved the heel of her hand through the blood, smearing it away, and found a small hole. A couple of inches above his left nipple, and over to the side.

'Mm! Mmmm!' The moans sounded urgent – or frustrated.

Jane tore the duct tape off Brace's mouth.

He gasped for air.

'I'll get you out of here,' Jane whispered.

He kept gasping.

'I didn't shoot you, did I?'

'Nuh . . . No.'

'Don't think I shot Mog, either.'

'Get . . . outa here.'

'Yeah.'

She looked for something to use as a bandage. It wouldn't take much of a bandage to cover such a small hole.

Setting the flashlight on his chest, she picked up the envelope. She shook the stack of money down to one end, and tore off two inches from the top. She let the rest of the envelope fall. It came to rest in the crease between

Brace's right arm and Jane's belly.

With shaking fingers, she folded the piece of envelope. Made a small, square pad of it. Placed the paper bandage against Brace's hole and fixed it there with the wide strip of duct tape she'd taken from his mouth.

'We'll get you to a hos . . .'

'JANE!'

The boom of the voice made her jump.

Brace's head jerked sideways.

'Up here, Jane! In the choir loft.'

She spotted his dim, dark shape up there.

And lowered her eyes to the pistol on Brace's belly. Its slide was locked back. Empty.

'You tricked me, you sly bitch.'

'I tried,' she called.

'Not hard enough. But the money is yours.'

'I don't want any of your fucking money!'

'That's no way to talk.'

'Fuck you!'

'I suggest that you read the note.'

'I suggest you eat shit and die!'

'Read the note, or you'll both die. I'll count to three. One.'

She grabbed the flashlight and swung its beam toward him.

'Two.'

He stood in the front row of the choir loft, aiming a strange device her way.

A crossbow?

'Okay, okay!' she shouted. She grappled blindly down by her belly, clutched the envelope and raised it. 'I've got it! Don't shoot!'

'Read your instructions. Read them out loud. I'm sure Brace will be amused.'

'Okay. Okay.' She fumbled the sheet of paper out of the envelope, leaving the money inside. She set the envelope on Brace, next to the pistol.

She unfolded the note. With one hand, she held it over Brace. With the other, she shone her light on it. '"My Dearest One,"' she read. Though she didn't speak loudly, her voice seemed to resound through the church. '"It is unfortunate that you chose to make life difficult for me – and impossible for your dear one, Brace. I blame him, in part, for your insurrection. He simply must go. But all is not lost. Far from it. After you've dispatched him, you and I shall resume the Game. With your combination of wit and spunk, my love, you stand . . . you stand to earn a fortune."'

She glared up at the indistinct figure in the choir loft. 'I'm not "your love," you bastard. And the Game is over.'

'Read on, Jane.'

She scanned the page, located the place where she had left off, and continued reading. '"Inside the back-pack, you will find the proper instrument for the job. Use it on Brace's neck. After you've done that, place his head on the silver tray – also to be found in the backpack – and . . ."'

Crumpling the note, Jane yelled, 'You sick bastard, there's no way . . .'

'Four hundred thousand dollars, Jane. Four hundred thousand, and change. All yours. Tonight. All you need to do is chop off his head and . . .'

'Fuck . . .!'

'Refuse and I kill you both!'

She shone the flashlight at him. The crossbow seemed to be aimed directly at her.

She suddenly had a very hard time catching her breath. Her heart was slamming. She felt dribbles of water or sweat running down her sides and back and legs.

'I'll put a bolt right through Brace's temple. Then it'll be your turn. But I won't kill *you* with a single, clean shot. I'll cripple you first, then come down and work on you. I'll cut you up a little bit at a time. And I'll fuck you till you can't see straight. Been wanting to do that for a long time, now. Oh, we'll have loads of fun.'

She shut her eyes. She felt herself swaying slightly from side to side.

'You can't ask me to kill him,' she said.

'Either way, he gets killed. If *you* do the honors, you'll earn yourself a fortune and you'll walk out of here alive.'

She opened her eyes. She looked down at Brace. His eyes were shiny in the candlelight and staring up at her.

'This,' she whispered, 'is where you're supposed to tell me to do what he says and save myself.'

'You think I'm nuts?' he whispered back.

Jane almost laughed, but her throat got thick and tears came to her eyes. Blinking them away, she raised her head, 'Okay,' she called. 'I'll do it.'

'Thanks a heap,' Brace whispered.

Jane took a deep breath, then stepped around the altar. In front of it, she squatted down and shone her flashlight into the backpack. It was half-full. But the meat cleaver was at the top, cushioned by a coil of rope. The silver tray was tucked down the back. She pulled out the tray, first, and set it down by her foot. Then she lifted out the meat cleaver.

Its big, gleaming blade looked heavy enough to whack off a head with one blow.

She switched off her flashlight, and left it on the floor beside the tray.

The cleaver in her right hand, she stood up straight.

Her back felt very much like a target. A huge target, bare all the way down to her rump – except for a couple of bikini strings.

Not turning around, she called, 'You promise you'll let me go?'

'If you follow orders.'

'I don't wanta die!'

'You won't be killed. That would put a crimp in the Game, you know.'

'Okay,' she said. 'You'd better keep your word.'

'I'll keep my word. Count on it.'

In a whisper to Brace, she said, 'I love you, don't move.'

She raised her arm high and swung the cleaver down in a silver arc toward his neck. And then she turned it in midair. As she lopped off the tips of the candles by Brace's shoulders, snuffing them, she heard the sound of a *thwung*.

She chopped down hard into the top of the altar beside Brace's ear.

Go for the temple!

As the blade chunked into the wood, the bolt struck with a noise like a hammer clanking an iron skillet. She felt the shock of the impact through the cleaver's wooden handle.

And then she let go of the handle. Grabbing Brace by the shoulders, she flung herself up and sideways. She dropped onto him, kicking at the two candles by his feet, hugging him to her body and rolling, tumbling him off the altar.

They seemed to fall through the darkness for a long time.

When they hit the floor, Brace was on the bottom. He let out a grunt.

'Sorry,' Jane whispered.

She pushed herself up to her hands and knees.

'Cut me loose.'

'Stay here and be quiet.'

'Jane!'

'Shhh!' She crawled off him. Keeping low, she scampered to the front of the altar and patted the floor until she found her flashlight. 'It's you and me, Mog!' she shouted.

No answer.

On her feet, she made her way through the darkness to the front of the sanctuary. She bumped into the railing. Climbed over it. Stood on the other side and switched on her flashlight. She aimed its beam at the choir loft.

He'd disappeared.

'I'm here, Mog,' she called. 'I'm here, and I want to play. So come on.'

She heard nothing.

'You aren't afraid of me, are you? What's to be afraid of? Look what I'm wearing.' She shone the light on herself, moved it up and down the front of her body. 'You can see I don't have a gun.' Turning around, she held the light over her shoulder to illuminate her back. 'See?' She turned toward the loft. 'I don't have any weapon at all . . . except my good looks.'

She heard a single, quiet huff of laughter. It came from somewhere in front of her. From the loft? From among the pews near the back of the nave? She couldn't tell.

She took a few slow, careful steps up the center aisle. After passing the first row of pews, she halted. 'What are you scared of?' she called.

'Let's see you take it off, honey.'

'Let's see *you* take it off me. Honey. If you've got the guts.'

She swept the front of the loft with her flashlight. No sign of him.

But she jerked with alarm when the double doors crashed open. She brought her light down and caught him in it.

Striding down the aisle, coming straight at her. Red and glossy in his leather suit and mask, zippers shiny as gold. He'd left his crossbow somewhere else. In one hand, he carried a very large hunting knife. His other hand held a long, black bullwhip.

Jane heard herself let out a groan.

'Whips and knives?' she muttered.

'All's fair in love and the Game, honey.'

Jane took a quick sidestep, reached in between two hymnals in a trough on the back of the pew, and pulled out a Smith & Wesson .357 Magnum long-barreled revolver she'd bought from a grinning fellow named Gatsby that afternoon with the help of Babe.

She cocked its hammer as she swung the muzzle, yelling, 'All's fair, Mog!'

He dived sideways as she pulled the trigger.

The blast stunned Jane. The recoil kicked the gun out of her hand. As she ducked and tried to catch it, she heard the clamor of Mog crashing down on a pew.

The revolver hit the floor. She crouched and lit it with her flash and picked it up and ran to the place where she'd last seen him.

She expected him to be gone.

She was wrong.

He looked as if he had stretched out on his back for a nap. But the seat of the pew was too narrow for him. He had one foot planted on the floor to keep himself from falling off.

Jane pointed the flashlight and revolver at him.

He didn't move.

She wondered if she had hit him, after all.

Where's the blood? Where's the hole?

'Just freeze right there,' she said.

She could see him breathing. Other than that, he remained motionless.

Both his hands were out of sight – one hidden between his side and the wooden back of the pew, the other down beneath the seat.

'Let me see your hands,' Jane said. 'They'd better be empty.'

Even as she spoke, she thought, This isn't a good idea. I should shoot him. This is stupid!

But she had shot three men in the back of the head at the house on Mayr Heights while they were watching a Barbra Streisand movie and having Pepsis and popcorn.

Shooting three men dead in cold blood, even though they had deserved it, was three too many for Jane.

Now that the choice was upon her, she didn't relish the idea of making it four.

Besides, this was Mog.

Master of Games.

The Answer Man.

His hands were still out of sight.

Jane thumbed back the hammer. 'Show me your hands right now or I'll blow your fucking heart out your back!'

Then came the splash.

A heavy, thumping collision with water – the water of the baptism pool?

Brace!

Trussed in duct tape.

Jane jerked her head sideways. 'Brace!' she yelled.

Should've cut him lose, damn it, why didn't I cut him lose before . . .

At the edge of her eye, she saw Mog bolt upright.

She faced him. The hunting knife had already been launched at her chest. With a yelp of surprise, she batted her revolver at the huge, tumbling blade.

Slammed it aside with her barrel.

As the weapons clashed together, Jane's gun went off. Part of the knife-handle disintegrated. The rest of the knife jetted off into the darkness behind the pew and disappeared.

Like before, the recoil tore the gun from Jane's hand.

This time, it pounded her hip. As it bounced off her body, she caught it.

But she jerked with a sudden spasm of pain, cried out and lost the gun as the bullwhip slashed a streak of fire across her arm and back.

In the glow of her flashlight, she saw the revolver bounce off the edge of the seat, fall between the pews, and vanish. She started to crouch and go after it, but heard the whistle of the whip.

Flinging up her arms to protect her face, she whirled away. The whip lashed her like a tentacle, cutting across her back and wrapping around to rip her belly. But then she was running. Sprinting up the center aisle toward the sanctuary.

Toward the baptism pool.

'Brace!' she yelled.

He didn't answer.

She heard only her own hard breathing, the slap of her bare feet on the church floor, the heavy pounding not far behind her back – and the whistling sound of the whip.

She glanced over her shoulder.

In the darkness, he was coming. One arm, held high, twirled the whip above his head.

Jane leaped the railing in front of the sanctuary. The flashlight was still in her hand. In its wildly prancing beam, she saw the altar ahead.

She raced for it.

And the whip came down over her shoulder, lashing down the front of her body all the way to her hip. Squealing, she fell to her knees and clung to the altar.

The backpack seemed to be gone.

The voice behind her said, 'Get up.'

She still had the flashlight.

She didn't even try to get up.

'Would you like another taste of the lash?'

Bastard sounds like a pirate movie.

'No,' she murmured. 'Just . . . give me a second.'

Wincing with pain, shivering and twitching, Jane struggled to her feet. She bent over the altar, hands on its top to keep herself steady. In her left hand, she still held the flashlight.

Its beam pointed toward the place where she had buried the cleaver in the wood of the altar.

The cleaver was gone.

This is good news, she thought. This could be very good news. Brace must've . . .

'Turn around.'

She turned around and leaned back against the altar. Its edge pushed into her buttocks. As she gasped for air, she felt fluids trickling down her skin everywhere.

Blood, tears and sweat.

Brace'll be popping up any second . . .

Unless he's dead at the bottom of the pool.

'You will do exactly what I say.'

471

'Don't count on it,' Jane said. She raised her flashlight and shone it on him.

He held the bullwhip by his side. 'Watch,' he said.

'I'm watching.'

A pair of zippers at the crotch of his red leather suit formed a big V. He raised one zipper, then the other. The wedge of leather was lifted high by a massive erection.

'I'm impressed,' Jane said.

'You'll be shrieking with delight. Now, strip.'

'You take off your mask first, and . . . then maybe I'll strip for you.'

'I'm the one who gives orders around here.'

'I don't follow them anymore.'

'We'll see about that.'

He gave the whip a quick snap.

Jane yelped and clutched her belly. Trying not to cry, she gasped, 'I want to see what you look like, okay? That's all. I mean, my God . . . After everything we've . . . Show me your face. Come on.'

After a few moments of silence, he said, 'Sure. Why not?'

With one hand, he reached behind his head. Jane heard the quiet buzz of a zipper. The smooth red front of the mask rumpled. A cheek of it sank in.

He peeled the mask off.

Jane shone her light on his face.

He had very short blond hair, blue eyes, broad features. She supposed that many women would consider him terribly handsome.

She had never seen him before.

'Who are you?' she asked.

He smiled. He had straight, white teeth.

'Tell me,' she said.

Where the hell is Brace?

472

'Who am I? Bradford Langford Crawford. My friends call me Ford. What else would you like to know before we proceed with the fun?'

'Why me?' she asked.

'Why not?'

'What's it all about? The Game?'

'Playing.'

'That's all?'

'Playing to win.'

'Ah.' She hurled the flashlight at his face. It tumbled end over end. She didn't wait for it to hit him or miss him; she flung herself around. Heard a thunk and a gasp. Vaulted the altar. Hit the floor on the other side – where she'd landed with Brace not very long ago (Where is he!) – and raced for the pool.

'NOW I'M REALLY GONNA HURT YOU, YOU FUCKING CUNT!!!'

Now it was dark.

It had gone dark at the same moment she'd heard the thunk and gasp.

She could only see dim shapes of gray and black.

The floor dropped out from under her.

She fell forward sprawling into the darkness.

Into the water.

Into the water where she had started out and where she had thought all the action would be, Mog having instructed her to 'take a refreshing dip in John's pool.'

She slammed down through the warm water, dug for the bottom, and grabbed the center post of the twelve-pound hand weight that she had put there. The weight lifted, but only slightly.

Where's Brace?

Jane kicked her legs about, stretched out with her free arm, but couldn't touch him.

473

Where, damn it?

Maybe at one end or the other. But Jane doubted it. The pool didn't seem large enough.

Doesn't matter.

Gotta nail Mog.

Holding the weight, she swept a hand down under one end and snatched up the knife that she had pinned underneath it earlier.

Not her little switchblade.

A hunting knife with a heavy, twelve-inch blade.

She'd bought it that afternoon at the sporting goods store at the mall. At home, she had slipped the sheathed knife onto a belt, and buckled the belt.

Now, fast as she could, she pulled the looped belt down over her head.

With the knife suspended from her neck, she peeled a plastic bag off the other end of the weight. The tape came off easily. She didn't bother to remove the .357 from the bag. Gripping it through the filmy plastic, she let go of the weight.

The revolver and knife were enough to keep her submerged. She turned herself around. Squatting, she gazed up through the water.

Saw nothing.

Come on, Mog. Come on. Any time, now.

She waited.

Her lungs were starting to hurt.

What's taking you so long?

It had been very lucky that he hadn't leaped on her back while she was trying to get her hands on the knife and revolver. But now she was ready for him.

With surprises.

Come on, Mog. Jump in. The water's fine.

She wouldn't be able to stay under much longer.

Can't just pop up and start blasting away in the dark. If he isn't right there . . .

Should've picked up some kind of underwater flashlight.

As if her wish for light were a prayer that had been heard and granted, lights suddenly bloomed around her.

Pool lights.

What the hell?

Startled, she gazed up. The water looked very clear. She saw the shiny, rippled underside of its surface. She saw the front wall of the pool, its submerged panel of light, its side above the waterline.

No sign of Mog looming over her.

Nothing but darkness above the edge.

She glanced to both sides.

No sign of Brace.

Nobody else in the pool, either.

Just me.

Jane looked down at herself. The bright lights and water gave her skin an eerie, pale shimmer. Made her look as if she were already dead, drowned. OBEY was hardly visible. Her bruises, scratches and gouges from last night's encounter with Mog were stark and vivid – but the lash marks from tonight were worse – long, thick trails of raw flesh.

So much for having a good-looking corpse.

I'm not dead yet, she told herself.

Just look that way.

She wondered if Mog was looking down at her. If so, he could probably see every detail: how she squatted on the floor of the pool, a huge revolver in a plastic bag in her right hand, a knife dangling like an enormous pendant from the belt around her neck.

If he *is* looking down, she thought, I've already

lost any chance to surprise him.

Maybe Brace nailed him.

Maybe it's Brace who turned on the lights.

I should be so lucky, but . . .

Jane could no longer hold her breath.

Gripping the revolver with both hands through the plastic bag, she shoved at the floor of the pool and thrust herself upward. She blasted through the surface, huffing, blinking water out of her eyes as she raised her arms.

Mog – Ford – stood just beyond the edge of the pool, swinging his whip overhead.

Jane pulled the trigger three times very fast.

Each time, the hammer dropped with a solid clank.

She felt no recoil, heard no gunshots.

She heard herself yelling, 'YAHHHHH!'

And she kept on pulling the trigger and yelling, thinking that this was simply not possible – she had bought the revolver herself from Gatsby and the ammo *had* to be good because the other .357 had been loaded from the same box and had fired as it should – she had *definitely* loaded it, had double-checked the cylinder just before sealing the gun inside the plastic bag and taping the bag to her hand-weight and placing it at the bottom of the pool.

This can't be happening!

Could water have gotten into the bag and ruined the ammo?

No chance. That sort of thing doesn't happen in real life – only in fiction written by people who don't know guns.

Why isn't it firing?

Through the keening noise of panic and disbelief coming from herself and the clanking of her hammer and the whistling of the whip, she heard laughter. She saw a big grin on the face of Bradford Langford Crawford.

He seemed to be very happy laughing and swinging his whip overhead. Happy and excited. His erection was still jutting up high through the gap in his leather pants.

He must've seen her looking at it.

He bumped his pelvis forward.

'We're gonna have a hot time, baby.'

She lowered her arms into the water.

She let go of the revolver.

'Take it off,' he said. 'Take it all off. Or I'll rip it off you with my whip. I can do that, you know. But I might nip off a bit of tit in the process. Wouldn't want that, would we?'

'Don't do that,' she said. 'I'll . . . just let me get out of the water, okay?'

'Climb on out. All the better to see you, my dear.'

Jane waded forward, boosted herself out of the pool, and stood on its edge.

'Get rid of the knife.'

With both hands, she lifted the looped belt over her head.

'You sure came prepared. Must be an old Boy Scout, huh?'

'Girl Scout.'

'Yes. You are a girl, all right. And you'd better drop the knife, now.'

She didn't drop it.

She clutched the handle of the knife and tugged. The long, broad blade came out of its scabbard.

'You must be kidding.'

She tossed aside the belt and sheath.

'Don't even think about it.'

'Who said anything about thinking?' she asked.

And then she went for him. She rushed in low, left

477

arm up to shield her face. The whip lashed her arm and licked a trail of fire down her back. The pain made her muscles feel watery, but she stayed up and kept moving, backing him away as he struck her again and again with the whip.

She heard herself yelling with pain.

I'm not really doing this, she thought.

Oh, yes I am! Oh, Jesus!

Kept lurching at him and he kept backing away and kept whipping her and she wouldn't let herself quit.

Because quitters never prosper.

And because sometimes it has all gone too far.

And sometimes tricks aren't enough.

'Stop it!' he yelled so loudly that Jane could hear him through the whistle and crack of his whip and her own cries of pain.

And, 'Are you nuts?'

And, 'Damn it, I'm gonna kill you if you don't stop!'

And, 'Last chance.'

And, 'Now you're in for it.'

And then, 'Fuck!' as he stopped abruptly.

Jane supposed he must've backed into something. She supposed his retreat was blocked.

The lashings stopped.

He struck her across the face with the handle of his whip.

She drove her knife at him in an upward sweep toward his belly. He caught her by the wrist.

'Now,' he whispered, 'you're really gonna get it.'

He twisted her wrist. She cried out. The knife fell from her numb fingers.

'BRACE!' she shrieked.

Her wrist was jerked upward. Higher and higher until her arm was stretched as high as it would go – then

478

higher. Her feet left the floor.

As she dangled in front of him, Ford tossed his whip aside to free his right hand. He grabbed the front of her bikini top. He ripped it off her.

His huge hand began to fondle her breasts. 'Ooo. Yes. Nice.' He squeezed one. He pinched the nipple or the other. 'Very . . .'

Her left fist punched him in the nose.

The nose made a crackle sound.

He growled like an outraged dog. Still holding Jane suspended high by her right arm, he stopped toying with her breast. He smashed his fist into her belly so hard that it started her swaying. He punched her two more times, then rammed his hand between her legs.

Clutching her groin, he lifted her. His other hand released her wrist and grabbed her by the throat.

And he raised her above his head.

He turned in circles, spinning her.

Then he hurled her across the darkness of the sanctuary.

She crashed against something – the pulpit? – and knocked it over.

Things fell on her.

A book dropped onto her face, crunching her nose.

Papers fluttered down.

This *must* be the pulpit.

And that was probably a *Bible* that hit me.

Her body rang with pain.

She didn't think she could move. She *knew* she couldn't breathe.

But her mind seemed strangely alert.

She thought, When the going gets tough, the tough get going.

She thought, I oughta kill whoever said that.

She thought, Brace or the Cavalry or some damn thing had better come to the rescue pretty fast, or I'm in very deep shit.

Nobody seemed to be coming except Ford.

Backlit by the glow of the pool, he looked like a giant. 'Rough landing?' he asked.

Jane concentrated on trying to get some air into her lungs.

He knelt in front of her. He didn't need to spread her legs; they were already thrown wide apart and she couldn't bring herself to move them.

He tore off her bikini pants with such a rough yank that her rump was jerked up off the floor for a moment. Then the fabric tore and her buttocks fell with a smack.

Her tailbone pounded against something hard and cool.

She wondered if she might be able to move her hand. *Maybe.*

'Time to rock and roll, honey.'

Leaning way forward, he grabbed her shoulders.

Yes.

He thrust and went in deep, big and hurting.

She cried out, 'NO!'

Oh yes.

Oh yes oh yes.

As he pumped and she whimpered (*yes*) she tugged the Colt .45 automatic out from under her rump (*yes! yes!*), the .45 she had bought from Gatsby that afternoon (*yes!*) along with four .357 magnum revolvers and three other .45 automatics and four .38 revolvers all of which she'd placed strategically about the church (*yes! yes!*) – the .45 on the bottom shelf inside the small wooden stand of the pulpit (*oh, yes!*) – because toughing it out was good but being tricky was better (*ha!*) – and because

God helps those who help themselves (*amen!*) – and as Ford thrust and grunted and Jane shrieked with the pain and horror of his invasion she shoved the muzzle against his ear and pulled the trigger.

The crash of the gunshot deafened her.

(*YES! YES! YES!*)

Chapter Forty-five

For a while, Jane thought she might not be able to get out from under the body.

He wasn't just on top of her.

'Bastard,' she gasped.

Summoning all her strength, she twisted and bucked and shoved at the body, and was finally able to squirm free.

She picked up the Colt.

She was sure that Ford must be dead.

But she fumbled through the darkness until she found his face. His mouth was already open. She thrust the muzzle inside until it wouldn't go any farther, then pulled the trigger twice.

All these shots, she thought, and no cops.

Not yet, anyway.

Just as well.

It was a long time before Jane was able to stand.

She found Brace stretched out motionless on the floor across the sanctuary from the demolished pulpit. He was still bound with duct tape.

When she put her face against his chest, she heard his heartbeat and felt the rise and fall of his breathing.

'Brace?'

He didn't answer.

Leaving him, she wandered the sanctuary. She found her hunting knife on the floor by the altar. She also found Ford's backpack. She staggered, carrying it through the darkness, and sat down beside Brace.

Feeling her way inside the backpack, she found a lighter and a few candles. She lit a candle, dripped it on the floor near Brace, then set it upright in the patch of melted paraffin. She did the same with two more candles.

By the light of the three burning wicks, she used her knife to slice the bands of duct tape around Brace.

He woke up while she was ripping the tape from his skin.

His first word was 'OW!' Then he squinted up at her. He looked as if opening his eyes all the way might be too painful. In a voice that sounded squeezed, he said, 'Jane?'

'Are you okay?'

'God . . . what happened to you?'

'It's all right.'

'You're . . . all torn up.'

'You don't look so hot, yourself.'

'What happened?'

'He's dead,' Jane said. 'I shot him. It's all over.'

'Thank God.' Brace lifted a hand off the floor. He lowered it onto Jane's thigh. His fingers tightened slightly, holding her.

She stroked his head. His hair felt wet. By the light of the candles, she could see that the wetness wasn't blood. Not up there. Sweat, probably. Or water.

'Did you fall in the pool?' she asked.

'Pool?'

'Under the cross.'

'No, I don't . . .'

'I heard a splash. I thought you fell in.'

'I don't think so.'

'What happened to you? You're not where I left you, and . . .

'Don't know. I . . . I remember you getting me off the altar. Hit the floor a good one, and . . . and you went after him . . . by yourself. Why didn't you let me . . . ?'

'Didn't have time. But you must've gotten up. Did you go for the cleaver?'

'Don't remember.'

'It's gone. I figured you'd gotten it. For a while there, I thought you were gonna sneak up on the bastard and give him forty whacks.'

'Don't know. Maybe.'

'Guess you fell,' Jane said.

'Wish I could remember.'

'Do you think you can get up?'

'Sure hope so.'

'Or should I get an ambulance?'

'No ambulance. If we can get out of here . . .'

'We can try.'

'Or we'll be in trouble.'

'A shitload,' Jane said.

'Yeah. Let's see if we can't scram.'

Squatting beside Brace, she helped him to his feet. Then she put an arm around him. Side by side, hanging on to each other, they made their way out of the sanctuary. Brace's body was slippery against her.

'You okay?' she asked.

'I don't feel . . . like I'm gonna drop. It's just my shoulder and . . . he cut off my ear. And I feel like I got my head caved in, but . . . what about you?'

She wondered if she should tell him about the rape.

Yeah, she thought. I should.

But I can't.

Just can't. Not right now.

Maybe never.

No, I'll have to tell him. Have to tell him before we make love next time. Have to warn him.

'Jane?'

'Huh?'

'What did he do to you?'

'Beat me up pretty good.'

'Did he . . . did he *whip* you?'

'Yeah. He had one of those big old bullwhips.'

'Jesus.'

'But I had a gun. He's deader than hell.'

Brace looked over his shoulder. As he peered backward down the aisle, he stumbled. Jane staggered with him, holding on, and swung herself around and caught him. They clung to each other, gasping.

'Sorry,' he said.

'It's okay.'

'Am I hurting you?'

Her raw, lashed flesh burned where he was pressed against it, but she said, 'It's fine.'

'Should've watched what I was doing.'

'No problem.'

'I wanted a look at the bastard.'

'Can't see him from here. He's over to the side where it's dark.'

'We shouldn't leave . . . the candles burning.'

'It's okay. I have to come back. Right now, let's just get out of here.' She eased him away from her body, moved again to his side, and slipped her arm across his back. She felt his hand curl against her hip. As they walked toward the rear of the nave, his hand glided upward. It caressed the side of her breast.

'You must be feeling better,' she said.

'Awfully glad we're both still alive.'

'Yeah. Me, too.'

'Can we go to your house?' he asked.

'We'd better visit an emergency room.'

'Better if we get cleaned up first. And . . . we oughta make up a story. To account for stuff.'

'Yeah. You're pretty smart . . . for a guy.'

He groaned, then asked, 'Where's your car?'

'By the bridge. You know where you picked me up after Crazy Horse?'

'That far?'

'Yeah.'

'You got any clothes? 'Cause I don't.'

'I noticed. Don't worry. I'll get the car and bring it back for you.'

'What about you?'

'I've got stuff.'

At the back of the nave, they pushed their way through the double doors and entered the narthex. 'Do you want to wait here or outside?' Jane asked.

'Better not go out like this.'

'You can claim you're Adam.'

'That'd go over big.'

'Wait here,' Jane said. 'I've got a few things to do, but I'll hurry. Would you rather sit or lean?'

'Lean. So I won't have to get up again.'

'Okay.' She guided him across the dark narthex to the space between two of the doors to the outside. 'Is here all right?'

'Fine.'

He sighed as he leaned back against the wall.

Jane moved in close to him. 'I won't be long.' She

kissed him gently on the mouth.

Two rows from the back of the nave, she found her nylon satchel underneath a pew. She dragged it out, lifted it onto a seat, and searched its dark contents until she found the backup flashlight she'd bought that day at the mall.

She switched it on.

The satchel, which she had carried into the church loaded with guns, now held only her purse and the clothes that she had worn over her bikini.

She stepped into the soft, denim skirt, then pulled a T-shirt down over her head. Though the T-shirt was big and loose, its touch set fire to her wounds. Trembling, she pulled it off.

Save it for when I have to go outside.

Feeling a little better, she sat down and put on her running shoes.

Then she picked up the satchel and began to hunt for the handguns that she had hidden about the church. She knew just where she had left them. She gathered them quickly, but stayed away from the sanctuary until the end.

There, she picked up the .45 that lay on the floor beside the red-clad body of the man who had beaten and raped her. Near his feet, she found the torn remnants of her bikini pants. She put them into her satchel.

She found the little .22 that had done her no good tonight, but had been so effective against the three men at Savile's house.

On the floor near the altar, she found the envelope that had been pinned to Brace's chest with the ice pick. It was spotted with blood. She glanced inside to make sure the money was there.

She found the note nearby.

The note telling her to cut off Brace's head.

It was wadded into a ball.

She tossed the envelope and note into her satchel.

She left the ice pick on the floor.

And she decided to leave the silver tray. She quickly wiped both its sides with her T-shirt to take care of her fingerprints. Not that her fingerprints were on file anywhere. And not that she wasn't certainly leaving prints throughout the church. But the tray was right at her feet and such a shiny surface and so obviously connected to tonight's mayhem that she thought it would be tempting fate *not* to give it a couple of quick swipes.

As she tossed the T-shirt back into her satchel, she remembered her handweight at the bottom of the baptism pool.

She placed her satchel on the edge of the pool. Not bothering to take off her shoes or skirt, she jumped into the water. She waded toward the dark shape of the miniature barbell, then ducked down. The lukewarm water felt cool and soothing against the heat of her wounds. She stayed under for a few seconds, savoring it. Then she picked up the weight.

Her skirt felt heavy and clinging when she boosted herself out of the water. Her shoes made squelching sounds when she walked, lugging the heavy satchel and searching the area with her flashlight.

What else do I need to take care of? she wondered.

Once I'm out of here, I'm not coming back.

And the cops will find whatever I leave behind.

So let's do this right.

The beam of her light fell on a revolver inside a clear plastic sack.

Her .357 magnum.

The gun that she'd counted on to drop Mog.

The gun that had failed her.

The gun that got me raped, she thought. And almost got me killed.

Her satchel thunked against the floor as she set it down. She crouched and picked up the revolver.

Flashlight clamped under her arm, she ripped away the flimsy plastic covering.

Even if water got in, it shouldn't have . . .

She swung out the cylinder.

Empty.

Empty?

It couldn't possibly be empty.

Jane remembered punching the big, magnum rounds into each of the cylinder holes. She'd done it in her kitchen only a few minutes before leaving for the church.

She had loaded it.

She had slipped it inside a plastic bag, and taped the bag shut.

And then later, at the baptism pool, she had taped the bag to the side of her hand weight and submerged it along with the hunting knife.

This revolver simply could not be empty.

But it is.

She shut the cylinder. As she lowered the gun into the satchel with the others, she remembered the heavy sound of the splash she'd heard during her showdown with Mog in the pews.

She'd been afraid that Brace had fallen into the pool.

She'd feared he might drown.

But he'd denied falling in.

Had he jumped into the pool? To unload the magnum?

Why the hell would he do a thing like that?

Ask him.

Jane stood up and strained to lift her satchel.

Maybe he's been in this from the start, she thought.

No. That's crazy. Mog cut off his ear, stabbed him with an ice pick.

Some sort of double-cross?

No, she told herself. You can't make Brace part of this. If he's part of it, there's nothing left – nothing to believe in, no one to love.

I can believe in myself, she thought.

I can love myself.

Love myself. Big deal.

'Damn it, Brace,' she muttered. 'You've gotta be a good guy. Gotta be.'

As she lugged her satchel through the sanctuary, the swinging beam of her flashlight revealed Mog's backpack.

'Thar she blows,' she said.

She'd been promised four hundred thousand dollars (and change) for chopping off Brace's head.

She hadn't played along.

But Mog must've brought the money with him. Probably in the backpack.

She hurried over to the pack, set down her satchel, and knelt on the floor. She dumped the pack upside-down.

The coil of rope fell out. So did one black candle, a couple of Bic lighters, a hammer and several nails, a screwdriver with its tip filed to a point, a pair of pliers, a road flare, a straight razor, a white envelope with JANE written on it, and a second white envelope.

A second envelope?

She clamped the flashlight under her arm and picked it up.

On one side of the envelope was written FORD.

She ripped it open.

No cash inside.

She pulled out a single sheet of lined notebook paper and unfolded it.

And glimpsed a handwritten message.

Her eyes darted to the bottom of the page.

Where three gleaming gems were fixed to the paper with cellophane tape.

Diamonds?

They sure looked like diamonds.

Big ones.

In the white beam of her flashlight, she read the message.

My dear lad,

Enclosed is an envelope that you may give to our lovely friend Jane after she has completed her assigned task.

If she follows through, three cheers!

She is a spunky lass, however. Be prepared for trouble.

If she refuses to play, you have my permission to dispatch her lover-boy in any way you see fit. Then you may have Jane for yourself.

Enjoy her to the hilt, so to speak.

But be careful. She might be hazardous to your health.

Your buddy,
MOG

Stunned, Jane tried to read the message a second time.

She couldn't. The paper shook too badly in her

hands, making the handwriting blur.

Can't be, she thought. No.

Then the bullet hit her in the head.

Chapter Forty-six

She cried 'Ow!'

As she reached up with one hand, the flashlight fell from under her arm and the cartridge dropped like a stone onto Mog's note. It smacked the paper down. The flashlight bumped the floor by her right knee, but didn't go out. Jane clutched the top of her head. The magnum rapped the floor in front of her knees and rolled.

Tears flooded her eyes.

The second cartridge struck her right breast.

Like getting flicked hard by a bully's finger.

It bounced off and clattered to the floor.

Jane looked upward, blinking tears.

Someone laughed.

She snatched up her flashlight.

Aimed it high.

Aimed it toward the quiet, mean laughter.

The beam made a path upward through the darkness to the huge wooden cross suspended by chains above the baptism pool.

She saw the man up there.

The sight of him made Jane go loose and shivery inside.

She suddenly felt as if a tub full of live spiders had been dumped onto her head and she was naked and the creatures with their thousands of tickling feet were

493

racing all over her, scurrying into every orifice.

She knew that the man on the cross was Mog, Master of Games.

So white his skin seemed to glow.

White – and shiny wet.

Skin and bones.

Hairless.

With a face like a grinning skull, but a skull that had full red lips and big pale eyes.

Perched atop the cross-beam, legs dangling, left arm hugging the upright, the cleaver gleaming in its hand. Right arm high and cocked, ready to throw another round at her – then throwing it.

The tumbling brass glinted in the light of Jane's flashlight.

Coming down toward her face.

With her left hand, she snatched it out of the air.

She shoved her flashlight between her knees.

Reached into her satchel for the .357, clutched the first gun she touched, realized most of them were already loaded *except* for the magnum, dropped the revolver and found an automatic and grabbed up her flashlight with her left hand.

Aimed flashlight and pistol at the top of the cross.

The huge cross was swinging slowly back and forth, groaning on its chains.

Abandoned.

Chapter Forty-seven

Jane slammed shoulder-first through the double doors. She staggered into the narthex, .45 in one hand, her ponderous satchel in the other.

'Brace!' she gasped. 'Brace!'

'Yeah?'

She spotted his dim figure against the wall. 'Let's go!'

'What?'

'*Let's go!*'

At the nearest door to the outside, she swung around. She slammed her rump against its crossbar and the door flew open. She backed her way through it and stood there to hold it wide for Brace.

He lurched out, one hand cupping his genitals, and glanced at Jane with frantic eyes.

The front of the church was well lit.

'Let's go, let's go!'

Rushing down the concrete stairs, Jane scanned the area ahead. Nobody in sight. The road empty. The wooded park across the road dark.

Brace stayed by her side.

She twisted her head around and glanced over her shoulder at the doors.

So far, so good.

At the bottom of the stairs, Brace blurted, 'What is it?'

'Mog.'

'You said he was dead.'

'I was wrong. It wasn't Mog I shot.'

'What?'

'He's after us.'

Brace glanced back. 'Where?'

'Don't know. He was up on the cross. But he . . . vanished. Could be anywhere. Just don't know. But he's got that cleaver.'

Side by side, they raced across Park Lane.

'Which way?' Brace asked.

'Into the trees.'

'Your car.'

'No point. He'll just . . . Can't run away from him.'

Jane ducked into the trees beyond the border of the park. She dropped her satchel to the ground and fell to her knees.

Brace knelt beside her. 'What're we doing?' he asked.

Jane slapped a pistol into his hand, then reached into the satchel for another. She gave it to Brace, too.

'Jane?' he asked.

'Yeah?'

She filled both her hands with guns.

'What're we doing?' Brace asked.

'We can't run away from him,' she said.

Brace looked at her. Light from the streetlamps came in through the foliage, making his eyes glint.

'I love you,' Jane said.

'Hey . . .'

'Are you with me?' she asked.

'You name it,' he said.

'We make our stand here.'

'You don't sound very optimistic,' Brace said.

'I'd feel a lot better if we had silver bullets.' Jane turned on her knees so that she was facing the road and the front of the church. Beyond the bushes and tree trunks, she could see the doors at the top of the concrete stairs.

Brace, on his knees next to her, eased closer until the warm skin of his side touched her.

'Tell me he's not a werewolf,' Brace said.

'I don't know what he is. Some sort of spook.'

'I'm not sure I believe in spooks.'

'I do.'

They never saw the church doors open.

They never saw Mog at all until he lurched out of the trees behind them. The only sound he made was a quiet, mean laugh.

The cleaver whistled on its way to Brace's neck.

But Jane had heard the laughter and swung around, both guns blazing.

A slug bashed Mog's arm aside in time to save Brace's neck.

Another punched through his cheekbone.

Brace, too, swung around.

Together, they filled the night with thunder and muzzle flashes and full metal jackets that pounded Mog backward and made him dance like the marionette of a madman until he slammed against a tree trunk.

The trunk knocked him forward.

He pitched facedown on the ground.

They stood over the torn, motionless body.

'Is it *him*, this time?'

'What?' Jane asked. Her ears were ringing from the gun blasts.

'Mog? Is this him?'

'Yeah. I guess. He's the guy from the cross.'

'Still think he's a spook?'

She wrinkled her nose. 'He looks pretty dead. I don't know.'

'We didn't even need silver bullets.'

'Keep an eye on him, okay?' Jane turned her back to the corpse and squatted over the satchel. She set her two empty guns inside. Then she tugged out the T-shirt.

She tossed the T-shirt to Brace. 'You can wear it to the car.'

'What about you?'

'I'll say I'm Eve. If anybody asks.' Bending over, she searched the ground and found the cleaver.

She picked it up.

From Brace, she heard a gasp. Then he blurted, 'Jane!'

She whirled around.

Mog got to his knees, grinning.

This can't be happening. Cannot. No.

Yes.

I knew it
knew it
knew it
a fucking spook!

Brace kicked him under the chin.

Barefoot.

And cried out with pain.

Mog's head snapped backward. The kick lifted him off his knees, sent him sprawling until the back of his head slammed the tree trunk.

As Brace hopped, clutching his toes, Jane leaped past him.

She heard herself whimpering.

She dropped and skidded on her knees through the litter of dead leaves between Mog's spread legs.

Stopped just short of his crotch.

Forced herself not to look at the huge white thing jutting up from there like a pike.

Jammed the heel of her left hand against his slippery forehead.

Chopped through the side of his neck with the cleaver in her right.

Chapter Forty-eight

People must've heard the gunfire. If not the shots inside the church, at least those that had crashed through the silence of the park.

Jane expected police cars to swarm in from all sides, lights aflash and sirens screaming.

But no cops showed up.

On the way back to the car, she saw nobody.

Except Rale.

Rale, the bearded and faceless wino, stepped out suddenly from among the trees on the far side of the bridge, held out a filthy hand and grumbled, 'Spare me a . . .' Then he made a choking sound.

Jane doubted that Rale's stunned reaction had much to do with confronting a young man who wore nothing except a T-shirt that was not quite long enough for decency.

It probably had little to do with encountering a torn and bloody young woman dressed only in a skirt and shoes.

Maybe he recognized her as the one he'd tried to rape.

More likely, though, the shock came from seeing what she carried upside-down beneath her left arm – the severed, hairless head of Mog.

Instead of finishing his request for a handout, Rale squealed and fled into the wooded darkness of the park.

Nothing else happened on their way to her car.

Early the next morning, clean and bandaged and nicely dressed, Brace presented himself to the emergency room of Donnerville's hospital.

He explained that he had tripped in his garage while carrying a window. He had plunged through the window, its shattered glass slicing off his ear. Then he had fallen on a board that had a jutting nail.

Two hours later, he returned to Jane's house with a new puncture from a tetanus shot, fresh bandages, and two prescriptions that would require a trip to a pharmacy.

According to the news reports that day, Satanists were believed to be responsible for the brutal slayings of two unidentified males found in and near the Calvary Baptist Church.

Nothing was mentioned about the missing head.

They buried Mog's head at midnight in the weed-choked back yard of the creephouse next to Paradise Gardens Memorial Park.

'That oughta keep him down,' Jane said, stomping the ground flat.

At dawn the next morning, they buried Brace's ear in Jane's back yard.

It was still frozen.

Jane wanted to leave it in the Tupperware bowl for the ceremony, but Brace objected. 'We don't wanta do that,' he said, peeling off the lid of the bowl. He handed the lid to Jane. Crouching, he placed his ear into the small hole. 'Ain't biodegradable.'

'You're right.'

'Besides, you might wanta use it again.'

Jane wrinkled her nose. 'You've gotta be kidding. Not that I've got anything against your rotten old ear, but I don't think I wanta put *food* in the bowl.'

'You women are all so squeamish.'

She laughed softly. 'That's me.'

With the edge of his shoe, Brace pushed dirt into the hole. 'So long, ear.'

'So long,' Jane said to it.

Gently, Brace rubbed her back. Already, he seemed to know where the worst of her wounds were – and he stayed away from them as he caressed her.

In a somber voice, he said, 'Nothing will ever be able to take us by surprise again.'

She grinned at him. 'Don't tell me.'

'Don't tell you what?' He raised his eyebrows, oh so innocent.

'Because,' Jane said, 'you'll always have your ear to the ground?'

Brace laughed. '*I* didn't say it,' he protested.

'You were gonna.'

'If I'm so damned predictable, what am I going to say next?'

'That's not fair. If I get it right, you'll just deny it.'

'I never lie, remember?'

'You lied to the doctor, and . . .'

'Never to you.'

'Oh, okay.' Jane grinned. 'So, what is it that you were planning to say next?'

'You're supposed to tell *me*,' he reminded her.

'Oh. Okay. Here's what you're going to say.'

'What?'

'"Jane, you're the most gorgeous babe in the world and I can't get enough of you."'

Brace laughed and shook his head.

Then he looked her in the eyes. His smile vanished. 'Jane, you're the most gorgeous babe in the world and I can't get enough of you.' Suddenly, his eyes bulged. His mouth fell open. 'My God!' he blurted. 'How did *you* know I was about to say that?'

'I can read you like a book,' Jane said.

Then he kissed her.

More Thrilling Fiction from Headline:

'IF YOU'VE MISSED LAYMON, YOU'VE MISSED A TREAT'
STEPHEN KING

RICHARD LAYMON

ALARUMS

'A BRILLIANT WRITER' *Sunday Express*

Melanie Conway is a pale and lovely violinist who has
strange visions of death. When she crashes to the floor
during a concert her boyfriend, Bodie, is at hand to
hear her fearful premonition of disaster...Penelope
Conway is even more stunning than her sister but her
looks frequently get her into trouble. Although she
takes herself seriously as a writer, men only seem
impressed by her beauty. The last thing she needs is a
series of obscene phone calls...

Captivated by these two alluring sisters, Bodie finds
himself drawn deep into a strange mystery that is fired
by sex and haunted by blood.

Richard Laymon is the author of several acclaimed horror classics including:
THE CELLAR, FLESH, FUNLAND, THE STAKE, RESURRECTION DREAMS,
THE WOODS ARE DARK, ONE RAINY NIGHT, BLOOD GAMES, DARK
MOUNTAIN, MIDNIGHT'S LAIR, OUT ARE THE LIGHTS, SAVAGE and
DARKNESS, TELL US, all available from Headline Feature.

'No one writes like Laymon, and you're going to have a
good time with anything he writes' Dean Koontz

FICTION/HORROR   0 7472 4130 9

More Horrifying Fiction from Headline:

RICHARD LAYMON
SAVAGE

'If you've missed Laymon, you've missed a treat'
STEPHEN KING

'HIS BEST BOOK EVER' *Northern Echo*

Whitechapel, November 1888: Jack the Ripper is committing his last known act of butchery in the one-room hovel occupied by the luckless harlot, Mary Kelly. And beneath the bed on which the fiend is cruelly and cheerfully eviscerating his victim cowers a fifteen-year-old boy...

This is just the start of the extraordinary adventures of Trevor Bentley, a boy who embarked on an errand of mercy and ran into the most notorious serial killer in criminal history, a boy who became a man as he travelled on a quest of vengeance across a wild and untamed continent – a boy who brought the horrors of Jack the Ripper to the New World.

RICHARD LAYMON

**is the author of several acclaimed horror classics including:
THE CELLAR, FLESH, FUNLAND, THE STAKE,
RESURRECTION DREAMS, THE WOODS ARE DARK,
ONE RAINY NIGHT, BLOOD GAMES, DARK MOUNTAIN,
MIDNIGHT'S LAIR, OUT ARE THE LIGHTS and
DARKNESS, TELL US, all available from Headline Feature.**

'A brilliant writer' *Sunday Express*

'No one writes like Laymon, and you're going to have a good time with anything he writes' Dean Koontz

FICTION/HORROR   0 7472 4120 1

A selection of bestsellers
from Headline

THE WINGED MAN	Moyra Caldecott	£5.99 ☐
COLD PRINT	Ramsey Campbell	£5.99 ☐
THE DOLL WHO ATE HIS MOTHER	Ramsey Campbell	£4.50 ☐
SIGN FOR THE SACRED	Storm Constantine	£5.99 ☐
ANGELS	Steve Harris	£5.99 ☐
THE FUNHOUSE	Dean Koontz	£4.99 ☐
OUT ARE THE LIGHTS	Richard Laymon	£4.99 ☐
SAVAGE	Richard Laymon	£4.99 ☐
ELEPHANTASM	Tanith Lee	£4.99 ☐
THE REVELATION	Bentley Little	£4.99 ☐
THE HOLLOW MAN	Dan Simmons	£4.99 ☐
VALDEREN	Roger Taylor	£4.99 ☐

All Headline books are available at your local bookshop or newsagent, or can be ordered direct from the publisher. Just tick the titles you want and fill in the form below. Prices and availability subject to change without notice.

Headline Book Publishing PLC, Cash Sales Department, Bookpoint, 39 Milton Park, Abingdon, OXON, OX14 4TD, UK. If you have a credit card you may order by telephone – 0235 831700.

Please enclose a cheque or postal order made payable to Bookpoint Ltd to the value of the cover price and allow the following for postage and packing:
UK & BFPO: £1.00 for the first book, 50p for the second book and 30p for each additional book ordered up to a maximum charge of £3.00.
OVERSEAS & EIRE: £2.00 for the first book, £1.00 for the second book and 50p for each additional book.

Name ....

Address ....

....

....

If you would prefer to pay by credit card, please complete:
Please debit my Visa/Access/Diner's Card/American Express (delete as applicable) card no:

Signature .... Expiry Date ....